In Broken Places

in broken places

Michèle Phoenix

Tyndale House Publishers Inc., Carol Stream, Illinois

Visit Tyndale online at www.tyndale.com.

For more on this novel, including photos and an interview with Michèle Phoenix, please visit www.michelephoenix.com.

TYNDALE and Tyndale's quill logo are registered trademarks of Tyndale House Publishers, Inc.

In Broken Places

Previously published as *Shards of Shell* by Dog Ear Publishing, LLC, under ISBN 978-1598583601.

In Broken Places first published in 2013 by Tyndale House Publishers, Inc.

Designed by Beth Sparkman

Edited by Kathryn S. Olson

Published in association with the literary and marketing agency of C. Grant & Company, www.cgrantandcompany.com.

Library of Congress Cataloging-in-Publication Data

Phoenix, Michèle.
In Broken Places / Michèle Phoenix.
pages cm
"Previously published as Shards of Shell by Dog Ear Publishing."
ISBN 978-1-4143-6841-2 (sc)
1. Self-realization in women—Fiction. 2. Christian fiction. I. Title.
PS3616.H65I5 2013
813'.6—dc23 2012045960

Printed in the United States of America

19 18 17 16 15 14 13
7 6 5 4 3 2 1

For Mom.

You taught me to love words.

These are my gratitude.

Acknowledgments

MY GRATITUDE TO:

Aaron, for your profound Seth-ness.

Grayson, for your exuberant Trey-ness.

Jane, for your nurturing Bev-ness.

Mari Ellen, for your instructive Miss Reeser-ness.

Kandern, for your enchanting and exasperating *Djohmany*-ness.

My students at Black Forest Academy, fascinating amalgams of innocence and world-weariness, fragility and fearlessness. You were both my vocation and my reward. In many ways, my healing too. I love each one of you.

The world breaks everyone and afterward
many are strong in the broken places.

—ERNEST HEMINGWAY

1

"THE ONLY DIFFERENCE between a German and a primate is his ability to read the label on his beer can," Bonnie said.

I'd spent a lifetime wondering what purgatory might be like and I'd found it here, at thirty-five thousand feet, confined in this garishly upholstered space between a sleeping child and a ranting parrot of a woman. Her voice was loud—as sharp as the bones jutting out of her seventysomething body—and ill-fitting dentures did nothing to soften her staccato consonants and shrilling vowels.

"Of course, they can't help it," the occupant of 41-C continued, oblivious to the silence coming from 41-B. "It's cultural. Like wearing those lederhosen getups and dipping their fries in mayonnaise. I'd bet money their waistbands are as tight as their arteries." She punctuated her sentence with a derisive snort and reached for her drink.

I counted off the seconds as she sipped orange juice from her plastic cup, relishing the silence while pleading with the gods of conversational relief that the sleeping pills Bonnie had taken minutes ago would kick in before I died of murder by monologue. I had predicted, when she'd entertained Frankfurt-bound passengers in the departure hall with a ruckus about her overweight carry-on luggage, that this diminutive woman would spell transatlantic discomfort for her seat companions. And fate had placed her next to me. My only consolation was in imagining how ugly the scene might have gotten if this Germanophobe had been seated near a native of the country to which we were flying.

Bonnie replaced her cup in the indentation on the tray in front of her and took a deep breath. I held mine, dreading the next chapter in Bonnie's Defamation of the German Culture, but it never came. With a weary "I think I'll rest my eyes for a few minutes," Bonnie let out a long, pesto-scented breath and deflated into silence.

My hand drifted over the head of soft blonde curls resting in my lap. The gesture had been foreign to me only months before, and it struck me, as I looped a curl around my finger and watched it unravel, that the concept of *foreign* was quickly becoming familiar. Shayla stirred and I pulled her airline blanket higher on her shoulders, amazed that she could sleep, contorted as she was around the seat belt the attendant had suggested we leave fastened. She coughed and opened one eye, squinting at the geometric pattern on the seat in front of hers, then craning her neck back to get a look at me. Apparently satisfied that I hadn't morphed into any of the "bad people" from her Disney cartoons, she closed her one eye and coiled back into sleep.

I considered it a compliment that the sight of me hadn't sent her into horrified hysterics. There were multiple reasons why it should have, the greatest of which was the physical ravages inflicted on me by six months of utter shock in which twelve weeks of disbelief had yielded to twelve more weeks of second-guessing, all culminating in the past seventy-two hours of rabid, nerve-numbing packing.

I was the poster child for post-traumatic stress disorder. My skin was dirty-eggshell pale, my hair had all the stylish flair of a brown Brillo pad, and my eyes, I was pretty sure, screamed a hazel shade of terror that churned with utter confusion. Post-traumatic Shelby was not a pretty picture. At all.

I looked out the window at cotton-candy clouds and the first pale hues of another day. There was a large foreign object—perhaps a boulder—lodged in my throat, and for months, nothing I attempted had succeeded in dislodging it. None of the crying or raging or peacemaking I'd done had put a dent in it. And I was pretty sure, as I gazed out at the day dawning on the horizon, that the rock was there to stay. At least for a while. I contemplated carving something pertinent like "Let me off this ride!" on it and making it a permanent feature of my emotional landscape. It would feel right at home among the bits of barbed wire, chunks of fortified wall, and steel-reinforced doors torn from their hinges that had washed up on the same shore during previous existential storms. They formed a panoply of failed self-protection I wasn't ready to dispose of quite yet. I figured broken barriers were better than none at all. At least they showed intent.

Right?

⌘ ⌘ ⌘

SEVEN MONTHS EARLIER

"She's beautiful, Shelby."

I stared at the social worker's face and wondered what *beautiful* had to do with the present circumstances. There were other words that described my dilemma. *Strange?* Yes. *Disconcerting?* Yes. *Completely and horrifically out of control?* Absolutely. But *beautiful?* No—it was not an adjective that belonged in this particular conversation, no matter how accurate it might be.

"Dana," I began, shaking my head and raising my hands in utter dismay, "I can't . . . I mean . . . Seriously? You're being serious here?"

This was only the second time Dana and I had met, but given the circumstances, we'd abandoned the formalities and gone straight to first names. She was old enough to be my mother, and there had been a frantic moment during that first meeting when all I'd wanted to do was curl up in her well-padded lap and have her shush me into oblivion as my mom had done when I was a child, but the official nature of our encounter had kept my instincts in check and my pride intact. Besides, I was sure not even the competent and sympathetic Dana would have known what to do with a thirty-five-year-old woman trying to crawl onto her knees.

Weeks later, I didn't remember many of the details of our first meeting. Only the general gist of the conversation and the mystification that had plagued me every day since then. My dilemma had done for my prayer life what trans-fat-free fries had done for my fast-food consumption. I was cranking out prayers as fervently as I was shoveling in fries, and though my decision hadn't gotten any simpler to make, my ability to use a drive-through window without guilt had vastly improved. But I hadn't given up on my praying. Not yet. This impassable imbroglio had proven two important facts to me. Firstly, I was helpless. A lifetime of learning to be strong and independent had left me more debilitated than I'd ever felt before. And secondly, my praying had gotten rusty. The first few times I'd tried to utter something profound, I'd sounded like a glossary of antiquated King James clichés. I was pretty sure God laughed at my initial attempts, but I figured he could use the entertainment as much as I could use the practice.

"I need you to make a decision," Dana now said, reaching across the gray Formica tabletop to press warm fingers around my frozen disbelief. Her oversize gold rings sparkled in the morning sunlight, somehow incongruous with the muddiness in my mind. "The paperwork is drawn up, and we can get this procedure started just as soon as you give us the go-ahead."

The go-ahead. Such an innocuous term. But in this case, it carried life-altering ramifications I couldn't even fathom. I grasped the edge of the kitchen table and found comfort in its realness. It was solid and predictable, scarred by time and use, but it was there—measurable and palpable and familiar. It seemed at that moment that everything else in my life had catapulted off a cliff, exploded like a clay pigeon into thousands of jagged fragments, and fallen scattered and unrecognizable into the dark abyss below. Giving anyone or anything the "go-ahead" while the pieces of my life were still settling in the muck of incredulity seemed about as wise as diving into a piranha-infested lake with pork chops strapped to each limb.

"Dana . . ."

"I know it's frightening," she said, tightening her grip on my hand, "and I know you have no point of reference for making this decision."

"It's just . . ." I searched her eyes for answers. "How did this happen? I mean, a month ago my life was . . . and now it's—"

"Kaboom," Dana said matter-of-factly.

"Exactly." I sighed and retrieved my hand to rub at my eyes and rake at my hair. Dana returned my gaze, unflinching, and I tried to absorb some of her calm as it wafted across the table toward me like the fragrance of cinnamon or freshly cut grass or White Shoulders on my mother's chenille robe.

"Will you at least come to meet her?"

"No." The word shot out like a reflex.

"I'll stay with you."

"No."

"We won't even tell her who you are."

"I can't."

"Shelby." Her expression was compassionate, but her eyes scolded my cowardice. "There's more at stake here than just you. I know it's overwhelming and I know you're still reeling, but think outside yourself for just a moment."

I laughed at that, mostly because that response seemed preferable to curling into a fetal position under my mom's old kitchen table and praying to God for the Rapture to come quickly. This was a choice of cataclysmic consequences, and I was known to get stumped by a Dunkin' Donuts display. How was I supposed to decide this so soon when glazed versus frosted could keep my brain in a knot for days?

"She needs a mom," Dana persisted.

"I'm not her mom."

"But you can learn. Even if you're not her real mom, someone's got to raise her."

"No." I shook my head as if the gesture would rid me of the excruciating decision. "I'm not mom material. He made sure of that."

"And yet it's you he wanted to take care of his daughter. No one else."

I laughed again, though the sound was completely devoid of humor. "He doesn't even know who I am."

"But he chose you."

"I can't do it."

"What other option do we have, Shelby?" Her voice was soft, but her words slammed a vise across my lungs that threatened my ability to breathe. "What other option does Shayla have?" She leaned across the table, her eyes seeking my averted gaze. "Take a deep breath, Shelby." She waited while I obeyed. After a few moments, she smiled and added, "If you don't let it back out, you're going to pass out."

I expelled the breath in a rush of frustration and helplessness and fear, tears stinging my eyes. "I feel like I don't really have a choice at all."

"Sure you do. Technically. But if you're feeling like there's only one *right* choice, I think that might be true." She fished a Kleenex out of her giant purse and handed it to me as if she'd done it a thousand times before, which she probably had. "I suggest you and I go for a little ride. We'll drop in and see her—just as casually as you'd like—and then maybe you'll be able to wrap your mind around all of this." She pushed her chair away from the table and rose.

"I'm not sure I can do this." I swallowed past the boulder in my throat and bit my bottom lip to steady it.

"I believe you. But you still need to."

"I'm scared, Dana. What if . . . ? What if . . . ?"

"You don't have to decide today. Maybe seeing her will help you, though."

"Help me what?"

"Help you to know."

"You won't tell her who I am?"

"It'll be our little secret."

"And you'll stay with me?"

Dana nodded and hung her purse over her shoulder. "You ready?"

"No." My laughter only *almost* masked my terror.

"You'll be fine," Dana assured me, coming around the table to squeeze my shoulder as I stood. "I'll be with you—and we'll take it nice and slow."

"I need to brush my hair."

"I was hoping you would."

"Don't insult me. I might change my mind."

"Then you're absolutely beautiful," Dana said sweetly.

"And you're a lousy liar."

"Hey, if it gets you to the car . . ."

"I need a donut."

"There are three Dunkin' Donuts between here and Dream Acres."

"Good," I said bravely. "We'll stop at all three."

❋ ❋ ❋

Bonnie's sleeping pill was still going strong when the captain informed us that we were beginning our descent. She'd slept through a breakfast sadly devoid of donuts, waking only enough to mutter, "Leave me alone," when a solicitous attendant had fastened her seat belt. The captain's announcement had done nothing to rouse her from her drug-induced nap.

"You okay?" I asked Shayla, tucking a stray strand of hair behind her ear.

She twisted away and gazed in rapt fascination out the window again. There were Shayla-size noseprints on the glass and fresh smears of strawberry jam and chocolate milk below them. How she'd managed to eat her entire breakfast without taking her eyes off the clouds was a mystery to me. It was the first time she had flown, and after her initial nervousness at takeoff, matched closely by my own, she had either slept or been enchanted by the skyscape for the remainder of the flight. It was nearing midnight in the time zone we had left behind, but a lengthy nap and her innate enthusiasm had Shayla virtually hopping with excitement.

An airline attendant collected our trays and commented on Shayla's riot of blonde curls.

"They're only cute until I need to brush them," I replied, trying to finger-comb them as I spoke. "Then they become the opening salvo of World War III."

The attendant smiled and stowed the trays. "Well, she's a beauty. And a great little traveler."

"Thanks," I answered, a little proud in spite of myself. That Shayla was beautiful had nothing to do with me, and yet . . . she was mine. There were times when the thought sent me whirling into a jumble of panic and amazement. I hadn't wanted any of this—I'd resisted it with all the fury of my fears, if truth be told—but Shayla had woven herself into the fabric of my life with wide, forget-me-not eyes, timid smiles, and satin-soft hands that had tugged at my resolve as surely as they now tugged at my sleeve.

"Hey, hey, hey!" She brought me out of my reverie with her trademark threefold plea.

"What, what, what?" I answered, taking her small hand from my sleeve to kiss her fingers.

"Look!" Shayla snatched her hand back, swiveled in her seat, and came up on her knees to lean as far into the window as she could. Through a gap in the clouds, she could see the random, irregular shapes of German fields, the crisscross of roads where tiny headlights strained to pierce the morning gloom, and the clustered homes and barns of farming villages scattered here and there across the hills. "Look!" she said again in her cute-as-can-be little-girl accent, pointing this time. "Look at Djoh-many!"

She reached behind her without taking her eyes from the window, grabbed a fistful of my shirt, and pulled me closer. "You see?"

Two thoughts simultaneously struck me. The first was that her seat belt couldn't be fastened tightly enough if she was able to kneel in it. The second was that there was no turning back now. That bank of light approaching like a luminescent storm front was not merely a pretty sight to get excited about as we descended toward Frankfurt. It was a reality so stark and final that it tore a gaping hole in the armor of my bravado. Germany was no longer a distant destination or a temporary lapse in sanity. As streetlights blinked off far below and the outline of a modern city emerged out of the early-morning gray, Germany became as real as the seat belt cutting me in half as I leaned toward the window and gazed at the beginning of my future.

There was a small town called Kandern nestled somewhere in those hills. And in that town was the American school for missionaries' kids where I was going to teach. The apartment where Shayla and I would live. The new life I would build—we would build together. I swallowed around the boulder and took a calming breath. There was nothing predictable about what waited for us in Kandern, and though I'd done as much Internet research as I could in recent days, I knew I was still sorely unprepared.

"Her seat belt should be tighter." The attendant's hand on my shoulder was a welcome distraction.

"Yes. Of course." I smiled, trying to tighten Shayla's seat belt while she strained away from me. "Shay? You've got to sit down, honey. We need to get your belt tighter."

"Look!" she said again, this time mesmerized by the outline of mountains in the distance.

"Can you sit down, Shayla?"

"No," she declared, ignoring my futile attempts to peacefully get her to sit. I hadn't had much experience with four-year-olds, but my time with Shayla had taught me that their attention span was not only limited—it was also selective. "Look! Look!"

I didn't take the time to follow her pointing finger. Grasping her arm and turning her toward me, I marveled at her ability to swivel her body without removing her nose from the streaked surface of the airplane's window. "Shayla, sit down!" I tugged a little harder and her nose came unglued from the double-paned glass.

"But I want to look!" She pushed the seat belt lower on her hips so she could rise toward the window again.

"Not right now."

"I want to see!"

"We're going to be landing soon and then you can look and look and *look*, but you've got to keep your seat belt tight until we're on the ground."

"But why?"

"Because," I answered firmly. Six months of parenthood had rid me of my original distaste for the pat answer. As much as I'd despised it when my parents had used it on me, I realized now that the only reasonable response to some questions was simply "Because." Why did she have to go to bed? Because. Why couldn't she have another piece of cake? Because. Why did the other kids get to stay at home while she had to go to Djoh-many? Because. Why did I want to be a missionary and not a normal person anymore? Because. "Because" was my new best friend. It was not, however, Shayla's. I fastened her seat belt as tightly as possible, unfazed by the squirming bundle of "I don't want to" fighting the process, then I pointed out the window with relief and said, "See, Shay? You can still see the mountains." And there they were, right outside the window. By any other standards, they were merely large hills. But having lived in the plains of Illinois all our combined lives, they might as well have been the Swiss Alps to Shayla and me.

❋ ❋ ❋

SEVEN MONTHS EARLIER

"What are you drawing, Shayla?" Dana asked. She overflowed a child-size chair next to the small desk where Shayla bent over a brownish piece of paper, her brow furrowed in concentration. She hadn't looked up when we entered. She hadn't stopped drawing.

"Mountains," she now said, quite unnecessarily. On her paper, the dark outline of mountain ridges split the space between earth and sky. She'd started to fill in the lines with greens and browns and blues, sometimes coloring just outside the edges of the shapes in a rush of creative zeal.

"Have you ever seen a mountain?" Dana asked gently, her face just inches from Shayla's. I stood at a safe distance, feeling tall in this miniature space where furniture seemed shrunken and pictures hung just above waist level on the walls. It was a room designed to make children feel safe. It had an entirely different effect on discombobulated grown-ups like me, whose inner world was suddenly unrecognizably askew.

I'd hesitated for a long time before entering Dream Acres, a small, family-owned farm that doubled as a foster home for children needing temporary housing. I'd lingered on the front steps, ignoring Dana's prompting. This was a pivotal and irrevocable moment in my life. Whatever happened after I passed through the wide, welcoming front doors would be largely out of my control. And control was a critical issue for me. It always had been. I'd discarded my violin when it had proved too hard to master. I'd given up on being a ballerina when teachers had started planning my career. And I'd declared myself a dedicated single when romantic relationships, most of them imagined, had exhausted my limited supply of optimism.

So, facing a moment of overwhelmingly human proportions in which any form of control and predictability was impossible, I'd stood on the steps before my encounter with Shayla and briefly but frantically considered fleeing from the unmanageable.

"I saw them in *Heidi*," Shayla answered Dana's question, drawing me back to the present with a voice fluffy and soft as rabbit's fur. "When she's living with her grandpa in the wood house on the mountain."

Dana looked up at me as if inviting me to join in their fledgling conversation. I shook my head and took a small step back, inexplicably unbalanced by the too-low paintings on the walls and the too-small artist entering my too-full life.

Dana was a natural. She coaxed answer after answer from Shayla, affirming her talent and revealing her heart.

"You're very good at drawing, Shayla."

Her button nose went up and down as she nodded.

"Would you like to see real mountains someday?"

"Yes." She sounded like she'd been taught never to say *yeah*.

"And what mountains would you like to see?"

"Volcanoes."

"Volcanoes!"

"Uh-huh."

"Why do you want to see volcanoes?"

"Because they're big and have the fi-yoh stuff that comes out of them."

"The fire stuff? Like lava?"

"Uh-huh."

"Is that a volcano you're drawing now?"

"No." The word *stupid* was implied in Shayla's tone of voice. "I told you. It's Heidi's mountain."

"Oh," Dana said with a smile. "I should have remembered that."

"My dad taught me how."

"He taught you how to draw mountains?"

The honey-blonde curls, like a wheat field in the wind, bobbed as Shayla nodded. "Uh-huh." She looked at Dana for the first time, her blue crayon poised above the sky. "He's not here anymore."

Dana nodded and smiled gently. "Do you miss him?"

Shayla went back to her coloring with renewed focus. She nodded and took in a quick, clenched breath. "He's not coming back."

I looked around the room for an escape route and wished Shayla's mountain were real. What I wouldn't have given to lose myself in the dense foliage of the trees covering its flanks. But in this warm sitting room where the sun and surfaces danced golden rays over drawings and toys and brightly colored books, the only plausible direction to go seemed downward. So, feeling the bottom drop out of my life as my stomach churned and my throat clenched, I took three tentative steps to Dana's side and sank onto the carpet next to the child who would unravel life as I knew it.

"This is a friend of mine. Her name is Shelby."

Shayla looked suspiciously at Dana. "I had a dog called Shelby. My dad gave her to me."

I felt the oxygen whoosh out of the room.

"Really?" Dana asked.

"Did you alweady know?" Shayla didn't like the coincidence. She picked up a pink crayon and started on a cloud.

"I promise I didn't."

"She wan away."

"Shelby?"

"Uh-huh."

"I'm sorry, Shayla. That must have been sad for you."

"Uh-huh." Another cloud took shape in Shayla's sky.

I cleared my throat and tried to sound natural. "Hi, Shayla. How are you?" Given the gravel-meets-phlegm texture of my voice, I half expected the beautiful child to grab her mountain and run.

Instead, she turned two of the largest blue eyes I'd ever seen on me and pursed her mouth in disapproval. "That's a wee-ohd voice," she said.

Dana covered a smile while I grasped at conversational straws.

"It's not . . ." I cleared my throat, attempted a sound, then loudly cleared my throat again. "It's not usually this bad. My voice, I mean."

The blue gaze was still focused on me, though her eyes scanned my face without ever truly making contact with mine. She turned back to the stack of crayons next to her drawing and picked just the right shade of yellow for the sun.

"You don't look like my dog," she said seriously.

"Oh—well. That's good, I guess. Isn't it?"

"Uh-huh."

Dana pushed up from her chair and arched her back. "I'm going to get some coffee, Shayla. Is it okay if I leave you here with Shelby for a few minutes?"

Absolute panic burned up my neck. "But . . ."

Shayla nodded, and Dana patted my shoulder as she walked rather stiffly toward the other end of the room. "You'll be fine," she said softly, closing the door behind her.

If "fine" meant dizziness, nausea, and mental paralysis, I was indeed going to be fine. I took a calming breath and instructed my heart to stop its nonsense. I think it laughed at me. Seriously.

But I might have been hallucinating from all the "fine" going on, so I couldn't be sure.

"Are you going to ask me a question?" Shayla asked.

I was stunned into silence.

"People always ask me questions," she continued, extending yellow rays from the sun's center. "Like my favowite color and my middle name and silly stuff like that."

I attempted a casual laugh. "Those are rather stupid questions, aren't they," I said, trying desperately to come up with questions that involved neither colors nor middle names.

This time her gaze did meet mine, and so directly that I thought I heard an audible thunk as my future settled into place. That was all it took. One direct gaze from strangely familiar eyes and a reproachful "You shouldn't say *stupid*. It's naughty."

As someone who had spent most of my adult life proclaiming that having children was a stupid idea, I realized I had a lot to learn.

2

It had taken two flight attendants and a wheelchair to get Bonnie off the plane. Whatever she had taken to help her sleep had all but knocked her unconscious. I'd stayed on board until a doctor had pronounced her alive (which the raucous snores, to my unmedical mind, had already confirmed), then helped Shayla into her pink backpack and pulled my own carry-on toward the exit.

Although I'd made a halfhearted pass at listening to language CDs in the weeks preceding my departure for Germany, the guttural sounds that assaulted my ears as soon as Shayla and I disembarked came as a nearly physical blow. The plane ride had convinced me that I was leaving the US, Bonnie had convinced me that I was in for some surprises, the landscape we had seen through the window had convinced me that this definitely wasn't Kansas anymore, but it was the language and the impatient glares of airport personnel that truly brought reality crashing home. I was in Germany. Or *Djoh-many*. My four-year-old pseudo-daughter of six months and I had arrived in a foreign land where the language was as mysterious as everything else, including where I would live, what I would do, and how we would both survive the changes.

After a cursory glance at our passports and the luggage stacked on my cart, a portly customs agent motioned us toward electric doors that swooshed open and ushered us almost directly into the arms of a woman I had never seen before.

"Shelby, Shelby, Shelby," she said, wrapping me in a bear hug that disconnected Shayla's hand from mine. I didn't want to seem rude, but Shayla's safety at that moment was more urgent than returning the hug, so I pushed away and quickly scanned the space around me for Shayla's blonde head.

I had been amazed, in the weeks following her arrival in my life, at how instantly and dramatically my view of the world had changed. I'd never been responsible for someone else's safety before, and a guardian's heart, until then buried under layers of determined singleness, had surged to the surface the moment Shayla had come into my care. It was that ferocious protectiveness that gripped my chest in panic as I looked around the arrival hall and failed to see Shayla's pink backpack in the crowd. With fear fueled by jet lag, I gripped the arm of the woman who had been hugging me moments before and stuttered, "Where's . . . where's Shayla?"

"Whatsa mattoh, Shelby?" came Shayla's sunny voice, a little rough around the edges from lack of sleep.

She was right next to me, her head level with mine, her supple body completely at ease in a stranger's arms.

"I'm Gus Johnson," he said amiably, extending his hand and meeting my startled gaze with a Santa Claus chuckle. "And this woman who forgot to introduce herself before she grabbed you is my lovely wife, Bev."

I looked from Gus to Bev, at a loss for words. "Oh . . ." I attempted a smile and expelled a tight breath. "Hi."

"I'm so sorry, Shelby," Bev said, her arm coming around my shoulders in a maternal hold. "I was just so happy to see you that I forgot all my manners." Her Southern accent had a soothing quality that threatened to unleash unexpected tears. "And this," she continued, reaching out to flick Shayla's nose, "must be beautiful Shayla."

"It is," I said, snapping my brain into gear. "And it's wonderful to meet you after all this time. Thank you so much for driving so far to pick us up."

"No trouble at all," Bev said. "We love a good excuse to get out of town now and then."

Shayla, who was amazingly unfazed at being held by a strange man, smiled tiredly in Bev's direction and settled more heavily against Gus's chest. I blamed his appearance for her lack of concern—his graying hair, rosy cheeks, rounded belly, and sparkling eyes evoked Christmas trees and presents.

"Say hello, Shayla," I prompted. "This is Bev and Gus Johnson. Remember the e-mails I read to you? They're going to help us get settled."

"Did you see my new house?" she asked, a yawn distorting her delicate features.

"We sure did," Bev answered. "I even went over there last night and put some flowers in your bedroom for you."

Shayla looked at me with a "she's nice" smile, and I reached out to squeeze her arm in agreement. There was something about Bev that inspired familiarity and confidence. She had a direct gaze and an energy that made her chubby, five-foot-three frame somehow seem taller than it was. She stood there grinning at us in her patchwork vest, white turtleneck, and denim skirt, and her smile held all the warmth and welcome of her Southern heritage. Though she'd hidden her graying hair under an artificial shade of reddish brown, she still exuded a grandmotherly charm that had made me like her on sight.

"Looks like this little one is ready for a nap," Gus said, plopping Shayla in the basket of our luggage cart. Her legs draped over the edge and her feet rested on the stack of suitcases. "How 'bout we head to the car and get you ladies home?" He set off toward some elevators, carrying on a warm, one-sided conversation with the small pink bundle sitting atop the cart.

"I'm so happy you're finally here," Bev said as she linked arms with me and followed Gus through the crowd pressed around the customs exit. "We've been counting the hours. Haven't we, Gus?"

"Indeed we have," he said over his shoulder, turning just long enough to wink in my direction.

And that was the moment the enormity of it all hit home. After so many weeks of frantic preparations and adrenaline-fueled activity, I had expected the breaking point to come. And I'd imagined that something upsetting like a disappointment or confrontation or frustration or one of Shayla's temper tantrums would set it off—but a mirthful wink from a friendly soul? This wasn't the way it was supposed to happen. It was embarrassing and completely out of my control. As Bev ushered me out of the elevator and into the parking garage, my tears began to fall. I told myself to think positive, and still they fell. I told myself that I was making a terrible first impression, and still they fell. I told myself that I was supposed to be the grown-up in this scenario, and still the tears welled up and overflowed my self-control. Bev, who seemed to have witnessed this kind of thing before, merely handed me a handkerchief, patted my arm, and prattled on about airports and airline food and Gus's driving.

I had always prided myself on being able to stifle the kind of emotion that was presently overwhelming me and, in order to do so, had developed various techniques. The *National Enquirer* technique required losing myself in the pages of a tabloid until my own woes seemed minor compared to women birthing chimps and aliens running for the presidency and Madonna claiming to be the reincarnation of King Tut. The Jon Stewart technique involved imagining what the caustic comedian might say about my emotional demonstration, like "Ladies and gentlemen, it seems icebergs are indeed melting" or "And this just in: the women's liberation movement has just been set back fifty years by the sheer spinelessness of an Illinois woman" or even "Yo, Shell, mascara landslides are not a good look for you."

My most effective approach, which I reserved only for desperate occasions like tears in very public places, was the Daddy Dearest technique. This was the most brutal of my emotion-avoidance mechanisms, and it was a surefire solution to my more acute meltdowns. *"Look at you,"* my dad's voice would say in my head, his words dripping with acid, *"carrying on like a two-year-old. You're an embarrassment, Shell. A disgusting humiliation. Stop your whining! Grow up! No one is ever going to give you the time of day if you can't get a grip on yourself. Get out of my sight until you're ready to be an adult. No daughter of mine is a sissy. . . ."*

And on and on his voice would drone, as it was droning now, though it had serious competition from Bev. By the time we reached the car, I'd been battered back into good-girl mode, completely in control and with the lid screwed firmly on. Shayla had fallen asleep in the cart, bent over at an impossible angle, and Gus lifted her into the rear car seat as if he'd had plenty of practice.

"Poor dear," Bev said as she reached into the car to fasten Shayla's seat belt. "Did she do okay on the flight?"

I nodded. "She fell in love with the clouds."

"Well then, she's in the right country! It's cloudy for most of the year around here."

Gus closed the door behind me and climbed into the driver's seat. "Brace yourself, Shelby," he said. "You haven't really driven until you've experienced the autobahn."

"Gus," Bev warned.

"I'll be good, darlin'. I'll be good."

Bev turned in her seat to look back at me, one eyebrow raised. "Gus's 'good' is everyone else's 'certifiable.' I swear—he thinks the autobahn is a challenge to his manhood."

I laughed in spite of myself and tunneled a finger into Shayla's fist, feeling a wave of exhaustion weighing down my limbs.

"You're going to be just fine, Shelby," my new friend said. "You and that precious child are going to be just fine."

"Seat belt on?" This from the man revving the engine in the front seat.

"Yes, sir," I answered, too tired to be seriously concerned about the driving ahead.

Bev handed her husband the parking receipt and pointed him toward the exit. "Get driving, Evel Knievel. The sooner we hit the road, the sooner we get to feed these tired little ladies their very first meal on German soil."

❋ ❋ ❋

SEVEN MONTHS EARLIER

"What is it?" I asked.

"Shut up and eat it," Trey said. He was in full-on chef mode and not amused by my dillydallying.

"Well, since you ask so kindly." I speared a piece of meat with my fork and piled what looked like boiled Honey Smacks on top, wrinkling my nose at the cook before popping his latest concoction into my mouth. "Mmmm," I said, my thumbs-up clarifying the unintelligible review of his masterpiece. I washed the first bite down with a healthy slug of Perrier and motioned for him to keep the food coming. "Hope you have a lot more of this back there, buddy. I'm in an eat-myself-into-oblivion kind of mood."

"Again?"

"Cut the sarcasm."

"Or . . . ?" He didn't look in the least intimidated.

"Or I'll sit on you."

He made a production of hurrying back to the kitchen for more food, mock terror on his face.

"If that's your attempt at making fun of my weight, you should know that I've lost five pounds in two weeks!"

"Good," came his voice from the kitchen. "Another sixty-five and you'll be back to your fighting weight."

"You know, that may have been funny fifteen years ago, but it just sounds dumb coming from a man your age."

"I'm sixteen months older than you," he declared with conviction, reentering the room. "Therefore I'm entitled to say anything I please." He set another plate down across from mine and folded his lanky, six-foot-one body into a wrought-iron chair.

"Oh, be quiet and grow some facial hair."

Trey put his hand to his face, where nothing much had ever grown below the bush of honey-blond hair that shadowed earnest eyes. "Don't threaten my manhood, Shell. I may be thirty-six and virtually hairless, but I'm doing my part for ecology. Think of the razor blades I'm saving."

"And razor-blade trees all over the world thank you for sparing them."

"Not to mention shaving-cream trees." He dug his fork into the steaming food in front of him. "And for the record—and for the thousandth time—you're not fat. Never have been, except in your mind. So get over yourself."

I looked around the empty tearoom. "Slow day?"

He smiled around a forkful of French cuisine. "They heard you were coming."

I mopped up some cream sauce with a piece of baguette. "You never told me what this is."

"Escalope de poulet à la zurichois."

"English, please."

"Chicken breast in cream sauce, with a zing of onion and a *soupçon* of *herbes de Provence*."

"I'll call it Trey's chicken."

"Works for me," he said, rising from the table to open the door for an elderly customer.

I watched him at work, pleased by the enthusiasm on his face that belied the strain around his eyes.

Trey was a passionate dreamer, which meant that he usually met his goals, but at the cost of extreme physical and emotional exhaustion. He was a walking contradiction. Always had been—which I blamed on our parents. From our mom he'd gotten an innate kindness and an appreciation of art, travel, and haute cuisine. And from our dad he'd gotten the kind of drive that had made him a high school soccer star. He was the only teenager I'd ever known whose top grades were in both phys ed and home ec, and though he'd majored in sports education during a truncated college stint, his higher ambitions had found their fulfillment in L'Envie, the homey French bakery and tearoom that also served lunch, from noon to two, to a handful of devoted fans. There was only one meal offered each day, on what Trey called his "Like It or Lump It" menu, but the dishes were so tasty and unique that none of his customers complained.

It was the contrasts I found most endearing in my brother. This chef-slash-coach who had been perceived for most of his life as a sissy-slash-jock had evolved into a functional paradox of the highest caliber, a human being whose spirit and wit and aspirations and compassion far surpassed the best prognoses for a product of our family. Though the term *family* only vaguely applied to us.

Trey ushered his customer out of the store and returned to the table where I sat in front of an empty plate. "Still living in the pantry?" I asked.

He smiled. "It's not a pantry, Shell."

"You know, I'm pretty sure there are apartments for rent in town."

"And I will look into those," he said patiently, "just as soon as I pay off the stove and the bathroom remodel."

"How many of your customers actually use that bathroom, Trey?"

"Not many. But those who do absolutely love the Italian tile and French art."

My brother the aesthete. He'd slept on a cot in a tiny room at the back of the bakery for the past few months to save enough money to transform a cesspool of a bathroom into an international artistic delight. Buying an imported industrial stove, I could understand. It was the kind of investment an astute businessman would make. But a bathroom? I shook my head in despair, neither for the first nor for the last time, I was sure.

"Want more?" he asked, eyeing my empty plate.

I shook my head. "I'm holding out for a decadent dessert later."

He observed me closely and I felt again that warm flow of recognition. We sparred a lot. We loved more. And when Trey looked into me like he was doing right now, I knew that my darkest demons were not only safe, but understood.

"Made a decision yet?" He'd been the first to know about Shayla.

"Yup. I think I'll keep voting Republican unless Roseanne Barr runs again."

"Good," Trey said. "I was worried something stupid like becoming a mom might interfere with your political wranglings."

I sighed. "Dana and I went to see her a week ago."

He put his fork down and clasped his hands in front of him. "And it's taken you this long to tell me about it?"

"I've been . . . Trey, if you could see inside my brain right now, you'd be calling the guys in the white jackets."

"What's she like?"

For the hundredth time, my mind went through an inventory of Shayla's most endearing features. "She's beautiful. Luminous. Artistic. Precocious. Sweet . . ."

"So not a chip off the old block is what you're saying."

"She seems to be everything he wasn't."

"And . . . ?"

"And . . . Trey, I'm terrified."

"Good. Then you're getting the big picture."

"I like my life," I said on a sigh.

Trey raised a dubious eyebrow.

"I do!" I repeated with greater conviction. "I like that there's only me in it. I'm the only one making decisions and living with their consequences. And I'm the only one decorating my house and paying my bills and picking out DVDs. Just me. It's not selfish; it's effective management."

"Yup."

"It's a good life, Trey. I do what I want when I want, I eat what I like, I go where I please. . . ."

"Uh-huh."

"My life is just the way I want it."

"Sure."

"Stop agreeing with me!"

"All right. I disagree."

A brimming silence passed between us. "What part do you disagree with?"

"Oh, you know. The great-life, just-the-way-I-want-it part."

"You don't think my life is good?"

"I don't think your life is as good as you think it is. There's a difference."

I let his words sink in, tasting them like one of his exotic concoctions before voicing my reaction. "So you think I should go ahead with it."

"I think you shouldn't let your 'perfect life' stand in the way of something meaningful."

"But Trey—"

"I know, Shell."

"She's his. His, Trey."

"And for reasons I won't even try to understand, he wanted her to be yours."

"I'd rather inherit his watch. Seriously. I really liked his watch. You know, the gold one with the filigree and the chain and—"

"Yeah, Shelby. I know the watch."

"They need my answer soon. So they can look for other options if I don't take her."

"How soon?"

"A week or two. I might be able to buy more time if I bribe Dana with some of your *esclep di pol . . .*"

He smiled. "I hate it when you try to speak French."

"I love that you hate it."

"Do it, Shell. What do you have to lose?"

His question dumbfounded me. "Uh . . . let me see now." I made an I'm-calculating face. "Yup. Just as I thought. Everything. I've got *everything* to lose."

"Okay, so think about how much you have to gain."

"Like what? How can I possibly know if there's anything to gain from any of this?"

"You can't. Not until you dive in."

"This is me, Trey. I'm not good at diving. And certainly not at diving blind."

"Look on the bright side. You've lost five pounds in two weeks. Shayla might be the best diet plan you've ever attempted."

"But what if she becomes just the latest one I've failed?"

❋ ❋ ❋

"And this," Gus said, "is Lady Shayla's bedroom." He rolled her suitcase across the room and turned to us. "It's little, but it's cozy. And that bed right there—" he pointed toward the small bed below the room's sole window—"is the most comfy bed in the whole town of Kandern."

Bev spoke softly by my side as Shayla and Gus tried out the bedsprings. "I made up both beds for you, so you're all set for now. There's no hurry to get the sheets back to me. I've stocked your kitchen cupboards with the essentials, and there's a water kettle and fresh bread on the counter. That should get you through 'til morning."

So this was home. The past twenty-eight hours of travel and discovery had been a prelude to this. I glanced around the small apartment with the stark white walls and large windows, taking in the hand-me-down furniture and lacy white curtains, and the exhaustion of too much stress descended on me like a lead-filled blanket. I wanted to sleep—desperately so. But I also needed to absorb some of the realness of this moment.

The ride to Kandern from the Frankfurt airport had been memorable, punctuated with multiple near-death experiences caused by Gus's enthusiastic driving. It had taken all the self-control I could muster to keep from throwing my body over Shayla's as a sort of human shield against the collision I knew was bound to happen sooner or later. Driving on a German autobahn was much like playing bumper-car tag at ninety-five miles per hour, but Gus, Bev, and Shayla had seemed oblivious to the danger. While the two adults had carried on a hearty conversation, Shayla had slept, her body warm and supple against my arm.

"That's Europa-Park," Gus had said after a couple hours of driving. "You'll have to take Shayla there."

"What is it?"

"An amusement park. Costs an arm and a leg to get in, but it's great fun. The school goes every year. We put our problem kids on the worst roller coasters and see if we can scare them straight."

"Gus . . ." Bev shook her head—again—and turned to whisper, "He exaggerates."

"I'm sittin' right here. I can hear you, darlin'."

"Only when you want to, love."

As we got nearer to Kandern, the Johnsons described in detail every point of interest we passed, but my mind was more on fear of death than on churches, ruins, and distant mountain peaks. Every time Gus turned to point at something, I pushed an imaginary brake pedal and prayed we wouldn't become the losers in a Porsche-versus-old-beater crash. It was a relief when we finally took the Müllheim exit and merged onto smaller roads that hugged the vineyards.

"We'll be there in a few minutes," Bev said. "I've got a pot roast cooking and plenty of caffeine to perk you up! Oh, and there are two families in town who have some furniture to donate, if you want it, so we might go out this afternoon and see if it's your cup of tea or not. How does that sound?"

I smiled at her kindness and reached over to stroke Shayla's hair, hoping she'd wake slowly from her deep, jet-lagged slumber. "You've gone to so much trouble," I told Bev, moved by the Johnsons' solicitousness. "If you'd rather just drop us off at our place and let us muddle through on our own, that's fine too."

"Nonsense," Gus said. "You're our special guests and we take that kind of thing seriously in the South . . . even if this is southern Germany. Besides, if we leave you alone, you're likely to sleep the day away, and that's just begging for jet lag to beat you. Nope, we're going to get you through your first day in style, Shelby Davis. It's the least we can do for important people like you!"

I observed the countryside as we drove the last miles to the beginning of my new life. The towns were small, some no larger than villages, and it seemed there wasn't a straight road to be found in them. We curled down main streets that wove along streams and tree lines, crowded at times by too-close homes in various shapes and sizes that made the roads and sidewalks appear impossibly narrow.

I loved the gentle slope of hills, the rhythmic lines of vineyards, and the surprising contrast of ancient and modern. Some barns looked centuries old and on the verge of collapse, but they were often flanked by homes so avant-garde in design and color that the two seemed to belong on separate planets. There were small *Gasthaus* restaurants everywhere, and I longed to stop at one and try my first German meal in a courtyard under a canopy of rustling vines. But Bev and Gus had different plans for us, and we rushed toward Kandern in a blur of speeding traffic and overlapping narratives to arrive at their home just in time for lunch.

Shayla woke with difficulty from her too-brief nap, clinging to my neck as I pulled her from the backseat and whining weakly every time I tried to put her down. Bev ushered me into their home and directly to an armchair, where I collapsed with Shayla, grateful for the high armrests that helped me support her weight. Though Shay's eyes were half-open, her mind was clearly still on pause, so I was content to sit there with her in my arms, listening to the Johnsons as they scurried around the kitchen in preparation for our meal. A few minutes later, while a whistling Gus took an electric knife to the pot roast, Bev joined me in the other room.

"Remind me how long you've had her?" Her eyes were compassionate as she watched me trying to balance Shayla and the before-lunch drink she had brought me.

"Six months," I said to Bev, amazed at how permanent such a recent situation already felt.

She smiled and absentmindedly used her dishcloth to polish the silverware she was laying on the table. "What an amazing story you two share," she said, her Southern accent melodious and sweet. "And what a miraculous thing that you've chosen this place to start your lives together."

"Only because of you, Bev."

"Are you kidding? When Gus asked me how I'd feel about watching Shayla while you're teaching, it's like God said, 'There you go, Bev. There you go. You wanted to feel useful, and here's your chance.' I tell you, Shelby, the hardest part of this missionary thing is being away from my kids and my grandbaby. Shayla here, bless her little toes, is going to make it all a lot more bearable for me."

"And for me. This single-mom routine is more complicated than I realized."

"You'll figure it out. There are tricks we moms develop that make life a lot easier."

"Like always carrying a Disney Band-Aid in my purse?"

"And never mentioning what's for dessert before she's finished eating the rest of her meal. That's another winner." Bev shook her head in amazement. "A new mom—in a new country. There's only so much 'new' a person can handle before it becomes a tad overwhelming."

"I passed that point about six months ago." I laughed. "And now I'm adding a new job and a new language to the mix. You think I might be overdoing it a bit?"

Bev chuckled. "And you haven't seen the last of it. The students at this school are—how shall I put it?—unique."

"I figured they would be, with missionary parents and international backgrounds."

"Actually, in most ways, they're not that different from American teens. They get in the same kind of trouble, believe me. But they've dealt with a lot heavier stuff than, say, a fifteen-year-old kid from North Dakota. So they develop some pretty interesting coping mechanisms. That's where the unique part comes in. Old souls and quirky minds make for a great combo. And I wouldn't be surprised if that uniqueness reached entirely new heights when they're involved in a creative project."

"Like acting in a play?"

"Exactly. So you, my dear, are in for a treat."

"I've never directed a play before, Bev."

"Gus hadn't ever been a custodian before either, but he caught on pretty fast. Though I'm sure directing plays is a whole 'nother ball of wax."

My worry was exacerbated by the fog of jet lag. "I don't know, Bev. I've taught English for twelve years, so that part won't be anything new, but . . . theater? I tried to tell them that I wasn't qualified when they gave me my assignment, but no one seemed overly concerned about it."

"Shelby, honey, a person learns two lessons mighty fast at Black Forest Academy. One, there's no business like God's business. And two, what you used to do, think, and be is entirely irrelevant to your presence in this place." She snapped her dishcloth at me and flashed a conspiratorial smile. "But don't tell anyone I warned you."

3

I'D JUST WANTED to make my dad a drawing. That's all. But my old eraser made red marks on my paper and smeared my pencil lines, so I went hunting for another one. I knew Dad had one somewhere in his desk, a white one that used to be square but looked rounder now that all the corners had been rubbed off. It was a good eraser. And it smelled—I don't know—helpful, somehow.

So I went to his desk and looked in the drawers and behind the stacks of papers, even though I knew I wasn't supposed to get into his things. I figured just this once would be okay because it was for him. Dad always watched John Wayne Westerns on TV, so I was drawing him a cowboy on a big black horse, with hills in the background and some Indians' feathers poking out from behind them in red and green and yellow. It was everything he liked right there on one piece of paper, and I was pretty sure it would make him happy—like Tootsie Rolls made my brain grow a smiley face. On days when Trey stayed after school for soccer, I really needed my dad to be less mad.

I didn't find the eraser, not even in the tin at the back of the top drawer where he kept old batteries and rubber bands and twisty ties and paper clips.

I finished the drawing anyway and put it up on the fridge with a basket-of-fruit magnet. Then I waited for him to come home. I could always tell by the way he closed the back door if he was happy or mad. Today he'd slammed it so hard that the glasses in the cupboard rattled and I was glad I'd done something that would—maybe—make him just a bit less angry. Actually, it was more about making me less scared than making him less angry.

Dad went straight to his office before I could tell him about John Wayne, and I could hear him fiddling around for a while. I was trying to get up the courage to interrupt him when he said, "Who's been in my desk?" He kind of growled it more than just saying it.

I could tell Mom was trying to be soothing when she said from the kitchen, "Just Shelby. She was looking for an eraser, I think. Where is that white one, by the way? We looked through every drawer in the house for it this afternoon!" Her voice sounded jittery.

My father stepped out of his museum-clean office and saw me leaning against the arm of the couch. I'd bumped into it backing away from his door.

"You've been going through my things?" he asked.

His voice was quiet. But it was that thunder-behind-the-clouds kind of quiet that made me want to cover my ears and sing "La-la-la" as loud as I could. I figured if I made enough noise, I wouldn't be able to hear it when the thunder really got close. The other option was running really fast and really far. But the rule was no screaming and no running in the house. So I had to just kind of stand there and be scared and hope he wouldn't notice and call me a coward. There was usually another word right before coward, *but it made me feel cringy to even think it in my mind.*

"Answer me," Dad demanded. His voice sounded like barbed wire. The backs of my legs were up against the couch. I couldn't have run even if I'd tried. "Have you been in my stuff?"

I fought the tears. I fought them and fought them. I tried to sing happy songs in my mind, but the stupid tears came anyway and I knew they'd make Dad go from angry bull to exploding bomb—like in the Road Runner cartoons. "I . . . I was making you a present. . . ."

And that's as far as I got. His fingers closed around my arm so hard that my legs gave out. I tried to pry his hand away, but he just held on tighter. I could see Mom peeking around the doorway, but she didn't say anything. She never did. "You will not touch my things again," my dad hissed at me. I could feel his spit hitting my face and smell old coffee on his breath. "If you touch them again, I'll give you a real reason to cry." His fingers tightened some more around my arm as his eyes squinted and slashed.

"Jim?" My mom had found her voice. A squeaky voice, but a voice.

Dad let me go so suddenly that I fell into the arm of the couch and slid to the floor in a humiliated tangle of limbs and loss and misery. It was my fault. I had made him mad with my dumb picture. I knew that he worked really hard and needed everything to be tidy and quiet when he got home. I was stupid, stupid, stupid.

"Keep her out of my office, Gail," my father barked. He turned like a soldier in a parade and marched out of the living room.

❋ ❋ ❋

It was well before dawn when I heard the door of my bedroom open.

"Shelby?" The clear, high voice close to my ear sounded like it meant business. "Shelby, you awake?"

I tried not to groan and pried an eyelid up just long enough to ascertain three facts: I was in a German apartment, it was just after four, and Shayla was looking way too wide-awake for this ungodly hour. By my calculations, she'd gotten just seven hours of sleep, which was roughly ten hours less than I'd hoped for. Her long afternoon nap the day before was coming back to bite us both in the you-know-what. Jet lag was nasty business.

"You wanna crawl into bed with me?" I asked hopefully.

"I'm hungwy."

"Well, sure, but how 'bout we snuggle for a little while before we eat?"

"I'm *hungwy.*" There was a telltale threadiness to her voice this time around. I'd heard it before, usually right about the time this child I'd thought was perfect had launched into an unprovoked crying jag. I pushed back Bev's lavender-scented sheets and swung my feet onto the chilly tile floor.

"You want a piece of bread?" I asked as Shayla and I padded down the hallway from my bedroom to the kitchen.

"Toast," she said.

The apartment looked no better after a night of sleep than it had the day before. There wasn't anything overtly wrong with it. It was just that the walls were all painted chalky white and everything was square and sterile. The off-white tile floors were cold and the furniture was hard and angular. I knew it would begin to feel familiar eventually, but for now, to my sleep-deprived mind, it felt more like a furnished science lab than a home.

I looked through the cupboards without finding a toaster. "There's no toaster, sweetie," I told the expectant child who stood no taller than my hip. "Can we just have bread this morning and we'll buy a toaster later?"

Her mouth twisted a little and her chin began to wobble. "But I like toast," she said.

"Shayla, there's no toaster. And I can't make you toast without a toaster."

"But . . ." A house without a toaster was an aberration to her mind. "But I want *toast*."

Toast was a big deal to my jet-lagged four-year-old. The wobble became a wail that started soft and crescendoed from there. Stream to torrent. Spark to blaze. Zero to sixty before I'd had time to quell it. I tried to reason with her.

"Shay, this isn't our old place. . . . We don't have everything we need here yet."

The crescendo grew to new proportions. So I got defensive.

"There's nothing I can do about it, Shayla. It's practically the middle of the night and . . ."

The wail rose to greater heights. So I decided to get firm.

"Stop that right now, Shayla!"

And off we went into a stratosphere of weeping I'd only visited on a couple of previous occasions. How Shayla managed to stay upright with her head thrown back and her body gone limp was beyond my understanding, but there she stood, tears sliding down her cheeks and neck and under the collar of her Cinderella pj's. While I pondered my options and feared another failure, Shayla gasped and sputtered and gathered another breath, then tore into the second chapter of her wail.

I sighed and lowered myself to the floor, pulling Shayla into my lap and holding her sideways against me. She resisted at first, leaning her body weight outward and down, her hands pushing weakly at mine. But I lifted her closer and kissed her hot, damp temple and shushed quietly against her ear and began to rock, side to side, like a metronome measuring her forlornness. She hiccuped once, twice, swallowed hard, let out another mini-wail, then ran completely out of steam. She burrowed a little deeper and rubbed her cheek against my chest, her lungs spasming in the wake of so much strain.

"Things feel really different this morning, don't they, Shayla." She took a tremulous breath, nodded, and wrapped an arm loosely around my waist. "Do you miss home?"

A tiny bubble of air sighed out of her. "I miss my daddy," she said, and I felt a familiar sinking in my gut. I knew this wasn't completely about her dad. I knew, on a rational level, that this was about a new place and new people and a new bed and a window that hadn't been where it was supposed to be when she'd opened her eyes this morning, but on the level of my own inner six-year-old, her words punched the confidence out of my courage. She missed her dad. She *missed* her dad. There was nothing I could do for that other than hold her a little closer and stifle my denials of her dad's wonderfulness. It was good that she loved him. A little girl needed that. It just made my own loss feel more empty.

We sat on the tile for a few minutes more, which gave me time to assess my response to this latest crisis and give myself a failing grade. I sang Barney's theme song for her, and then she joined in a faltering rendition of "You Are My Sunshine," which never failed to bring back memories of the bright-yellow sun she'd drawn during our very first encounter. "What do you want on your bread?" I asked when we'd sung ourselves dry.

"Stwawberry jam."

Of course. "Have you used the bathroom yet?" She padded off toward the insanely small bathroom while I opened the fridge and prayed for strawberry jam. Bless Bev's saintly heart, there was one jar of jam in the fridge and it had strawberries on the label.

There were three more teary episodes in the hour that followed, which may have set a new record. The first was when she discovered that German bread was harder than the Wonder Bread she was used to; the second was when I suggested she go back to bed and lie quietly for a few minutes as the rest of the world wasn't awake yet; and the third was when we discovered that shower hoses apparently didn't hang from the wall in German bathrooms but had to be held by hand. I knew this would be a bit of a sticking point for me, too. If there was one thing I loved in life, it was a long, hot shower. But I was trying to look on the bright side that morning, so I remembered what I'd been told about the exorbitant price of water in Germany and tried to be grateful that my contortionist showers would probably save me money.

"I want to go home," Shayla wailed as I aimed the water at her hair and rinsed off the shampoo suds she had been shaping into horns and halos minutes before. They coursed down her back between her chicken-wing shoulder blades.

"This all feels pretty weird, doesn't it."

"Wee ohd," she repeated with passion, tears in her voice.

"We'll take a walk around town later, okay? Get to know it a little better. It looked really pretty when we drove in yesterday, don't you think?"

"It's wee-ohd."

"You're right. It is. But you do like Bev, right? She's not weird at all."

"Gus, too."

"They're good people," I agreed as I wrapped her in a thin blue towel Bev had left for us. "And Bev's going to be taking care of you while I'm at work, so you'll get to spend lots of time with her."

"She makes good cookies."

I laughed and wondered if all women were plagued, from such a young age, by an obsession with food. “We’ll get you cookies today too,” I said, and the news seemed to comfort Shayla immensely. So at five o’clock in the morning of my first full day in Germany, I sat on the edge of the tub with a sopping-wet child wrapped in my arms and had a long conversation about cookies and cake.

❋ ❋ ❋

The air felt taut. It was streaked with Daddy’s spittle and tinted gray-green by his wrath. “You will finish your meal!” he screamed into Trey’s stricken face, his bullhorn words a blistering burn, a stab, a hammer strike. “And you will finish it now. So pick up your fork and get shoveling, boy!” He punctuated his tirade with a string of expletives that made my brother shrivel and slump.

Trey looked across the table at me and I tried to wing some courage to him with my eyes, but I knew he couldn’t really see me. It was a weird side effect of my dad’s temper tantrums, as if the loudness of his voice took so much out of us that there was nothing left for seeing or smelling. I’d felt it often enough that I recognized it in my brother—my gentle, tough brother whose eyes looked stubborn and scared.

“Eat!” *my dad yelled again, and when Trey, frozen by fear, didn’t budge, he grabbed a fistful of zucchini and mashed it against his son’s mouth. I saw tears spring out and balance on Trey’s lower eyelids as he clamped his jaw shut and furrowed his eyebrows in a superhuman effort to keep emotions at bay. He had never liked zucchini, had always gagged on it like I gagged on mushrooms, and I knew he’d rather have eaten worms at that moment than chewed on the green triangles he’d so meticulously separated from the rest of his stir-fry. I looked at his plate where the vegetables had been stacked in neat little piles until moments ago. We’d both learned early on that tall stacks made quantities look smaller, and I’d often felt a little jealous that*

Trey's most detested food was so much more stackable than my despised fried mushrooms.

But the ploy hadn't fooled our dad today. He'd come home from work with so much tension ricocheting around inside him that I thought he should have sounded like a beehive. Instead, he sounded like one of those bad guys on TV that hold up banks with masks on their faces—and as a result, my brother looked like one of those dogs that live at rest stops on the highway. I wouldn't forgive my dad for reducing him to that. Not ever. Trey seemed to have shrunk—so much so that I thought I might be taller than him at last. But I knew that was only a for-now kind of thing. He'd grow back to his normal size once my dad slammed out of the house and took off, tires squealing, in his fancy black car.

Right now, though, there was only razor-sharp anger and ugly bullet-words that seemed to be striking my brother from the inside out. I wanted to run around the table and hit my dad's chest until he turned his wrath on me. It was okay for me to cry—I could take it—but I was afraid of what would happen to Trey if those shimmering tears ever fell from their perch onto his flushed cheeks. They would hurt him much more than any of my father's words.

We'd been well trained by now, though. We knew to sit still as statues while my dad ranted and raved. Still as the green soldier on the pedestal in the park. Still as the air when my dad's anger ran out and all we could hear was pieces of our souls drifting to the gouged linoleum like shards of shattered shell.

"You did this," my dad screamed, turning his bile on my mother, who stood clutching the back of a chair on the other side of Trey. His voice sneered as he continued. "You sissified him with your cooing and fawning and now we're stuck with a mama's boy that doesn't have the guts to eat his ve-ge-ta-bles. . . ." He yelled the last word right into Trey's ear and I saw my brother flinch, bits of zucchini still stuck to

his face. I looked to my mom, but there was no salvation there. Only a grown-up reflection of my brother's gut-sick fear.

So I did what I always did when my dad went all Wicked Witch of the West on us. I locked eyes with Trey, whether he could see me or not, and designed stuffed animals in my mind. I was on animal number three when I heard the door slam and my dad's car peel away. I wondered if the stuffed animal in Trey's mind was blood-red too.

❋ ❋ ❋

Shayla was excited that she'd had two mornings today—the first one with the bright-red sunrise, the shower, and the strawberry jam, and the second one without the sunrise and shower, but with more strawberry jam. Strawberry jam was a big item in Shayla's little life. I was only grateful that she'd fallen back to sleep for a couple hours between her two breakfasts. Toward the middle of our "second morning," we ventured out of our new home and into the streets of Kandern. A short walk brought us to the *Hauptstrasse*, a street lined with small stores and restaurants that ran the length of the town. I'd read on the Internet that Kandern was actually classified as a city, the smallest city in Germany by some accounts, but the narrowness of the streets and the smallness of the buildings gave it that barely-larger-than-a-village feel I found quaint and endearing.

I decided that if Kandern were human, it would be a middle-aged man with a big, rounded belly, weather-chafed cheeks, and a hesitant smile. He'd be wearing tuxedo pants below the waist and a plaid shirt above it, equal parts sophistication and down-home charm. Kandern was a farmer looking for a banquet and hoping he'd fit in when he got there.

Shayla and I walked up the street hand in hand, pausing to stare into storefronts at homemade pottery and thick-heeled shoes, then halting again for Shayla to run her fingers under a fountain's waterspout. Though the rest of the town seemed deserted for a Saturday, one plot of real estate was bustling with activity. A farmer's market filled the small square, and stands brimming with fresh fruit and vegetables begged me to spend some of the money Gus had loaned us yesterday on an apple for Shayla. I listened to the conversations going on around us as we wandered the market and waited in vain to hear a word I recognized. There were none. That would come eventually, I told myself—but still, I had never felt more foreign, and I found it disconcerting.

When Shayla finished her fruit, we headed into a nineteenth-century church just behind the market and decided in unison that its garish, life-size crucifix, complete with profusely bleeding wounds and dying grimace, was a little too graphic for our tastes. High above us, in the rear balcony, an elderly gentleman brought a pipe organ to life with hands and feet and soul, and the broad chords of "Ode to Joy" filled the church with a warmth and power that made my heart smile. Shayla, unfortunately, wasn't as entranced as I was with the music, and she dragged me out of the church after just a few minutes to continue our exploration of Kandern.

The square at the center of town, the *Blumenplatz*, was framed by knobby trees and paved with cobblestones. By the time we got there, we'd become accustomed to the greetings we received from just about every person we passed. At first, I'd figured they were mistaking us for someone else, but as I observed other travelers on Kandern's sidewalks, it became clear that these curt greetings were a common thing in this culture. The word they said sounded like *tuck*, and after a bewildered "They don't even know us" from Shayla, she'd taken to the game with vigor. She had no clue what she was saying, but she uttered her *tuck*s with the kind of verve that earned her smiles and pats on the head.

We found a small paper store, on the corner of the *Blumenplatz*, with racks of postcards displayed outside. "Let's get this one for Twey," Shayla said, pointing to a picture of a cow posing in front of snowcapped mountains.

"You sure?"

She nodded vigorously. "Twey likes cows," she said with conviction. "He dwinks milk all the time."

There was no arguing with that kind of logic, so we bought the card and headed home. Bev and Gus were waiting on our doorstep when we got there.

"Are we late?" I asked, embarrassed to have kept them waiting.

"Not at all!" Gus swung Shayla off the ground and perched her on his shoulder. "We old folks tend to get places early, and today's no exception."

Bev wrapped me in a motherly hug. "Did you sleep all right, honey?"

"Right until Shayla woke up."

"I had two mohnings this mohning," came Shayla's voice from above me.

"How'd you manage that?" Gus said.

"I woke up and I ate hawd bwead and then I went to sleep and then I woke up and ate hawd bwead again."

"You think the bread made an impression on her?" I said to Bev.

"But Shelby said we'd get some diffewent bwead this afternoon and maybe a toastoh to toast it."

Gus raised an eyebrow at his wife. "Who's going to break the news?"

"Here's the bad news, ladies," Bev announced. "Only grocery

stores are open on Saturday afternoons in Kandern. All the rest of the stores are closed. And they stay closed until Monday morning."

"They do?" It seemed like a pretty poor economical choice to close stores on the two days of the week when people were actually home, but who was I to question it?

"We can't get a toastoh?" Shayla asked.

"I'll loan you mine," Bev assured her. "But before we do that, how 'bout we go to school and show your mo—and show *Shelby* where she's going to be working?"

Shayla seemed to think she had a say in the matter and pursed her lips in thought. I laughed at the independent streak that was already so strong in her and wondered what her teen years would be like. For her *and* for me. "Let's go, Shayla." I lifted her down from Gus's shoulder so she could walk next to me on the narrow sidewalk.

We arrived at the school a few minutes later, and Gus gave us a royal tour of the premises. One building was nondescript, four stories high, and had recently had a gym and auditorium built onto it. The second building, which stood behind the first, had just been renovated and was home to a state-of-the-art library. The school's classrooms were divided between the two buildings, and it was in the second, newly renovated one that I found mine.

As the academic year had started five weeks before, the teacher covering for me had already made herself at home in the space. There were posters on the walls, pictures and quotes, a portrait of Shakespeare and a poem by Frost. The desks were arranged in two arching rows. I counted just twenty-two of them. A good sign indeed. My last teaching assignment had involved inner-city classes of nearly thirty students, and this, in comparison, looked like a cakewalk.

Gus finished our tour with the gym, a tall, broad space flanked on one side by bleachers and on the other by high windows. I figured I might as well get this visit over with on my first day at school, because chances were slim I'd ever enter the space again. Gyms, in my experience, had nothing to offer but sweat, which I considered humanity's greatest design flaw, and pain, which only looked noble in the worlds of *Braveheart* and *Saving Private Ryan*. So I looked around, acknowledged the gym's size and technology, and mentally checked it off my list of places to see.

Gus was giving me a rundown of the competitive sports in which the school's teams participated when a door above the bleachers opened and a man carrying a bucket entered the gym. Years of effort had trained me well in the art of greeting men who, even from a distance, appeared to be rather attractive. I looked away and focused on my double chins, which Trey insisted I didn't have. But in the distorted mirror of my mind, they were the size of a cherub's rear—and nowhere near as cute.

"Hey, Gus," the sandy-haired man said, raising a hand in greeting.

"Scott! What are you doing working on a Saturday?"

"Beats sitting at home," the younger man answered. "Where's Bev?"

"I traded her in for a younger model!" Gus laughed. "Actually, she's giving a little guest of ours a tour of the ladies' room. Don't go too far—she'll be wanting to see you."

"Not going anywhere," Scott answered, hiking up his jeans and hunkering down to peer more closely at the benches in the bleachers. "I've got a boatload of gum to scrape off before I'm through here."

"Great thinking, my friend! That's one less thing for old Gus to do!"

"A custodian?" I whispered to Gus, my chins swinging against each other in my mind as I spoke.

"The head coach and health teacher," he answered.

"Scott Taylor!" Bev shrilled from right behind me, scaring me so badly with her deeply Southern exclamation that I thought I'd have to make a trip to the ladies' room myself. "Get your buns down here so you can meet my new friends!"

Her voice echoed around the gym as Scott threw up his hands in mock surrender. "Yes, ma'am!" he yelled down to a beaming Bev.

"Smart boy," Gus whispered to me, traces of husbandly pride in his smile. "When Bev gives an order, the only correct answer is a resounding 'Yes, ma'am!' Learned that on my honeymoon."

Scott trotted over to us moments later, and I realized he was taller and younger up close than he'd appeared from afar. A quick glance took stock of his short, wavy hair, his deep-brown eyes, and the shadow of stubble across his jaw. I added love handles to my chin obsession and bent down to straighten Shayla's blue hair clips.

"Scott, my boy," Gus said, "I'd like you to meet Shelby Davis, your future wife."

I straightened slowly—dumbfounded. If Shayla's eyes could have outgrown her face, they would have done so at that moment. Just as my embarrassment was outgrowing my poise. I looked from Gus's cheerful smile to Shayla's frozen stare to Bev's Cheshire grin. I looked into the rafters, I skimmed the gym's blue floor, and I sent up a prayer, once again, for a spontaneous Rapture.

"Well, it sure took you long enough," Scott said, and I could see from my peripheral vision that he was extending a hand toward me. "Where've you been all my life?"

The smile in his voice proved either that he had a healthy sense of humor or that he shared a delusional disorder with my *former* friend, Gus. "Running from humiliating moments just like this one," I answered his question, shaking his hand without ever actually making eye contact.

"She's the English teacher we've been waiting for since the beginning of the school year! And this," Bev added as if this were the most normal conversation in the world, "is Shayla. Shelby's daughter." She caught herself. "I mean . . . Shelby's . . ."

"'Daughter' is fine." I laid a hand on Bev's arm, distracted from my embarrassment by concern for the little girl who still stared up at all four of us as if we'd suddenly sprung horns.

"You getting *ma-wied*, Shelby?" she asked, eyebrows drawn.

I rolled my eyes. Then I rolled them again for good measure. I stopped there because I felt a headache coming on. I picked Shayla up and brought our faces nose-to-nose. "Remember when we talked about this before?" My little girl nodded seriously, her knees digging into my midriff. "What did I tell you then?"

"You're too busy to get ma-wied."

"Right."

Shayla pushed away from me, and I set her down on the floor. With eyes riveted on Scott, who'd been observing our exchange in amused silence, arms crossed, the pale little girl in the blue turtleneck took a step toward him and, hands on hips and forehead furrowed, stated, "She's *not* going to ma-wy you!" She said the words with such conviction that part of me was offended.

Scott hunkered down in front of his pint-size confronter and looked very seriously into her eyes. "Do you know any jokes?" he asked.

Shayla was taken aback by the question. Then again, so was I.

She looked up and around, scanning her memory for a joke, and burst into a smile when one came to her. "Why didn't the man see the elephants?" she asked.

Scott appeared to think hard and then give up.

"Because they were weawing sunglasses!"

Three of the four adults in the gym frowned in confusion. We were still racking our minds for a trace of humor in Shayla's joke when Scott chuckled and said, "See? That's a joke. And Gus here was just making a joke when he talked about your mom getting married."

I held my breath. I'm pretty sure Gus and Bev did too. Shayla, on the other hand, was holding nothing back. She leaned in and, in a conspiratorial whisper, said, "Gus's joke wasn't vewy funny."

"Hey!" Gus was mildly insulted and immensely entertained.

"You tell 'im, Shayla!" Bev said.

"You'll get used to them," Scott told me, pointing his chin toward my new friends as he stood. "They grow on you." He paused. "Kind of like a parasite, come to think of it." He bent low to flick Shayla's chin. "It was very nice to meet you, little girl."

"I'm four!"

"Well then, it was very nice to meet you, big girl."

Shayla found my hand and slunk behind my leg.

"Back to work!" Scott declared, walking toward the door to the bleachers, then turning back to level a pleasant "You two really need to get a hobby" at Gus and Bev.

We exited the building without another word spoken, but once we were well out of earshot, I turned on Gus with an incredulous "What was that?"

Bev took Shayla's hand, crossed the street, and headed toward home. Gus patted my back as we followed after them and met my wild-eyed disbelief with a long, hearty chuckle. "Oh, Shelby," he said when it had passed, "if you could have seen your face!"

"Do you introduce all your friends like that?" I tried to keep my voice cheerful, but there was lead spreading in my lungs.

"Only the ones I like!"

Bev said, "Actually, I don't recall him ever doing that before."

She smiled at me over her shoulder while Shayla gripped her hand to jump over a puddle.

There was something dirty-brown in my mind as we walked toward home. Gus's bold introduction had destabilized the part of me I'd so carefully kept calm over the last two days of change—the part that wanted to flinch like a patient in a dentist's chair every time something new or unexpected came along. I'd done well so far, taking all the newness in stride while I'd stifled my more natural instincts to run and hide with comfort words like "This will pass with time" and "Change never killed anyone." I'd expected the language barriers and feelings of alienation. I'd expected the jet lag and the pervasive, gnawing lostness. But I hadn't foreseen being introduced to a perfect stranger as his future wife. It had never crossed my mind. And it had jolted all kinds of fears and insecurities out of their carefully assigned cages.

I shouldn't have been surprised. Well-meaning people who wanted to introduce me to every available, nonsenile bachelor they knew were old hat to me. Old hat and insulting, although I knew there was a compliment hidden under the strategy of well-planned "chance encounters," blatant hints, and sudden disappearances that left me face-to-face with unmarried specimens of the masculine persuasion. The subtext of the ploys was positive. It said, "We think you're too good to be wasted on a collection of stray cats." Though I appreciated the sentiment, I also found the meddling intrusive and the exhortations belittling. I didn't want a husband any more than I wanted a festering rash. I had never had a serious boyfriend. I had never made a list of proposal scenarios. I had never designed wedding gowns in my head. Other girls' dreams were my "nevers," and I intended to keep it that way. But I *had* sworn off felines years ago in an attempt to outwit the old-maid stereotype.

And here I was in Germany, with just over twenty-four hours of international living under my belt, facing the same brand of matchmaking I'd battled all my life. I wasn't sure if it was the jet lag or the impending start of a new career or the sight of the little girl galloping like a pony ahead of me, but the overt matchmaking didn't feel funny at all this time. It felt invasive and insensitive and just a few notches too close to impossible on my sliding scale of life's probabilities.

4

SIX AND A HALF MONTHS EARLIER

"DANA'S COMING OVER," I said to Trey, pocketing my cell phone, "so I guess you're finally going to meet her."

"She's coming here?" He was arranging pastries in his display window while we talked, stacking golden croissants in a basket and flanking it with twin towers of cream-filled *religieuses*.

"She wants to drive to the lawyer's together so we can talk on the way." I reached into his lighted display case and grabbed a coffee éclair.

"Hey! Put that back!"

I took a bite out of one end and went to put it back on the tray.

"You can't put it back now," Trey said in exasperation, pulling my hand away and rearranging the remaining éclairs to mask the gap where mine had been. "You owe me a buck twenty."

I bit off another large chunk of éclair and spoke around it. "I left my purse in the car."

"Then you can work to pay off your debt. I have another tray of those right over there that need to be filled."

"I'll help you with them if you help me figure my life out." The last piece of pastry disappeared into my mouth.

"Not exactly an even trade," he said, reaching for the pastry tube.

"Gimme the baggie," I muttered, grabbing the bag of vanilla pudding from his hand. Filling éclairs just might offer the kind of distraction I'd been craving. I sincerely doubted it, but it was worth a try. Trey placed a tray of baked éclair shells in front of me and I picked one up. I twisted the top of the bag to force the pudding into its metallic tip, then inserted it into the end of the éclair and squeezed until the pudding evenly filled the pastry's belly.

"So have you seen Shayla again?" Trey appeared next to me with a bowl of frosting. He took the éclair I'd just filled and proceeded to frost it.

I nodded. My eyes felt heavy from thinking, my mind a little raw. "We had a tea party."

"And?"

"And she's still an amazing child. And I'm still the furthest thing from a mother."

Trey said nothing, and we worked in silence for a while.

"He was such a great guy, wasn't he?" I said.

Trey glanced at me. "Dad?" He'd always been able to identify daddy thought lines on my face.

I nodded.

"You mean *great* as in he-beat-the-tar-out-of-his-wife-and-kids-because-he-couldn't-stand-a-noisy-house or *great* as in he's-a-loser-who-should-have-died-a-painful-death-before-he-got-old-enough-to-have-kids-of-his-own?"

"*Great* as in please-God-don't-ever-let-me-turn-into-my-father."

"That's highly unlikely."

"It could happen, though. You know what they say about the apple and the tree."

"I know what I know about you. Period. Fear of becoming Dad should have nothing to do with this decision."

I'd grown accustomed to the heaviness in my chest and the anxiety that came in viscous, lumbering waves anytime I allowed my mind to drift. And standing there beside Trey with images of Shayla superimposing their guilt on everything I saw and touched, I felt my mettle slip again. I was caged in by the dilemma. Trapped between a life that was me-shaped and comfortable and a beautiful child who threatened the predictability that defined my bland existence. I bit my lip to stop it from trembling and looked up into my brother's compassionate face. "Tell me what I should do, Trey." My voice was hoarse with urgency and doubt. My fingers clenched around the éclair as my eyes blurred with tears.

Trey wrestled the damaged pastry from my grip and turned me toward him, his hands warm against my arms. "I can't make this decision for you," he said.

"But I can't, either."

"You've got to make it alone."

I let out a tremulous breath and dabbed at the tears in the corners of my eyes. "But what if—?"

"You're not Dad," he interrupted softly, his eyes sincere and strong. Then he smiled and added, "His mustache was way fuller than yours." He took the pastry tube from my hands and started filling éclairs.

"She looks like you," I said.

He smiled. "Then how can you say no?"

I shook my head and bit my lip again to stanch my emotions. "Trey . . . I just don't know."

Chimes pealed and Dana breezed in, her purple trench coat perfectly matched to her dangly earrings and beaded necklace.

"Hello, Shelby," she said cheerily as she walked up to the counter, looking from me to the handsome baker with the pastry bag in his hands.

"Dana, this is my brother, Trey."

She took in the bush of blond hair, the mischievous gray-green eyes, and the general overgrown-teenager appearance and declared her approval with a heartfelt "Where's Shelby been hiding you all this time?"

"In the back of her closet with that size-two pair of jeans she says she's going to fit into someday."

"It's nice to meet you, Trey Davis," Dana said, reaching over the counter to shake his hand. "Now if I could just remember where I left that fountain of youth . . ."

Watching the two flirting was a little disconcerting. Dana had at least fifteen years on Trey, which, coupled with a husband and three college-age kids, made flirtation pointless, but she had fallen victim to the debonair charm that had always made my brother popular with women of all ages and persuasions.

"Uh, before I turn the hose on you two, how 'bout we get going, Dana?" I rinsed off my hands and went to grab my coat from the rack near the door.

She tore her eyes from my brother's face. "Right," she said, reluctantly backing toward the door. "Much as I've enjoyed making your acquaintance, young man, I'm pretty sure it won't stand up as a valid excuse for wasting Steve Kotz's time!" She took my arm and walked me toward the exit. "He can only give us a half hour, Shelby, so you and I need to figure out exactly what to ask him on our way there."

I met Trey's eyes as I left L'Envie. They gave me courage.

Steve Kotz was the kind of lawyer who inspired both confidence and comfort. His competence was matched by his people skills, and the framed recognitions on the wall of his office proved that the combination had served him well. He looked like a past-his-prime movie star. His features had been softened by age and weight, but the sharpness of his gaze and his thick mane of graying hair still made him look more Alan Shore than Denny Crane.

This was an unofficial, off-the-books meeting Dana had orchestrated merely to put my mind at ease. Steve invited Dana and me to sit in the two luxuriously upholstered chairs facing his mahogany desk and opened a file that bore Shayla's name.

"So, Shelby," he said, folding his hands on top of the file and aiming a warm half smile at me, "your life has certainly taken an unexpected turn."

I tried to smile back, but the sound of waves in my head was making it hard for me to concentrate. It was a sound that had been coming more frequently of late, particularly when I'd tried to formulate a yes or no answer to the Shayla dilemma.

"With everything that's happened in the last few weeks," Dana explained to the family law specialist sitting in front of us, "we thought it might be good to get some explanations from you, Steve. It's a complicated situation, and Shelby's . . . well . . . she's still kind of reeling from it all."

Kind of reeling? Sure. Like Elizabeth Taylor is kind of beautiful and a tidal wave is kind of powerful. There was no "kind of" to my reeling. It was the full-on variety of reeling, which, coupled with the crashing waves in my head, I found exhausting.

Steve glanced down at the picture paper-clipped to the front of Shayla's file. "She's a beautiful little girl," he said.

"And sharp as a tack," Dana answered. They sounded like doting grandparents, not like the advisers I needed them to be.

"What are my options?" I asked before they launched into an inventory of Shayla's most adorable traits. I didn't need to like her more. I needed to make a decision. Soon.

"Well," Steve said, glancing at the sheaf of documents in the file, "this is a perfectly valid, well-executed will. Shayla's father certainly covered all his bases. With the amount he's left for you in savings and investments, I'd suggest you get a financial adviser. If it's well managed, this nest egg could make your life a lot easier."

I didn't care about the money. Or the condo. Or the three-generations-old cuckoo clock. "What about Shayla?"

I felt Dana glance at me, but she kept quiet, waiting for the lawyer's response.

"His wishes are clear. He wants you to be her guardian. That doesn't mean you *have* to be her guardian. It's just his wish and request."

"What about her mother?"

Steve shuffled through the papers. "It looks like she formally renounced any rights to the child—" he scanned a sheet of paper for the date—"six weeks after Shayla was born, give or take a couple days."

"Why would anybody do that?"

"There aren't many details in the paperwork, but Shayla's dad added a few notes to his will, which I'm sure have been passed on to you. He just states that Shayla's mother abandoned her shortly after the birth, that she had never wanted a child to begin with, and that the initiative to rid herself and her family of any future responsibility for the baby came entirely from her. He requested full custody, and as her sole parent, given the mother's voluntary termination of rights, he became a single dad."

"And now I'm inheriting his daughter." The concept seemed so heartless.

"Not inheriting, per se. He named you as her guardian—"

"Without my consent."

"Without your consent. Which means you have a right to refuse Shayla."

"But aren't there other people—people Shayla actually knows—who should take her instead of me?"

"Not that he listed," Steve said, his voice soft and encouraging. "A man of his age raising a child alone . . . He left you everything—including his daughter—which tells me that there probably weren't many other people in his life. And even if there were, you're named as his primary choice, so we'd need an answer from you before considering other options."

I looked at Dana.

"I think Shelby needs to know what the other options are, Steve."

He sighed. "The usual, unfortunately. We'd need to do some research into relatives Shayla's had contact with, but again, as no one has come forward yet, I suspect we won't find any. If that failed, she'd become a ward of the state unless something better could be worked out."

"A foster child?" The term brought Shayla's face to my mind in a rush of guilt and distress.

"Shelby . . ." Dana must have sensed my affliction. She reached over to pat my knee. "The foster care system isn't what it used to be—"

"I've seen the documentaries, Dana."

"The bottom line," Steve said, "is that Shayla's father made his wishes clear, as these documents attest. But you are in no way obligated to take on Shayla's guardianship. It's up to you, Shelby."

I felt nausea clawing at my gut. Steve straightened the documents and closed the file. I saw him hesitate before he added, "Off the record?" I nodded. "His will—the savings, the assets, the condo, Shayla—it could be a new beginning for you if you wanted to see it that way. A new life."

I leaned forward in my chair, resting my elbows on my knees and covering my face with my hands as I expelled a deep, painful breath. Dana's palm against my back was warm and comforting, and I wished she would make this decision for me.

"Why don't you take a few more days to think about it," she suggested gently. "You don't have to start your new life just yet."

❋ ❋ ❋

Play tryouts—the next phase of my new life. I stood before a roomful of eager high school students and questioned my sanity, which wasn't a very original activity. My sanity had been a frequent subject of concern in recent days. I'd questioned it while I'd unpacked a grand total of four suitcases, which contained every scrap of Shayla's and my earthly belongings. I'd questioned it when I'd made my first trip to a grocery store and recognized only a handful of items on the shelves. I'd questioned it when I'd driven my new used car to the school for the very first time and nearly gotten broadsided while turning right on red, an illegal move in this country where driving inspired a need for drugs and therapy. I'd questioned it when I'd met my landlady and gotten only as far as *"Guten Tag"* in what would go down in history as my most awkward conversation ever. And I'd come to the absolute certainty that my sanity had migrated to another planet for the season when I'd walked into the school's auditorium minutes ago and come face-to-face with thirty-eight students auditioning for only ten roles.

I'd been teaching for two weeks already, and though the newness of the circumstances had posed some challenges, the familiarity of teaching English to juniors and seniors was comforting. I knew what I was doing in a classroom. There were well-tested techniques that yielded predictable results. There were curricula and study guides and mathematical assessments of progress. But in the world of theater, the only certainty I'd reached so far was that I knew nothing. And I didn't like it.

I briefly considered being flattered by the turnout for auditions. In a school of just over three hundred students, the nervous teenagers in front of me formed a sizable chunk of the population. But there were too many other concerns on my mind to focus for long on self-congratulation. I'd never directed a play before, and the first step in the process held all the clarity and predictability of, say, a drugged sumo wrestler trying to negotiate a high wire on one foot with a piano strapped to his back. It was a metaphor smorgasbord, but it got the point across. In plainer words, I was petrified.

Being petrified was starting to feel natural to me. The terrifying ride from the airport to Kandern on our first day here had only been an appetizer in the feast of fear of our introductory weeks in Germany. I'd started to invent *-phobe* words to accurately describe my emotions. I was now a card-carrying languageophobe, bratwurstophobe, and bigspendingophobe. That last one sounded a bit contrived, even to my own ears, but after buying a car, a toaster, a pink bicycle, and enough pastries to gorge an army, I was feeling broke enough to warrant my longest *-phobe* word yet.

And, standing at the front of the auditorium, another one came to my mind, perhaps the most pertinent of them all. I was officially becoming an I-have-no-idea-what-I'm-doing-ophobe.

This audition session marked my leap into the chaos and mystery of drama, which was scaring my hair gray. I was relieved to see some of my English students among the prospective actors, but I doubted that our tenuous connection would do much to mask my stunning ineptitude. Months ago, the school's personnel director had assured me that my limited experience would be sufficient for the task. By *limited*, I was sure he'd meant *nonexistent*, as participating in a junior-high speech contest twenty years ago held little relevance to directing a serious high school play. And Bev had done nothing to soothe my nerves in recent days by raving about the productions of previous years, the extraordinary talent of the students, and the high expectations of the entire community.

I cleared my throat, gave the assembled students my patented don't-waste-my-time stare, and stifled the urge to yell, "I'm clueless!" at their expectant faces. Instead, I thanked them for their punctuality and explained to them the challenges of a play like *Shadowlands*. I'd discarded dozens of comedies, musicals, and dramas in my search for something that felt just right. When I'd first read *Shadowlands* and been enthralled by its scope and depth, I'd declared myself deluded and gone on to something else. How were teenagers supposed to bring such human vulnerability and complexity to life? No—this wasn't *the one*. But all the scripts I'd subsequently read about murders and mayhem and monsters and madness had paled in comparison to the story of C. S. Lewis, a famed English writer whose work I'd always admired and whose life somehow touched mine. And here we all were, all thirty-eight students and me, gathered three months later to embark on a voyage of nerve-knotting importance.

The auditorium was a semicircular carpeted space with a wooden ceiling that sloped from the stage to the highest point above the balcony. The stage wasn't much to look at. A raised platform devoid of curtains or wings, with a bare, white wall behind it, it was as conducive to acting as the stomach flu is to cooking. Turning the room into a theater would be a challenge indeed, but that was a concern best left for a much later date. A wall of windows on each side of the auditorium extended from floor to rafters and, as the evening darkened outside, reflected the tense body language of the students assembled for tryouts.

Most of the prospective actors had come well prepared. They'd read the play packets I'd placed in the library and had memorized the scenes we'd be using for auditions. Only one of them truly stood out as the session progressed—both in stature and in talent. His name was Seth. He stood six foot six and had a voice like molten chocolate. But it was his countenance and spirit that caught my attention. Though he was young and enthusiastic, his carriage spoke of strain. His face revealed a melancholy intelligence and a sort of world-weary passion I'd seldom seen in one so young. He took to the stage in long, loping strides and addressed the gathered students in a tortured monologue so authentic that I briefly forgot he was speaking from a script. It was in the silence that followed his last words that I wondered for the first time if the burden of this play might bloom into a blessing.

But I quickly dismissed the notion as a by-product of Lewis's inspirational words and shoved my cynicism firmly back into place. The process was aided by many less stellar moments in the proceedings, culminating in the performance of a freshman girl from Tennessee who went, quite perfectly, by the name of Meagan. She had all the acting talent of, say, a telephone pole, but her giggle was boundless and entirely too rare to ignore. While attempting to bring the role of C. S. Lewis's dying wife to the stage, she stood in front of Seth, as tall as her five-foot-two frame allowed, and craned her neck back so far to see his face that she choked on her own throat in the middle of a profound dialogue and went into a coughing fit. She then collapsed in a giggling jag that ended with a high-pitched Tennessee wail that went something like "Oh—my—gosh! Wait, wait, wait—let me try it again!" It was like watching Betty Boop attempting to tackle a Meryl Streep role. The result was disconcerting and memorable—in an is-this-for-real? kind of way. Two failed attempts later, I made a mental note to invent a job, if need be, that would keep this little lady with the world-brightening giggle involved in the play . . . though not onstage.

Save for Seth's discovery, I was no closer to having picked a cast when the bell rang at five thirty. The students headed in a mass exodus toward the buses that would carry them home to their dorms for dinner, which left me alone in an empty auditorium, shaking my head in dismay at an empty stage. I decided to leave my dilemma for another day and, locking the door and the play behind me, hurried to Bev's to pick up Shayla.

Every school day until now, I'd been met at the door by a happy "Shelby!" and a small, warm body catapulting itself against mine. That wasn't the case today. I rang the doorbell and heard Bev's slippered feet shuffling up to the door. I could tell from her smile that all was not well. "She's in the kitchen drawing," Bev answered my inquiring look.

"Is she okay?"

"Well . . ." She ushered me into the sage-green living room and we sat on either side of her faux-wood coffee table. Looking over her shoulder toward the kitchen, she went on in a hushed tone. "Today was a little hard."

"Hard how?"

"A snowball kind of hard. First it was her missing hair clip, and then it was the bread."

"Again?"

"She's definitely got a Wonder Bread obsession." Bev smiled. "Then it was the crayons."

"What's wrong with the crayons?"

"The red wasn't red enough."

"It's the exact same red it's always been!"

"Well, it wasn't red enough today."

I was confused. "And then?"

"And then she wasn't tired enough to take a nap, and then she didn't like my cookies anymore, and then her leg hurt, and then the spoon made her teeth feel weird, and then she put her coat on and hasn't taken it off since then. . . . It was a hard day is what I'm saying. But I don't think it has anything to do with crayons and bread."

I ran a hand over my face and tried to clear my thoughts. "She's been so good so far."

"She's been wonderful. She's *still* wonderful. I just think it's all starting to hit her. And your staying late tonight probably didn't help."

"I had play tryouts."

"She knows that."

"And I'll have play practices nearly every evening starting next week." I felt familiar walls closing in around me. They were labeled in Shayla's favorite red with glaring words like *motherhood*, *responsibility*, *dependence*, and *failure*.

"It's not just that, Shelby. You realize that, don't you?"

"I'm not sure I want to. . . ."

"Kids are resilient, but they still feel loss. They live it and then they relive it, and it gets triggered by small things that seem completely insignificant."

Insignificant. "Like moving halfway across the world with a new mother who isn't really her mother?"

"Like losing a hair clip her daddy gave her. It's a matter of grief."

I laughed without humor and sank lower in my chair, my head against the backrest, the strain of the last two weeks suddenly weighing heavy on my limbs. I was doing my best to handle teaching in a new school and not knowing the language and directing a play that so far had only one actor. But a four-year-old child whose grief was making her leg hurt and her teeth feel weird? It felt like the proverbial last straw, and I could hear the camel's back straining. "She hates being here," I said.

"I wouldn't say that."

I took a long, deep, resigned breath. "Maybe we should've . . ."

"Don't you go second-guessing yourself, Shelby." Bev's voice was soft but firm.

"I knew it might be too soon. . . . I knew it before we came."

"And you haven't been here long enough to gauge anything yet. Give yourself time."

"But Shayla's . . ."

"Shayla has lost her dad."

"And her country and her day care friends and her Wonder Bread . . ."

Bev leaned across the coffee table, grabbed my hand and pulled it toward her, clasping it in both of hers. "Shayla has lost her dad," she repeated, more firmly this time. "All the rest is just more losses that remind her of that one. She's not accumulating loss; she's reliving it. And there are going to be days like today when the loss makes her life feel a little less red than she wants it to be."

"I'm still pretty new at this mothering thing, Bev. How do I know if I'm doing it right?"

"You are doing it right. You're setting firm boundaries and loving her fiercely," she assured me, squeezing my hand in hers. "That worry you're feeling in the pit of your stomach? It means you've got the most important part right."

"Play season starts next week." I felt backed into a corner. "I'll be getting home late and . . ."

"So she'll have a few more days like today and she'll throw a temper tantrum or two and you'll reassure her that you love her and she'll still love you no matter what."

I sighed and straightened. "I promised her we wouldn't stay if it got too hard."

"And I promise you I'll let you know when you have real cause to be worried. Right now, she's just acting exactly the way she should under these circumstances."

"Are you sure?"

She smiled. "I'm sure."

The mystery and responsibility of motherhood both baffled and exhausted me. "How old were your kids when you finally figured it all out?"

"Oh, twenty and twenty-two." She laughed. "It's not a learning *curve*, Shelby. It's a learning *slope*. It just keeps on going up."

When I entered the kitchen, Shayla was slumped over her drawing in her fuzzy pink coat, fast asleep.

"You want Gus to drive you home when he gets back from the store?"

I shook my head. There were few things in life that brought me the kind of marrow-deep peace I felt when I held Shayla's softness in my arms. When I picked her up, partially waking her in the process, she wrapped her legs around my waist and both her arms around my neck and held on tight. And we walked home like that, me embracing her and her embracing me, me rescuing her and her rescuing me. And the sun setting over Kandern seemed just a little redder somehow.

5

SIX MONTHS EARLIER

"Nice," Trey said.

I looked around the condo and wondered what he was seeing that I wasn't. Nice? The walls were straight and the windows were clean, I'd give him that. The laminate floors weren't bad either and the fairly new kitchen held definite potential, but nice? No. The condo was an eclectic collection of old-man smells and single-guy knickknacks and way too many small-child toys. The only draperies I'd seen were in the balloon-themed bedroom upstairs, and the furniture from top to bottom was a tribute to the worst the '70s had to offer.

"Sure, Trey," I said. "This is nice. Nice like *All in the Family* meets *Sesame Street*."

But it was tidy and warm and spacious and in a good part of town, and most importantly, just a few blocks from L'Envie.

"Maybe I'll buy you a lava lamp as a housewarming present," Trey said.

I swatted his arm and walked to the bay windows overlooking a small, man-made pond. I tried to picture a younger Shayla out there feeding the ducks, her two-year-old bowlegs pumping stiffly as she chased them into the pond. And I tried to picture a tall, sixty-year-old man, slightly stooped with age and regret, trying to catch her before she fell in, then both of them walking slowly back to the condo, hand in hand, while he pointed out trees and flowers and stones to his tiny, adoring daughter.

It was the "adoring" part I had the most trouble imagining. Yet every surface in the condo seemed to hold pictures of a devoted father and his loving child picking pumpkins, decorating Christmas trees, swimming at the beach, and posing with Mickey Mouse. I hadn't seen one picture that didn't reflect utter happiness and mutual affection. Even in the snapshot of Shayla in the hospital that I'd found in a kitchen drawer, the little girl, dwarfed by her big bed and the monstrous teddy bear she was hugging, had something that looked like serenity in her eyes. The note on the back of the picture said, "Shayla—tonsils—Apr. 15," and I had stared at the handwriting until it blurred, trying to find a trace of familiarity in it.

"So what do you think?" Trey asked from right behind me.

"About what?"

"Oh, you know, the price of gas. The condo, Shelby! What do you think about the condo?"

I sighed and smiled. "It looks just the same as it did last week, and just the same as the week before that."

"And . . . ?"

I took a deep breath and held the keys up so they dangled between us.

"You're going to keep it?" He sounded pleased, unaffected by the conflict between the hand-me-down home and my hand-me-down wounds.

"Sorta." I took his hand and dropped the keys into it. "Can I use the couch if I stay overnight?"

His gray-green eyes got wider. He opened his mouth, then shut it and frowned. When he opened it again, I held up a finger to stanch the flow of perfectly rational arguments I knew was coming and launched into a monologue of my own instead.

"It's perfect, Trey. Perfect for you. It's close to work. It's furnished. . . ."

He wrinkled his nose.

"It's got a new kitchen."

He looked more hopeful.

"It's in a good neighborhood, and—" I grabbed his shoulders—"it's not a pantry!"

"I don't sleep in a pant—"

"You do. You've moved a cot and a lamp into it, but Trey, it—is—a—pantry!"

"This is your place. He left it to you."

"And I want you to have it."

"All right, we've got to talk," he said grimly, taking my hand and dragging me to the couch.

"Trey . . ." We sat facing each other on the green-and-orange hide-a-bed that squeaked when we moved, and Trey kept my hand firmly in his.

"Shell . . ." He paused and shook his head with a smile that said "my sister the doofus." "You are not giving this condo to me. Period. It's paid for. It's cute."

I raised a dubious eyebrow.

"You know what? It's everything you just told me it was. So use it! Live in it!"

"It was his," I said. The words sounded brittle.

"And you think that has any less of an effect on me?"

I shook my head. "I think you're stronger, though."

He laughed at that. "And you're . . . what? Weak? Helpless?"

"Furious."

"I know. It's a terrible cut, but seriously, Shell, your hair will grow back."

"Trey . . ."

"I don't know why he left it for you, but he did. So . . . be thankful. It's your place now. At least, it will be once you've burned all the furniture and painted some walls. And I know a great bathroom guy if you want to remodel that."

"You know," I said, finally voicing the thought that had been on the tip of my mind for the past three weeks, "you should be furious too. You were just as much his kid as I was, and you were hit by just as much of his shrapnel. You were his firstborn, Trey, and I can't figure out for the life of me why you're taking all this so well. You should be hating me for being on the receiving end of his last will and testament."

He shrugged and smiled some more, but there was something bruised in his eyes.

"In any other family," I continued, rolling my eyes at the ridiculousness of the whole thing, "Mom and Dad would leave a nice little bundle of junk for their kids to inherit. A stamp collection. A few picture albums. A time-share in Aruba. Maybe even a dog. But in ours?" I laughed. Then I laughed again, harder.

By the third laugh, I knew I was on the verge of hysterics, so I reeled in the humor and put a lid on the levity. "In our family, Dad leaves, Mom dies, Shell and Trey move on; then Dad dies too and . . ." I wasn't sure where the tears had come from. They weren't part of the plan.

I swallowed hard. "Dad dies," I resumed, "and we inherit what? No—wait. Not *we*. Just me. What's up with that? *I* inherit—me, Shelby Davis—I inherit a condo, a truckload of money, and a four-year-old half sister he had with heaven knows who. Trey," I said, my voice brimming with incredulous anger, "*weak* doesn't begin to cover what I'm feeling—what I've been feeling since Dad's lawyer knocked on my door. I am winded, stunned . . ."

The tears came in earnest then. "I don't know what to do," I groaned, leaning into Trey with abject devastation forcing sobs from my constricted lungs. Three weeks of utter desperation burst through my restraint and rained a bruising hail of betrayal, fear, and anguish down on me.

And Trey? Trey remained the person he had always been—my anchor, my defender, my friend. He was the eight-year-old boy who patted my back and dried my tears, the twelve-year-old rescuer who convinced me we'd be fine, the sixteen-year-old knight who promised to make it better, and the thirty-six-year-old champion who persuaded me that this latest assault would not shatter me either. Nothing else my dad had done had managed to destroy me, and this—this aberration both for Trey and for me—would not undo us.

"I need you to keep the condo," I told him when reality had grown more bearable again. "And we're splitting the savings. I want you to have a home, Trey. I've already got my own and it feels like me. So take this one. Take it just to infuriate him, wherever he is, because he didn't leave it to you."

"You make a good case."

"He was your father too."

"Don't remind me."

"And if this is his last-ditch, posthumous attempt at hurting us, we need to show him that he can't."

"I don't know, Shelby."

"I do," I said, and for the first time in forever, I actually felt certain of one thing. "This is a good thing for you, Trey. It's what you need. And it's what I need because it's driving me nuts picturing my brother sleeping in a pantry."

"I—"

"Shut it, Trey. You're taking this place off my hands. And that's it. Done. 'Signed, sealed, delivered . . .'"

"'. . . I'm yours.'"

We spent a few moments talking about other things. Another tactic we'd developed in thirtysome years of deliberate denial.

Then Trey came back to the trauma at hand. "So . . . can we talk about this?"

"I thought we just did."

"No, about Shayla."

Shayla. "Well, I've pawned this place off on you and the money off on an accountant. What do you think? Can I pawn Shayla off on the state of Illinois?"

He didn't answer. He just looked at me. I suddenly understood what microwave popcorn felt like. He was watching me pop and waiting for me to be finished.

"What do you think I should do?" I asked.

"Be true to yourself."

"So helpful."

"I try."

"And 'myself' is . . . ?"

"'Yourself' has a good heart. A warm heart. Something you didn't inherit from our dad."

Deep breath. "Trey . . . She's so—"

"You know, there's a chance—a very small chance—that the old man got a couple things right in his life. The first was marrying Mom. No one else would have put up with him for so long."

"And the second?"

"Giving his daughter to the best possible person for the job."

"You mean giving his *illegitimate* four-year-old daughter to his *estranged* thirty-five-year-old daughter."

"Hey, I never said this family didn't put the *fun* in *dysfunction*!" He wandered to the kitchen and started opening cupboards. "And in his defense, it looks like he actually put some thought into things this time. I mean, it's not like he just handed off his daughter and expected you to make do. She comes fully loaded with a condo, a college fund, a cuckoo clock, and a babysitting uncle."

"And a '64 Impala." I smiled at his incredulous look. "Convertible. Cherry red."

"He left you his car, too?"

"Two of them, actually. I'm donating one, but the Impala's for you. Custom-restored and kept in mothballs since Shayla was born." I held up a second set of keys. "Congratulations, my friend. You're the new owner of your very own chick magnet."

He shook his head. "A '64 Chevy, huh? Too bad I don't have a thing for fifty-year-old broads." He took the keys and stared at them for a moment, considering the emotional strings he knew would be attached. Then he pocketed them and let his dimples reveal his conclusion. "You sure?"

"I'm sure," I answered.

"About the condo, too?"

"Yup." I followed him toward the kitchen and took stock of the time and effort he'd need to invest to rid the space of my father's presence. "So—you think you can do something with this mess?"

He leaned against the counter and surveyed the small room.

"I think I know just the right shade of Italian tile to make the cupboards pop."

❋ ❋ ❋

From where I sat on the edge of the stage at the front of the auditorium, I could hear Italian, French, and a couple other languages I didn't recognize. It was round two of the play auditions, and there were only a little over twenty students in attendance this time. I'd thanked the rest of them for their efforts and, squelching the part of me that wanted to throw myself at their feet and beg for their forgiveness, had informed them that there just weren't parts that suited them in this year's play. So the twenty-three pairs of eyes begging me for mercy on this cloudy afternoon were all the more nervous about the verdict to come, and their performance jitters had made them revert to their comfort languages to express their insecurities.

The vulnerability of these young people had become increasingly evident in my first couple of weeks in Germany. At the beginning of my time here, they had shown few differences from the teenagers I'd taught back home. They had the same scattered study habits, the same discipline issues, and the same aversion to rules. All of those were familiar to me—and somehow comforting, too. But there were other facets to these students that I was only beginning to discern.

A handful of them had asked if they could eat their sack lunches in my classroom every day, and I had allowed it, as the only alternatives were a crowded, noisy cafeteria and the bleachers in the gym. So Grace, Nicole, Liz, Sunny, and Fiona had become regular lunchtime companions. Instead of talking among themselves, though, they'd drawn me into their discussions, asking my opinion on topics as varied as morality, global warming, and Lindsay Lohan's latest scandal. They wanted more from me than a good grade and a manageable homework load. They wanted my input and my guidance, and I found it disconcerting to be personally involved in the lives of students in a way I'd never been before. I was happy to try, though, because I was coming to love these contradictory creatures—self-sufficient and dependent, mature and naive, complex yet still simple enough to play duck-duck-goose in the school parking lot when there was nothing else to do.

But it was another kind of play the students had on their minds this afternoon. I'd cast four parts already, though I'd told no one yet, but I was still looking to fill several major roles, including C. S. Lewis himself and Joy Gresham, the New York native who had blown into Lewis's life like a tornado of cynicism and somehow managed to transform the stodgy scholar into a man softened and empowered by love. Needless to say, the role was a challenge of monumental proportions, and my sights were set not so much on finding the best actress as on finding the least bad one. It was an approach I'd used in the past for buying cars and choosing shoes, and I'd found it to be immensely practical, if not entirely gratifying.

The tryout scene I'd selected was Lewis's declaration of love to Joy. I'd been a victim of enough misguided declarations in my life that I knew just how complicated and awkward the practice could be, and I figured I should set the bar high for this first face-to-face scene between wannabe Lewises and potential Joys. In the script, Joy eventually forces the issue by saying, "Back where I come from, there's this quaint old custom. When a guy makes up his mind to marry a girl, he asks her. It's called proposing. . . . Did I miss it?" But a sadistic streak that scared me just a little had made me deviate from the script on this afternoon and instruct the students to spontaneously make up their own proposal, in keeping with

C. S. Lewis's character. And to push the meanness just a little bit further, I had announced that all the actors would have to submit to the torturous scene, not just the ones trying out for lead roles.

Oh, the sheer entertainment of watching teenagers trying to be at once intensely romantic and casually credible. The attempts ran the gamut from gut-wrenching to sidesplitting. One actor seemed to be doing an imitation of a British Rocky Balboa, all emotionally battered by philosophical cogitating, begging his beloved to marry him as if some sort of horrendous physical harm would befall him if she were to say no. Another less dramatic young man opted for a more lighthearted approach and simply mimed clubbing Joy into unconsciousness before slinging her over his shoulder and carrying her off to his . . . Oxfordian den?

My personal favorite, however, was the scene between Seth and a young lady called Kate. Seth was a senior and she was just a sophomore, so there was a good chance neither of them had really spoken to the other before. Still, I thought they might be a good match. There was a bit of a rebellious edge to Kate, the kind of countenance and carriage that said, "Your welcome only extends so far." And Seth's response to her defiance was an expression and body language that were at once awkward and curious. The pairing looked promising, and I gave them the signal to start. I should have known something noteworthy was in the offing when Seth took a moment to gather his thoughts before stepping onstage. The other actors hadn't so much as marked a pause before launching into the scene. Kate, on the other hand, walked onto the stage with her usual purposeful stride and struck a stance that reminded me more of a wrestler than of fortysomething Joy.

They moved to sit on the make-believe bench we'd fashioned out of three chairs, and then, for seconds that stretched to the breaking point, neither of them said anything. Seth sat in hunched bewilderment, and the eyes he turned on Kate spoke of such reluctance and yearning that the air between them grew taut. She returned his gaze with a sort of competitive defiance and provocation that seemed to shrink him for a moment even as it grew her into an imposing presence.

Seth looked away, wiped sweaty palms on his pant legs, then gathered the courage to meet her gaze again. Only this time, there was something of a challenge in his eyes, and the bravado that had masked Kate's frailty yielded to a femininity that instantly softened her lines and gentled her carriage. Their eyes held as a blush crept up Seth's neck. He reached toward her, his hand visibly shaking, then withdrew it. When he turned to face away from her, there were protests from the students watching the scene unfold. Kate hardened a little again, though there were cracks in the armor this time, and just as she stood to leave the stage, Seth whispered, "Will you marry me?"

It was so quietly uttered that I wondered if I'd imagined it, but a Korean girl in the front row let out the kind of heartfelt "Aw" that confirmed how real and stirring the moment had been.

I didn't know much about play directing, but I did know that the kind of improvised acting I'd just witnessed was rare—even more so at a high school level. If truth be told, I'd felt a little pang of envy at the scene, and I knew enough to jot down two names next to the parts of Lewis and Joy. It may not have been true love I'd seen on that stage, but it was something worth exploring further.

I was hurrying to Gus and Bev's at the end of the session when a figure in shorts and a torn sweatshirt emerged from an alleyway at a dead run. Night was falling and the street was deserted, so I stepped off the curb to change sidewalks and avoid the oncoming runner. I knew this was Germany, where the odds of being stampeded by a herd of cows were probably higher than being attacked by a jogger, but survival instincts and a college self-defense class propelled me across the street nonetheless. I hadn't gone two steps when the runner slowed his pace and, coming to a full stop, said my name. I was so surprised that I didn't respond immediately, and the jogger walked up to me and peered more closely at my face. "It's Shelby, right?"

"Uh . . . yes. Yes, it is." I took a deep breath and covered my heart with my hand to muffle the beating I suspected Scott could hear.

"Sorry—didn't mean to jump out at you like that."

"Oh, it's okay. I was just a little startled, that's all."

"Hey, it's getting dark out here. Would you like me to walk you home?"

Fierce independence reared its ugly head. "Oh, no. Thanks, though. I'm just going as far as the Johnsons' to pick Shayla up."

"I'll walk with you."

"Uh . . . You know, that's really kind of you, but it's only a little bit farther and it's still kind of light out and I really enjoy the time to think before I pick Shayla up."

"Hey, that's fine. No problem." He used his sweatshirt to wipe his face and stood there a moment longer. "I haven't seen you around since you got here."

"Well, you know, you live in the gym." I attempted some humor to cover my awkwardness and send him on his way. I failed. All he did was scrunch up an eye in confusion. "I don't do gyms," I clarified. "They give me the heebie-jeebies. Too many jumping jacks when I was a kid."

He grinned at that and wiped his forehead with his arm. "So you're not into sports."

"I'm into fork lifting. I hold the world record. But only when cheesecake is on the fork and there's a glass of milk nearby. Otherwise I stick to stepping on my scale once a day for exercise."

Being funny was exhausting. But his chuckle was gratifying, so I attempted one more zinger. "Besides, I have this rare medical affliction that makes me yodel if I sweat, so . . ." Yup. No reaction. One zinger too far. "I'll see you later then," I said into the lengthening silence. The streetlights came on and I saw a sparkle in his eyes. He was laughing on the inside—I was sure of it. "So, uh . . . enjoy the rest of your run!" It was a cheerful dismissal, which he was kind enough to obey.

"Thanks, Shelby," he said with laughter in his voice, and he took off down the street yodeling like a maniac.

❋ ❋ ❋

My father was singing. Which was a frightening thing. It was frightening for two basic reasons. One, he had the musical ear and sensitivity of a foghorn. Two, it meant he was happy—chipper, if such a word could apply to someone like him. And the higher the high, the harder the fall. So it was a walking-on-eggshells kind of day again.

My mom was so solicitous over breakfast that I knew she was bracing us all for the worst. It was an unspoken language between us, a sort of codependent shorthand Trey and I had PhDs in—when Mom made chocolate chip pancakes and beat up real whipped cream to go with the chocolate sauce, we knew there was something unpleasant on the way. And by unpleasant, we meant out of control, out of proportion, and completely out of his gourd. My dad, that is.

Dad joined us late for pancakes. He'd been singing while shaving, which always made the process take longer. But he liked the resonance in the bathroom and I think he imagined the whole neighborhood was listening in rapt attention. His face was never smoother than on a day when he'd been singing.

My dad was the only man I knew who wore a tie to mow the

lawn, and he was wearing one today. It was that kind of professionalism that had propelled him so quickly to the top position in the first investment firm he'd worked for, then allowed him to start his own firm two towns over from where we lived. We weren't poor, but you'd never know it. Dad believed in making money, not spending it, and he was perfectly content living in my grandmother's old house with squeaky floorboards, water-stained ceilings, and decades-old wallpaper on every square inch in sight.

My dad took his place at the head of the table. To be honest, the table was pretty much square, so there was no geometric head. But it seemed to make him happy to think there was one, so we all played along and made him feel important. He stacked four pancakes on his plate, and Mom poured so much chocolate syrup over them that I half expected them to float off the edge of the plate and onto the floor. Which might have caused the outburst we all feared. So I sat in front of my own melted-cream-saturated pancakes and willed his to stay in place. Please, God, let them not make like a barge and flow downstream.

"Thermos, Shelby," he said. Which was my dad's way of saying, "May I please have the thermos of coffee, my beautiful daughter?" I liked his voice better in my head. I watched him spoon enough sugar into his coffee that it should have permanently sweetened his countenance, but life wasn't fair that way. After all, this man who was devouring four pancakes and already eyeing the ones coming off the griddle, this man who could order two McDonald's meals without blinking, this man to whom oversweetening was a culinary habit, not a character trait, this very same man was so thin that seeing him without a shirt on made me want to feed him butter. I, on the other hand, seemed to be wearing my butter—mostly around my hips and chest. And at the ripe old age of thirteen, it felt not only ugly, but icky in a can't-I-just-be-a-skinny-man kind of way.

"Got practice before the game?" he asked Trey. There was a game

that afternoon, and Trey's team was so riddled with incompetent newcomers to the sport that they often resorted to pregame scrimmages to try to get their act together.

Trey nodded yes. Then he went back to eating.

It had become something of a hobby trying to imagine the subtext of conversations that happened on my dad's happy days. Under normal circumstances, there would have been no subtext needed. He would have hit us right between the eyes with his personal brand of overt insult and not-so-subtle disdain. But on his happy days?

"They're lucky to have you," he said. Translation: Anyone says anything bad about my son and I'll have their head. Insulting you is my job.

"Thanks, Dad." Translation: I hate it when you're happy—makes me squeamish. *Trey gulped some orange juice and caught my eye-rolling. His eyes crinkled. I liked making him smile.*

"Cleats still feeling okay?" Translation: You should be kissing my feet for spending so much money on your cleats, young man. I'm a wonderful dad.

"Yup. Fine." Translation: I'd rather kiss Sonya Roland than say thanks to you, and she's got zits and braces.

"Well, try to score one for the old man." Translation: I've got a belt and I'm not afraid to use it. You stink, you sting. That's the rule.

"Sure, Dad." Translation: Like I'm ever going to put any effort into making you happy, you pompous bag of bones.

I wanted to play too. "It's too bad you hurt your ankle skateboarding," I said. "Maybe you'll be able to play anyway, though." Translation: Let's see if we can make Dad crazy by letting him think you might not get to play.

"What's wrong with your ankle?" He put his fork down and narrowed his eyes. Translation: How stupid have you been, Son?

"It's fine, Dad." Translation: Please don't get mad, please don't

get mad, please don't get mad. *Trey sent me an are-you-nuts? glare and swallowed a too-large bite of pancake.*

"What's with the ankle, Son?" The distant sound of thunder was in his voice.

"Nothing," Trey answered, an almost imperceptible tremor weakening his words. I knew it meant fear, but to my dad, it sounded like guilt.

He leaned across the kitchen table, the napkin he'd stuck in his collar brushing the chocolate syrup on his plate. "What—did—you—do?" Strange that a minute before his face had looked clean-shaven. Now, with the blotchy red creeping up from his collar and the dirtiness of his scorn flaking out from his eyes, it looked like a kind of threatening stubble was growing out of his skin.

Trey saw it too. "I didn't . . ."

My dad pushed away from the table with so much force that a couple of plates went flying and the milk container tipped over. Mom, who had been standing frozen at the counter, rushed in with a dish towel and mopped up the milk before it spilled onto the floor along with more of Dad's wrath.

"Dad, I didn't mean—"

His hand came down so hard on the top of my head that I bit my tongue and felt my jaw go weird. He pressed his fingers into my skull like it was a watermelon he was trying to crush. I felt his pancake breath wetting my ear when he hissed, right next to it, "Shut up, Shell."

There were stars behind my eyes when he released me, so I didn't actually see him shove Trey's chair back so hard that it toppled over. My brother looked like one of those beetles that can't figure out how to get up off their backs. So I guess my dad decided to help him by flipping him over onto his stomach with his shoe. He flipped him hard and Mom yelped and I jumped off my chair and went to grab Dad's arm because I knew what he was thinking and Trey kinda crawled away as fast as he could, but his knees kept slipping in the mess of his pancakes.

I grabbed my dad's arm harder and said, "I didn't mean it, Dad! I was just being funny! Trey's ankle is fine! Really, it's fine! He hasn't been on his skateboard in forever!" But he wasn't hearing anything right then except Trey's cowering. He flung me off his arm so hard that I hit the fridge. Then he leaned down to pick my brother up by the front of his shirt. My mom had retreated to the sink by then and I wished she would throw herself on her husband's back and ride him and pummel him until he stopped, but she twisted the towel in her hands instead and kept saying, "Jim. Jim, stop. Please, Jim." Which I thought was a very ineffective approach.

My dad had Trey shoved into the corner of the wall and cupboards, and Trey had gone from looking scared to looking mean. He hadn't been able to do that until the last couple of years or so. But somehow he'd managed to figure out how to stop being frightened and start being mad. It hadn't really changed the outcome of my dad's happy days, but I think it left Trey feeling somehow less destroyed.

"I'm not injured, okay?" he croaked bravely, trying to pry my dad's fingers from the front of his shirt. "Let go of me, Dad!"

I tried to squeeze between my mother and the sink, thinking maybe her towel would protect me from what I knew was coming.

"Let go of you?" My dad was going rigid. "Let go of you?" he repeated, as if Trey's request were colossally insulting. And he did let go then. He released Trey's shirt and used that hand to slap him across the mouth—hard.

"Dad!" I yelled. "Dad, I was just joking. There's nothing wrong with his—"

When my dad turned on me, I realized I'd crossed the kitchen and grabbed his arm again. I felt something wet on my face, but it couldn't be tears. I wouldn't let it be tears.

"His ankle is fine," I said, trying to look like Trey, but I could feel my chin wobbling, so I clamped my jaw to stop it. "I was just being funny, Dad! I was just—"

The look he gave me dried up my words. He stood in front of me smelling like sweat and coffee and injustice. He was shaking—I could see it. And there was a vein popping out near his hairline. But it's his eyes I remember most clearly. He looked at me like I was at once invisible and intolerable. He didn't really see me. I was sure of it. He saw a weak, whiny, repulsive, and unwanted distraction. He made a kind of snorting sound that would have been funny under any other circumstances. Then he gave my mom the same kind of look he'd given to me, turned on his heel, and slammed the door on his way out of the house.

Mom rushed to Trey, who'd slid halfway down the wall and was bracing with his legs to keep from slipping farther. She helped him to a chair and got a wet rag to put on his lip. It was split a little. But he didn't look mad anymore, which was good. It scared me when he looked that way. I picked up his plate and put it on the table in front of him, then I sat down on the chair next to his and kinda waited. We never knew quite how to bridge the gap between terrified and normal.

"I was just trying to be funny," I finally said.

He turned his eyes to me and I could see he didn't hate me. I couldn't ever figure out how he did that.

He smiled a bit, but I could tell it hurt him, so he settled for smiling with his eyes instead, which always made me feel like warm bread.

"You gotta stop being funny, Shell," he said. But I knew he didn't mean it.

I nodded and put a pancake on his plate.

6

THERE WERE RITUALS in Kandern that seemed so well orchestrated that I wondered if I'd missed a memo somewhere along the way.

Every Sunday around 7 p.m., identical shiny black garbage cans appeared on the curbs, their contents devoid of plastic, glass, and paper. Consequently, every Saturday, before and after lunch, a parade of cars headed toward the recycling center behind the school and disgorged trunkfuls of reusable goods. Upon their return home, Kandern's dutiful residents grabbed brooms and dustpans and headed out to the street to sweep the sidewalks and gutters. If sidewalks could shine, German sidewalks would be blinding.

On Sunday mornings, another smaller parade took off on foot and headed to the bakery, which stayed open only long enough to provide fresh rolls and thick-crusted loaves to Kandern's bread connoisseurs. And every Sunday afternoon around two, a procession of the young and elderly headed to the hills for their traditional, slow-gaited hike.

There were other less pleasant traditions, I discovered. It was apparently an unwritten law that Germans were required to tell their American neighbors how to park their cars, where to park their trash cans, and when to park their butts. I discovered the hard way that there was a window of time, between one and three every day, when silence and rest were not only a preference but an obligation. The same was true all day long on holidays. No work. No noise. Nothing. I was quite firmly informed of this fact when Shayla and I went out to the street to wash our car on a day off, and a neighbor I'd never seen before came stomping out of his house to tell me . . . something. My German hadn't improved very much in our first four weeks in the country, what with spending all my time in an English-speaking school with my English-speaking colleagues or with my English-speaking pseudo-daughter. So though he wagged a finger at me and was sufficiently forceful to communicate that he was giving me an order, all I knew to do was freeze and instruct Shayla to freeze too—which actually managed to make the unhappy man smile a bit as she froze in midgiggle with suds on her nose.

The smile seemed to deflate his frustration. He said a couple more words to me, which could have been "Get a haircut" for all I knew, then grinned a little stiffly at Shayla and returned to his home. Shayla thought she saw him wink before he turned, but she had this wonderful habit of expecting people to love her. I, on the other hand, spent the rest of the day feeling stupid and nursing a humiliated ego.

I was beginning to understand that Shayla, besides being my half-sister-daughter, was also going to be my only ticket into the good graces of Kandern's population. Her unabashed smiles and clear-voiced *tucks*, which we now knew were actually *Tag*, drew outright friendliness from some of the people we encountered and curious stares from the more austere strangers we crossed. I just got the stares—and a less pleasant variety of them, at that. It seemed that no one had ever informed the German population that gawking was rude, and they had elevated the brazen impoliteness to a sort of national pastime.

The first time I fully experienced the even-greater discomfort of a group stare was when Gus and Bev took us to a restaurant in the nearby village of Hammerstein. The restaurant was actually a train car dating back to 1882, which had been attached to a large building where the kitchen and bar were located. There were still small metallic signs on the paneled walls warning passengers not to lean out the windows. It was a small, cozy space, and the curve-backed wooden benches on either side of each table gave it an old-world charm. Shayla went a little crazy with excited questions when we arrived. Where were the tracks? Was there a conductor? Why weren't we moving? Did we have to pay to ride it? And lastly, what was this "shishel and pomus" Bev was talking about?

As it turned out, "shishel and pomus" was *Schnitzel und Pommes*, the most traditional of traditional German meals. Breaded pork cutlets and fries, to be exact. The dish lost some of its exoticism in translation. But not as much as *Schwein Nippel Suppe*, which I found out, to my horror, was pig-nipple soup. The Johnsons had wanted to be the first to introduce us to schnitzel, but they hadn't bargained on Shayla's reaction to the train, or on the effect her excitement would have on the evening.

It started with me trying to get her to sit down. It had been an easier feat on the plane ride to Germany, because the seat had been equipped with a seat belt and the patrolling airline attendants had made sure we used it. But there were no seat belts on the restaurant benches, and Shayla was determined to spend the meal standing on her seat and staring out the window.

"Shayla, you need to sit down."

"Why?"

"You're not allowed to stand on the benches, honey. You might fall and hurt yourself."

"I won't. Look! A cat!" she shrieked with glee, pointing out the window at a barnyard tabby crossing the road.

"Sit down, Shayla." I was painfully aware of the Johnsons' eyes on me and even more painfully aware that I was new at the mom thing. An unfriendly waitress brought us our drinks and ordered Gus to tell *"das Mädchen"* to take her feet off the bench.

"The nice lady wants you to sit down, Shayla," he coaxed, and I wondered on what planet the waitress's personality would be defined as nice.

"No!"

I took hold of Shayla's arm with one hand and turned her face toward me with the other. "You will not speak to Gus that way, little girl." I tried to sound motherly and firm.

"I'm not little!" she yelled, trying to tear her arm from my grip and losing her balance in the process. One of her feet slipped off the edge of the bench, and her cheek connected with the hard wood of the backrest.

"Shayla," Bev said, jumping up to prevent any more of a fall, but Shayla was well beyond fear by that point.

"I'm not sitting down! You can't make me! I'm not! I'm not!"

I'd learned early on in my pseudo-motherhood that Shayla was a generally well-behaved child with a naturally sunny disposition. *Generally* meant that the sunniness was not a permanent fixture and that the reverse side of *well-behaved* was *raving maniac*. But

Gus and Bev had never made the acquaintance of the *One Flew over the Cuckoo's Nest* version of Shayla, and her banshee-meets-hyena screams clearly took them by surprise.

As I tried to lift her off the bench and away from the glassware on the table, she threw her upper body back and used her feet to kick at me. And she screamed. She screamed so much that patrons at the other tables started to protest. I redoubled my efforts to appease her, finally lifting her stiff body onto my lap in a flurry of thrashing arms and kicking legs, but I simply couldn't quiet her. She was mad. Spitting mad. And I couldn't figure out what I had done to set off such a ferocious response.

Bev said something to me across the table, but I couldn't hear her. As Gus made a comment to the diners at the table next to ours, she stepped close to me and whispered, "Do you want me to try?" in my ear. Coming from anyone else, I might have taken the suggestion as an insult, but Bev's face was so full of compassion for my predicament that I numbly nodded my appreciation and mouthed my thanks. She gathered a squirming and still-wailing Shayla into her arms and stepped outside.

Now why hadn't I thought of that? It was October and the nights were getting colder, but a few goose bumps were a small price to pay for extricating myself and my daughter from a humiliating situation. Through the window, I watched Bev talking to Shayla, keenly feeling the stares of the other diners in the train car, all of whom had interrupted their conversations to observe the battle raging at our table. Gus stacked his forearms on the table and said, "You know, Christopher used to throw such bad fits that the neighbors called the cops on us once."

I tore my eyes away from Shayla long enough to give Gus an incredulous look.

He nodded in confirmation and went on. "You'd be amazed

at what set him off. Mostly it was not getting his way, but sometimes—and don't quote me on this—sometimes I think he just did it for the fun of it. I think it felt good to the little guy to let it rip once in a while."

"But did he do it in public?" I was ashamed at the scene we'd caused.

"If he really wanted to get his way, he did. There's nothing like a little public embarrassment to make a parent give in!"

After a very brief time outside, Bev reentered the restaurant with a sullen Shayla walking next to her.

"What do you say?" she asked the little girl whose bottom lip stuck so far out it looked glued on. "Shayla?" Bev coaxed.

"Sowwy," Shayla said, and though her eyes were trained downward and her body turned away, I was pretty sure the words were intended for me.

Bev deposited Shayla in her seat and placed her napkin in her lap, then circled the table to sit by Gus.

"Have a nice talk out there?" he asked.

"Shades of Christopher," she answered.

I glanced at Shayla while Gus and Bev perused their menus. She looked dwarfed by the bench, her little hands clasped in front of her and her chin against her chest. I saw her take a hiccuping breath as tears gathered in her eyes. There was "I miss my daddy" written all over her face, and it broke my heart. I scooped her into my arms and held her like that while I ordered our meals and waited for them to arrive. She never really cried outright, which was more heart-wrenching to me than overt tears would have been. She just sat there, occasionally answering the questions we asked her, but mostly staring at the door every time it opened. I think she was waiting for a conductor to come by.

And after it was all over, every patron in the train car smiled at Shayla as she walked toward the exit, as if she were the best-behaved little girl in the whole wide world. Me? I got stares. But Bev had explained to me, after the earlier scene, that the stares only meant "You're interesting" and not, as I had assumed, "We dislike you intensely." So I squared my shoulders, pasted on a smile, and left the restaurant under the patrons' stares with as much dignity as I could muster.

Back home and ready for sleep, Shayla sat against me in her bed while I finished reading *A Fly Went By.* She smelled of toothpaste and baby shampoo and was so soft and snuggly that I had trouble associating this sweetness with the tantrum I'd witnessed earlier.

I closed the book and scrunched down a little farther in the bed, turning sideways so her head could rest on the pillow. "Did you like the train restaurant?"

Her head nodded against me.

"What part did you like the best?"

She took her time answering. "The cat," she said.

Of course. We'd gone out to dinner in a train and eaten all new foods, and the memorable item of the evening had been a cat wandering past in the street. Children—how had I managed to inherit one?

"Is that why you got so mad? Because you wanted to see the cat?"

She shrugged and I sighed. "You need to obey me when I ask you to do things, Shayla. You might not understand why I'm asking you to do them, but you need to obey anyway."

"Or you'll get mad at me?" she asked in a hesitant voice.

"Did you think I was mad at you tonight?"

She nodded.

I knew the taste and texture of a parent's wrath. It was acrid and coarse—noxious. It had no place in Shayla's world. "I wasn't really mad," I said, stroking the hair back from her forehead. "I just wanted you to sit down because that's what you're supposed to do in restaurants. I was annoyed and frustrated, but I wasn't really mad."

She shrugged again.

"What did Bev tell you when you went outside with her? Do you remember?"

"She said scweaming's not helping."

"That's all?" Trust Bev to make it simple.

"And she said my mom loves me."

I felt my heart turn a cartwheel and softly asked, "Do you believe her?"

Another nod.

"Well, good, because it's true." I kissed the top of her head. "Shayla, do you mind when people call me your mom? I mean, I know I haven't been taking care of you for very long, but . . . people are going to just figure I'm your mom since we live together."

"It's okay." Her voice sounded younger than usual, or maybe just more hesitant.

"And is it okay if they call you my daughter too?"

"Uh-huh." There was less hesitation that time.

"Here's the deal," I said, turning myself around in the bed so I could face her. She snuggled down against her pillows and looked at me with large, tired eyes. "Let's just let people call us what they want, okay? And you can call me whatever you want, too. You can keep calling me Shelby for the rest of your life if you'd like, and I'll . . ."

She reached out and grabbed my hand. Just like that. I was in the middle of my we-don't-really-have-to-be-mother-and-daughter speech, and this little girl whose little life had impossibly stretched my selfish little heart wrapped her soft, warm hand around my fingers and smiled in a way that made me want to . . . It made me want to call her *daughter*, to be honest. It made me wish I was her mother. It warmed me and enveloped me. It also scared me senseless.

So on that night when the only words roiling around in my brain were *I want to be your mother,* the words that came out of my mouth were "It's past your bedtime. We can talk about this again later, okay?"

I avoided her gaze as I kissed her satin cheek and tucked the blankets under her chin. She said her prayers and I said mine. Then I let myself out of her room and went to sit on the secondhand couch in the living room. There was something about secondhand that I found disquieting, especially on that night. I didn't like it much. Not in furniture. Not in scars.

And not in daughters.

❋ ❋ ❋

Trey and I sat in the attic under a sheet draped across the backs of four rickety chairs and secured with clothespins. We called it our Huddle Hut, but for all intents and purposes, it was our bunker—a place where we could talk about the ickiness outside without fear of its nastiness actually bruising our souls.

It was a tradition we had started when we were much younger, on a day when my mom had screamed a bad word at my dad. We'd been so shocked to hear both the word and the volume coming out of her mouth that we'd scattered to our bedrooms. But that had left us all alone with our thoughts and our fear that Mom had lost it and joined the ranks of compulsively cursing grown-ups, so we'd catapulted back out into the hallway, where we'd very nearly smacked into each other.

We needed to debrief. Quickly. Before our minds came to any conclusions about Mom and lost the very last vestige of security we still had.

But going outside required passing through the kitchen, where Mom and Dad were still locked in combat, and talking in one of our bedrooms carried the risk of being overheard, so we'd headed to the attic instead. Feeling too exposed under the dusty beams and a little grossed out by the moth-eaten piles of junk, we'd erected the first of our Huddle Huts and crawled into it, all conspiratorial and confused.

We concluded that day that our mother wasn't really losing her mind. Nor was she ever going to be as mean as our dad. She'd just caught a bug, probably—the kind that gives you fevers and broadens your vocabulary. It would pass, we decided—like those migraines she got.

We were a little older now and well past the age for building forts and playing hide-and-seek, but still the Huddle Hut tradition endured. We didn't wait for something terrible like cursing to send us to the attic anymore. We just decided, when things got too murky, to run away for a bit. Our tradition had gotten a little more elaborate with time, and we now sat on a rug rescued from a trash heap with an assortment of candies and soda cans in front of us. Trey never told me where he got the snacks, but I had the feeling he might have stolen them from Mr. Karzakian's 7-Eleven on the corner of Elm and Main. That was just a guess, though.

Trey made a production of opening a Coke can and handing it to me. Then he got one for himself and clinked it with mine as if they were crystal goblets and we were at a cocktail party.

"To the brotherhood . . ."

". . . of Davishood."

"And to the muddlehood . . ."

". . . of huddlehood," I finished. It was pretty lame, as toasts went, but we'd invented it when we were little and it sorta had sentimental value.

Trey leaned back against a garbage bag full of old curtains, and I lay on my stomach with my face above the stack of candy. Again, it was traditional, and who was I to mess with history?

"Sylvia's knocked up," he said.

"But not by you, right?"

"Nope. Bobby Stevens."

"To Bobby Stevens," I said, raising a Rolo in salute.

"And to his kid. May he live long and forever be happy he doesn't have Jim Davis for a father." Trey smirked and slurped at his Coke can.

"He called Mom the B *word again. Do you think he knows he's repeating himself?"*

"He's going to have to make up new words. He's overused all the old ones."

"How 'bout . . ." I thought hard, the Rolo pinging at my brain. "How 'bout kryphip*?" I suggested and spelled it for him because I thought the letters looked cool.*

He pondered it for a moment, then gathered a big lungful of air and bellowed, "Get out of my face, you pathetic kryphip!" It was a dead-on impression of Dad. "Yeah, I think that'll work," he said. "You'll have to suggest it to him."

"I'd rather eat dirt."

"I'd rather eat worms."

"I'd rather eat monkey brains."

"I'd rather eat rabbit turds."

"Okay, you win," I said. "I don't want to get gross."

"Too late."

I knew he was trying to make me mad by implying I was gross, but I also knew he'd feel horrible if I did get mad, so I threw a marshmallow at him instead. If anyone had witnessed our exchange, they would have pegged us as being maybe seven or eight. We were nearly twice that, but it still didn't bother us that our huddles were embarrassing. Nobody was there to see them but us, and it felt kind of freeing to talk about eating bugs and poop and stuff.

People like Bobby Stevens made it hard to stay on the funner topics, though. He was a couple of years ahead of us in school, but he still reminded us of how old we really were and made us wonder when we'd be the ones God spit on.

The concept of God spitting on us was also one of our Huddle Hut inventions. But we didn't mean any disrespect. We knew God was out there because Mom prayed to him a lot—and I did too, when I remembered. And we knew he was out there because when we said something like "God's been spitting on us again," we felt guilty, like we'd hurt his feelings. And you can't hurt the feelings of someone who doesn't exist.

"Is she going to keep the baby?" I asked.

"Sylvia?"

"No, Joan of Arc."

"Yeah, I think so. Her parents don't know yet, though."

"Dad would kill me if I ever got pregnant." The thought alone made us both shudder. "He'd probably send me away to one of those knocked-up farms where girls go to have their babies without anybody knowing."

"Would you want to keep it?"

I pondered his question awhile and turned it over and over in my head. "No," I finally said, and I was sure of my answer.

"Why not?"

"Because what if I end up like Dad? That wouldn't be good. Even if I ended up with someone like Bobby who kinda deserves to have Dad for a wife."

"You have a crush on Bobby?"

"No. Do you?"

"No."

"Glad we got that straight."

"So you're not having kids," Trey said, and I knew he was getting at something.

"Nope."

"Are you ever getting married?"

"Nope."

"Me neither."

I wasn't liking this huddle. It was more fun to talk about what other people would never be than about what we would never be. Big difference there.

"I think you should," Trey said.

"Get married or have kids?"

"Both. I think you could do it and not turn into Dad."

"I'd rather have another Rolo," I said and popped one in my mouth.

"Seriously, Shell."

I sighed. "Why should I if you don't?"

"Because you're a girl."

"And . . . ?"

"And I think maybe the bad-parent gene is a male one."

I pondered it for a moment. "Well, I'm not going to risk it. There are enough screwed-up Davises in this world without adding any more. Besides, I haven't exactly seen any guys hovering around me."

"That's 'cause you've been scaring them away."

"With my hair or my weight?"

"Are we going to discuss this at every single huddle?"

"Um . . . yeah."

"You're not fat and your hair is fine."

"So what's scaring them away?"

Trey looked at me as if he was trying to figure it out. "I don't know," he finally said, and I was pretty sure he really didn't. "Maybe if you actually, you know, got girly around them."

"What are you saying? That I'm not girly enough?"

"Not around guys. You get all competitive and stuff."

"I do not. What do I have to compete about?"

"It's not that kind of thing. It's like they can't get anywhere with you. You're always shutting them down."

I raised my eyebrows and assumed a Southern accent. "Who, me? Why, surely you jest."

"I'm just saying," he concluded.

I saw the serious look in his eyes and the way his mouth was pulled kinda tight and I knew he was worrying about me. I didn't like it, so I tossed another marshmallow at him. He caught it in midair, quick as a rattlesnake, and launched it back at me with a bellowed "Get out of my face, you pathetic kryphip!"

7

ANOTHER REHEARSAL, another stab at the chaos theory. I used the term like I knew what it meant, but it was way too mathematical for my brain. All I knew was that play rehearsals tended to feel like too many free radicals bouncing off too many parameters and never quite achieving homogeneity. That was a fairly random succession of science-type terms, all inaccurately used and with absolutely no scientific value, but it sure felt like a play practice to me.

Though Seth and Kate were doing a great job learning their lines, they were—much to my surprise—being a tad less successful at re-creating the kind of intimate moment that had earned them the roles in the first place. Seth seemed afflicted with compulsive awkwardness, and Kate, with her take-no-prisoners approach to everything, did nothing to put him at ease. In the scene where Joy, who had bone cancer, was supposed to be lying in a hospital bed in unbearable pain and Lewis was supposed to be proposing to her, the best they could muster was a dynamic that made Seth look like a bumbling idiot and Kate come across as an ailing tyrant. And when I tried to add a tender gesture to the mix, merely asking Seth to run his fingers down Kate's cheek, the lid came off the pressure cooker.

"He's not going to touch me," Kate said before I'd even finished my instructions. "He doesn't even look me in the eye when he's proposing to me, so how on earth is he supposed to touch me?"

Seth looked pleadingly my way. "I just . . . It's hard to remember the lines and the motions at the same time. And the text is so . . ."

"Mushy! Go ahead. Say it. Can we change it, Miss Davis? It's really kinda gross."

I looked from one to the other and tried not to laugh out loud. You'd think a scripted romance would be easier to manage than a spontaneous one. All around us, the rest of the cast was trying to look absorbed in either homework or learning lines, but it was obvious that their ears were really trained on the quarreling not-quite-couple in front of me.

"Okay, you two," I said. "We're going out to the cafeteria to work on this. And the rest of you—" I paused to make sure I had their attention—"are going to run the opening scene with Meagan standing in for Seth." There were grumbles—which I understood. Bubbly Meagan had ended up being my right-hand man, which meant she was an errand runner, an actor fetcher, a snack cleaner-upper and a whatever-Miss-Davis-needs-er. She'd already proven invaluable to me, as much for her helpfulness as for her bright and cheerful spirit. But—and this was the reason for the cast's groans—she was not an actress by any stretch of the imagination, and her voice and accent did nothing to convey the solemnity of 1950s Oxford. So whenever she stepped onto the stage to replace a missing actor, the scene invariably dissolved into something akin to auditory slapstick.

"It's only for a few minutes," I told the cast. "And it's more for the memorization than for the acting, so give Meagan a break."

"Seriously, y'all," Meagan added, her voice too high for her age but oh-so-cute.

Seth, Kate, and I found a table in the cafeteria just outside the auditorium.

"Okay," I said. "Seth, read your line again and try to put some real affection into it. Then touching her face will come from a whole context of emotions and might not feel so forced. Go ahead. The actual proposal."

I'd discovered, in the short time I'd been a play director, that acting had as much to do with psychology as with stage technique and vocal production. This had come as a relief to me, as I had much more experience with being an armchair psychologist than with teaching amateur actors to become juvenile De Niros and Hepburns.

Seth's tall frame hunched a little as he first read the words silently, then attempted to speak them. "Will you marry this foolish, frightened old man, who needs you more than he can bear to say, and loves you even though he hardly knows how?"

"To which you reply, with feeling . . ." I prompted Kate.

She dutifully said her line. "Okay. Just this once."

It was the Edsel of proposals, the Pacer of all things intimate. "All right, Seth," I sighed, "what do you think was wrong with that?"

He looked at me as if I'd asked him for the square root of an astronomical number.

I tried another tack. "What's missing that would make it sound like an adult man who is finally—at long last—asking the woman he loves to marry him?"

"How's he supposed to know?" Kate asked in frustration. "He's not a man yet!"

I was just about to lecture her on respecting her castmate when she caught sight of something over my shoulder and rose from the table, waving her arms.

"Hey, Coach Taylor! Coach Taylor!"

I froze. In fact, I think my lungs might have suffered some sudden-onset frostbite because for a moment there, they felt like they didn't really want to work anymore.

"What's up?"

I turned to find Scott sauntering up to the table in a tracksuit and a knit hat. I assumed my best nonchalant voice. "Kate, I'm sure Coach Taylor has other things to—"

"If you were an adult man . . . ," Kate interrupted, blushing when Scott tilted his head a little and gave her a look. "I mean, *since* you are an adult man, tell us how you would do it if you were proposing to a woman who was dying of cancer."

"Sounds cheerful." Poor Scott. He did a great job of not, say, busting out laughing and leaving the cafeteria as fast as he could. He did, however, get that I'm-about-to-launch-into-a-yodel look I'd seen before, so I knew there was some laughter in there somewhere. I felt a little sorry for him, but I felt sorrier for myself. I just wasn't very good at real-life awkward situations. I preferred them on a stage.

"Please feel free to tell Kate to find another guinea pig," I told him. What I really wanted to say was, "This was not my idea and I'd really rather not have to deal with you." I turned on Kate. "This isn't Coach Taylor's problem, Kate; it's yours and Seth's. So how 'bout we concentrate on the two people who can actually do something about it?"

"What are the lines?" Scott asked, pulling a chair up to the table and sitting on it backward.

"Don't you have a practice to run?" I asked as Seth handed him his script and Kate pointed to Lewis's proposal.

"They're running the *Wolfsschlucht*," he said, referring to the cross-country course in the woods behind thc school. "Besides, I haven't been in a play since high school, so this might be fun."

"You used to act?" This from Seth—with a little more desperation than he'd probably intended.

"Scott, really, if—"

"Wow. Pretty serious stuff," he said, ignoring my second attempt at allowing him to leave. He glanced at Seth. "So you're telling her you want to marry her?"

"He's supposed to be," Kate interjected.

"And you're supposed to love her—I mean really love her. Like a guy who finally gets the guts to propose. Right?"

"*Guts* is the key word there, Seth. *Guts.*" Kate was on a roll.

I, on the other hand, was not. My body was anchored to my chair and so, apparently, was my brain. I wasn't sure what was most traumatic at that moment: Kate's behavior, my inability to change the situation, Seth's bordering-on-physical discomfort, or the fact that Scott—whom I really did not want to know—was about to utter intimate words in what I feared would be a powerful way. I didn't want to be there to witness it. At all. But I did have an overwhelming craving for cheesecake.

Scott cleared his throat and took a moment to focus. While he did that, I took a moment to look for the nearest emergency exit, but as my brains were anchored to the chair, running for my life would have been a dangerous proposition. So I sat there and tried to assume a casual expression.

Scott began. "Will you marry this foolish, frightened old man . . ."

I snorted. It was very unladylike and very insulting and very, oh so very, unintentional. Scott shot a be-quiet look my way and continued in the most horrendous faux-British accent I'd ever heard, his voice crackling so badly in a semblance of age that an audience would have thought he was the one dying of cancer. ". . . an old man who needs you more than he can bear to say, and loves you even though he hardly knows how?"

Kate was speechless, which, after the last hour of rehearsal, was a bit of a relief. Seth was dumbfounded and hugely disappointed. And I was desperately trying to regain the composure that seemed to have slipped out the door along with Scott's real accent. At first, I'd feared that Scott had been serious in his interpretation, and if that had been the case, my snorting and carrying on would have probably irreparably damaged his self-esteem. But one good look at his grin had convinced me that his self-esteem was intact, as intact as the sense of humor that had apparently motivated the world's worst *Shadowlands* performance.

Scott slapped Seth on the back and flashed Kate a smile. "Sorry about that, guys," he said jovially. "Guess I'd better stick to sports!"

"Coach Taylor," Kate said suspiciously, "what play were you ever in in high school?"

"Play 99—full-court press, man on man," he answered. "We won the game 89 to 33. It was fabulous." He turned to me. "You walking home tonight?"

The headlights were coming my way, and I was a deer. "Uh . . ."

"Maybe I'll see you then." He smiled and trotted away.

"All right, Seth," I said, firmly forcing ridiculous panic to the back of my mind, "let's talk romance."

❈ ❈ ❈

I was halfway to the Johnsons' an hour later when I heard someone jogging up behind me.

"Don't be startled. It's Scott!" he called to me.

"Who?" I kept walking.

"The world's greatest actor."

"Oh, him. You come near me, I'll douse you with Mace."

He slowed down beside me and matched his pace with mine. "That bad, huh?"

"By Academy Award standards, you were on par with, say, Dorothy's dog."

"Toto? That's a compliment. I would have ranked myself more along the lines of what he'd leave behind."

"Speaking of . . ." I sidestepped to avoid a little pile of doggie doo. "You really don't have to walk me to Gus and Bev's, you know," I said when the silence had outstayed its welcome, which was about one and a half seconds after it had started. I wasn't good with silence. Actually, I was, just not when it involved other people.

"I was a Boy Scout. I have to protect the weak and beat up on the bad guys."

"And I'm . . . ?"

"Going to hit me if I call you weak, so I guess that leaves the bad guys."

"I doubt I'll be mugged in the streets of Kandern. It makes Mayberry look like a crime capital."

"Which means it's boring as all get-out, but kind of nice for raising a daughter, huh."

"Beats Chicago any day."

"So does the weather."

"Except for the rain."

"I'm from Seattle—the rain just feels like home. So how's your daughter doing?"

"Shayla?"

"No, your other daughter." There was a little bit of Trey in him, but I tried not to register that fact.

"Shay's doing okay. Bev's wonderful with her."

"Can I ask you something . . . personal?"

"Too late," I said. "We're here." And sure enough, we'd reached the Johnsons' front door.

"Wow. Time flies when you only have thirty seconds to talk."

I smirked. He hesitated.

"So . . . do you want me to wait and walk you back to your place?"

Absolutely not. "Actually, that's kind of my time to catch up with Shayla. She tells me something else about her day with every streetlight we pass. You know."

"Wouldn't want to stand in the way of a mother-daughter streetlight routine," he said, and I wondered if there was a simple way of just slipping "She's really my half sister left for me by my dead abusive father along with a condo and a '64 Impala" into the conversation. But I figured what he didn't know couldn't harm me.

"Well, it's been nice talking to you, Shelby," he said lightly. "Thanks for not Macing me, or we'd have had even less time to chat."

"No problem. Guess you'll just have to talk faster next time."

He smiled and raked his fingers through his wavy hair. "Next time, huh?" I decided his dimple was dangerous. "Say hi to Shayla from me."

"I will. Thanks for the escort, Cub Scout. This damsel's safe and sound."

He raised a hand in a half wave, pivoted, and took off jogging down the road at a leisurely pace.

Me? I told myself not to be flattered and that I didn't have time for the likes of Scott Taylor. Then I opened the door to greet the sunshine of my life.

⁂

SIX MONTHS EARLIER

Dana held the car door open while I got Shayla out of the backseat. She smelled of soap and sun and felt impossibly small in her oversize jacket and matching pink boots. I felt like Peter Pan introducing Wendy to his world—an emotionally weary Peter Pan with a serious is-this-for-real? buzz going on. Things had moved fast since I'd made my decision. One minute I'd been sitting in Dana's office trying to pick the right words to change the course of my life, and the next I'd been signing papers in Steve's office, rushing off to Dream Acres, and then driving extremely carefully back to Trey's bakery. I wasn't used to having a pseudo-daughter strapped into the backseat. As it turns out, the words I had used to change my life were "I'll take her," which, as life-altering statements go, wasn't exactly poetic, but it beat "I'm terrified but I can't help myself" for clarity of purpose.

Everything had gone so fast that Trey didn't know he was an uncle yet. A pseudo-uncle-half-brother, I supposed. So Dana and I had decided that I should make L'Envie the first stop on my way home. And Dana had come along, I suspected just to get another look at my brother, but her presence in the car had been comforting, especially when Shayla had asked, "Are you taking me to Daddy?" from the backseat. I knew she knew that her daddy was gone, but I guess we all need to ask the tough questions again every so often. Just in case.

Given the difficulty I was still having realizing that this pint-size human being now belonged to me, I didn't know quite how to introduce her to Trey. *Belonged*, of course, was an overstatement. *Depended* was more accurate. This agreement between my dead father and me was a nebulous thing, a tenuous connection I both wanted and despised. The *wanted* part was Shayla, who had crayoned her way into my future on our very first encounter, all sunshine-yellow and cloud-blue. The *despised* part was her father, who was mine, too, but only by birth. This man who had punctuated my childhood with emotional whiplash and affective dissension, the sound of which could still be heard in the squeaky hinges of my relational impairments, was now intimately linked to me—and in a permanent, irreversible way. I had tried to distance myself from him all my life, and in recent years successfully. Yet Shayla had brought him back inside my fortified walls with such intimate finality that a part of me—the fragile, damaged part—instinctively braced itself for rejection, aspersion, and pain.

I gazed into Shayla's eyes after I pulled her from her car seat, and she gazed right back, unwavering and just a little numb. If this new beginning was overflowing my adult capacity for comprehension, I couldn't imagine the havoc it was wreaking in her uncomplicated world where, until recently, home had simply been Daddy. I asked Dana to watch her while I went inside and prepared Trey for the news.

Trey was handing change back to a classy-looking lady when I entered the bakery. He sent me a wait-a-minute look and finished his business with her, turning his attention to me only as she exited in a fog of Chanel No. 5.

"Shell! What are you doing here?"

"Nice to see you too."

He checked his watch. "Shouldn't you be teaching?"

"I'm playing hooky."

"Nice. Add to that ripping off a 7-Eleven and spending your allowance in the arcade, and we'll have to start calling you Trey."

"Um . . . I have some news." I sat down at one of his pretty French tables and, as there were no other customers in the shop, he joined me.

"News?"

"Kinda big news."

He had a suspicious look about him all of a sudden. "And the big news is . . . ?"

I had trouble believing that I was about to tell my brother that I'd just become the legal guardian of our father's child. He must have misread my incredulity for hesitance, because he sighed a little and said, "Do we have to play twenty questions every time something big happens with you?"

He was referring to the day I'd gone shuffling into his bedroom many years ago, my head low and my gaze averted. He'd tried to coax my problem out of me, but my mortification had prevented it. So he'd resorted to twenty questions.

"Are you in trouble?"

"No."

"Are you sick?"

"No."

"Is someone we know in trouble or sick?"

"No."

"Are you covered in hideous warts from the frog you had in your pocket last week?"

I rolled my eyes. "No."

He looked at me more closely and I blushed. My body language said, *I'm so embarrassed I'd be happy if the ground opened up and swallowed me,* and it didn't take long for Trey to figure it out.

"Are you . . . ?" He blushed a little. I had to love him for it. "Are you . . . a woman?"

I hit the floor and pulled the blanket off his bed to cover my head.

"You are?" He wasn't supposed to sound so perky about it. He was supposed to get all awkward and kick me out of his room, then act weird around me for months and years.

I couldn't breathe very well under the blanket and I had a bit of a claustrophobia problem too, so I didn't dillydally any longer. "I don't know how to buy the . . . stuff," I said, hoping he could hear me through the knit fabric draped over my bruised pride.

"Go ask Mom."

"She's in the den with a box of Kleenex." Which was code for "She's curled up in a fetal position on the couch, sobbing into a cushion like we can't hear her, and jumping out of her skin every time she thinks she hears Dad coming home." Mom in that state was like a car without tires—it could still kinda move, if it had to, but you knew it really shouldn't.

Trey had suspended every smidgen of male pride on that day and had walked with me to the Jewel-Osco on Cross and Willow. He'd shielded me with his body so nobody could see me reading the labels on the boxes of girl stuff I'd studiously ignored all my life, and then, seeing my nearly apoplectic shame, had boldly walked to the checkout and paid for my icky things himself.

I realized at that moment that the only way I would ever be able to pay Trey back for being my brother would be to buy an island in the Pacific, build him a palace on it, hire professional soccer players to populate it, and equip it with state-of-the-art Dad repellents. Since I couldn't quite afford any of that yet, I just kept quiet on the walk home. I knew he appreciated that, too—though not as much as an island. What I really wanted to do was hold his hand and say thank you over and over again until I turned blue.

But it was a much different bit of news I had for Trey on this day, twenty-odd years later, and as we sat at the table in his cozy French bakery, I was once again at a loss for words.

"Question one: Are you in trouble?"

I laughed a little jaggedly. "You don't have to twenty-questions it, Trey."

"Oh, good. Just tell me who the guy is and I'll take a baseball bat to his car."

"I want you to know that I've finally made my decision about Shayla."

I had his full attention. His gray-green gaze narrowed and he kinda squinted at me, waiting.

I went to the door and found Shayla and Dana playing hopscotch on the sidewalk. When I reentered L'Envie, Shayla was propped on my hip, her legs around my waist. I hadn't really realized before then how convenient those hip bones were, and I wondered if there wasn't a bit of genius in God's design plan after all.

Trey stood as we approached, and his astonishment melted into a lopsided grin.

"This is Shayla, Trey," I said.

"Shayla," Trey said, as if testing the name's flavor. He bent so his eyes were on a level with hers. "I'm Trey. And I'm going to be one of your favorite people. Seriously. You'll be telling all your friends about me when you grow up." He pulled back as if suddenly struck by a thought. "I think . . ." He peered at her more closely, assessing what he saw. "I think you may be the most beautiful little thing I've ever seen."

Shayla looked up at me and I shrugged. "Trey goes a little poetic when he gets nervous," I said.

"Don't listen to her. I'm always poetic." He smiled a crooked grin at me that held both approval and support. Then he ran the back side of a finger over Shayla's rosy cheek and said, "How 'bout a pastry? I've got these great chocolate croissants."

And this little girl who had known him for only a handful of seconds followed Dana's lead and became instantly smitten. She smiled a little and hid her face in my neck, which was a new experience for me and made my stomach do strange things. Then she peeked at him again, smiled more broadly when he wiggled an eyebrow, and let herself fall forward into his arms as he held them toward her.

Dana looked like she'd have done the same thing had his hands been pointing her way. There were tears in her eyes, and I was grateful for that because I couldn't seem to muster any of my own right then. I figured I'd borrow hers for a while.

A few minutes later, with Dana and Shayla engaged in a coloring contest at a table near the window, Trey and I huddled in the kitchen at the back of the bakery. He'd been shaking his head a lot since I'd arrived with Shayla, and he was still shaking it now.

"What do you think?" I asked.

"You may be the most courageous woman I've ever met."

"Wait a minute. You were the one telling me I should just take a risk and go for it."

"Yeah, but I never actually thought you would!"

"Trey!"

"Don't get your undies in a bunch. You made absolutely the right decision. She's . . . Is it possible that something that sweet really came from our dad?"

"I figure the mother's genes were pretty potent."

He glanced out the door to make sure Shayla was securely out of earshot. "So this is Dad's idea of a parting gift, huh?" He leaned a hip against the stainless-steel countertop mounted to the wall.

"Beats a potted plant any day. More upkeep, though." I was sitting on a tall stool with a half-finished plate of *mille-feuilles* in my hand.

"Can you believe it?"

"What part—the part where I'm a mother or the part where I have a daughter, neither of which is entirely accurate?"

"The part where the woman who vowed she would never have children suddenly has a little girl to take care of."

"You're just jealous 'cause all you got was a condo."

"About that . . ."

"We're not going back over this, Trey. It's yours. Deal with it."

"The fact is, you're a mom now."

"A guardian half sister, actually."

"And your place isn't really big enough for both of you."

"Is that a crack about the five *mille-feuilles* I've eaten in ten minutes?"

"It's a one-bedroom apartment, Shell."

"Which is why I think we need to move."

"Exactly my point."

"But it's not going to be to your condo."

"Dad's condo."

"Whatever."

I let the silence lengthen. There was something about my conversations with Trey that made me feel loved, even if he did make veiled comments about my eating habits. There hadn't been many people in my life who had actually listened to me and worried about me and been willing to make sacrifices for me. Trey was one of those rare ones. He felt like thick, soft slippers and feather comforters and the hollow of a shoulder. I loved my brother. He reminded me of a past I'd never had but could have had, if he'd been in charge.

"So you're moving," he said, bringing my mind back to the bombshell at hand.

"It's . . . um . . . probably going to surprise you."

He raised an eyebrow. I think he'd reached his surprise quota for the day, but he let me go on anyway.

"Remember John Burkhart?"

It took him a moment to place the name. "That missionary dude who used to come by the church and guilt us all into moving to Timbuktu?"

"Yup. He lives in Naperville now. Retired. I ran into him at church."

"Aw, man," Trey whined melodramatically, "I knew he'd get you to Timbuktu!" He raised his voice in a fairly decent imitation of Burkhart's impassioned sermons, getting louder with each word he uttered. "'Don't waste your lives on materialism and ambition! Bring God to the lost in the jungles and the ghettos, to the outcasts and the hopeless and the poor!'"

John Burkhart was a dynamic speaker with an extraordinary gift for capturing an audience, but he had the bad habit of always ending his talks with a rising crescendo that bordered on comical. I laughed at Trey's only slight exaggeration.

"Everything okay in there?" came Dana's voice from the other room.

"We're fine, Dana! Trey's just feeling the spirit and channeling Billy Graham."

"So," Trey said, his face serious again, "you're not going to the jungle, are you?"

"Not exactly."

"Well, as long as whatever it is is within a twenty-mile radius from here, I'll allow it."

"That's the problem. Trey, I think Shayla and I may be moving to Germany."

Trey's face looked like the bottom had dropped out of his stomach. I saw him swallow—hard—and take a steadying breath. "Germany, huh?"

"The land of Beck's beer."

"You going for the beer?"

"No. To try something new. With Shayla."

He didn't say anything for a moment. "Did you ask her?"

"Dana told me to wait awhile. See how she adjusts in the next few months."

"You've got a good job here. And now a daughter to raise. You've got me, too," he added, and I could tell there was something fragile bending in his heart. "Why are you going, Shell?"

It was the question I had dreaded, but only because I didn't really have an answer. Why was I going? Because it felt right. Because I could. Because I needed to. Because . . .

"Because I can't raise Dad's daughter on Dad's turf," I said.

Trey nodded like it made sense. "What's in Germany?"

"A school. For missionary kids. In English."

"So you'll be teaching?"

"Maybe doing some synchronized swimming on the side."

"And they'll pay you well?"

That made me laugh. "They won't pay me a dime. I'm going to be a modern-day John Burkhart, ministering to the tribes and ghettos of Deutschland."

"A missionary?" He was having trouble with the concept.

"I blame it on the guy who taught me to say prayers."

"I had to. You couldn't sleep if you didn't."

"I still can't. My life is too . . . messed up to sleep without prayers. And it's not getting any simpler." I paused. "Is it really the God thing that's bugging you most?"

"You know, even when we were little, I wondered how you could believe in God with Dad screaming loud enough to scare off the Holy Spirit."

"That's just it. Dad screamed and ranted and raved and cursed, but God never left. He stuck around to hear it all."

"He didn't spare us."

"No. And I still don't get that. But when I think of what it would have been like if I hadn't known he was there when I said my prayers at night . . ." I didn't know how to put it into words. "I really want to do this, Trey. I think I need to. For me and Shayla. But if you don't think we should . . ."

Trey filled the silence with nervous little tics like scratching his ear, rubbing the back of his neck, and shifting from foot to foot. When he spoke again, it was with a sort of reluctant capitulation.

"Don't you have to raise money or something?"

"My church is helping me. And the rest will come from the Jim Davis Atonement Fund."

"How long before you go?"

"School starts in August, but they said they'd cover for me if I had to get there a little late. They know the circumstances are . . . unusual."

"They know about you and Shayla?"

I comforted a sigh with a piece of *mille-feuille*. "They know. And they're concerned—think I should probably take more time to adjust before launching into work over there, but . . . two of the English teachers they were counting on just fell through, so they're a little desperate."

"They might be right about you needing time to adjust."

"They might. But they've assured me that my commitment is dependent on Shayla doing okay, and if she doesn't, we'll pack up and come home."

"Sounds fair."

"I'm sure it's not a normal arrangement, but they're out of options and I'm willing and eager, so . . ."

"You should take my half of Dad's money back."

"I'm not taking it."

"You should. Shayla's going to be growing up. She'll need things."

"We'll be fine, Trey. I've talked it over with my money guy and we've worked it all out."

Trey smirked. "Your money guy."

"Yup. I got me a money guy. How un-me is that?"

Another silence settled like static electricity over the kitchen and I wished we'd been able to have this discussion in our Huddle Hut. But we were grown-ups now, and the Huddle Hut had gone the way of most other great childhood inventions. Except that special, indefinable connection that made Trey and me the toughest unit around. There was a twoness to us that had withstood some of the worst life had to offer, and here I was preparing to break it. Remorse choked me. But a giggle from the other room strengthened my resolve.

I speared a piece of *mille-feuille* with my fork and raised it in salute. "To the brotherhood . . ."

". . . of Davishood."

"And to the muddlehood . . ."

". . . of huddlehood."

I clinked my bite of *mille-feuille* with his imaginary fork and tried to swallow past the boulder in my throat.

8

"Is IT GOING TO BE good this time, Shelby?"

I knew Shayla was trying to be as diplomatic as a four-year-old could be, but I found the question mildly insulting. "I'm trying, Shay," I said, adding something called quark to the ground beef I'd just fried up and praying it would be more edible than the last three meals I'd attempted. It had gotten so bad that Shayla had complained to Bev about my cooking, and Bev, bless her missionary heart, had taken it upon herself to teach this Lean Cuisine and Stouffer's addict how to cook an edible meal from scratch. She had informed me that preparing Lean Cuisine and Stouffer's dinners didn't amount to actual cooking, and I had tried to convince her that they did require some kitchen skills compared to my other best friends: Arby, Wendy, and Mickey-D, which, in Germany, were as scarce as, say, sauerkraut in North America.

So I was trying out one of Bev's easy recipes, and Shayla was watching closely to make sure I didn't dump the whole box of salt into the sauce as I'd done on a previous attempt. I hadn't expected cooking to be among the more challenging aspects of a life abroad, but my first trip to the grocery store had proved me wrong. The Germans weren't big into prepared meals, and that was an understatement. They apparently liked to waste vast amounts of time on, say, chopping vegetables, browning raw meat, and frying potatoes. And if they wanted something sweet for dessert, they didn't seem to have any aversion to measuring and stirring multiple ingredients rather than just adding an egg and some water to a Betty Crocker mix.

"What do you think, Shay? You think it's going to turn out this time?"

"I don't know," she singsonged, trying to look hopeful, though I knew she was anticipating another supper of hard bread and strawberry jam if this last-ditch effort failed.

"Well, Bev gave me very specific instructions, so I think we might have a winner." I poured a tiny box of gravy spices into the mixture of meat and quark and gave it a stir. The smell was promising.

"Do you think we should invite Bev and Gus for dinner?" We hadn't had any guests yet, and this seemed like a good occasion for an inaugural meal.

"Yeeeeeees," Shayla squealed.

I left the meat simmering on the stove and called Bev.

"I'm cooking," I declared. I hadn't actually introduced myself, but I knew Bev would figure it out from the sheer pride of my statement.

"You are! Shelby, that's great."

Shayla tugged at my sleeve. "Tell her it might be good."

"Shayla says it might be good this time."

That made Bev laugh. Bev laughed a lot at Shayla, but in a good—no, wonderful—way. "So we were wondering if you and Gus might want to come over and sample it with us. Take some Pepto-Bismol before you come . . . just in case."

I heard a muffled conversation on the other end of the line before Bev came back on. "We'd love to, Shelby, but we've invited Scott over tonight and . . ." Bev covered the mouthpiece for another conversation with Gus. "Gus says it probably wouldn't bother Scott if we just dragged him over there instead, though."

Oh, the agony of trying to say something frantic in a calm, composed way. What I wanted to say was, "What—are you kidding? I'm having enough trouble outrunning him on my way home from school each night without inviting him into my house. Absolutely not. No. *Nyet. Nein.* Period." What I said instead was, "You know what? We really don't need to do this tonight, not if you've already made plans. Let's just postpone it 'til next week. It'll give me the chance to make sure I've got it right."

"Are you sure?"

"Absolutely."

"All right then. We'll take a rain check. Let me know how it turns out, okay?"

"I will."

"And congratulations on cooking a meal from scratch."

"I'm tackling Mount Everest next!"

She laughed. "Gus says to give a kiss to Lady Shay from him."

"Done."

"Thanks for thinking of us! We'll look forward to next week."

"No problem. Bye, Bev!"

I hung up the phone and answered Shayla's look. "They're coming next week, honey. They have company of their own for dinner tonight." I gave her a kiss. "That's from Gus. I think he kinda likes you."

She grinned and got back to important things. "Can we eat?"

I loved that girl. And it frightened the you-know-what out of me to admit it. She might have been my father's daughter, but she reminded me of me. Another reason to be scared. "Sure. You get the usual and I'll bring the usual." Which, in Shay-Shell talk, meant, "You set the table and I'll bring the food over." Of course, I ended up doing most of the table-setting, too, as Shayla wasn't exactly the quickest table-setter in the land, but I thought it was good for her to have little jobs around the house.

We'd gotten into so many natural routines lately that this pseudo-mother-daughter thing was starting to feel comfy, like the steam off a cup of hot chocolate—warm and sweet. And again, that scared me. It scared me so much, sometimes, that I felt a near-panic while performing some of our routines, as if I couldn't let myself get too used to them in case my dad suddenly came back from the dead and took Shayla away from me and started calling me the names he used to hurl at me. They weren't pretty names, and just the thought of them turned the world a little blotchy in my mind. But we stuck to our routines despite the thoughts that made me feel kooky. There were bedtime routines and Sunday routines and garbage routines and reading routines and after-school routines.

The after-school routines weren't so much Shay-Shell affairs as Scott-Shell and *then* Shay-Shell. No matter what time I left the school after play rehearsals, and no matter what door I used to exit the school (I switched them up—just for the sport), he always managed to catch up with me. After our first trek to the Johnsons' had yielded little information other than his Boy Scout history, he'd started to come prepared for conversational blitzes that went something like this:

Sound of jogging feet. "Hi, Shelby."

"Low, Scott." Sometimes I had to resort to kindergarten humor. I found it refreshing.

"How was rehearsal?"

"Seth actually touched Kate's cheek without any visible seizures, so I think we're making progress."

"And all because I was able to inspire them."

"Right. I'm sure that's what did it."

"So do you think God has a sense of humor?" He tried to get down to the serious stuff by the time we got to the halfway mark, just so I couldn't use Gus and Bev's house as an excuse not to answer.

"He created Meagan, didn't he?"

"What's your position on predestination?"

"I was predestined to eat cheesecake. You were predestined to harass cheesecake eaters."

"Do you really not like any sports at all?"

"I like to watch them if I know someone who's playing. If I'm expected to participate, I'd rather throw myself off a tall building and get my eyelid caught on a protruding nail. Or something more painful—like conversational whiplash from these little talks with you."

I tried to throw in the occasional barb or two just to keep things light, but they never really seemed to hit home.

"Did you name your daughter Shayla so both your names could start with the same sound?"

I made a noise like a buzzer and declared the round over. We'd reached the front steps of the Johnsons' house.

"Thanks for talking," he said.

"It gave me a headache."

"I wouldn't have to talk so fast if you walked more slowly. Or took a longer road. Or . . . you know . . ."

"It's not so much the speed as the topic-hopping."

"Just trying to cover some interesting bases in the two minutes and forty seconds you allow."

I smiled. "There's no practice tomorrow." Fridays were our down days, and I didn't want him walking the sidewalks alone, carrying on a monologue.

"You could always come by the gym and have an orange with the guys."

"I don't do oranges. They're too much like fruit."

"Invitation's open."

"Duly noted."

"Bye, Shelby."

I did my best imitation of a flight attendant. "Buh-bye now."

I'd lie in bed at night and rack my brain trying to figure out what kept him coming back for more day after day, barb after barb, buzzer after buzzer. I couldn't ever figure it out. Maybe he was just a glutton for punishment. Maybe he felt sorry for me. Maybe he was bored and would move on in time. I liked that last option best. It made me feel safe and less off-balance. And feeling safe was a big deal for me.

I think Gus and Bev caught on to the after-school ritual pretty fast. Sometimes I saw the living room curtain rustle a bit when we reached the front steps, and I suspected they waited to tell Shayla I was there until Scott had started trotting back down the street. They always welcomed me warmly, but their smiles, some days, made me wonder if they hadn't plastered their ears to the front door and gotten a sampling of the Scott and Shelby Show. There was an undertone of plotting in the air and it made me uncomfortable. Like seeing German bicyclers in spandex shorts riding by on too-narrow seats. Uncomfortable.

❋ ❋ ❋

Germany's weather was an accurate reflection of its people. It was generally mild, though it tended toward cloudy. But there were times when the clouds seemed to suddenly march away as if by celestial decree, instantly making way for the kind of brightening that left me squinting and confused. The greenness of the German countryside was a wondrous result of so much gloom and drizzle, which only went to prove that there were silver linings around every cloud, green fields under every downpour, and friendly smiles behind every scowl. It was just a question of sticking around long enough to see it happen.

The Germans hadn't been unfriendly so much as just blank. No frowns, no smiles, no scowls. Nothing that let me know they even noticed my existence, let alone welcomed or resented it. Just rigid backs and mildly disapproving stares. We did exchange *Tag*s in the daytime and *Abend*s in the evening, but I knew they were merely a pleasant German custom that fostered little personal connection and certainly didn't bridge the gulf of miscommunication and suspicion between us.

Shayla, of course, had been on the receiving end of smiles and pats ever since her arrival in Kandern. But me? I'd been the woman standing next to her, living in perpetual certainty that I was doing something culturally wrong and that, someday soon, someone was simply going to tell me to go back to the States, where I belonged.

I kept reminding myself that all the newness in my life had left my morale weakened, and I commanded my mind to think positively—mostly because the alternative would have hampered my sanity. And there were times, on my more optimistic days, when I actually thought I glimpsed a bit of a softening from the man at the post office, the lady at the bank, and the gentleman across the way who had reprimanded us for washing our car on a holiday, though I was fairly sure that none of them were about to shed their natural reserve and try to engage in a full-fledged bilingual conversation with me. And there was probably no hugging or high-fiving in our future either. They were German, after all. But the smallest of thaws was a positive sign indeed, and I clung to each one with all the fervor of my fears.

It might have been a desire to finally bridge the abyss that lent me the courage, one Saturday afternoon, to attend a small gathering of German ladies in the Johnson home. Bev hosted twice-yearly *Kaffee und Kuchen* get-togethers for the handful of German women she knew, and she had invited me to the next one. Though the socializing was a daunting prospect, the coffee-and-cake theme quickly overcame my reservations.

I hadn't realized, until five German ladies overtook Bev's living room, how much German my friend spoke. I was pretty sure it was heavily laced with a syrupy Southern drawl, but the ladies seemed to understand what she was saying, albeit with the occasional help of some gesticulating and an English-German dictionary. Not only was my German limited to a very restrictive collection of phrases—I had yet to use "Hans and Regina went to the pool" in conversation—but it was also crippled, on that afternoon, by the sheer panic of being trapped in a room crackling with such an abrupt-sounding language. I spent two hours smiling politely, speaking English very slowly in response to the few questions Bev translated for me, and gorging on Linzer torte. By the end of the get-together, my stomach was fairly happy, but my brain and self-esteem were mush.

Bev and I cleaned up the kitchen together after her guests left, and I basked in the single-language conversation.

"That wasn't too bad, was it?" she asked.

"It was . . ." How could I put it? "Actually, Bev, if it hadn't been for the torte, I probably would have gone home an hour ago."

"Are you saying my tea party was boring?" She smiled and dumped leftover coffee down the drain.

"Boring? No! It's just that . . . I tried to listen for words I understood, and I did catch a few, but not enough to follow even the main topics of the conversation. I tried to smile when everyone else smiled and look concerned when everyone else did too, but I was pretty much lost from the moment they walked in until the last lady left!"

"But you stuck it out in spite of the challenges, right? That's an accomplishment in itself."

"I need to learn German," I said emphatically. Bev opened her mouth like she was about to tell me when and where to go for lessons. "*After* my life settles down a bit!" I amended. The last thing I needed to add to my challenge-saturated life was language study.

"Well, when you think the time is right, I know a lady who'd be a great tutor for you."

"Maybe in a month or two—give or take a decade."

Bev laughed and plopped down at the kitchen table.

I sat opposite her. "How did you learn? Did you take lessons when you got here?"

She smiled like there was a good story there. "Gus would tell you I had to learn German because nobody was obeying my orders when I barked at them in English."

"Your orders?"

"I was a bit of a battle-ax in a previous life."

I had trouble believing it. "How 'previous'?"

"Oh, you know . . . ongoing."

"Really?"

She nodded and leaned back in her chair. "I was one of those women whose world isn't so much their oyster as their kingdom. And that worked just fine in South Carolina. I could walk into Walmart and boss the customer service people around like nobody's business. I'd give waitresses a run for their money demanding this and that and complaining about it when it came. There was a teller at my bank who refused to deal with me—she actually took a coffee break every time I walked in the door."

I was dumbfounded. "Really?"

"Really. And that's not even mentioning the way I treated my kids' teachers or the elders at my church. . . ."

I gave her a disapproving look. "What did you do to your poor elders?"

"I was the church secretary for nearly ten years before we came over here. And I figured the position gave me the right to turn First Baptist Church into Bev's Private Playground. If they didn't do things the way I thought they should be done, I made enough noise about it that it became a bigger issue than it ever should have been. The pastor finally had to ask me to tone it down a little or a couple of his elders were going to resign. Now that, Shelby, is a battle-ax."

I shook my head, looking across the table at this woman who seemed the epitome of the genteel Southerner. "Well, I haven't seen anything battle-axish about you since I've been here."

"Oh, I had most of it knocked out of me when I got to Germany. You don't get very far in the grocery stores here by yelling, 'I demand to speak with your manager!' in English."

"I can't believe you were like that."

"Well, I was. And Gus will tell you I can still be. But it took moving here to cure me of the worst of it. Nothing like a little humility to drive a lesson home. But my need to be understood made me learn German, so I can now kindly tell the mailman that he should leave our packages under the balcony rather than in the pouring rain, and I can gently suggest to the waitress at our favorite restaurant that my pork steak is so rare it's still oinking. A few years ago, I would have demanded a new dinner—and on the house, too!" She laughed at my astonishment and added, "Gives you a whole new appreciation for my husband, doesn't it?"

"The guy's a saint." I laughed. "I just . . . I just can't picture it."

"Lucky for you."

We sat there grinning at each other for a moment.

"I should get going," I finally said, remembering Shayla and suddenly missing her.

"Can you hold off just a minute? I've been meaning to talk to you about something, and this seems like a good time to do it."

"Is Shay still refusing to eat her vegetables?" Not that I could blame her. It showed she had good taste.

"Oh no, it's not that. I've just been wondering if it wouldn't be good for her to start going to kindergarten in the mornings. There's a great one right here in Kandern. It might be healthy for her to have more contact with other children, don't you think? She'd probably pick up the language in a matter of weeks, too."

"Kindergarten?" I had visions of Shayla alone on a foreign-speaking playground.

"It's just half days."

"Is she . . . Is it too much for you to take care of her?" I'd worried that Bev's child-care duties might have been too taxing, and this suggestion seemed to validate my fear.

"Oh, heavens, no, Shelby! Having her around is as easy as it gets. This has nothing to do with me. I just hate to see her cooped up with an old lady all day long when she should be out playing with kids her age. And since you're in Germany now, why not give her some contact with the language and the culture? If there's a good age to learn it, believe me, it's hers."

I felt irrational fear tightening my throat. "Really? You really think it would be good for her? I mean, with all the changes she's gone through already this year . . ."

"Well, it would be another change, for sure, but the payoff might outweigh the adjustments. She'd be able to play with other children again, for one—something she really hasn't done much since you've gotten here. And it's so important to have that kind of social contact at her age. It'll stimulate her mind and broaden her world a little in the process."

"I don't know. . . ."

"Hey, there's no hurry. Think it over and let me know if you'd like to try it. I know one of the ladies who runs the place, and we could go visit the school together. You can ask around, too—find out how other BFA faculty children have fared. She wouldn't be the first to go there."

"I'll think about it," I said.

And I did. I thought about it from that moment all the way until supper, fretting and weighing and pondering, until Shayla's wide eyes, gazing across the table at me, made me just blurt it out.

"How would you feel about going to kindergarten, Shay?"

She frowned a little. "Is that school?" She sounded suspicious.

"It's school for kids your age."

"Djoh-many kids?"

I nodded. "Bev said you could go a few mornings a week if you wanted to. Doesn't that sound like fun?" I hoped with all my heart that she would shake her head and refuse to consider it. Maybe even throw a tantrum. Fling some macaroni.

Instead, she frowned a little less and said, "Only if my wabbit can come with me."

Huh? Someone suggesting that I go to school in a foreign language, even at the ripe old age of thirty-five, would have encountered Hysterical Shelby, the one with the bugged-out eyes, shrill voice, and permanently shaking head. But Shayla? Four-year-old Shayla? She just frowned a little, like she wasn't sure she liked the flavor of this particular conversation, then shrugged and decided her stuffed animal should come along. I wasn't sure who was teaching whom in this relationship.

"You're sure? I mean, you don't want to think about it some more?" I told myself to shut up. This was about Shayla, not about me.

"Will there be Legos?" she asked.

"Um . . . probably. Or something like Legos."

She pursed her lips. "Okay," she finally said.

"Okay," I repeated, a little reluctantly, peering at her closely to detect any minute sign of misgivings. But Shayla was back to concentrating on her macaroni, so I figured the conversation hadn't exactly traumatized her. "Well," I said lightly, "I'll talk with Bev and maybe we can go visit the school this week."

"Uh-huh."

I had expected anxiety and tears and refusals from this child who had suffered such an overdose of change in recent weeks. Instead, her matter-of-fact agreement had put my own fears to shame. What felt like the beginning of a loss to me, to my pseudo-daughter was merely the start of something new.

9

THE DAY MY DAD left had started pretty well. It would go down from there for a few hours, then up again for, oh, about a couple decades. Trey and I followed the smell of bacon frying to the kitchen and observed our usual rituals of breakfast in pj's, doing dishes to the Beatles, and getting dressed to the smell of the lawn being cut. It was a day that felt cheerful—kelly-green around the edges—and that somehow brought out the sports fans in us. So Trey donned his lucky Bulls championship cap, and I donned my lucky McDonald's Walk for Life T-shirt, which always felt disloyal to Wendy's. But I was getting over that.

I think it's the sports theme that dismantled our lives. That may explain the hate-hate relationship I've had with sports ever since then, though I'm pretty sure I was already of that mind-set in preschool, when I staged a sit-in every time my teacher told us to climb the monkey bars. Monkey bars *was a deceptive term.* Monkey *sounded like fun, in a goofy, screechy kinda way. And* bars *sounded yummy, in a Mars or Snickers kinda way. But* climbing? Climbing *sounded like something that required physical effort, and that's where five-year-old Shelby drew the line.*

Trey and I wandered outside in our sports gear, and Dad told us he was going to the hardware store to have his lawn-mower blade sharpened. He took Mom's car since it was parked behind his and she wouldn't be needing it as she had walked to the hair salon to have her ends trimmed. We stood in the driveway after Dad drove away and had our usual Saturday conversation.

"What do you wanna do?"

"I dunno. What do you wanna do?"

"I dunno. We could go to the arcade."

"Yeah."

"Or we could watch MTV."

I didn't like MTV. It made me feel like I'd drunk too much Coke. "Or we could go to the grocery store and try their free samples."

Trey and I weren't very good at Saturdays. We could never decide what we were going to do—except when Dad had one of his fits. When that happened, life became predictable and manageable and we no longer had to plan our day or come to an agreement. We knew the drill. It took all the frustration out of Saturdays. But Dad had been in a pretty good mood so far, so we were left to our own devices.

Why Trey stayed home on weekends with little old me was a mystery. He had friends on the soccer team and at school, though he mostly just hung out with them between classes and during games and scrimmages. They never came over to the house, but I think that's because it was too hard to explain my dad to them. And not just the neckties-on-Saturdays thing.

We were about to throw in the towel and head to the video arcade when the sport of basketball decided to turn our lives upside down.

See, Trey had his Bulls cap on, and when he was wearing that, he tended to suffer from Michael Jordan delusions. I saw him eyeing the basketball hoop that hung above our garage door and concluded I'd have to find my own entertainment for the next hour or so while my usually fairly rational brother bounced a ball in rhythmic monotony and yelled, "Three-pointer!" at the top of his lungs. I did, however, see an impediment to his plans.

"Don't you think Dad's car is too close to the hoop?" I asked.

"I'll shoot around it."

"Trey . . ." Dad loved his car. The first deadly sin in our household was messing with Dad's car. The second deadly sin was everything else.

"Don't worry about it, Shell." He was already bouncing the ball and lining up his first shot. "I've got all the precision of my man Jordan."

He had neither the skin color nor the height, so I doubted he had the precision. The first shot went wide and bounced off the backboard directly onto the shiny hood of Dad's Chevy. I cringed and covered my eyes like it would undo the hollow thunk that I knew must have left its mark on the finish.

"It's okay," Trey said a few seconds later, and I uncovered my eyes to find him polishing a blemish off the hood with his shirt. "It's coming right off."

"Maybe it's a bad idea to pretend you're a Bull while the car's in the driveway," I suggested. He got a look on his face that made me want to tie him to a tree with duct tape. It was a look that spelled mischief*— only it spelled it* d-a-n-g-e-r-o-u-s. *"What are you thinking, Trey?" I really didn't like the glint in his eyes.*

He looked into the car and his smile broadened. "You know how I've been taking driver's ed at school?"

"Trey . . ."

"I'm going to be sixteen in two and a half months."

"Only if Dad doesn't kill you before then."

Trey leaned down and eyed the garage doorway like a golfer lines up his shot. "All I've got to do is put it in gear and let it coast into the garage."

"Uh, Trey . . ." I was trying to figure out how to express my true feelings without resorting to nasty words.

Trey opened the driver's-side door and got into the front seat. I was rooted to the spot with a combination of terror and reluctant admiration. My brother, the idiot, was truly a courageous guy.

"You sure you know what you're doing?" I yelled as the engine came to life and he put it in gear. The car inched forward and I could see how it was perfectly lined up with the garage. I think Trey and I were both so focused on that, neither of us realized he had left the car door open. I saw it just as it was about to make contact with the garage's doorframe and yelled, "Trey! The door!" so loudly that I startled myself.

I apparently startled Trey, too, because he panicked. He didn't know what I'd yelled, but he knew it had sounded urgent, and in his frantic attempt to bring the car to a halt, he hit the wrong pedal, just for a second, and jolted the Chevy into the workbench on the back wall of the garage.

I've heard it said that time stands still at critical moments in life, like when someone says they love you or you win the lottery or your brother plows your dad's prize possession into the garage wall. But time didn't actually stand still in the aftermath of what we would come to refer to as the Big Bang. Time actually took on a life of its own and started to rock and swirl around me, and I think the whole earth kinda bucked along in rhythm. It was a cataclysm of unimaginable consequences, and time was thrashing around in a desperate effort to reverse itself. It didn't succeed. When the earth settled a little under my feet, I heard a lone wrench fall off its wall hook and land on the hood of the shiny black Chevy.

This was not good—a very bad, very scary, very irremediable version of not good.

When Dad returned, he found us sitting on the stoop at the front of the house. We'd passed the minutes trying to make light of the situation, but I could see from the sweat on Trey's forehead and the wideness of his eyes—like the top lids were stuck on something—that we hadn't succeeded. That was a little disappointing, because we'd tried so hard.

"So do you still feel like Michael Jordan?" I'd asked.

"This is the end of my life."

"Maybe we should run away to Mexico and build a Huddle Hut on the beach."

"He's going to kill me, Shell."

"We could make up a story. We could say some homeless guy jumped in the car and rammed it into the garage. Or maybe a druggie."

"Or maybe the pope."

"Yeah—the pope's a good one too."

"The damage isn't too bad, right?"

I hesitated. I didn't know much about cars. "Well, the door is . . . It just has a few scratches, but . . ."

"He's going to kill me."

"Maybe if you tell him how sorry you are, he'll understand. Or maybe he's one of those people who get all upset about stupid little things but don't really worry about the big things."

He gave me a my-sister-the-moron look. We were in deep doo-doo and both of us knew it.

"I hear Mexico's really nice this time of year."

That's when my mom's car, with my dad in it, pulled into the driveway. It took a while for him to open the door, and that was scarier than anything that came after.

Trey stood and waited. I could see he had dark spots on his back and under his arms where the sweat had soaked into his shirt. When

Dad got out of the car, Trey took a step back. I stood and touched his arm, and then he stepped off the stoop and went to stand in front of the man whose lips had disappeared and whose neck was popping with veins and sinews and fury.

Dad didn't take his eyes off the car and the mess of tools and paint cans on the floor around it.

"Dad, I—"

He backhanded Trey so quickly, like a lightning strike, that it was over before I'd seen it coming. Trey fell against Mom's car so hard that his back curved over the hood. My dad kept him plastered there with his hand on his throat, pushing down on his neck like he wanted to crush it.

I felt like I was watching the scene through a wall of buzzing bees, so thick and seething was the air.

The sky lowered and added its weight to my dad's. The trees in the yard bent forward, forcing more air out of my brother's lungs.

"What have you done?" Dad raged, disgorging a crush of poison words. "What have you done to my car?" I could see the spit flying out of his mouth, even at a distance, and the veins around his eyes were starting to stand out. He was red. Mottled. Rabid. His body taut and straining. His teeth bared in a snarl that belonged on a sick, caged animal—not on my dad. This was not my father. This was my worst nightmare in human form, my greatest, most horrendous fear choking the life out of my brother in Technicolor and surround sound. My legs wanted to buckle and my mind wanted to flee into insentience, but the only good part of me was being broken, that part that walked and talked and breathed as Trey, and I couldn't let it happen. There was a bright-blue flash at the back of my mind and I launched off the porch, pushing through thick air toward my brother. My friend. My protector.

"I'll kill you for this! I'll kill you!" my dad was shrieking, his voice like broken glass. Then he ran out of words and just screamed and

howled and thundered while I tried to pry his vicious hands from my brother's neck. I pulled at his arm, pitting my full weight against his grip, but I was a moth throwing myself against a fortress, feeble and frantic and impotent.

In a desperate last effort fueled by the churning lava in my chest, I jumped onto Dad's back and braced my feet against Mom's car and tried to pull him away from the hood, away from Trey, away from the hell of seeing my brother, shattered and helpless, dying before me. And still, my efforts were in vain. I reached around to my dad's face and started to claw. I clawed at his eyes, I clawed at his cheeks, I clawed at his mouth and ears and nose. I felt wet against my fingers, and I didn't care whether it was spit or blood or tears. All I cared about was that he was staggering back and releasing his hold on my choking, convulsing brother.

And then he turned, his hands tearing mine from his face, and slammed backward into the car with me on his back, knocking the terror from my lungs, before throwing me over his shoulder like a wrestler onto the ground. I felt my wrist bend too far, but it was only the mechanics of the injury that registered, not the pain. I heard shrieking in the background that sounded like my mom. Then my face hit the pavement in a streak of fire-yellow and blood-pounding red and I passed out.

My first thought when I woke up on the living room couch was, Shoot, I didn't kill him. *I'd really hoped my clawing would have severed an artery somewhere in his face and made him bleed to death. But there he was, sitting off in the corner of the room in the chair that was so pretty that none of us ever used it. My eyes were seeing things a little blurry, so I couldn't tell if it was blood or just scrapes crisscrossing his face. I hoped it was blood.*

"Trey . . ." I croaked, turning my head to find Mom's face above mine. She was holding my wrist like you hold a dead bird.

"It's just a sprain," she said, and I squinted a little to make sure it was really my mom. She didn't sound like her.

"Trey," I tried again. "Where's Trey?" This time my voice sounded less like a bullfrog and more like a cricket. But Mom was so busy staring at my dad, all slumped over in the pretty flowered chair, that I don't think she heard me. Her face looked stony, like those gargoyles we'd studied in art class. Except she was prettier—but not by much. Hate had turned her ugly just then. It suddenly dawned on my mushy brain that maybe she was ignoring my question because the answer was too horrible to say. I felt like the couch folded up beneath me and I fell through, butt first, and went spiraling into an endless, dark, suffocating hole where the absence of Trey would shred me.

There were weird pictures flashing through my head, like pages of a notebook being flipped so fast that they all blurred together. I saw bits and pieces of Rolos and basketballs and zucchini and Coke cans and the Huddle Hut and the arcade and all these fragile pieces of Trey I wanted to gather up and press into a ball and swallow so he would be a part of me—inside me—even if he wasn't in the world anymore. The darkness of the hole was blackening my vision and snuffing out my thoughts.

Life without Trey. Life without Trey. Life without Trey. *My heart tried to beat through my ribs so it could run away screaming into the attic and curl up in the Huddle Hut and just shriek.*

"Is she okay?" The voice was raspy like the smell of burned toast, but it was Trey's and it was alive and it came from somewhere down around my feet. So I pulled my head off the couch's armrest and looked down my body through the spinning, rocking world . . . and there he was. He was sitting in Mom's armchair, holding a bag of frozen peas against his throat. I could see there would be bruises there tomorrow. Tomorrow. Trey would be alive tomorrow. I laid my head back down on the armrest and heard a sob and thought, How embarrassing *for*

whoever was making such a pathetic noise. And then Trey was beside me, his frozen-peas hands cold against my arm. He knelt by the couch and shushed me like a baby, stroking my arm, while Mom stood there and stared at the corner with the pretty chair.

I didn't know what to do to stop sobbing, and I think I looked at Trey like, Help me! *because all the crying was hurting my ribs and my head and my wrist. But Trey just kept on shushing me. And then his shushing got a little jagged. And then he put his face down next to my head, kind of burrowed it into the pillow under my neck, and I could feel his sobbing matching mine.*

❋ ❋ ❋

I couldn't stop the tears. They had started when I'd gotten into Gus's car, and they hadn't abated during the fifteen-minute ride home. He had tried to console me as best he could, but his reassurances had been weightless on the scales by which I judged the good and bad of my life.

"You couldn't have seen him coming," Gus said. "It's a blind intersection and you did everything you should, but he just came around that corner too fast to miss you."

"He didn't listen," I said, swallowing the sobs that tried to overcome my self-control. I would not let them out in front of Gus. "I kept telling him that I don't speak German and he just kept on yelling at me. I even told him *in German*—but he kept pointing at his car and at me and . . ." I had to pause because the exertion of trying to maintain my dignity was making it hard for me to catch my breath. "And I don't have a cell phone!" I finally wailed.

"It all worked out," Gus said in a soothing voice, reaching awkwardly to pat me on the shoulder as he drove. "That store owner let you call Bev, and she got ahold of me."

I felt another wave of humiliation and horror rushing up from my stomach to my throat. "He just wouldn't stop yelling, Gus!"

"The damage isn't bad." He was trying hard to drag my mind off the yelling, but it had apparently made quite an impression on my conversational skills. "I'll go over this afternoon with someone else and drive your car home. We'll have it back in shape in no time. And it probably won't even cost that much."

That launched another tears-versus-self-control battle. Money. Money had become more of an issue than it had ever been before. I did have the income from my dad and from my church, but every month still felt like a desperate countdown from one paycheck to the next.

"We can help you pay for the repairs," Gus said, misinterpreting my increased crying for concern about the bodywork my car's rear fender would require. He didn't realize how much deeper and wider my anxiety was. This wasn't about an accident. This wasn't about another bill. This was about the utter foundationlessness I felt in every facet of my out-of-control life.

When we got home, Bev was waiting on the doorstep for me. She rushed over and helped me out of the car, while Gus took the keys from me and opened my door.

"Oh, Shelby, honey, I'm so, so sorry," she said, wrapping me tightly and rubbing my shoulders as we walked. "Is the car badly damaged?"

"Just a scratch and a dent," Gus said as we passed in front of him and entered my apartment. "I'll keep your keys so I can get your car later, okay, Shelby? And I'll pick Shayla up from kindergarten in an hour, so don't you worry about that."

"We'll be okay," Bev said, walking with me to the couch. Gus told her to call him if we needed anything, then left.

Now that I was in my own home and in the comfortable presence of my friend, I had no command left over the torrent of emotions that had been months in building up. Bev went to my bedroom and came back with my pillow. "Here," she said, "hang on to this. It's no good to cry without something to hold on to." And she sat down beside me on the couch and patted my back while I hugged the pillow to my stomach and let the torrent rage. The force of my crying was terrifying, so powerful that I pitched slowly sideways as I sobbed, my head finding the armrest and my legs curling up under me. Bev's hand never ceased its movement on my back and shoulder. She just sat there quietly and let my anxiety flow.

"I don't know why I'm doing this," I sobbed, minutes later, when I couldn't seem to get a grip on my emotions. "I don't know what's happening to me."

Bev's voice was gentle and laced with understanding. "It's been a long time in coming, hasn't it."

I nodded, powerless to gain control.

"And it's not just about your accident," she said. "But you know that, too."

"He wouldn't understand me," I cried. "I kept saying it over and over—'I don't speak German.' But he kept on ranting. And when the cops came—" I buried my face in my pillow to stifle the sounds coming out of my throat—"they laughed, Bev." I turned my head to look at her. "They laughed and said something about Americans."

"Well, that was uncalled for."

"I can't do this," I said, and the resolve of that statement relieved me somewhat. It also made me angry enough to sit up. "I can't live here. I can't keep trying to convince myself that everything's fine. I can't keep putting Shayla through this."

"Don't make any decisions now, Shelby, not while you're in this state."

"But I can't do it, Bev! I'm sick of this. I'm sick of being a foreigner. I'm sick of not being able to read any labels at the grocery store. I'm sick of being scared on the roads and of getting mail that doesn't mean anything to me even though I know it's important. I'm sick of having to beg people for help and being treated like a dimwit!"

"Shelby . . ."

"I can't take it!" Another crying jag threatened to overwhelm me, so I got off the couch and began to pace, anger adding an edge to my tears. "I thought I was doing okay. I kept telling myself that this is normal, that it's going to get easier. I keep telling Shayla that too, but how can I convince her when I can't cope either? I knew it was going to be hard, but nothing like this. Nothing like this, Bev!

"I haven't even made friends with anyone aside from you and Gus. It's like every moment I'm awake is consumed with trying to keep Shayla happy, and trying to be a good teacher, and figuring out how to direct a play, and cooking with foods I've never seen before, and feeling like an absolute idiot because I still can't speak German, and . . . and I'm tired of it!"

"Give it time."

I stopped my pacing long enough to give her a disbelieving look. "How much? I was expecting some tough stuff, but nothing like this—and I feel it all the time. On the outside *and* the inside. Like my organs aren't even in the same place anymore. I can't handle it, Bev. I thought I'd be able to, but I can't!"

"This is *normal*, Shelby," Bev said from the couch, her own eyes bright with tears.

"Well, it's too much," I said wearily, my sobs subsiding but my lungs still heaving. I sat at the dining room table and looked at my friend in utter despair. "It's all too hard. The Germans are always staring at me and correcting me and acting like I'm an imbecile.

Nothing is easy here—nothing! I mean, it takes an hour and a half to do a load of laundry! I can't find a donut to save my life, I can't buy clothes because none of them fit right, I feel guilty driving because gas costs so much, I only get to talk to Trey once a week . . ."

Bev came to the table and pulled a chair up close to mine. "You're transitioning. It's supposed to feel this way."

"And then," I added in desperation, "I go to the doctor this morning for a sore throat and he makes me strip to my waist—to my waist!—and he doesn't give me anything to cover up with. Nothing. No paper robe, no sheet . . . I can't do it," I said again, shaking my head in resignation. "And I can't do this to Shayla."

"She'll recover too."

"Have you *seen* her since she started kindergarten?" I asked angrily, motherly protectiveness hardening my tone. "She's come back every day *so* unhappy, Bev. The other kids won't talk to her, the teachers refuse to listen to her if she speaks English. How is she supposed to learn when no one cares about her?"

"I've seen her when she comes home," Bev said with the kind of firmness in her voice that told me it was time to become rational again. "She comes straight to my house, remember? So I've seen it firsthand, and you know what?"

I shook my head and swiped at my nose with the Kleenex she'd brought me from the box next to the couch.

"The two of you are suffering from exactly the same adjustment pangs. Too much newness and weirdness all at the same time. Too many things that feel like you somehow need to survive them."

"I need to pull Shay out of kindergarten. It's killing her."

"Give her another couple of weeks."

"Bev! She cries herself to sleep at night and begs me every morning not to send her back. It's been like that for two weeks! How can I force her to do something she hates so much?"

"You're not forcing her. You're allowing her enough time to get used to it before pulling her out of the one thing in her life that gives her contact with others."

My lungs spasmed a little and I swallowed hard. My eyes were pulsing with the intensity of my emotions, and my chest felt hollowed out. Nausea came and went like a veil across my eyes.

"And I can't stand the rain," I said, every ounce of my rebellion in the words.

Bev laughed and reached across to pat my hand. "Well that, my dear, is the one thing you *really* can't do anything about!"

I allowed a smile, but it didn't feel very hopeful.

"None of this is easy, Shelby. That much you've got absolutely right. And combined with everything else you're coping with, it's got to feel so overwhelming that you can't see straight right now. But give it time. Just like Shayla needs a little more time before you decide whether to leave her in kindergarten or not, you need more time to see just how strong you really can be. You've only been here a few weeks, and I don't want to depress you, but culture shock like this can sometimes take a couple years to put behind you."

I rolled my eyes. "Great. That's encouraging."

"Except that you're doing it right. You're trying as hard as you can and giving it all you've got, which is exhausting considering you're juggling motherhood and teaching and learning to direct a play. You've been through monumental changes in the past few months, and you've somehow maintained your sanity."

I raised a dubious eyebrow.

"You have," Bev persisted. "This—" she pointed at my swollen eyes and salt abraded cheeks—"this is sanity. It's acknowledging that it hurts and that none of it makes sense. And once this passes, once you get your car back and Shayla starts to do better, once you master a few more easy meals to make and get a few more German phrases under your belt, it'll start to feel better. Just don't expect it to happen overnight."

She patted my hand. "What feels overwhelming now won't be quite so confusing in a month and even less in a year. Every challenge is part of the process. Give the changes the time to become familiar, and give yourself permission to be scared or frustrated or confused. Just like you give permission to Shayla."

"Hans and Regina went to the pool," I said in German.

"Come again?"

"That's the one German sentence I know really well, and I'll probably never get to say it." The last words turned into a wail, and I launched into chapter two of Shelby's Epic Meltdown.

"Hey, consider yourself lucky," Bev said. "The only sentence I know in French is *Voulez-vous coucher avec moi, ce soir?*"

I put my wailing on pause long enough to give her a *Huh?* look.

"From 'Lady Marmalade,'" she explained. "You know what it means?"

I shook my head. I had heard the song all my life without ever wondering about the French.

"Well, it's a surefire way of meeting the natives," Bev said. "It means, 'Do you want to sleep with me tonight?'"

I laughed so hard I snorted.

❊ ❊ ❊

"Your nose is red," I said to Trey. He was lying on the floor next to the couch, his bag of frozen peas still pressed against the livid traces of my father's shame around his neck.

"I've been sneaking out and doing a clown act after dark every night," he croaked, his eyes closed. "Can't seem to get all the makeup off, though."

"Oh, good," I said, "'cause I thought maybe you'd been crying or something."

He opened an eye and glared at me. We'd never been very good at crying together.

Mom and Dad were in the kitchen. They'd been in there forever. After I'd come to on the couch, Dad had sat there for a while in the pretty flowered chair. Then, while I went to the bathroom to throw up, he'd gone into the kitchen with Mom. It hadn't been his idea. Mom had approached him, trying to keep her voice low so we wouldn't hear what she said. But she was so angry that it was like her words had ultrasound. They weren't loud, but we felt them vibrate in our bones.

"Go to the kitchen," she'd hissed, the words sharp and brittle in the silence of the living room. It was the kind of tone we'd used on the dog we had when we were really little. We'd sent him to the kitchen too when he'd peed on the rug or chewed on the furniture. But I never, not in my most psychedelic nightmares, ever thought I'd hear Mom speak to my dad that way.

They'd been in the kitchen for several minutes now, and all we could hear was the occasional word.

"You want me to go put my ear to the door?" I asked Trey.

"Only if you want to."

"My wrist hurts too much."

"Okay."

That's when Mom yelled. She yelled so loudly that both Trey and I sat up like someone had set firecrackers off under our backs.

"Get out!" she yelled. "Get out of the house and don't come back!"

I had never heard Mom yell that way before. Never. Not even when her brakes had given out when she was biking down a hill during a camping trip. Even then, she'd just kinda kept quiet and aimed her bike at the pond off to the right instead of at the trees to the left. She hadn't even screamed when the bike had gone off the road, across a bumpy patch of grass, then right into the water. She'd just put her feet down when the bike sank in the silt and walked out of the knee-deep water, leaving the blue Schwinn standing there in the pond all by itself.

We heard Dad go upstairs and rummage around for a while. Then he came through the living room on his way to the door, a garbage bag full of stuff slung over his shoulder, left the house, started up his Chevy, and just kinda poofed out of our lives.

Mom told us over lasagna that night that Dad was going to be staying at his other house for a while.

"He has another house?"

She got that look like she'd said something she hadn't meant to say. "He's got a place to stay."

"Is he coming back?"

"I don't know."

I looked at Trey.

"You shouldn't let him come back," he said to Mom. I liked it when he said things in that tone of voice. Strong. Like he knew more than Mom did.

Mom had been spending a lot of time moving the lasagna around on her plate with her fork, so I knew she wasn't feeling too good. She let a long silence pass, the kind of silence that feels like smooth water. Like if you say anything or breathe or move, there will be a ripple and the smoothness will be gone. I don't think any of us were in the mood for ripples. We'd had enough. So we all ate in silence for a few more minutes, enjoying the smooth surface while we could.

"I want you to know that what your dad did this afternoon was . . ." She paused.

"Bad?" I offered the word, but I knew it fell short.

"Reprehensible." Better word. Score one for Mom. "And I need you to know that I never would have let it happen if I'd been home." Like

she'd never let him cuss at us or yell at us or shove us around? But her intentions were good. I knew that.

"Why didn't you call the police?" Trust Trey to jump right in.

"They would have . . ." She put her fork down and rubbed at her eyes like she was sleepy. "They might have . . ."

"They might have given him what he deserves," said the boy with the purple-red bruises around his neck.

Mom got teary, but she kept the drops from falling off the edges of her eyes. She'd always had a gift for that. "I don't want you to think your father hates you," she said.

Trey and I exchanged eye rolls. Right. He loved us. He'd nearly loved us into oblivion, the pig. I didn't say the word out loud because part of me still thought he was with us, listening to us, waiting to pounce on his kids' major sins—like not eating zucchini or, you know, calling him a pig.

"He's got some problems," Mom continued. "In his head. And he knows he's hurt you really badly this time."

"I'm not going to forgive him." I looked around to see who had spoken and realized it was me. "I mean—not for a very long time." I knew in my head that it would be never.

"If he comes back, I'm moving out." This from Trey. I guess having the life choked out of you makes you see things in a more definite light. He had that look about him—like he meant it—and it scared me. If Trey left, I'd have to leave too, and I wasn't quite ready for that.

Mom stood after Trey's statement and took her full plate to the counter. "We'll see," she said, her back to us, and we knew that meant she wanted him to come back. She reminded me, sometimes, of the fish we used to catch in the inland lake near the cottage we rented in the summer. It's not like we were subtle about it. We didn't have real fishing rods, so we'd wade in up to our thighs, fishing line and hook tied to the end of a stick. And we'd just walk around dangling the baited hook in the water, kind of like human trawlers, waiting for something to be dumb enough to bite. And there was this one sunfish—we called him Ringo—who kept coming back for more. He'd bite, we'd tear his mouth off the hook and throw him back in. Then, the next minute, while we waded around the edges of the pond and talked loudly and did everything you're not supposed to do if you're fishing, Ringo would come back. He'd bite again, get hooked again, we'd tear him off again and let him go again. After about an hour of this, we'd have to give up and go home. Neither of us could stand the sight of Ringo, his mouth and cheeks all torn up, coming back to bite our icky worms for the umpteenth time.

Mom was like Ringo.

10

THE SILENCE in the auditorium was burdened with emotion. The rehearsal had been going well—so well, in fact, that I'd begun to design play posters in my head as it looked like the whole project wasn't going to be declared dead on arrival after all. I'd instructed Seth to run through his final monologue, just so we could get a sense of it, and I'd asked him to make sure he put some feeling into it—which sounded like good advice from a play director, but this play director had no idea what she was talking about.

Seth, however, apparently did. He walked through an imaginary curtain from the back of the stage and began his speech. "God creates us free, free to be selfish, but he adds a mechanism that will penetrate our selfishness and wake us up to the presence of others in the world, and that mechanism is called suffering. To put it another way, pain is God's megaphone to rouse a deaf world."

The other actors scattered around the room quieted and turned toward the stage, where Seth was taking a deep breath, eyes closed, before going on.

Meagan said, "He's doing good," from the chair beside mine and I nodded. He certainly was.

"Why must it be pain? Why can't he wake us more gently, with violins or laughter? Because the dream from which we must be awakened is the dream that all is well. All is not well. Believe me, all is not well." He took another breath, and there was something ragged in the sound this time. A muscle contracted in his jaw as he seemed to brace himself before continuing, his eyes at once haunted and luminous. "Suffering . . . by suffering . . . through suffering, we release our hold on the toys of this world, and know that our true good lies in another world. But after we have suffered so much, must we still suffer more? And more? And more?"

I was entranced. A herd of tutu-wearing elephants could have pranced through the auditorium just then, and I don't think any of us would have paid them much attention. Because Seth—Seth who couldn't hold Kate's hand without turning five shades of red, Seth who never joined the other guys in stress-relieving rumbles during breaks between scenes, Seth who avoided looking me in the eye at all costs out of excessive timidity or guilt or who-knew-what—that same Seth was standing on the stage reciting his lines with tears dripping off his chin onto his chest. Much like the day I'd first met Shayla, I realized at that moment how deeply I loved him. Mind you, I wasn't planning on officially adding him to my already-complex pseudo-family, but oh, how I loved this giant man-boy whose sensitivity and talent were so far beyond his years.

Shayla was with me at rehearsal that night because Bev had a commitment elsewhere, so I didn't have much time afterward to debrief with my young actor. But Seth and I did sit for a few minutes in the last row of the auditorium after the others had gone outside.

"Tell me about the monologue, Seth."

He shrugged and looked away, apparently enthralled by the white wall off to his right. He'd been a little shaken for the rest of the rehearsal, probably as much because of his emotional display as because of the reaction of his peers. They had walked around the auditorium for the remainder of the evening like pilgrims in a holy place—speaking in whispers, their eyes a little wide, their faces serene. And since it had seemed we'd reached something of a pinnacle, I'd called off the rehearsal a half hour early. Now the other actors were outside engaged in some rip-roarin' game that had the boys screaming, the girls squealing, and the neighbors probably calling the police to complain about the noise. But I could hear Shayla's high voice among all the others—I'd developed mom ears somewhere along the way—and I knew it meant she'd be tired early tonight, so I didn't do anything to intervene.

"Was it the text you were saying?" I asked Seth. "Or is there something going on in your life that makes it hard for you to be a part of the play?"

"I . . . I used to have this . . . this thing," he said. "And the lines I have to say are . . . Well, they mean a lot to me, I guess."

I wasn't sure how to proceed. He was clearly still in a vulnerable state of mind, and I didn't know whether further questions would help or harm him. "What do you mean by 'this thing'?" I asked, giving him the chance to elaborate or be succinct.

"It's called pectus excavatum," he said. He might as well have said it to me in Uzbek. I wasn't familiar with the condition, whatever it was. While my mind tried to piece it together from the Latin terminology, he shifted in his chair and extended his impossibly long legs in front of him, still looking slightly away from me.

"It's a disease," he said. "It means my chest was permanently caved in. My sternum and my ribs." He shook his head and shifted again. "I couldn't breathe normally or exercise because it was messing with my lungs and my heart. And I . . ." He trailed off.

"What, Seth?"

"I looked deformed. You know. When I took my shirt off."

"Seth . . ." His vulnerability awakened my own. "Is it treatable?"

He swallowed hard and nodded. "I had surgery a year ago."

"Well, that's a step in the right direction." I wanted to be encouraging.

"But then I got injured." He took a deep breath and scooted down a little in his chair, aiming his eyes at the ceiling as he relived his pain. "Seven ribs got disconnected from the sternum. And it killed. I mean, the pain . . ." He blinked a few times to dispel the tears in his eyes. "But the doctors couldn't see it. They didn't do an MRI or anything and just kept telling me it was normal to feel bad after surgery, but . . . I knew it was worse than that. Anytime I moved . . . or breathed too deeply . . . or someone bumped into me . . . And the pain pills they gave me to try to deal with it made me moody . . . you know, mad and tired all the time, and . . ." He paused and bit the inside of his cheek to quell his emotions.

"Oh, Seth . . ."

"It lasted four months before anyone figured out that my bones were detached—and that whole time I just felt like someone was constantly sawing at my chest. Then a doctor in Munich did an MRI and they had to go back in and operate again."

"After four months?"

He shook his head to dispel the memories, and his mouth pinched into a line. "It was . . . It was bleak," he said. "Wanting-to-be-dead bleak."

"Seth, I'm so sorry."

"So when I get up and give that monologue about pain and death and stuff . . ."

"It hits close to home."

"Yeah. Every time."

"And is that okay? I mean—will it hurt you too much to relive it over and over?"

He shook his head again. "It'll help me, I think. I'm still dealing with the whole God thing, and saying Lewis's thoughts . . . it screws my head on straighter."

"Well, I'm sure you know it's a powerful scene from the audience's perspective too."

He looked genuinely surprised. "It is?"

"It's . . ." I looked for the right word. "Redemptive." Seth was one of the few students I knew who would understand the significance of the word. "You mentioned the 'God thing.' I think it's a God thing that you're part of this cast, Seth. That you're C. S. Lewis."

His hands were rolling and unrolling the script they held. He nodded.

"Please let me know if there's anything—anything at all—you need help with." I remembered some of the tough rehearsals we'd had recently. "How are you doing with Kate?"

He shrugged.

"Listen, I know it's not always easy dealing with her. But I think she really respects your acting, and she clearly wants to get this right. So if you can just let Kate be Kate for a little while longer and not let her Joy-ness fluster you . . . She doesn't mean any harm."

"I know," he said as a blush crept up his neck.

"All right." I stood. "Time for me to get Shayla home."

Seth rose too and pulled on his trademark trench coat before shouldering his backpack.

"I'm proud of you, Seth."

He just ducked his head and exited the room.

Minutes later, Shayla and I were walking up three flights of stairs to the front of the school and Shayla was whining about being hungry. I wanted to tell her that she wouldn't know what hungry was until she went on a no-carbs diet, but I informed her instead that we'd be home soon and could eat then.

"But I'm hungwy *now*, Shelby!"

It was the I'm-about-to-lose-it variety of Shayla's whining. And it usually came right before the much less socially acceptable I'm-going-to-scream-until-I-get-what-I-want variety.

As always, knowing this left me with a dilemma. Should Shayla learn that sometimes you don't get everything you want when you want it? Yes. Was it an important life lesson? Absolutely—as any number of her future boyfriends would probably attest. Was teaching her that lesson on this particular evening worth the drama of sweet Shayla turning into Cruella de Vil? Uh—no. Not really. So, as all good parents do (or so I chose to believe), I took a long look at her pre-explosion face and decided I needed to find some food, and pronto. It was not exactly a groundbreaking thought for me.

I rummaged through my briefcase and found nothing. I mentally rummaged through my classroom desk and concluded there'd be nothing there either. I could hear the sound of basketball practice coming from the gym, where I knew there'd be at least oranges for Shayla to dig her teeth into. But I was a closet sufferer of post-athletic stress disorder, so rather than spurring me forward, the thought of entering the gym for oranges made me redouble my efforts to coax Shayla home, where an assortment of not-yet-ready meals was waiting to be cooked. Maybe she could chew on a hard noodle while she waited.

"It's only a few minutes from here to home," I told her. "If you can wait that long, we can have the chicken casserole Bev taught us to make!" I was becoming a regular Martha Stewart—hold the fancy aprons.

"But I'm hungwy now," Shayla wailed, big old tears rising in her eyes. My mistake had been letting her think I had something in my briefcase. That had gotten her taste buds all fired up, and I knew from experience how painful it could be to dash their hopes.

"Honey, I don't have anything with me."

"Not even gum?"

"No. And you're not allowed to chew gum anyway. You get it in your hair." My mind flashed memory cards of Shayla screaming and me calling Bev and having to find sharp scissors.

"Not even gummy bears?"

"No, Shayla. I have no food, no candy, nada." She looked at me askance. I think she thought I'd made *nada* up. "So . . . we're going to walk home and get into our slippers." The floor tile in the apartment was frigid. "And then we're going to have *chicken casserole*."

I'd tried to make the dish sound dramatic and enticing, but Shayla scrunched up her face and began what I now called the Crescendo Wail—the kind that starts soft and low, then grows steadily into an all-out fire siren. I couldn't let that happen for two reasons. Firstly, her siren tended to push my buttons and I didn't want to lose my patience. Losing my patience was a fear that obsessed me—always. And secondly, the acoustics were so good in that stairwell that I feared the Crescendo Wail would have the neighbors calling the police for the second time that night, and that just wouldn't be good.

So, with a deep, calming breath, I picked Shayla up and carried her into the gym.

The first impressions that assailed me brought back memories I'd thought were safely deleted from my failure treasure trove. The smell of dirty sneakers reminded me of Johnny Dunbar, a boy who had tormented me by sitting on my chest, for no apparent reason, and holding his sneaker over my nose until our second-grade teacher, Mrs. Dailey, had pulled him off. The sound of balls bouncing reminded me of the ridiculous habit I had of actually looking up when someone called, "Heads up!" to warn of incoming basketballs, volleyballs, and baseballs. It was a flaw that had earned me more bloody noses during gym class than I cared to remember. How was I to know that "heads up" actually meant "heads down"? The sight of two opposing teams reminded me of all the times I'd stood midcourt in junior high and high school waiting for the two captains selecting teammates to earn me by elimination. And the sight of Coach Taylor reminded me of countless conversations with Trey in which I'd promised—no, vowed—to never, ever risk getting attached, which would guarantee that I'd never pass on the Davis family genes.

Needless to say, our entrance into the gym was not a pleasant thing. Scott, whose radar was apparently functioning well, saw us almost immediately and came over with a surprised smile for us both.

"You're two weeks late," he said.

"We ran into traffic."

"Rush hour in Kandern can be a mess." He winked at Shayla and squeezed her foot. "How're you doing, Lady Shay?"

"Gus calls me that."

"I know. Do you mind?"

"Nuh-uh."

"Then Lady Shay it is." He turned his attention to me, which was helpful, as my mind had started to wander back down Memory Shame. "We'll be through in a couple minutes."

"Oh, we're not here to see you," I said breezily. "Shayla's hungry."

"No, I'm not."

"What?"

"I'm not hungwy anymoh." She tried to push out of my arms and it was all I could do to keep her from running out onto the court. "I want to *play*," she protested.

I wasn't amused. "We came in here to get you some oranges," I whispered into her ear, loudly enough to be heard over the noise of shoes and dribbling.

"I want to play!"

Scott leaned in to say, "She's welcome to go out there. The guys won't hurt her."

"They'll trample her!"

"I promise they won't."

"Let me down!" This from Shayla, who was fighting me so hard that I was starting to sweat. If I was going to sweat, I was certainly standing in the right place, but sweat was my enemy anywhere.

Scott blew his whistle and Shayla snapped her head around, scared motionless by the sound. "Lady on the court, guys!" He took Shayla out of my arms and set her on the ground. Handing her a ball, he winked at her and said, "Go get 'em, tiger."

She ran out onto the court, smiling at the faces around her, and the army of teenage boys parted like the Red Sea. One of them pointed toward the basket and told her to throw. The ball only went a couple of feet, but another player, a student I had in English class, snatched it up and rolled it back to her.

"What's her name, Coach?" It was the team captain asking, and I recognized him as Kenny, a muscular player who also had a reputation for being a gentleman and an all-round good guy.

"Lady Shay! Treat her like one!"

Kenny picked her up by the waist and ran with her to the basket. She dunked the ball like a pro and beamed as a cheer went up from the players. It wasn't long before they were all involved in a quirky game of basketball, with Shayla riding high on their shoulders, up and down the court, answering to Lady Shay and living one of the highlights of her short life.

"She's a natural," Scott said.

"She was a *hungry* natural two minutes ago. I promise."

"Guess she changed her mind."

"They won't drop her, will they?"

"They know the rules. 'You break it, you pay for it.'"

"That's comforting." There was a silence. "Kenny seems nice."

"He's a class act."

"He's got a way with kids."

"I think it goes both ways. Shayla has a way with strangers."

"No kidding. You should see her and the landlady cozying up."

I let out a startled yelp when I looked over to find Shayla hanging from the rim with her little hands, then letting go and dropping into the arms beneath her. "Shayla!" It was instinctive. As instinctive as the need I had to get out there and rescue her. But Scott's hand on my arm halted me midstride.

"She's fine," he said.

And looking out onto the court, I could see he spoke the truth. Shayla was off down the court again, perched on Kenny's shoulders, her ball resting on his head, a glowing smile on her face and her eyes riveted on the approaching basket. She giggled and squealed and dunked the ball again.

"And I'm supposed to get her to bed after this?"

"Have you ever been to Sausenburg?" he asked, changing the subject abruptly, which was his modus operandi.

I rolled my eyes—but that took them off Shayla for too long, so I decided to stop that for now.

"It's the ruins of a castle," he continued, unfazed. "Just above Sitzenkirch. Shayla would love it."

Sitzenkirch was a tiny village about five minutes from Kandern, where the elementary school had found a home. I had been there once, just to see what it looked like, but I hadn't seen any ruins.

I didn't answer Scott. I'd learned that answers led to conversations, and conversations that didn't have the Johnsons' house as a punctuation mark gave me the heebie-jeebies.

Scott blew his whistle again. "Okay, guys! Outta here!"

Every head on the floor except Shayla's snapped around to look at the clock.

"But, Coach, we still have ten—"

"Pack it up!"

The players clearly weren't used to aborted practices. They looked at each other, mumbled, then shuffled off the court. Kenny deposited Shayla at my feet, a ball still in her hands, then went back out to gather the rest of the balls into giant nets.

"What's the rush?" one of the guys asked as he was passing Scott.

"Lady Shay needs a ride home."

I was outraged. "She does not!"

Scott raised an eyebrow. "You want me to tell them why I really cut our practice short?"

"You're hurrying home to catch *The Young and the Restless*?"

"No—I'm hoping to have an actual conversation with you."

"Oh."

"Right. This two-minutes-and-forty-seconds thing is for the birds."

"Well, Shayla and I need to get home to make a casserole, so . . ."

"I'd love some."

"What I was going to say was that we need to run and you need to lock up, and we don't really need a ride, so . . ." I was bending over at the waist and trying to pry Shayla's hands off the basketball she held like a lifeline.

"I'd like to talk."

"Why?"

He looked exasperated and entertained. It was an interesting combination. He fished a quarter of orange out of a bowl and handed it to Shayla. She immediately let go of the ball and focused her attention on devouring the snack.

"I knew that would work," I said a bit defensively.

"Of course you did. You're her mom."

I bit my tongue.

"And I'm a guy who's either got a death wish or a challenge disorder, because I'd kinda like to get to know you."

"I'm not good with people."

"You're a teacher."

"I'm not good with grown-up people."

"Gus and Bev adore you."

"I'm not good with . . ."

Scott crouched down so he was eye-level with Shayla. "Shayla, is your mom crazy?" He said it with a mock-serious face as he wiped some orange dribble off her chin with his thumb.

Shayla had been helping herself to more of the leftover oranges, and she had her mouth so full that she had to swallow twice before she could say, "She's not my mom." The subtext was "dummy"—as in, *"She's not my mom, dummy."*

Scott looked at me, his eyebrow raised in question.

"She's not technically my daughter," I confirmed.

If Scott was taken aback, he hid it well. "See why we need to talk? I don't even know the basics."

I looked away.

"You can have your Mace within arm's reach at all times."

I bit my lip.

"I'll help you with the dishes."

He was getting warmer.

"I read a killer bedtime story."

"Sounds a bit morbid for a four-year-old."

"I mean I'm a good bedtime-story reader."

"Had a lot of practice?"

"My niece and nephews think I'm pretty cool."

"I'm sure that's comforting."

"After conversations like these? You bet it is."

"I've got a rock," Shayla said. Scott's conversational skills were clearly rubbing off on her.

"Really?" He was down on her level again.

"A blue one on the inside."

He looked up at me. "Quartz?"

"She found it at the flea market."

"Maybe you can show it to me someday."

"But not tonight. We've had a big day and Shayla needs to get to bed early." It sounded hollow even to my ears.

Scott straightened and ruffled Shayla's hair. "Some other day, then. And maybe I can show you a castle, too. Would you like that?"

"A weal castle?"

"What's left of it. You can even climb the tower."

Something rasped over my nerve endings. In one overwhelming moment, the walls and ceiling around me shrank and closed in until they became the pale-green walls of my mother's kitchen. The sensation was so vivid and stark that I could hear the angry impotence of the air conditioner propped on the windowsill above the sink and feel the grip of something dark pressing in around my mind. I knew, in a remote and rational part of my thinking, that I was still standing in a high school gym, but something about Scott and his castle plans had suffused my senses with the smells, sounds, and crippledness of my youth. There was nothing truly menacing in the moment, yet I felt trapped by Scott's exchange with Shayla, backed into a corner, barred from an escape route, and robbed of both choice and independence. I felt manipulated, bulldozed, and helpless.

Scott must have read the anger on my face. He frowned and looked like his mind was on rewind, trying to figure out what he'd said wrong.

"Don't back me into a corner," I said. The tremor in my voice shamed me. "And don't use Shayla to do it." I could feel the flush of anger on my cheeks and was as shocked by it as Scott.

"I wasn't . . ."

I picked Shayla up and headed toward the door. "Thanks for the oranges."

We left.

I'd like to say Shayla and I walked home in silence. It's what my brain needed. But Shayla's mind had been so stimulated by her first pick-up game that she couldn't seem to stop talking. She talked about her rock, she talked about oranges, she talked about hanging from the rim, she talked about a cat that crossed the street in front of us and about the bright-green shoelaces on her sneakers. She talked, in other words.

As much as I craved silence, I found solace in her chattering. In the days following her enrollment in kindergarten, Shayla had become subdued and pensive, but the last week had marked a change. After Bev and I had talked with her teacher and encouraged her to acknowledge Shayla's English questions and respond to them in German rather than ignoring them altogether, an awkward, bilingual dialogue had begun between them. Some of the girls in the class had started to include Shayla in their playground antics, and the newness of German kindergarten rituals had become less startling to her. She no longer cried herself to sleep, and though she wasn't always excited about going to school in the morning, it didn't terrify her anymore. Which was good for both of us—she had fewer meltdowns and I had fewer guilt-ridden, sleepless nights. So we were both a little happier.

But as Shayla talked all the way home from the gym that evening, my mind wasn't really on her brighter spirits or on the meal I still had to make. It was on the abrupt and frightening end of my conversation with Scott. I couldn't understand what had led from A to B, from bearable present to intolerable past, from relatively sane Shelby to raving-lunatic Shelby. I didn't have any answers. Scott's bullheadedness had made me put up my defenses; that much I knew and understood. But losing it that fast over a harmless invitation to a castle? That was perplexing—and, given my gene pool, terrifying, too. I remembered the heat of anger that had suffused my face and how it had made my voice shaky and my hand too firm around Shayla's, and a familiar fear gripped me. The apple and the tree.

Shayla and I retired Martha Stewart for the evening and had cereal for supper. This made Shayla happy, in part because she could eat immediately and in part because of the sugar high cereal gave her. Go figure. Consequently, our bedtime ritual became a little more drawn out and a lot more competitive. Shayla wanted to color instead of brushing her teeth. She wanted to sit on the floor and pout instead of picking up her toys. She wanted to point out the window at nothing instead of getting into bed. When she decided she'd rather belt out the Barney song at the top of her lungs, singing over my admonitions and squirming out of my grip instead of saying her prayers, I again felt that flush of anger, that quickening in the chest and stomach that made me want to slap myself . . . or her.

I left the room with Shayla still blasting "I love you, you love me. We're a happy family" in a way that might have scared Barney back into prehistory and, closing both her bedroom door and mine, reached for the phone.

It was midafternoon in Illinois, and Trey was at his post at L'Envie.

He picked up the phone and did his business-owner greeting.

"I'm turning into Dad."

"Sounds like a personal problem."

"Trey . . ."

"Hey, Shell. How are you doing? Things going well over there?"

"Guess that was a bit abrupt."

"Just a tad."

I sighed. "I'm sorry."

"I'm not. It's good to hear your voice."

"Are you busy?"

"I'll let you know when the Japanese tour bus gets here to buy me out of house and bakery."

"So it's a slow day is what you're saying."

"Slow *time* of day. It'll pick up later."

"I went to the gym tonight . . ."

"I'm sorry, let me replace the batteries in my hearing aid."

"Trey . . ."

"Sorry."

"I went to the gym to get something for Shayla to eat after school tonight."

"Uh-huh."

"And I lost it."

"You lost Shayla?"

"I lost my temper. Over nothing."

"Okay . . ."

"And now Shayla is in her bedroom shrieking a heavy-metal version of the Barney song and I can't get her to stop, and when I grabbed her arm to make her lie down for the hundredth time . . . Trey, I wanted to . . . I mean, I almost . . . I wanted to just plaster her to the mattress and hold her there—hard." I felt the emotion tightening my muscles again.

"She's singing 'I love you, you love me' like Marilyn Manson?"

"Trey . . ."

"Hold out the phone. I want to hear."

"Trey!"

"You're not turning into Dad, Shell."

I let out a shaky breath. "I need a Huddle Hut. And maybe a Valium."

"Did you yell at her?"

"I thought about it."

"Did you tell her she was worthless and repulsive and stupid?"

My stomach churned as I pictured Shayla on the receiving end of such a maiming diatribe. "No."

His voice got softer, more serious. "Did you slap her or physically hurt her in any way?"

"No, Trey."

"You're not turning into Dad."

"But I wanted to. I mean . . . I felt angry, Trey. You know—the face-getting-hot, might-have-to-scream variety of angry. I just wanted to, you know, shake some sense into her and make her stop *yelling* and tell Scott to go take a flying leap off a high place. . . ."

"Scott?"

"Never mind."

"So how's the weather . . . ?"

"It's—"

"Who's Scott, Shell?" I swore I could hear a twinkle in his voice, if such a thing were possible.

"This is about me, Trey. My anger. My personal failures as a pseudo-mom."

"So egocentric."

"I'm serious."

"Number one, lose the 'pseudo-mom' thing. It's insulting to you and to Shayla. Number two, getting mad isn't a crime. Picturing how mad you could really get if you let yourself is not a crime. Having instinctive urges to hit something or hurt someone or throw a tantrum are not, in themselves, criminal, Shelby. Should we all be figuring out how to deal with things before those urges rear their ugly heads? Absolutely. But the fact that you didn't scream, that you didn't shove her into the mattress, that you didn't start throwing dishes or heavy furniture . . . Shell—that's proof that you're not turning into Dad."

I sighed. Loud and long. The singing in the other room had lowered a few notches.

"And number three," Trey continued, "who's Scott?"

"Don't you ever worry? That you've got too many Davis genes, I mean."

"Sure. But I also try to figure out where Dad went wrong. I'm of the school of thought that genes can be deprogrammed."

"If that's the case, why are you still single?"

"I'm not completely clear on the deprogramming yet."

"Maybe I'm not either."

"Maybe Shayla is part of the process."

"As long as she doesn't become a victim of it."

"I know you, Shell. Is there anyone else who knows you better?"

I thought for a fraction of a second. "Nope."

"I've seen you at your best and at your worst—and no, a bathing suit is not what I'm referring to—and I have never, *ever* seen a hint of Dad in you."

"Even when I jumped on his back and clawed his eyeballs out?"

"You were protecting me. Just like you'd protect Shayla. And this fear you've got going, Shell? That's exactly what it is. You protecting Shayla—against yourself."

"Huh."

"But there's no need to. I know that like I know . . . like I know you used to Ace-bandage your chest in junior high."

"I wasn't happy about being a woman."

"No kidding."

"You knew about the Ace bandages?"

"Yup. The only thing I apparently don't know anything about is Scott. So, hey, Shell . . ." He tried to sound casual. "Who's Scott?"

"Are you coming for Christmas? Please come for Christmas! Shayla needs to spend time with her favorite uncle."

"How can I be her uncle if you're only her pseudo-mom?"

"Shut up."

"You're going to have to deal with this, you know."

"When I'm sure I've deprogrammed my genes."

"Who's Scott?"

"He's a coach." I rolled my eyes.

"Stop rolling your eyes."

"How'd you know?"

"And . . . ?"

"He keeps wanting to talk to me!" I said *talk* like it was a horrible thing—like playing bingo.

"And?"

"And I don't want to talk to him. But he keeps backing me into a corner—"

"Figuratively or . . . ?"

"Figuratively, Trey."

"Which makes you feel powerless, which makes you get angry, which makes you think you're Dad, which makes you blow a gasket at Shayla's AC/DC impersonation."

"This call is getting expensive, Dr. Freud. Tell me about you."

"*Me* wants to hear about Scott."

"Then I guess we've reached an impasse."

There was a pause. "I miss you, Shelby."

"I miss you, too." I allowed my hopes to rise just a little. "Christmas?"

"We'll see."

"I think Marilyn Manson's losing steam."

"Give her a kiss for me."

"I will."

"To the muddlehood . . . ," he said.

". . . of huddlehood."

"Thanks for calling."

"Bye, Trey."

Shayla was half-asleep when I stepped into her bedroom. She was lying on her side, a stuffed animal in the crook of each elbow, humming Barney's song in a misty, cottony voice. I knelt on the braided throw rug next to her bed and slung an arm over her waist.

"You getting tired?"

She nodded.

"You had fun playing basketball with the boys, didn't you."

Another nod.

"Shayla . . ." I wasn't sure how to broach this subject. It felt like shoving a porcupine into a wool sweater—not easy, at best. "There's something I think I need."

Tired eyes opened a fraction more. "You want a donut?"

I loved this child. "Actually," I whispered, adjusting my seating so I could prop my head sideways on my arm and be nose-to-nose with her, "I think it would make me really happy if I could call you my daughter." Shayla's eyes were so close to mine that I could see the dark flecks in the blue and her pupils dilating and retracting. "When we meet new people," I continued, trying to make it clear to her young mind, "I'd like to be able to say, 'This is my daughter, Shayla.' You know what I mean?"

A shy smile curved her lips and she tightened her hold on her animals.

"So, beautiful—" I could feel a tear escaping from the corner of my eye and running down into my hairline—"is it okay if I call you 'my daughter, Shayla,' from now on?"

She watched another tear follow the path the first had taken and looked into my eyes, worried.

"I'm not sad," I assured her, and I knew my smile proved it.

Shayla let go of the blue rabbit she'd been holding and reached out to hook her arm around my neck, pulling my face down to touch hers. We stayed like that until she was asleep, me kneeling next to her bed, cheek to cheek with my daughter, her breath warm against my neck, the smell of her sweet and heavy like warm honey in my lungs. And it struck me with so much force that I had to hold back sobs that this was the antithesis of a God-spitting-on-me moment. This was God pouring such a deluge of wondrousness and overwhelmingness and profound healingness on me that I could hardly stand it. As I knelt there by Shayla's bed and tried to absorb the enormity of the moment, it was all I could do not to crawl up under the blankets and huddle there all night with Shayla—with my *daughter*—in my arms.

11

Trey and I had been huddling a lot in the week since Dad had gone all Godzilla on us, though it had taken a couple tries for me to figure out how to make it up the ladder to the attic without using my injured arm. We'd been off school all week, and I wanted to think that was because Mom was giving us time to get our heads sorted out. After all, last Saturday had been the kind of thing that muddles the brain a little. I wasn't used to seeing my brother being strangled by my dad, and the image kept coming back to me, no matter what I did. Opening a carton of orange juice—Dad strangling Trey. Cleaning up my bedroom—Dad strangling Trey. Watching game shows on TV—Dad strangling Trey. It had been a Dad-strangling-Trey kind of week.

But I knew my mom hadn't kept us home from school just because we needed to get over the shock to our brains. I figured it was also to allow time for Trey's neck to heal. Explaining that her daughter had sprained her wrist in a fall was one thing. But explaining how her son had gotten bruises all over his throat and a bad cut to the side of his mouth? That would take a little more creativity than my mom possessed. We hadn't complained about the weeklong vacation, though. Instead, we'd spent it reading books, playing video games, eating tons of food (Mom always cooked when she was stressed), and turning the Huddle Hut into Ali Baba's cavern. We brought up pillows and comfy blankets; we moved in lamps and extension cords; we even dangled Christmas tree lights over the wardrobe at one end of the attic so we could lie in our tent at night and imagine they were stars. I'm not sure what had prompted the Huddle Hut overhaul. There was just so much uncomfortable going on inside that we felt compelled to build something comfortable on the outside, I guess.

It was shortly after lunch, and Trey and I were lying on our backs shoveling trail mix into our mouths. Mom had discovered our attic hideaway. I knew that because we'd crawled up today to find a bowl of trail mix and two glasses of Kool-Aid sitting in the middle of the hut on a tray.

Trey dropped an M&M into his mouth. "One week ago this minute, I decided I wanted to shoot hoops."

"I always told you sports were unhealthy."

"Maybe it's just basketball."

"I think he'd have been mad if you'd wrecked his car for soccer, too."

"Yeah, probably. We should make a movie."

That was a new one. "Of what?"

"The things you see in your head when the life's being choked out of you."

He had my attention. "You saw things?"

"Yup."

"Like what?"

"An Easter egg hunt."

"Weird."

"You were there too."

"What was I doing?"

"I don't know. Just kinda smiling and looking at me."

"Trust me—I wasn't smiling in real life."

"And I saw something orange. Really orange. Like, burn-your-eyeball orange."

"It wouldn't make a very good movie," I said.

"No, you're right."

"You think he's coming back?"

"If he does, I'll kill him."

His words made my stomach do a little thunk. *That was the weird thing about my dad. I knew he was evil and capable of hurting us—I wore the bandages that proved it—but hearing Trey talk about killing him still made me feel not right. He may have sprained my wrist, but he was still my dad.*

"Do you think he ever liked us?" I asked my brother.

"Nope."

"I used to give him things to make him like me more. Like leftover candy from Halloween and clay bowls from art class. I even made him a macaroni necklace once. I was supposed to give it to Mom, but I figured he needed the cheering up more."

"He never loved us."

"You sure?"

He pointed at his neck.

"Right." I didn't want to push it, but . . . "It's just that sometimes he was really nice."

"Like when?"

"Like when we went to Disney World that one time. He let us go on all the rides we wanted and stay until the park closed. And when he took us out to movies 'cause we got good report cards," I added,

recalling more and more instances when he'd seemed a little less horrible. "He even bought us popcorn that one time when you'd gotten good grades and scored three goals in your soccer game."

"And then he came home and made me stand outside the front door for three hours because I dropped the pickle jar when I was getting it out of the fridge."

"Yeah, but we got popcorn."

"He didn't love us, Shell. He still doesn't."

"Maybe he'll realize he does—because he's away from us—and come back and say he's sorry." There was something light and fluttery brightening in my lungs. "Maybe if I send him a card or something—"

"What?" Trey came up on his elbow and glared so hard it made me shiver.

"Or maybe if I went to see him, wherever he is, and told him that we don't hate him bad. We hate him like we hate the dentist—not like mass murderers."

Trey looked at me and I could tell I should be quiet. His nostrils were flared and his eyes were squinty. He got up off the floor and took a few steps away, his hands on his hips, breathing like he'd just run up the stairs. When he turned around, his lips were curled in and the skin of his face looked stretched too tight. "What's wrong with you, Shell?" His voice was hard, as Trey-less as the sneer distorting his features. It scared me bad enough to make my face feel prickly. "He's out of our lives," he said, and there was cement behind his eyes. And then his voice got really hard, like cold metal, and he said, "He's gone. You hear me? Leave him wherever he is!"

He stood there, glaring, for another minute or two, then stalked back to the Huddle Hut, threw himself down next to me, and crammed a fistful of trail mix into his mouth, chomping hard and squinting at the sheet above us. "Leave him wherever he is," he said again, more softly this time. A little faded. I put an M&M in my mouth, but my stomach didn't seem to want me to swallow it. Maybe I was coming down with the flu. Or cancer. It wasn't normal, anyway.

After a few minutes had passed, enough for me to sing "Eye of the Tiger" in my mind, I tried to reason with Trey one more time. Actually, I was probably trying to convince myself more than him. It just felt wrong not to have a father—guilty, somehow.

"We should have waited until he got home to move the car."

"Shut up, Shelby!" He sat up and spit a little trail mix at me when he added, with gravel in his throat, "He's not coming back! He's dead!"

I knew my dad wasn't really dead, but it made me cry anyway. Trey's yelling made me cry and my not-dead dad made me cry. I thought of the drawing of John Wayne I'd made him when I was little and wished I'd just used the red eraser. If I hadn't gone into his desk, maybe he'd still be here today. But I couldn't say that to Trey. His anger had made his bruises look deeper red, and I could tell he didn't want to talk about Dad anymore. Not for a long time. So I closed my eyes and listened to the squirrels running back and forth on the roof. I hoped they were playing, maybe with their dad watching them through the leaves of a tree to make sure they were safe. I hoped it so hard it made me dizzy.

⁂ ⁂ ⁂

After an unseasonably warm fall, the weather had turned wintry. The leaves, it seemed, had browned and fallen overnight, and we'd gone from Kool-Aid weather to hot-chocolate weather just as fast. My walks to the Johnsons' after school were now drives, and though I disliked the cold, I was grateful for the change. It made it less obvious that Scott had stopped performing his Boy Scout routine. We'd crossed in the hallways and on the street several times since the gym fiasco, and he'd always been friendly. I'd tried to keep the zingers down to a minimum—my form of penance—but sometimes they just popped out. He'd become one of Shayla's favorite people, and she tended to launch herself at him whenever she saw him, which made extricating myself from banal conversations a little complicated. But I did get one thing straight when I ran into him in the doorway of the Lacoste bakery one Saturday morning.

"Where's Shayla?" he asked, surprised to find my usual sidekick nowhere in sight.

"My daughter is having a playdate with Lizzie Robinson," I said, putting sufficient emphasis on *daughter* to make my subliminal message not quite so subliminal.

He looked pleased—happy, actually—and said, "Well, say hello to your daughter from me." There were three cement blocks and a Humvee stacked on the word *daughter* when he said it, so I knew my message had gotten across.

I thought that would be the extent of our conversation and slung my bag higher on my shoulder, prepared to leave the bakery, but Scott didn't move. I was standing inside the door, waiting to go down two steps to the street, and he was standing on the sidewalk, blocking my exit while his mind was engaged in what appeared to be some pretty intense internal dialogue. The baker's wife finally bellowed that we were keeping the sliding door from shutting, and that spurred him into motion. German women yelling had a tendency to do that. He stepped into the bakery and moved me aside to allow other customers to exit.

"Would you like a cup of coffee?" he asked, jutting his chin toward the small dining room just beyond a glass wall.

"Um . . ."

"Please. We don't have to stay long, but . . . I've been unfair to you and I'd like to make up for it."

"Unfair?"

He pointed to the dining room. "Coffee? Or tea? I'd like to explain myself, but not standing here."

This was not the usual fearless Scott standing in front of me, the conversational warrior who had submitted me to a hailstorm of questions so many times with zeal and confidence. This was a more guarded man who seemed more deliberate than spontaneous, more considerate than impulsive.

It must have been pity that made me say, "Just a few minutes," as I pushed through the glass door into the smoky dining room beyond, wondering as I went what had possessed me to accept his invitation. "I'm not really comfortable with this," I added to make sure he knew I wasn't used to this kind of thing. He nodded and motioned toward a table. We sat in an alcove at the back of the room and ordered two cappuccinos. As soon as the waitress left, Scott leaned his forearms on the table and assumed a contrite expression.

"I've been selfish."

"You said *unfair* before, but I'll accept *selfish*, too."

He nodded and allowed a lopsided grin. "I've got to admit that I'm . . . confused," he said after a hesitation, "about what happened at the gym and . . . and a bunch of other stuff, but that's not why I wanted to talk to you. The fact is, I've done my share of interrogating you—"

"Ya think?" Sarcasm crackled.

"And I've given you absolutely no time to get even—to counter-interrogate. Which leaves me knowing some stuff about you, but you knowing nearly nothing about me. And I can't expect you to trust me if you don't have any information to base it on, right?"

I frowned. "Who says I want to trust you?"

My question didn't keep him from making his point. He'd apparently put some time into thinking it through and was intent on saying it all. "So I've got no right to ask you any more questions until you've had the chance to even things up."

"Even things up."

"Reverse the conversational blitzes."

"I get to ask questions?"

He took a deep breath. "As many as you want."

"What if I don't want to?"

He clearly hadn't anticipated that option. "Then I guess—"

"What's the time limit?" I asked abruptly. It was a strange proposition, but I could see some potential there. Maybe I'd decide he really wasn't very likable after all once I'd had my chance to question him.

He pondered it for a moment. "As long as you want."

"Actually, I'm supposed to pick Shayla up at the Robinsons' in a half hour, so . . ."

"So I guess you need to start firing."

The waitress appeared with our cappuccinos and gave us odd looks, perhaps perceiving the hum of tension between us. We were being cordial, but our guards were up. Our conversation in the gym, as unfinished as it was, had left us both in a kind of limbo that made this tête-à-tête feel a little surreal. Yet there was something reassuring in the emotional distance. It made me feel less vulnerable. So I launched into my questioning, subdued but purposeful.

"Middle name."

He raised an eyebrow as if saying, *That's the best you've got?*

"I'm working up to the good stuff," I said.

"Adam."

"Place of birth."

"Seattle."

"Siblings."

"One older sister. Two nephews, one niece."

"So forthcoming." I smiled sweetly.

"Keep going." He had the focused look of an athlete before a game.

"Do you get along with her?"

"We do now."

"You didn't before?"

"I wasn't always as lovable as I am now." He grinned. "She'd tell you I was the worst brother who ever lived."

I gave him a disapproving look. "What did you do to her?" We sisters had to stick up for each other.

"I threw all her bras into a tree outside her boyfriend's house when she was fifteen and I was twelve. That's the worst thing. I'll spare you the snake and lizard stories."

I rolled my eyes. Boys. "Education?" I was spitting out topics like a drill sergeant on steroids. It was kind of nice being in charge for a change.

"BA from MSU, master's from U of O."

"Oregon?"

"Yup."

"Phys ed?"

"Educational leadership."

"Impressive. Good student?"

"Terrible all the way through high school. Things picked up after my first year of college."

"Why?"

"I like sports."

"No kidding. Parents?"

"Mom is a Mary Kay sales phenomenon. She could sell lipstick to a monk. Dad owns a roofing business. Retires next year."

"Were you supposed to take over the business from him?"

"That was the original plan. He figured out pretty fast that it wasn't my thing."

"How'd he take it?"

"I think it was probably hard at first, but he's made his peace with it."

"How long have you been at BFA?"

"This is my fourth year. I came for a year and was hooked after a month."

"So you're planning on sticking around for a while?"

"Until it's time to move on."

That gave me pause. "How will you know?"

"Not sure," he smiled. "I think I'll know it when it comes, though."

"Got any friends here?"

"A men's group—we meet for a Bible study every week. And a couple of the other coaches."

"I don't see you hanging out a lot."

"We're guys. We get together for a purpose; then we go home. Some of us are going skiing next weekend. Does that count?"

"Sure."

"Come on—give me something a little harder."

I looked at him like he had no idea what he was asking for.

"I'm a big boy. I can take it."

Hey, who was I to resist a challenge? "Most memorable girlfriend."

"Jeanie Bledsoe. Our braces got locked when I tried to kiss her."

"That'll teach ya."

"It really didn't."

"Greatest personal flaw."

He didn't hesitate. "A short fuse."

"Really?"

"It's mostly under control, but if you'd known me when I was a kid . . ."

"So you're over it?"

"Been to any basketball games?"

"Not yet." But I'd heard some stories about the fiery coach.

"I'm not completely over it. Working on it, though."

"I should come to a game just to see you lose your cool."

I could tell by his face that he'd rather I went for another reason. "It's a pretty tough habit to break," he said. "You get a bunch of guys out on the court, the testosterone's flowing, the score's tight, the other team starts fouling my players . . ."

"What—you throw chairs?"

"No. But I get a little hot under the collar. It's stupid. I know it. And I'm working on it—the refs don't call me on it half as much as they used to."

"I'm sure they're impressed that you're growing up."

"I don't care so much about them as about the guys. They don't need to see their coach losing it."

"Punching other coaches in the nose, throwing Gatorade at the refs . . ."

"Never that bad. But losing my grip on what's important. Using some colorful language. Like I said—I'm working on it."

I had to ask it. "Ever been violent?"

He considered the question for a moment, and I wondered if he was deciding how much to reveal. "When I was younger," he finally said. "My first year of college was pretty rowdy. A lot of partying. Too much drinking. Too much freedom, really. So I got sloshed a few times and got into a couple of fistfights."

I didn't like this revelation. It reminded me too much of bruises and broken wrists. "Injure anyone?"

He shook his head. "It was never anything really bad. Bruises and black eyes. Stupid, macho, one-too-many-beers stuff."

"So what happened after your first year of college?"

He closed his eyes for a moment. When he opened them, they weren't as present as they had been before—like they'd drifted. "A drunk-driving accident. I wasn't involved. Two guys walked away, the third one's in a wheelchair for life."

"A friend?"

"Point guard on the basketball team." He sighed and rubbed his hands over his face. "I decided in the hospital waiting room that drinking wasn't worth it."

"So you stopped."

"Mostly. I still have a glass occasionally. That's it."

I'd hoped that the awkwardness that had preceded our conversation would have allowed me to interrogate Scott dispassionately. But I was suddenly uncomfortable with the personal honesty of his answers. I wanted to bolt, yet there were just a couple more questions I needed to ask before ducking out of the contrived intimacy.

"Anything else?" Scott asked.

"Just one or two more . . . if that's okay."

He nodded seriously. The guard that had slipped a little with the last series of questions fell back into place. He was braced and ready.

"Greatest personal quality."

He hadn't expected that one. "Mine?"

"No, Pee-wee Herman's."

His grin made my neurons jiggle. "Greatest personal quality, huh? I'd say . . ." He was having trouble with this one. I'd learned long ago that the good stuff was infinitely harder to come up with than the bad stuff. "I'd say it's a willingness to recognize my flaws. I can be a jerk and I know it. I can be stubborn and I know it."

"Doesn't stop you."

"Helps me try."

"Right. Last question before I run off to rescue my daughter from a horde of sugar-crazed monsters."

"Okay."

"Why, oh *why*, won't you leave me alone?" The question had come out a little more intensely than I had intended it to, perhaps because this conversation had pushed me dangerously close to admiring him, which was the opposite of the result I'd been hoping for.

His eyes narrowed and he leaned a little toward me. "Because my second-greatest quality is obstinacy."

"Really? Most people file that one under personal flaws."

He smiled—and I could see relief in it. "Thank you for the conversation."

"Thank you for the coffee."

"So are we even?"

I didn't know how to answer. "This isn't a competition," I said with a tight smile, rising to leave and eager to get away from the ambivalent tension hovering like an electrical current between us.

"Say hi to your daughter from me."

"I will."

⌘ ⌘ ⌘

"It looks like a baby," I whispered.

Trey and I crouched without moving just inside the attic. We'd been frozen there for a while, ever since a certainty that something wasn't right had brushed against my consciousness and sent me to the space beneath the roof. I hadn't heard a sound, and yet . . . I'd known. I'd known there was something desperate above us and had forced a sullen, reluctant Trey to climb the ladder into our intruder's agony.

It had flown in through the broken pane of glass at the other end of the attic and battered its wings against the rafters in its desperation to get out. Now it huddled there in a fold of the mussed-up Huddle Hut blanket we hadn't used in months, its protruding eyes wide open, its rounded chest heaving.

"You think he's badly hurt?" I asked.

Trey tried to shrug like he didn't care, but he'd been doing that so much lately, I could see right through it. "He's fine."

"We should help him."

"He'll get back out the same way he got in."

"He's scared. It's hard to know what to do when you're scared." I knew that for a fact.

We crouched there for a while longer and my thighs began to burn. I didn't like being sixteen. A few years ago, I could have crouched all day without a thought of aching legs. "You think he'll take off if we get closer?"

"Probably."

"Maybe if you circle around and we close in from different sides, he'll stay put."

"It's just a bird."

"Yeah, but he's our *bird!"*

Trey looked at me like he didn't have the time for this.

"He's in our Huddle Hut," I said. "And he needs our help."

"Just go back downstairs and let him be. If he dies, he dies."

I couldn't figure out what had happened to Trey. The gray-green of his eyes had turned the color of a dirty swimming pool lately. Something in him had broken the day over a year ago when he'd mistaken the accelerator for the brake and rammed what was left of our crippled family into the rear wall of the garage. I figured the bruises on his neck had inked their way into the cells and synapses of his mind like a tattoo.

For a couple weeks after the Big Bang, he'd been fine. Kind of sad and moody, but I figured that was because his neck still hurt. And then, after a month or so, he'd turned angry, snapping at Mom and cussing at stupid things like toast that got too dark or shoelaces that came undone. He'd started sneaking bottles into his room too, and hiding them under his bed where he thought no one would find them. But I always found things—even my Christmas presents, no matter how well Mom hid them. So I'd found his stash of bottles, but I hadn't emptied them like I wanted to. He needed them for now, and I figured he'd outgrow them when the worst of this was past.

After a few months, he had finally gotten better enough that we'd gone back to talking and hanging out, but not the same as before. It was like when someone leaned against the wall at the back of the school's meeting hall and hit the switch by mistake and half the lights went out. Trey was half-out, and I couldn't find the switch to fix him. I had a feeling that my carefree brother—the one who acted half his age sometimes and didn't care, the one who did the moonwalk and took me up on my stupid dares—had stayed pinned to the wall in the garage between some twisted metal shelves and the Chevy's shiny hood. I missed that Trey.

He said I'd been acting odd too, but I didn't feel much different. On Saturday mornings, I'd still wake up and listen for the sound of singing in the shower. And then I'd remember and crawl out of bed and tiptoe to the window and see that the lawn needed mowing. And that would make me happy because it told me I could have my chocolate chip pancakes for breakfast without the usual stomachache afterward.

Trey and I hadn't really spent any time in the Huddle Hut lately. He said he was too old to be crawling up there—he was going to start college next year, after all. I didn't like it when he talked about college, even though I should have been proud that he'd gotten a full scholarship for soccer. Instead, his imminent departure just made me feel trapped and homeless.

"I'm going downstairs," Trey said, standing a little stiffly.

The bird got scared and tried to move away but one of his wings wasn't flapping like the other, so he kinda did a sideways walk across the ripples in the blanket, teetering onto his damaged wing, righting himself, then teetering again.

"He's hurt bad," I whispered, moved by the small creature's desperate eyes.

"Don't be stupid," Trey said, squinting at the tears in my eyes like they were embarrassing to him. But he couldn't look at the bird, so I knew he felt it too. Like a sinking in the chest.

The bird teetered into a higher fold of the blanket and leaned there, one leg bent, his head turned forward so his eye could see us better. He blinked.

"We've got to help him," I said. My voice cracked and Trey's back stiffened.

"We don't have to help him. He's only a bird."

"But he needs us."

"He's half-dead!"

The bird was looking right at me. "I'm going to help him," I whispered, mostly to myself.

"Fine," Trey said in a sharp, clipped voice. "You help your bird. I'm going downstairs."

This was the Trey I didn't recognize, the one who lived in his skin but somehow left it empty. As Trey headed toward the ladder, I inched over to the bird, still crouching, one hand outstretched, making tsking *sounds with my tongue. Every time he started, I paused, waiting for him to accept my nearness. I hadn't heard the ladder creak, so I knew Trey was still there.*

"I'm not going to hurt you," I whispered to the bird.

He looked at me with wide, unblinking eyes.

"Let him die, Shell."

"You're okay, buddy," I cooed in a breathy voice. "You're okay. . . ."

"You're such a moron. Just let him die!"

"No," I hissed at my brother with all the fury I could muster. "I'm not going to!"

"Fine, then! Waste your time on the stupid thing! I'm outta here!"

"Fine!"

I could see the bird's pulse beating on the side of his neck. Mine beat nearly as fast as his. I crawled as slowly as possible toward the petrified creature, the Huddle Hut transfigured by his fear into a terrorizing space. My hand was inches above him, and I lowered it slowly, ready to wrap my fingers firmly around his back and immobilize his damaged wing.

I acted a moment too late. Spurred into motion by sheer panic, the injured bird made one last, desperate attempt at evasion, vainly flapping his defective wings as he tried to run away from me. His claws got caught in the blanket and hampered his escape, but the frenzy of his agitation made me rear back, losing my balance and toppling one of the chairs that supported the Huddle Hut's roof. The clatter seemed to rip the bird's claws from the blanket, and he lifted off in a floundering flight that stuttered and pitched and rose directly toward my brother's scowling face.

Trey reacted without thought as the bird rushed at him. "Hey!" he yelled, slapping it away, flinging it out of the air onto the dusty floor of our protected, sacred space.

"No!" I cried, too late. The bird lay pitiful and broken on the floorboards, its legs twitching. "Trey!" I uttered hoarsely, willing him to do something—anything—to undo his brutal act.

"It came right at me!" Trey yelled, his voice laced with panic. "It

came right at me—you saw it!" He looked around like he wanted to escape, his legs unsteady, his face a rictus of shock and shame.

"But you didn't have to hurt him!" There was a sob in my voice as I stared with stricken eyes at the brother whose love for animals had always mirrored mine. This person standing across from me couldn't be him. He looked and sounded and smelled too much like Dad to be the gentle, caring Trey I used to know. "What's happening to you?" I cried. "How could you do this, Trey?"

"Shut up!"

Incomprehension bled in a steady stream of tears from my eyes. I begged again, "What's wrong with you?"

"Nothing!" *he screamed, his weakness hardening into something fierce. His gaze turned flinty. I could almost see the self-abhorrence burrowing into his rigid chest. Every syllable was jagged rock when he half hissed, half snarled, "It's—just—a—stupid—bird!"*

And with those words, maybe to prove his callousness, he took a step and kicked the bird across the room.

"Stop!" I screamed, lurching forward to rescue the small creature. The bird went rolling across the floor in a ghastly twist and turn, and I lunged toward it, desperate to halt its torture. "How could you?" I pleaded as I reached shaking hands toward the mangled form. "How could you, Trey?"

I stared at my brother—my gentle, compassionate brother—outraged by his merciless act, his obscene destruction of fragility. "Trey . . . ," I wailed, my voice breaking as I took the shattered testament to his own agony into my hands.

I saw horror fissure his steel-masked face before it hardened again into rigid pride. He would not weaken now. He could not show his fear. And as the world that was my brother shattered in a hail of woundedness above our Huddle Hut, I held the bird against my chest and felt it slowly die.

12

My life these days was a collage of mothering and teaching and directing that left little space for actual socializing. It also kept me busy enough that there was no time for self-pity and even less for major culture-shock meltdowns like the ones I'd experienced during my first weeks in Germany. I'd come close to mini-meltdowns on several occasions, but Bev's advice had proven true. The moment I'd told myself that it was all right to be unbalanced by the change of life Shayla and I had undergone, the tough days had gotten more bearable. I'd also started to put considerable effort into focusing on the endearing and quirky aspects of the German culture rather than on its more frustrating traits, and that alone had brightened and opened my attitude. So I'd gone from a love-hate relationship with the country to a love-tolerance relationship, and the change had done wonders for my emotional well-being.

I found teaching at Black Forest Academy to be easier than elsewhere in some ways. It sure beat inner-city schools. But the nature of the student body made for inherent differences I hadn't noticed at first. The students were walking contradictions. Some of them could speak three languages fluently but consistently botched English idioms. Alyssa once announced that she would have to rewrite an entire research paper by saying, "Well, I guess it's back to the ironing board!"

And Ahram was prone to declare, "That's just not my bag of tea" when something wasn't to her liking. Bag of tea, cup of tea. It was all the same to this Korean young lady whose parents lived in Mongolia and who studied in an American school in Germany.

At the end of each class period, the school hallways turned into a virtual United Nations, with so many languages being spoken and yelled that I sometimes wondered how any of the students were able to study in English. Yet the students awed me with their adaptability and mutual support. Because they were all foreigners, to one degree or another, they could laugh at each other and commiserate with each other and convince each other that the worst times would pass. I loved to watch them together, their shared experiences fueling relationships that were surprising in their intensity and uniqueness. They formed a three-hundred-strong student family, complete with conflicts, growth, and the kind of bonds that I found rare indeed.

To me, of course, one of their greatest appeals was their love for Shayla. She was the unofficial school mascot, often carried aloft by members of the basketball team when she was on campus with me. They called her Lady Shay and taught her their worst jokes and generally did their part to de-angelize her. And she relished the attention, which meant Bev and I had to deal with the consequences at home. But I was learning that children are children, and the more childlike they act, the more they force adults into grown-up roles. Consequently, every encounter with Bev had become a parenting tutorial. I craved our times together. They felt like tiny steps toward reprogramming those Davis genes I loathed and feared. Bev was a patient teacher and a compassionate listener, and both Shayla and I thanked God for her in our bedtime prayers.

My own prayers had become more frequent in the months since I'd taken Shayla in, and more frequent still since our arrival in Germany. Seldom an hour went by that I didn't feel the compulsion—urgent and visceral—to seek solace and counsel from God. During my childhood, he'd been a vague entity that had kept me from feeling completely bereft of comfort apart from Trey. God had been the unseen adult who somehow made up for the neglect and abuse of the Davis dysfunctional duo. But now—now he was a presence in every way but tactile. And though I'd learned not to expect immediate responses from him—like a voice or a nudge or the Bible suddenly opening to, say, "Thou shalt not eat the fruit of the deep fryer"—I knew he was there with a certainty that defied logic. I'd sensed his compassion and patient understanding too often to deny it. And though I sincerely questioned the amount of time he wasted on me when there was so much more wrong with the world, I was immeasurably grateful that he did.

I had gone by the Johnsons' one Saturday afternoon while Shayla was at a birthday party to see if Bev could explain to me the mystery of yeast. She was going to teach me how to make bread, and that bread, in turn, was going to forever hush Shayla's complaints about hard crust. At least, that was the plan.

I had no idea that bread-making required so much time. It was like watching grass grow—only with more tasty results.

"Shayla told me a secret last week," Bev said, looking like the Pillsbury Doughboy had exploded in her hands.

I feigned dismay. "She told you she peed red after she had beet salad?"

"Nothing that earth-shattering! But she did mention that you call her your daughter now."

I could feel myself blushing, a sensation I'd despised since eighth grade when Tony Masolli had made me turn red just by staring at me—right after I'd told him he couldn't make me do it. I wasn't sure why I was blushing this time. Perhaps because the information seemed so intimate. "Did she sound okay with it?"

"Are you kidding? She acted like she'd just won the blue ribbon at a mom-earning contest!"

Bev had known from the beginning that Shayla was a recent addition to my life. It was something I'd revealed even before arriving in Germany, as she was going to be spending so much time with my daughter. My *daughter*. The word was a polka-dot rainbow in my mind. We'd talked about the circumstances only vaguely. She knew I'd been named as Shayla's guardian after a relative had died. The rest was still hard enough for me to make sense of without trying to explain it to someone else.

But on that cloudy afternoon in Bev's kitchen, with Gus out helping a family with a move, it seemed natural to bring it up.

"Does she ever mention her dad?"

Bev shook her head. "Only with reference to things or memories. A book her dad read to her or her trip to Disneyland. She's very casual about it."

"Her dad was my dad." There. It was out.

Bev stopped kneading for a moment, then resumed. "So she's your . . . half sister?"

I laughed at that and shook my head at the contortions of my family tree. "My daughter is actually my half sister," I agreed, still amazed by the strangeness of it all. "My dad left the family when

I was fourteen. My mom died eight years later. And we didn't find out until my dad died—last December—that Shayla even existed."

"So your mom never knew."

I thought back to that conversation we'd had after Dad's Godzilla imitation. Mom's reference to Dad's "other house" had planted seeds of suspicion in my mind. "She didn't know about Shayla's mom. But there were probably others before that. Dad was . . ." How could I reduce "a-monster-of-a-man-with-the-parenting-skills-of-a-certified-sociopath" to one word? "Dad was not a nice man." I took a deep breath and added, "He was actually an incredibly abusive son of a—" I clapped my hand over my mouth like Shayla did when she said *stupid*, ashamed that I'd almost used the term out loud. A fine missionary I was.

This was the point at which I expected Bev to launch into a kindhearted discourse on the fallenness of man, the challenges of parenthood, the sovereignty of God, and the virtue of forgiveness. Oh, and with something about washing my mouth out with soap thrown in. I braced myself for the guilt and slapped a "Repentant" sticker across my brain. *Lay it on me, Bev.*

Instead, she shook her head a little, like a mother mildly disappointed in her child, and said, "Well, isn't it a miracle that the filthy son of a—" she mouthed the word—"managed to hatch a little angel like Shayla and give you the chance to show her how parenting's done! If that's not divine irony, I don't know what is!"

I started to laugh. And then I realized I couldn't stop. Part of it was Bev's attempt at cussing—it struck me as funny in a Bambi-goes-R-rated kind of way. Part of it was sheer relief that I'd revealed the dreaded Davis secret and not been shamed or pitied or exhorted. Part of it was that Bev hadn't looked in the least inclined to call social services and have my daughter removed from the care of someone who was undoubtedly branded by her experiences and would in turn become a child abuser—the thought had never seemed to cross Bev's mind. And part of it was that the only alternative to giggling was crying, and I wasn't sure how well I'd be able to control the tears, given my happiness, my missing Trey, my fear of failure, and Scott. In that order.

So I giggled. I giggled until Bev sat in a chair and raised an eyebrow like she was waiting for me to stop but her patience was running out. When my giggling finally petered out, she said, "Now get off that chair and start kneading. I'm too old to sweat." As she'd done more for my morale in the last two minutes than anyone else had done in weeks, I took off my rings and dug into the dough.

We were staring at two gorgeous, rounded loaves of bread an hour and a half later when she said, "You should stay for supper. Scott's coming and he'd probably appreciate the young blood."

"I need to pick Shayla up from her party."

"Scott can bring her. He lives right next door."

The thought of Scott picking Shayla up and bringing her for dinner felt so intimate that I think I blushed again. "We've got leftovers at home we need to eat before they go bad."

"Stick them in the freezer—they'll be good as new."

"I need to call Trey tonight. His birthday's on Sunday and . . ."

Bev turned on me, hands on hips, and gave me an unhappy-mother glare. "What's with you and Scott?" she demanded.

"Nothing. It's—"

"Don't 'nothing' me, young lady!" Bev the Battle-Ax was back in business.

Just at that moment, Gus walked in. He saw my face and paused. "What's going on?"

"Shell's suffering from something Scott-related, and it's up to us to cure her. I invited her to stay for dinner and she turned me down."

Gus smiled. "Nobody turns down a Bev Johnson invitation."

"Precisely. And I think I feel a twinge of the old Bev coming on, so, honey," she said to Gus, taking off her apron and hanging it by the door, "this one's yours."

And she walked out. I was confused. Okay, and a little peeved. My business was my business and I couldn't figure out why she was taking it all so personally. And I didn't like having Gus sicced on me! Gus, on the other hand, didn't seem in the least put out. He sat down at the kitchen table and patted the chair next to him.

"Come have a chat with Uncle Gus," he said.

"Ew."

"Okay, so just Gus."

I sat. "Look, I'm not sure what Bev's expecting you to do, but—"

"Scott's a great guy, Shelby."

"Good for him."

"And given the number of times he's walked you here, I'd wager he's got something of a thing for you."

"These things pass."

"And you're a beautiful single girl . . ."

"Oh, for pete's sake, Gus, get to your point."

"Spend some time with him. Have a few talks. Get to know him."

"I don't have time. We've had a few talks, and I already know him."

"And?"

"And . . . what? And he's a nice guy. And I'm a busy woman. And I'm just learning to get the Shayla thing right. And . . ." I gave a very unladylike harrumph. "Why is this any of your business anyway?"

Gus sat back in his chair, arms crossed, narrowed his eyes, and stared. I didn't like it. It felt like I was being appraised, and I was neither a show horse nor an antique. Though I felt well on my way to the latter.

"You're scared," Gus said.

"Oh, please."

"It's written all over you."

"I'll admit there are some things in life that scare me—snakes, treadmills, spandex, empty donut boxes, scorpions . . . But Scott Taylor?"

"You're not scared of him?"

"Of course not!"

"Then prove it. Stay for dinner."

I really hated it when people saw the smallest crack in my argument and barged right on through it like a platoon of well-meaning nuns on a Shelby crusade.

"No."

"What do you have to lose?"

"My time."

"That's it?"

"I'm a busy woman."

"So you've said." Gus leaned forward and twinkled at me with his eyes, which I immediately recognized as manipulation but somehow failed to resist. "He's coming over for dinner. What's the harm in you and Lady Shay joining us too?"

I had roughly forty-three thousand rejoinders bouncing around in my brain, but none of them seemed to carry much weight against the brutal simplicity of Gus's "What's the harm?" We did an eyeball tug-of-war, each daring the other to back down; then I threw my hands up and tossed in the towel.

"Fine." I sounded as exasperated and unnervous as I could. "Call him up and have him bring Shayla."

Gus slapped the table and bellowed, "Bev! I'm better at this than you are, honey!"

❋ ❋ ❋

As it turned out, Scott had come down with the flu and didn't join us. I spent the meal chitchatting with Shayla about her party, getting caught up on Bev and Gus's children, and telling myself over and over that I wasn't disappointed. Which I wasn't. Really.

The next day, Scott didn't turn up for church, and I pictured him alone at home with a raging fever and no food to eat. In my picturing, he looked a lot like Trey, and that made me feel even more sorry for him. Scott wasn't Trey. Of this much I was sure. But he was enough like my brother that he brought out the caregiver in me. I didn't want him to feel alone and shut out because he was sick.

So, in an as-yet-unheard-of move, Shayla and I hopped in the car after lunch and took a sample of our latest culinary creation to Scott's apartment. It was the kind of gesture I'd heard of other people making, but had never actually contemplated making myself. Bev, I could see doing it. Or Dana. Dana would be good at it. But me? On my scale of mental clarity, this scored a one. Ten being sanity and zero being Barbra Streisand in *Nuts*.

We found Scott's apartment in a three-story building next to the market square and were let in by a grumpy gentleman who was apparently intent on living up to international German stereotypes. Shay had trouble climbing the stairs with the Tupperware of soup in her hands, so I took it from her, but only until we reached Scott's landing. Then she snatched it back and, giggling with anticipation, reached way up to ring the doorbell. It took Scott a while to open the door, and he obviously hadn't spent the time grooming. His hair was a mess, his stubble was out of control, and he wore sweats and a T-shirt that looked big enough for two of him. The ice-skater in my stomach did a salchow with a triple lutz thrown in, just for show. Not sure why. Maybe I was coming down with the flu too. When Scott saw Shayla standing on his doorstep with a Tupperware container in her hands, he blinked and scratched his head. When he looked up and saw me, he seemed to go through a mental checklist—brain in place, check; neurons firing, check.

"Hi," Shayla said.

"Hi, Shayla." He sounded like a laryngitic toad.

"We made you soup." She pushed the container at him.

"You did?" I could tell he wasn't putting on the surprised expression just to please her.

"Shelby and I made it."

"Well—" he took the soup—"thank you." Looking up at me, he raised his shoulders in a what's-going-on-here gesture.

"We heard you were sick," I said. "And since we had some leftovers . . ."

Apparently, it wasn't as obvious to him as it was to me. "So you just came over to drop off some soup?"

"I put the cawwots in." Shayla clearly didn't want to be left out of this conversation.

"She did," I confirmed.

"I . . . Thank you, Shayla. And Shelby."

I had an idea for a brand-new law: disheveled, handsome men suffering from unknown illnesses and possessing expressive brown eyes would heretofore be forbidden by law from saying my name out loud. Or they'd be put in prison for crimes against hormonity. Or exiled to Africa. Which would be a terrible waste, considering the Western world was sadly lacking in disheveled, handsome men suffering from unknown illnesses and possessing expressive brown eyes. "Scott, it's soup," I said, and with those words, something in a remote corner of my mind triggered a verbal tidal wave of ridiculous proportions. "It's not like we made you a turkey dinner, not that either of us would know where to start with turkey . . . or the stuffing or the mashed potatoes or the green bean casserole, for that matter. I'd probably manage to open a can of cranberry sauce, but even that might be a challenge. I mean, I've been cooking for all of three months, and my brother really got the cooking genes—though we both got the Davis genes. But that's another story. . . ." I wasn't sure who'd given the adrenaline injection to my mouth, but I couldn't seem to stop the verbal overdrive. "He's a chef, by the way; did I tell you that? Owns his own bakery and everything and makes the world's best éclairs; and, man, what I wouldn't give for an éclair right now. Shayla likes them too. Right, Shayla?"

You know those commercials for emergency lifelines where an elderly lady says, "I've fallen and I can't get up"? Well, I was talking and I couldn't shut up. I clamped my jaw shut to avoid any further verbal spillage and said, through clenched teeth, "Okay, we should probably be getting home and leaving you to your soup. . . . So . . . hope you feel better."

"Yeah." He cocked his head to one side. "Thanks, Shelby."

"Come on, Shay. We're going home."

Shayla and I flew down the stairs, out the door, and into the car. Once in the driver's seat, I looked back at the child who was contemplating me with a frown and wondered if she understood just how kooky her guardian really was. I figured she'd sort it out soon enough, as we were going to be hanging out for a while.

13

I WAS FAST ASLEEP *when Mom barged in. I think I'd been dreaming about touring Italian vineyards with George Clooney, so I wasn't exactly in the mood for interruptions.*

"Shelby! Get up!"

"Wh—what?"

"Get up." She pulled the blankets off me and threw me the clothes I'd left on the back of a chair a few hours earlier. I was eighteen and still living at home, which was embarrassing enough without tossing in the kind of wake-up call that reminded me of my first day of school.

"Mom, what—?"

"It's Trey."

The air rushed out of my lungs and something thick passed in front of my eyes. The look on her face didn't belong with Trey's name. Not in a world where things made sense. I shook the cobwebs from my mind and dressed while Mom found her keys and grabbed her purse. I was in the driver's seat before she was out the door.

"Where?"

"Memorial," she said, handing me the keys with unsteady fingers. "Drive fast, Shelby."

It took us twenty minutes to get to the hospital, twenty minutes of speeding through red lights and blowing through intersections and trying not to shriek at my mom to give me more details. She knew so little, which was the way she'd always liked things, but I needed facts. I needed to know times and places and diagnoses and prognoses and anything else I could wedge into the chaos of my brain to still it. Trey was in the hospital. He'd been brought in by his roommate. We needed to get there fast. That's all we knew.

I ran from the car to the reception desk, unsure of where Trey was, leaving my mom to follow alone. I sprinted from there to the south wing and rushed down an endless hallway of fluorescent lights and gaping doorways and starched-white nurses with concern and boredom on their faces. Somewhere at the end of that hall was the emergency room, and somewhere in that room was my brother, the boy I loved, the man who needed to be alive. Please, God, let him be alive.

A nurse saw me coming and intercepted my flight.

"My brother. Trey Davis!" I would have screamed it if my lungs had allowed it, but they'd stopped doing their job back in the vines with George Clooney.

"Are you a relative?"

"He's my brother. Is he okay? Is he alive? What happened to him?"

"You need to calm down, honey." She forced eye contact, and the connection helped me breathe. "I'll find out where he is, and we'll see if we can let you in to see him."

My world was spinning as she walked away. I braced my hands on my knees and took a few deep breaths while the lights got brighter and the sounds got clearer. I saw the nurse's feet returning and didn't dare look up. What if . . . ? What if . . . ?

"We're about to move him to a floor, but if you come with me, you can sit with him for a few minutes."

I straightened. He was alive. "Please," I said to the nurse, then followed her through a maze of screaming children and drunks and bloody dressings and beeping monitors to my brother's side.

They'd dressed him in a hospital gown and covered him with a blue blanket. His head was turned away from the door. The nurse patted my arm and stepped away.

"Trey?"

He turned his head and I could see a five-year-old in his eyes. They were scared and sad and battered.

"Trey," I said again. My body carried me to his bed without conscious thought. I ran my hand down his arm to the bandage on his wrist, so white and clean and terrifying. I wrapped my fingers over his and held them fast. There were black streaks around his mouth and down his chin. And in his gaze . . . It was his gaze that undid me. I sat on the edge of his bed and held his hand against my chest and raged mutely, my head thrown back, my throat clenched and convulsing, my eyes on the ceiling, on the lights, on God. . . . And when it passed—when the swollen air deflated and the sharp, crude fear abated—I held his hand to my lips and prayed. And prayed. And prayed. While his hollow eyes, torpid and spiritless, stared through me.

They moved him to another floor, where the nurses were friendly and the bedrooms were yellow-beige. There was moaning and misery filtering through the walls, so I stayed close to Trey, hoping to absorb most of the ambient pain with my body before it got to his. Mom went off to fill out papers and talk to his roommate and arrange for follow-up care, and I sat by his bed, wiping the charcoal residue from his mouth and laying my palms across his wrists as if my desperation could speed their healing. He didn't speak when Mom came back, nor when we tried to feed him, nor when the nurses came on rounds in the morning. A doctor asked us to wait outside, and apparently Trey answered his questions. He was silent when we reentered the room. He met my gaze when I said his name, which was the only word I seemed capable of formulating. He knew the subtext.

"Trey." Why did you do this?

"Trey." Your eyes are scaring me. Please come back. Please come back, Trey.

"Trey." I should have known. I should have guessed.

"Trey." We said he wouldn't break us. We—said—he—would—not—break—us.

We spent the rest of the day at his bedside. Mom tried to be chipper. She failed. I suggested that she go home after supper. Get some sleep. Maybe bake some lasagna. It was the Davis family crisis dish. She left and I pulled a large brown pleather chair up to Trey's bed and went back to holding his hand, covering his wrists, and saying his name. After a while, I put my head down next to his arm and fell asleep.

The nurses woke me some time later. Trey was still there, still staring, still silent. I brushed back his hair and told him his color was improving. He closed his eyes.

The nurses allowed me to stay the night. They told me the chair reclined into a bed and wished me a good sleep. I was just about to settle down when I heard Trey's voice.

"Shell?" It was raspy and raw, but it was life.

"We said he wouldn't break us, Trey." The words were out before I could stop them, before I could even sit up and touch his arm.

"I'm alive."

"Oh, God," I said on a sob. "Oh, Trey, you're alive."

Several minutes of silence passed while I looked at him and tried to smile and searched for words. Anger, fear, and gratitude were clashing in a brutal battle above Trey's bed, and the air was brittle with the strain. I could feel its stranglehold on my muscles, eyes, and lungs.

Trey dozed for a while and seemed less murky when he woke. He turned his head toward me.

"I'm sorry I scared you."

"Trey . . ."

He stared at me for a long moment. It felt like he was drawing strength from me, like he was delving into my own limited supply of hope and vitality and siphoning it out for his survival. "Did Ian find me?" he asked.

I nodded. "He said he was worried by your last phone call, so he ran home to check on you during a break in his shift."

"Great security guard he is."

I let a long silence fill in the details of the horror in my mind. "If he hadn't sensed something was wrong . . . Trey . . ." I didn't know how to ask, but I needed so desperately to know. "Why?" I finally blurted, fresh terror seizing my throat.

He looked at me like I should know.

"We said we'd get through it. No matter what," I whispered.

He sighed and shifted, turning his gaze on the ceiling, frustration tightening his jaw. "I'm just tired of it, Shell."

I felt anger at his weakness. He was supposed to be the resilient one. "Tired of what?"

"Of being pissed off," he said, his eyes firing shrapnel at the ceiling. "Of nothing making sense. Of wanting to scream or hit things or . . . whatever, all the time." His passion made him cough, his abraded throat constricting around the failure of his act.

"But, Trey . . ." I wanted to say something powerful to fix his world so it wouldn't be so treacherous, but I knew that his scars—like mine—required more than words.

"He's supposed to be dead to me, Shell. I've done everything I could to make him dead to me, but he keeps . . . he keeps coming back."

"He's gone, Trey. He's been gone forever."

"But not in my head."

I knew what he meant, but my indignation and distress outweighed my sympathy. "So you tried to kill yourself?" My voice was hard with disbelief. "You decided to bail out on me and leave me alone? Thanks a whole lot!"

"I wasn't—"

"You promised me! You swore you'd stick with me." I tried to stand, but my muscles were too stunned by the past twenty-four hours to lift me out of my chair. I felt electrocuted by horror, dismantled by sorrow.

"Shell—"

"We haven't heard from him in four years, Trey."

"I know. But he's in my head. He's—in—my—head," he said again, anxiety reverberating in his voice. "I can't get him out of my head."

I tried to think of something comforting to say, but nothing came to mind. It was Trey who was supposed to be the strong one, Trey who was supposed to have the answers, Trey who was supposed to convince me, as he had done so many times, that life was worth fighting for.

"Did something happen?" I asked, desperate to know the impetus that had sent him hurtling into the abyss of self-destruction. "Should I have seen something . . . or known something?"

He shook his head. "It's just too much," he said, and his voice held the forlorn emptiness of an abandoned home. "I try to hate him so much that he won't matter anymore, but . . . it's like he's still watching me and forcing me to be who he wants me to be." His eyes roiled with need and anger and pain. "But I don't want that. I don't want anything he wants anymore." Tears welled in his eyes for the first time since he'd tried to end his life. "And then sometimes . . ." He swallowed convulsively, averting his eyes.

"What?"

He shook his head and bit his lip. I laid my forehead against his arm and listened to him breathing. After a few moments, he said, "Sometimes I look at myself and all I see is him. And when it gets really bad," he added raggedly, "when it gets really bad, you look at me like you see him too."

I raised my head and opened my mouth to protest, but the honesty of his gaze halted my disclaimers. He was right. There had been seconds, fleeting seconds, when his incoherence and anger had revived the fear and guilt I'd so often felt around my father. "I know you're not Dad," I said quietly, stroking his arm with my hand. "It's just . . ."

"I know, but I could be. You know? I think I could be." He sighed.

I sighed too as I contemplated the tortuous journey that had led us to this place—Trey in a hospital bed, broken and confused, and me at his side, relieved and terrified.

"I never once thought you were him," I said again with all the conviction of my fear. "Never once—not even when you did things that weren't like you."

"Okay." It was a mechanical response, devoid of faith. He didn't know how to trust me. His self-condemnation left no room for extenuation.

"Never once, Trey. I promise you." I squeezed his arm to force his attention. "And if you'd succeeded—if you'd died . . ." A sob lodged in my throat, and all I could do was continue to convince him with the passion in my eyes. I could tell he was far from believing.

When I found my voice again, I took a deep breath and asked, "What do you think he wanted you to be?"

It took him a while to answer. He looked toward the window and his eyes got distant. "I don't know," he finally said. "A world-class businessman. A soccer star. Or something else I'm not."

"So you did this to get even with a dad we haven't heard from in four years?" I touched his bandages and felt a shiver ripple down my

neck. I'd come so close to losing him. "I can think of simpler ways of getting the message across." My voice was hoarse and overfull.

"Yeah, but not as dramatic. This is the drama-queen side of me." He managed a smile.

"Who knew?"

"She's a late bloomer." He coughed.

"Want something to drink?"

"Yeah."

"You can be whatever you want, Trey—a bouncer, a ballerina, a candlestick maker . . . Just be alive, okay?"

I got him a glass of water and he fell half-asleep in the seconds it took me to return to his bedside.

"Guess the muddlehood got a little out of hand this time, huh?" he said in a weary voice.

"Yeah. And it's probably going to take a while to unmuddle it too."

"I'm going to go to cooking school," he said, eyes closed.

"Right now?"

"Someday."

I knew "someday" would come much later, only after he'd recovered from this day. "Yeah?" I said. "I'm going to become a football coach."

❊ ❊ ❊

Coach Taylor was on the move, striding up the steep, uneven path like there was a mountain of Twinkies waiting for us at the top. Shayla was hot on his heels, though she took three steps for each one of his, and they were miraculously managing to carry on a conversation as they climbed. I, on the other hand, was a fair distance behind, breathing like an asthmatic heifer in a marathon and squinting up into the distance with the hope that Sausenburg's tower would suddenly materialize out of the forest.

I had three problems with the adventure at hand. One, it required physical effort. I was okay with physical effort if I could work at my own pace and self-medicate with my foods of choice along the way, but this was most definitely Scott's pace we were keeping, and the food of choice he'd brought along was oranges. Oranges. 'Nuff said.

My second problem was the fact that it was cold—bitterly cold—and I didn't like it much. It had taken me ten minutes to get Shayla decked out in so many layers that she now moved with all the grace and agility of the Michelin Man. This fact, however, wasn't slowing her down, what with her growing infatuation with the guy in the lead, whose enthusiasm and energy made me feel like I was moving at the pace of, say, a tree stump. A tree stump with screaming calf muscles and something wet trickling down the middle of her back, but I didn't think I had the fortitude to consider that just yet.

And my third problem was causing the kind of internal head-slapping that threatened to dismantle the precarious can-do attitude I'd brought along for the hike. The problem was that I had no one to blame for this excursion but myself. And maybe the Betty Crocker syndrome. Back in the good old days when my idea of cooking had been boiling up some water for Kraft macaroni and cheese, I hadn't had any delusions of grandeur. I'd gone about my business in the kitchen in the five to seven minutes it took to cook the noodles; then I'd plopped down at the table and declared myself a genius. That simple. But now that I was possessed by Betty Crocker's ghost, I'd been doing things that were as foreign to me as, say, bringing soup to ailing men, which had led to climbing up a mountain to a castle on a frigid day with a four-year-old and her way-too-fit partner in crime.

Scott had returned to school on the day after the soup incident and had tracked me down in my English classroom during lunch. He'd handed over my Tupperware and cocked his head to the side again, which had the unpleasant effect of making me wonder how weird I really was.

"Stop looking at me like that. It was only soup."

"It was great soup. I think Shay's carrots put it over the top."

I'd been wondering since yesterday what had put me over the top. "She was adamant about bringing it to you," I lied. "I'm glad you enjoyed it." Score one for being a mom—you got to blame things on the kid.

He took a deep breath. "Okay, so I'm going to go out on a limb here and revisit the battlefield of skirmishes past," he started.

I held up my hand. "You sure you want to go there? 'Cause I tend to pull out my zingers when things get weird, and I wouldn't want you to get, you know, injured or anything."

He laughed. I loved it when he laughed. It made me feel less fat and more funny. Which was good. He propped against one desk and I propped against another.

"Can you maybe keep them sheathed until I'm finished talking? Then you can let 'em fly."

I made a mental leap back to the humiliating monologue about turkey I'd submitted him to and decided that the least he deserved was a chance to put me through the same.

"Shoot," I said.

"First, I need to apologize."

Huh? I felt a monologue coming on. "What for?"

"Pouting."

I fiddled with some papers on the desk and said a clueless, "Uh-huh . . ."

"It's a character flaw—another one. And not very adult of me."

I smiled and wondered if that was the appropriate response. I was a bit outside my comfort zone here.

"So anyway," he continued, raking his fingers through his hair and shifting to sit on top of the desk, "remember the gym?"

"Yeah, it's right over there." I pointed over my shoulder.

He did his play-along-here-will-you? look. "I *mean*—do you remember the last conversation we had in the gym?"

"Sure." It was on a par with the time Trey had crushed my thumb in a car door when we were little.

"I acted like a jackass."

"Is that any way for a missionary to talk?" I was trying to lighten the mood.

"And I've been acting like a jackass ever since."

"I prefer 'horse's patooty.'"

"Shelby . . ."

"Sorry—please go on."

"So I apologize for that."

"You've been fine."

"I've been distant. Like I said, I was pouting."

And here I'd blamed it on my hair. I really liked Scott at that moment. One, because he looked good in forest green, and two, because he was acting like a grown-up—and doing so for my sake. It felt kinda flattering, in a dangerous sort of way.

He let out a quick breath and said, "So here's my question."

"Is this the battlefield part?"

"I really think Lady Shay would like the Sausenburg ruins. And I think you might enjoy the view from the tower. And I guess what I'm saying is that I'd love to take you ladies on a field trip—to make amends for being a horse's patooty." He paused. "And . . ." It was what you might call a pregnant pause, and pregnancies—real and metaphorical—had always made me nervous.

"We'll be happy to!" I jumped in. Maybe too fast and too loud, because he looked a little taken aback.

He cocked his head again.

"Stop doing that."

"What?"

"Looking at me sideways."

"Was I doing that?"

"You were."

"I'll try to stop it."

"Good."

"Saturday?"

"Whatever."

"Two o'clock?"

"Sounds like optimum castle-climbing time to me."

"Good—looking forward to it."

"Okay."

"Okay."

He walked to the door and turned back. "No zingers?"

"I'm being good," I said. "But you should see the verbal constipation in my brain."

He laughed.

And here we were, days later, turning a field trip into a fitness test. The air was like a sheer sheet of ice, and it seemed to amplify the brightness of the sun.

"You okay, Shelby?" Scott called from up ahead.

I'd stopped to catch my breath and work on my attitude. "Just enjoying the view!"

"You're surrounded by trees!"

"I like trees!"

He trotted down the path to me with a grin on his face that looked like it said, *You're so cute when you're winded.* The winded part made sense. But the cute part? I dismissed it as a figment of my imagination.

He came alongside me and matched his pace to mine. "You doing okay?"

I nodded. He had his hand on the back of my neck, a gesture I'd seen him use a hundred times while talking with his players, and certainly the furthest thing from an intimate touch, as my scarf and coat formed a pretty thick barrier, but still . . .

"You coming?" Shayla was waiting for us up ahead, her purple knit hat a little askew on her head.

"Coming, Shayla! Wait right there, okay?" She crouched down to peer closely at something on the path. "How much farther?"

Scott looked around for landmarks. "Not far. Maybe another couple of minutes."

"Well, good," I said, "'cause you're starting to look a little tired, and I'm sure you could use a rest."

"Not your idea of fun?"

"Put it this way," I said, and I realized that the walk had gotten much less painful since he'd turned up at my side. My lungs were even starting to work better. "Would I enjoy sitting by a fire with a good book? Yes. But it's good for Shayla to get outside and it's good for me to get exercise, so . . ."

"You really don't like exercise, do you?"

"Exercise is okay. It's exertion I despise."

He smirked. I liked his smirk. "Want a piggyback ride?"

"I can't afford your hospital bills."

We reached Shayla and spent a few minutes admiring the entirely unadmirable stone she'd found on the path. She taught us how to say *stone* in German, clearly disapproving of our accents, then declared that we should set off toward the castle again. I wasn't pleased that my daughter had gained an elementary understanding of German in the time it had taken me to forget the fifty words I knew.

When we got to the ruins, Shayla went a little nuts. It's not like it was anything extraordinary. The tower was impressive, but only the bottom half of the castle's outer walls still stood. There were piles of rocks and gaps where windows used to be. These were definitely ruins. Except in Shayla's mind. To her, this was an ornate vestige of the days of kings and queens and princesses with long, flowing hair. Though she didn't really have the verbal skills to paint the picture of what she was seeing in her mind, the expression on her face said it all.

She and Scott started up the tower together. It had a circular wooden staircase that wound up into the dark interior before changing, toward the top, into a zigzagging section of steps. As this wasn't really a tourist attraction, there were no lights inside, just a dank darkness and uneven steps that scared Shayla into whining. Her voice reached me from inside.

"I don't like it. I don't like it anymore. I want to go out!"

I could hear Scott's softer voice trying to coax her up a few more steps to where daylight streaming through a narrow window would make the space brighter, but Shay's voice was rising as her panic increased. Like a dutiful mom, I entered the tower and started to climb.

"Shayla, honey, are you up there?"

"I want to go *dooown*!"

"But you're almost at the top! Look up—do you see more light, Shay?"

There was a little hiccup from far above me. "N—no . . ."

I heard Scott's voice whispering, "Here—let me carry you."

"I want to go *dooown*!"

She had to be nearly at the top. "I'm coming up too, honey. You go on up and tell me what you see, okay?"

"Look, Lady Shay, see the door up there and the light shining through it? We're almost there." Scott's voice was soothing and calm. "Just a few more steps and . . . Here we are!"

I climbed the last few steps and came out on top of the tower, where a panoramic view of mountains and valleys stole my breath. Or maybe it had been the climb. I preferred the beautiful-view scenario. Stepping to the edge of the platform where Scott stood with Shayla in his arms, pointing in the direction of Kandern so she could get her bearings, I marveled at the simplicity of the moment. Shayla wasn't even aware of my presence, so entranced was she with the height of her vantage point, the breadth of the view, and the now-clearly-visible outline of the castle's ancient perimeter. I caught myself wanting to hook an arm through Scott's and stare out at the scenery with them, but I held back and merely stood next to them, contemplating the view.

A few minutes later, after a mildly traumatic descent back through the darkness, Scott and I sat on a wall and watched Shayla gathering leaves. We were deep into November, so they were half-decomposed and sodden, but she was building a princess bed with them, and in her mind, they were golden.

"She's a keeper," Scott said, his eyes on the little girl so absorbed in her task.

"Yeah, I figure I'll hang on to her for a while."

"A while?"

"Oh, you know, until she's forty. Maybe fifty."

"You're lucky to have her."

I contemplated my pre-Shayla life and felt tears stinging my eyes. "You have no idea."

"So . . ."

I giggled. Sometimes I did that when anticipating tough questions.

"Shayla told me you weren't her mother; then you told me she wasn't your daughter. I asked Bev and Gus and they told me to ask you, so . . ."

"I'm her guardian. I kind of . . . inherited her when her dad passed away."

"Really?"

"Really."

"How long ago?"

"He died last December. I got her in February."

"Were you close?"

"Shayla's dad and I?"

She came running up to show us a tattered leaf. We dutifully told her it was beautiful and she ran back to her task.

"No, we weren't close," I said.

There was a silence while Scott absorbed the fact and sifted through the questions it brought up.

I didn't know how much to say—what to explain. The sordid details of my family's derailment hung in the air, suspended like strands of spiderweb. I feared his reaction were he to know the truth. Would he find me too sullied? Too broken? Too complicated? If he knew all the facts, would he step back to a safe distance and become polite-Scott again? Friendly-Scott, who smiled when we crossed in the hall and greeted me when we passed in the street but didn't initiate Sausenburg hikes?

I braced myself for the worst and started to fill in some of the blanks that resonated like voids in the stillness around us. "Her dad was—not a kind man. He left my life when I was much younger and I didn't hear from him again until . . . until his lawyer told me he had died and left something in his will for me."

"Shayla?"

"A cuckoo clock."

He turned his head to look at me.

"And Shayla. He'd designated me as her legal guardian should anything happen to him."

"Wow." Scott looked over at the mound of dead leaves Shayla was trying to shape into a rectangle. "And you took her in right away?"

"Look at me, Scott. Do I look like I suffer from any Mother Teresa delusions?" He glanced at my *hellooo* face and cracked a smile. "No, I didn't take her in right away. I'm way too convoluted for anything that simple. I tried every trick in the book to talk myself out of it and finally gave in because it was the only right thing to do. And because I fell in love with her a little bit, with the Heidi mountains and the sunshine and all."

He raised an eyebrow.

"The bottom line is—I took her in and haven't looked back."

"And coming to Germany was . . . ?"

"A new beginning. For both of us."

"Her dad must have trusted you."

I laughed out loud before I could stop myself. But I could tell from Scott's expression that it hadn't been a very humorous sound—again.

"No, Scott, he didn't really trust me."

"So . . . who was he to you?"

"You know, that's probably a question best left for another day." Shayla, bored with the bed idea, kicked the pile of leaves and giggled as they rained down around her, a dull-brown waterfall. "But she's mine now—and we're here. And I don't think I'd change anything about that part of the story."

"You think she'll ever call you Mom?"

"When she's ready."

He stood, shoving his hands into his pockets and turning to look out over the valley. "You must have gotten a lot of questions around BFA with her calling you Shelby and all."

I shook my head. "Actually, I haven't gotten many. I think Bev and Gus did a pretty good job of telling people I was a single mom and leaving it at that."

"But . . . she calls you Shelby," he repeated.

"And if people ask, I'm happy to tell them it's an arrangement that works well for us. Period. Some of them seem to think it's weird, and that's okay. Any more details would require more explanations than I'm willing to give right now."

"What do the students call you?"

"Miss. Mrs. It depends. Half of them think I'm divorced."

"And you're okay with that?"

"Sure. I know what the truth is, and when Shayla understands it, we'll be able to make it a little more public."

"Sounds wise."

"I try."

"You're a good mom."

"Yeah? You're a good hiking coach."

"Sorry you came?"

"Ask me tomorrow when my calf muscles are screaming for mercy."

"Make sure you stretch them before bed and first thing in the morning."

I looked at him in fake exasperation. "Don't go all basketball coach on me. I need a friend, not a tyrant."

"Well, you've got that," he said, sitting beside me again and pulling me in for a quick squeeze.

"The friend part or the—"

"The friend part, Shelby."

"Well, good, 'cause the tyrant part reminds me of that time in fourth grade when Miss Nicholson sent me to the principal's office because I'd drawn a picture of her backside with flowers growing out of it and—"

"You're not going to start the talking thing again, are you?"

I bit my tongue and counted to twenty. That squeeze had done weird things to me. I didn't like it. The side effects, that is. The squeeze itself, I didn't mind.

I pushed off the wall and walked over to put Shayla's hat back on her head. It had fallen sideways onto her shoulder, exposing a matted mess of blonde that made me itch to grab a brush. She protested right on cue as I set the hat straight and tied its strings under her chin.

"Wanna go up the tower again?" This from the guy who'd nearly not made it up with her the first time.

"Yeah!" On the decibel scale of agreement, her answer ranked right up at the top.

He slung her onto his back and took off toward the thick metal door at the bottom of the tower, turning to wink at me just before they disappeared inside.

Triple salchow, double lutz, and a mind-numbing axel. My stomach was getting good at the ice-skating thing.

14

THE PLAY WAS coming together well, much to Meagan's excitement, and we were closing in on the last two weeks of rehearsals before Christmas break. I'd been seeing a lot more of the cast than just during our practices, as some of them had acted on their threats and invited themselves over for the occasional dinner-and-games evening. It was apparently a common thing in this place where half the student population was in the boarding program, but I'd never encountered anything like it in other schools where I'd worked.

Because the students came from all over the world to study, they were given fewer but longer vacations, which allowed them to fly home at Christmas and Easter to spend much-needed time with their parents. So there was a three-week break coming up—in which I hoped the actors' talent and memorization wouldn't atrophy—followed by just five weeks of rehearsals before their two performances.

Given that timeline, it was with renewed focus and drive that I approached our pre-Christmas practices, though my focus seemed increasingly undone by random and not-so-random encounters with a certain sandy-haired coach. My frantic monologues had subsided and I now faced our times together with a mixture of expectation and dread. Expectation because I really enjoyed spending time with him—in a daydreaming-then-smacking-myself-upside-the-head kind of way. And dread because, in the back of my mind, it was always Saturday and my dad was singing in the shower again and there was a faint whiff of chocolate chip pancakes in the air.

The actors had grown accustomed to Scott's impromptu visits, and I had grown accustomed to ignoring the meaningful glances and eyebrow wiggling that went on while he was there. The visits had been coming more frequently lately, and I wondered who was teaching the boys how to throw big balls through little hoops in the gym while their coach was loitering downstairs in the auditorium. He'd always have a word or two for me, like asking about Shayla's tummyache or planning a trip to the hot baths nearby ("Ix-nay on the athing suit-bay" had been my immediate reply). Then he'd get drawn into whatever argument or deliberation or joke-telling contest the actors were involved in. He had a casual way with students, entering into their lives without losing his authority, and I loved to watch them being drawn to him like . . . well, like Shayla. He'd become something of a fixation for her, and she never drew anything, learned anything, or lost anything that she didn't want to tell Scott about. She clung to his attention and hung on his words and responded to his remonstrances better than she did to mine. And that chocolate-chip-pancake part of me feared for her heart.

But I just kept shoving down the fear—forcing it away—because the Scott I saw at school and out, as a teacher and a friend, was not the singing-in-the-shower type.

Mind you, he wasn't exactly perfection incarnate either. There were days when he was preoccupied and barely even verbal, and there were times when his energy seemed too diffuse to do anyone any good, and there had been one occasion, when one of his players had been suspended for drinking, when it had taken every bit of persuasion in me to get him to gain some perspective again. The irony. But Scott was a good man, and getting to know him had been fascinating and stimulating . . . in a completely terrorizing kind of way.

Life was . . . Could I say "good"? Not yet. There was too much expectation attached to the word. So I stashed it away in my "to be determined" file, along with "I am a good play director," "I can be a good mother," and "Losing control over my heart could be a good thing." *Good* it was a word that bore investigation.

Kate and Seth were at it again on this particular day, but we'd all come to the conclusion that this was merely the way they functioned best, so we allowed the friction and oddly supportive disagreements. Off to the side of the stage, Thomas, the sole member of the cast who had British blood, was trying to teach a bunch of American boys how to speak with convincing accents. I'd found that the students often resorted to good-natured ribbing about the limitations and peculiarities of the multiple cultures represented in the school, and that habit had extended into the auditorium on this noisy afternoon.

"Ben!" Thomas yelled in exasperation—he was a bit dramatic that way. "You've got to sound bored. Terminally bored. Otherwise, you'll sound American." His phlegmatic accent took all the authority out of his instructions.

"What—are you saying Americans are less bored than Englishmen?"

In a long-suffering voice, Thomas responded, "The English sound polite and bored, and Americans sound obnoxious and way too friendly. It's not a good or a bad thing; it's just the way it is!"

"Hey!" Kate said from the stage, pausing in a conversation with Seth to address Thomas's declaration. "Just because we're friendly doesn't mean we're obnoxious!"

Thomas threw his hands up and said, "Just say the line like you're a stuffy old Englishman, Ben!"

Ben did his best to say, "Where men have intellect, women have soul," in a convincingly bored British accent, but he failed so miserably that a chorus of dejection went up around him.

I left Thomas to his ranting and approached the stage, where Kate and Seth had been working on a critical scene in which Joy found out she was dying of bone cancer and Lewis discovered how deeply he cared. Kate had lived up to the potential she'd shown during tryouts. She'd come to the play with the fiery temperament her character required, but she'd learned in the weeks since then to modulate her strength and mollify her bluntness, and her acting, in turn, had become infused with the heart of a tough American woman coping as best she could with imminent death and the tender, sweet bloom of love. She was mesmerizing.

"You ready to run the scene again?" I asked. The two actors nodded and stowed their scripts under their chairs. I stepped back and gave the rest of the cast a be-quiet look. Seth and Kate whispered something to each other, then marked a pause and began.

"Can I say anything I want, Jack?" she asked softly, resting her hand on Seth's arm and inflecting her voice with just enough roughness to express her illness.

"Yes."

"Anything?"

"Yes."

"You know it anyway."

Seth covered her hand with his and paused a moment. "Yes."

"I'm still going to say it." There was a bit of humor in that last statement and I loved Kate for it.

"You say it."

"I love you, Jack."

Seth seemed startled by the words, as if he'd never read them in the script before, then he grasped her hand more tightly on his arm and, blinking away an invisible fog, masked his own need with his concern for her by gently asking, "Better now?"

"Better," she said.

❋ ❋ ❋

Trey was determined to get better. And by "better," he didn't just mean "over it." He meant stronger in every way than he'd ever been before. He was so diligent in his recovery that I worried about his mental health for entirely different reasons. He faithfully downed his happy pills and was on time to all his appointments. He attended two support groups like elderly women go to bingo. He even started going to church occasionally. He was the poster child for suicide recovery, and I knew it was because he'd faced off with his demons, thrown himself into their hades, dared them to take him, and somehow survived. They hadn't destroyed him, and he wouldn't allow them to maim him anymore.

He still had down days occasionally. He'd get a little too quiet—his face would seem to harden and shrink, and his eyes would fade back to dirty-swimming-pool gray—but those times never lasted long. He'd learned what to do with them, I guess. I was so proud of him for that.

Trey also took stock of what he wanted from life in the months after his hospitalization, and that led him to do some major purging. No more borrowed soccer dreams for Trey Davis. He gave up his full-ride sports scholarship, quit college, and enrolled in a prestigious school of culinary arts in Chicago. I guess he figured he'd rather be in debt up to his ears and in flour up to his elbows than kick a ball around a soccer field in honor of a man who'd abandoned him years before. It seemed like a logical conclusion to me.

As the end of my freshman year of college approached, I got busy with my own career plans. Well, kinda. It was more like tiptoeing around my options and hoping a vocation would rear up and smack me in the face. The problem was that I had absolutely no ambitions. I didn't have a burning need for recognition or a passion for, say, stocks and bonds. And I didn't want Imelda Marcos's shoe collection any more than I wanted Donald Trump's fleet of private jets. I was actually quite happy with one nice pair of pumps and Trey's hand-me-down Civic.

Trey and I seldom saw each other during the week, as he was a commuter who spent too much time on trains going in and out of Chicago. But we always made it a priority, at some point on Saturdays, to crawl up to our hut and solve the world's problems.

"The problem with soufflés," Trey said on one rainy afternoon as we gazed up at the sagging sheet above us, "is that they're incredibly finicky."

"Uh-huh." It was my standard response to Trey's culinary monologues. Not that I wasn't interested, but my fascination with food was more practical than theoretical. I wanted to eat it, not discuss it.

"If you don't pull it out of the oven at exactly the right moment, it'll either fall or overcook."

"I liked you better when you were a sports geek," I said.

He turned his head. "You did?"

I nodded. "Our talks made me less hungry." I popped a Reese's Pieces into my mouth.

"So have you decided yet?"

"I think Tom Cruise. He'll make a better husband than Bruce Willis because he's shorter—therefore he has more to prove."

"Oh, good. I was afraid you'd settle for Rob Lowe." He came up on his elbow. "I mean," he said patiently, "have you decided on a major?"

"The serious answer or the sarcastic answer?"

"I have a choice?" He seemed genuinely surprised, which made me wonder if I didn't overdo the sarcasm sometimes.

"I'm going to major in nutrition—the donut variety; minor in potatoes—the deep-fried variety. And if I get bored, I might do an independent study on the health hazards of slimness."

"So I didn't have a choice."

"Nope."

*He smiled. I liked it when he smiled. It reminded me of those months when all he'd done was snarl and sneer and generally be un-Trey. This post–*Looney Tunes *version was a vast improvement. I felt healthier when he was happy.*

"I think I might need another decade or two before I decide on a major," I said.

"You have a year, max."

"Don't pressure me."

"What do you like to do?"

"We've been over this before."

He sighed and tried again. "What do you like to do other than eat and watch I Love Lucy *reruns?"*

"I like to read. And I like to watch you bake. But as far as I know, a person can't major in Erma Bombeck and minor in vicarious baking, so . . ."

"Shell."

"Well, science and math are out. That narrows it down."

"And underwater basket-weaving is a made-up thing, so that's out too."

"Really? Darn."

"That leaves . . . ?" He raised an eyebrow and waited for me to fill in the blank.

"That leaves way too many options."

"Your adviser's got to hate you."

"I think we've come to terms with it. She doesn't tell me I have to make a decision quickly, and I don't tell her plaid went out with the '70s. It's a great arrangement. Tell me more about soufflés."

He laughed and plopped back down on his back. "You don't care about soufflés."

He was right. I really didn't. But I did have an issue that I'd been tangling with for a while. I figured this was as bad a time as any to raise it, and I dove right in.

"Does life scare you?"

He didn't laugh or sigh or anything like that. He pursed his lips and thought about it. That was one of the things I loved most about Trey. He only laughed at me when I was being really stupid. The mildly stupid stuff, he actually considered.

"There are things about life that scare me," he said after a while. "But life in general? Not really—not anymore. I've learned a few lessons that have kind of de-scary-ized it for me."

I pushed myself up into a cross-legged position, my mussed-up hair touching the lowest part of the Huddle Hut's sheet. "I'd like a Trey Davis tutorial on de-scary-izing, please."

"Tutorial?"

"On what you've learned. The main lessons. Maybe if I get those out of the way, I'll be able to concentrate on choosing a major rather than sitting around waiting for the sky to cave in."

He smiled and squinted at me. "You know you're a nutcase, right?"

"Flattery will get you nowhere."

"The lessons I've learned . . ." He pondered the concept, concocting an answer.

"And please hold the sports metaphors."

"Well, that eliminates lessons one and two."

"Trey . . ."

"Things are never as bad outside my brain as inside."

"That's a lesson?"

He nodded.

"What does it mean?"

"It means my worst-case scenarios hardly ever happen in real life."

"Mine usually do."

"They do not," he said.

"Marie Fallon," I said. He raised his hands in an I-give-up gesture. "Tenth grade?" He still wasn't remembering it. "She invited me to a dance at her house and I refused to go because I was fairly sure I'd make a fool of myself, but you told me I should go anyway. Which I did. And I came out of the bathroom halfway through the evening with my skirt tucked up in my panty hose, and—because you'd told me to be bold—proceeded to dance up a storm in the middle of the floor. Now that, my friend, is a worst-case scenario. Next lesson, please."

He laughed and didn't push the issue. Now that I'd jogged his memory, I was sure there were a lot of other worst cases of mine running through his mind. "Fine," he said. "Second lesson." He thought for a moment, and then his eyes widened as he figured it out. "Here it is."

I put on my eager face. "Oh, please, Yoda, your wisdom with me share."

"The best things in life take risk."

"Survey says . . ." I made a sound like the Family Feud *buzzer. "Nope. Don't like that one. Lesson number three, please."*

"You can't just pick and choose," he said.

"Sure I can. What's number three?"

He thought for a while, and I could tell he was wondering if his lessons would do me any good, given my casual approach to all things requiring an honest assessment of my life. He had a point, but his lessons did make for better conversation than soufflés, so I let him go on.

"My third and final lesson is that you can't pick what life throws at you," he said.

"That's encouraging."

"But you can pick what you do with it."

I'd been hoping for something a little more optimistic. Like "You'll develop miraculous analytical skills and coping mechanisms the moment you turn twenty, and nothing will ever be confusing to you again." I guess that was asking a bit too much. "That's supposed to be helpful?" I said.

"Sure. It means you get to determine how much you'll be affected by things that happen to you."

I had a vision of my future, dark and ominous, creeping in for the kill. There was no part of me that wanted to determine what to do with it, as Trey had suggested. I just wanted to run from it, screaming. And maybe hide in a closet until it passed. "I don't think your lessons work for me."

"I didn't think they worked for me either."

"Until . . . ?"

He pulled back his sleeves and showed me his scars.

"Maybe next time I ask you for life lessons, you could recycle an old standard like 'self-fulfilling prophecy.' It's less taxing on the brain."

"Fine," he conceded. "Next time, I'll tell you that if you expect something bad to happen, it probably will." He looked at me. "Happy?"

"Yeah." Like a flailing spider circling the drain. But at least this latest lesson required less self-assessment. Life was safer that way. "So there's a chance I'm going to wake up in the middle of the night sometime in a casket filled with rattlesnakes?"

"You're like conversation cyanide. You know that, right?"

"And yet you still attempt it. You're my hero."

"Just remember me when your prophecies come true."

I knew what he was getting at. "I like being alone, Trey. There's less guilt when my head's in the fridge and less turbulence when I'm trying to sleep."

"You don't really enjoy sleeping alone. Nobody does."

"Well, I do. Except in the winter. But that's why God created hot-water bottles. They keep your toes warm, but you don't have to cook for them and they never, ever burp."

⁂ ⁂ ⁂

I was used to Illinois winters, where the wind-chill factor decided everything from the undergarments I wore to the moisturizer I used. Winters in Germany were quite a bit milder, and I found myself less prone to weather-induced funks. Which was nice for anyone who had to live with me—namely Shayla. As quirky and scenic as Germany was in the fall, it turned whimsical and ethereal in the winter, particularly in the small towns and villages, where snowplows were scarce and salt was even scarcer. So the beauty was somewhat unevenly balanced with danger. Germans were so intent on protecting the grass that grew along the side of the road from the damage salt might cause that they were willing to sacrifice their cars in the process. I wasn't quite so generous with my own wheels, and the lack of road upkeep scared me so much that I actually bought myself a large box of salt and sneaked out into the street at night to keep at least my part of Germany safe from slips and accidents.

Shay and I had risked life and limb driving up to Marzell to go sledding on a couple of occasions. Marzell was a small village fifteen minutes out of Kandern—fifteen *straight up* minutes. Because of the difference in altitude, there was often snow galore in Marzell when it was gray and rainy in Kandern, snow enough for Shayla to wear herself out dragging her sled to the top of a hill and squealing down to the bottom, then dragging the sled back up again. I'd never really understood the appeal of spending so much time and effort climbing only to enjoy a fraction of the time sliding, but Shayla seemed to love it, so I was happy to stand at the bottom, cheering her down the hill and telling her what a great job she'd done when she got there.

Christmas in Germany was a sight to behold. It seemed each of the larger towns in the area hosted elaborate markets that lasted all of December, filled with stands displaying ornaments and other items made by local artisans, wooden toys, live manger scenes, lots of fatty food, and hot spiced wine. We took Bev along to a Christmas market in Gengenbach one afternoon, as much because we loved her company as because we didn't quite know how to get there. I'd heard that it was one of the more beautiful markets in the area, about an hour from home, so off we traipsed on a sunny afternoon, the three amigos out to conquer the world.

Darkness had fallen by the time we reached the medieval city, and the crisp night air was saturated with sounds and smells that made my heart sing and my mouth water. We walked down narrow cobblestone streets in search of the main square, past crooked homes with half-timbered facades, through alleyways that practically rustled with the whispers of centuries past. It was an enchanting fairyland that drew us in, and we walked slowly, hushed by the mystery and charmed by the simple, otherworldly beauty.

When we reached the town's historical square, Shay immediately declared that she wanted a gingerbread cookie, which, lucky for me, was a staple of German markets—so were candied peanuts, waffles, wurst in fresh rolls, warm apple cider, and steaming hot chocolate. It was an overeater's paradise and I felt right at home. Shayla, however, declared an instant dislike for the hard, nearly tasteless cookie I'd bought her. Fortunately, a kindly gentleman at a bakery stand gave her a free Berliner that reconciled her to the tradition of Christmas markets.

We wandered around for a while, tasting, touching, and absorbing as much of the festive uniqueness as we could. We bought two hand-painted glass ornaments, kept a safe distance from a slightly overzealous Saint Nicholas, watched a children's choir sing "O Tannenbaum" from the balcony of the town hall that overlooked the square, and finally declared our adventure complete. We decided on the way home that Americans really had a lot to learn from their German counterparts, especially when it came to community Christmas activities.

In other areas, however, Shayla felt they fell a little short.

"Do they know they're doing it wong?" she had asked on a trip to the grocery store.

"Doing what wrong?" It took so much self-control not to imitate her accent.

"The Christmas stuff. It's all blue."

"What's wrong with blue?"

She'd looked at me like I ought to know better. "It's supposed to be wed," she'd said in a patronizing voice. And she was right, of course. Christmas was supposed to be red. But in Germany, where they did things decidedly differently, the decorations were largely blue. So when Shayla and I did dishes to the sound of her favorite Christmas CD, we sang our own words at the top of our lungs, trying to drown out Frank Sinatra's voice.

"I'm dreaming of a *blue* Christmas," we'd sing. And Shayla would find it so funny she'd forget to keep drying.

It was on a particularly chilly December evening that we invited Scott to accompany us on a tree-hunting expedition.

"He's here! He's here!" Shayla screamed. She'd been kneeling on a chair by the living room window, her nose plastered to the glass, waiting for Scott to appear. She was at the door waiting for him before he'd had time to stamp the excess snow from his boots.

"Ready, Lady Shay?"

"Yes, yes, yes!" She was a little excited.

"How 'bout your mom? Is she ready too?"

I waited to hear Shayla say, "She's not my mom," but she'd been saying it less and less these days. I rounded the corner into the entrance hall, pulling on my gloves. "Ready."

Scott carried Shayla upside-down into the street, then fastened her securely into her car seat.

We spent the next hour trying to figure out how two finicky adults and an overexcited four-year-old could possibly come to an agreement on the shape and dimension of the perfect Christmas tree. Scott liked tall and skinny, I liked short and fat, and Shayla liked anything with a price tag outside my budget. The person running the tree lot finally came to our rescue and virtually ordered us to buy the one he selected for us.

"Schoen! Schoen!" he said, pointing at the straight trunk and the way the branches sloped down close to it. It was an okay tree, if you liked them shaped like marathoners. I liked mine shaped like sumo wrestlers, and Shayla, apparently, liked hers shaped like dollar bills.

Shayla wrinkled her nose at the tree the salesman held up for us to see, I shrugged my shoulders, and Scott said, "We'll take it."

As he'd been holding my hand for a few minutes, I didn't put up a fight. I was busy trying to keep my neurons firing and my Jell-O legs from buckling.

Scott secured the tree on the roof of my car, installed Shayla in her usual spot, and walked me around to my door, pulling me into him just long enough to say, "We done good," plant a kiss next to my ear, and assist me into my seat.

When he was settled behind the wheel, he looked at me like he had something to say, but the moment was interrupted by Shayla yelling, "Home! Home! Home!" at the top of her lungs.

And off we went to my apartment, where Scott got a little testy trying to get the tree to stand up straight and Shayla did all she could to distract him from the task. She tried on her ballerina skirt and twirled around him like a top. She told him the story of Rudolph and the Seven Dwarfs. She tried to measure his arm with the tape he'd used to determine how much of the trunk to cut off. And then she brought him the hot cider I'd made for him, which gave him a reason to sit down and contemplate his handiwork.

I joined them in the living room and took a seat on the couch.

"What do you think? Is it straight?" Scott asked.

I pursed my lips and squinted an eye. "No, but I've always wanted to see the Tower of Pisa, and this'll save me the trip."

"What?" He was out of his chair and standing in front of me, trying to see the tree from my angle. "It's straight!" he protested.

"Well done." I smiled.

He pointed at a giggling Shayla. "Don't laugh, young lady. Your mom's messing with my mind!"

She giggled some more, so he picked her up by her middle, swung her around in a circle, then plopped down on the couch next to me with Shayla sprawled across him.

He turned his head on the backrest—which meant his face was alarmingly close to mine. I stared straight ahead and tried to concentrate on the marathon-runner tree while the ice-skater in my stomach tried some new, original leaps.

"Wanna go to Riedlingen for supper?" he asked.

I turned my head and looked at him, which took way more courage than, say, wearing a bathing suit in public. Up close and personal, he was no less attractive than from a safe distance, and the fact that my daughter was sprawled across him, perfectly content as she played with the measuring tape, was all the more endearing.

"What's in Riedlingen?" I asked.

"A museum-café I guarantee your daughter will love."

His breath was warm against my face. My inner skater slipped and fell—flat on her back, breath knocked out of her. The Russian judge was not amused.

"But will *I* like it?" I tried really hard not to look at his mouth. Really I did. Really.

"The food?"

Uh . . . "Yeah, the food."

"How 'bout we drive over there and find out?"

Or maybe we could just stay like this for a decade or so—staring at the tree or something—and let whatever was uncoiling in my chest finish what it was doing.

But Shayla had other concerns. She slid off Scott's lap to the floor and looked up at us with a frown. "Are you mushy?" she asked.

Scott laughed.

I tried to cough around the cider that had gone down the wrong pipe.

And Shayla giggled.

15

The *Puppenmuseum* in Riedlingen was a little girl's dream. A local lady had turned a big old farmhouse into a toy museum where dolls and teddy bears covered shelves and chairs and miniature dollhouses. There were only six tables in the café, spread out over three rooms. The lighting was dim and the ambience so cozy that it felt a little like being in someone's home.

Shayla, still excited from the Christmas tree shopping, immediately took herself on a tour of the toys with firm instructions not to touch a thing. Scott seized the opportunity to lean across the table and ask, "Is this okay?"

"Scott, it's perfect. Shayla's going to want to eat here every day."

"Not the restaurant," he said, and he was wearing the same expression as earlier, in the car.

"Oh."

"Is it okay if I . . . ?" He reached across the table and linked his fingers with mine. "Is this okay?" He was as earnest as I'd ever seen him, and I realized his question had a lot more to do with our relationship than with our hands.

"Scott . . ."

"I just need to know, Shell. If this makes you uncomfortable . . . or if it's too soon. I don't want to rush anything or . . . you know." His eyes met mine with an intensity of sincerity and hope that frightened me.

I knew this was a pivotal moment and I knew his vulnerability required my utmost care, yet I couldn't help myself. It was sheer panic that made me do a terrible Scarlett O'Hara impression and say, "Why, Rhett, I do believe you're blushing!"

He didn't move, but something steel-gray came down over his gaze as he slowly disconnected his fingers from mine. He had risked rejection and I'd given him worse than that—I'd given him ridicule. There was nothing I could think of that would allow me a do-over.

"I'm sorry, Scott. I . . ." My mind felt sluggish, hampered by remorse. There was something crippled in the silence between us.

Shayla came bounding in with a giant teddy bear clutched in her arms, and I saw muscles clench in Scott's jaw just before he shifted and tried to assume a casual position.

I was an idiot.

But this idiot had a daughter who'd swiped an animal off of a display shelf, and I had some explaining to do. The restaurateur was friendly, thank goodness. She just requested that I accompany Shayla on any future tours. She asked Shayla if she understood, and my fast-becoming-bilingual daughter responded in German that she would not touch any stuffed animals again. I think. I pried Shayla's fingers from the bear's thick fur and returned the animal to its owner under Scott's somewhat-brooding gaze.

We made polite conversation over our *Flammen Kuchen*, and I was grateful for Shayla's oblivious cheer. Then Scott drove us home and waited patiently while I put Shayla to bed.

"She'd like to say good night," I told him after Shayla had whined about it for a while. "I tried to convince her that you'd already said your good-nights, but . . . you know."

We walked into Shayla's room, where she was busy making shadow animals on the wall with her hands. It was a trick I'd taught her several weeks ago, and it hadn't yet lost its appeal.

"Okay, little girl," I said, "say good night to Scott."

"But we haven't said pwayohs," she said, temporarily distracted from the mean dog on her wall.

"Say good night first; then we'll say prayers." I was trying to remain patient, but nervousness about what would happen next had me a little on edge.

"No—with Scott. Please?"

I sighed and looked over at Scott. He was wearing his usual Lady Shay smile, the one that was so real and gentle and, somehow, proud. "Do you mind?" I asked.

He shook his head and went to sit on the edge of Shayla's bed. I took my usual position on my knees at her side.

Shayla knew she'd gotten her way and was emboldened by the victory. "You pway," she said to Scott.

I held my breath. The intimacy of that moment was so visceral that it felt fragile and taut.

Scott took hold of Shayla's hand and she grabbed mine with the other, squinting her eyes shut and waiting for the prayer.

"Jesus," Scott said, holding her hand in both of his and using words Shayla would understand, "please be with Shayla tonight. Keep her dreams happy and her spirit sweet. And be with Shelby too—there's a lot going on in her life. And in mine. We rest in you. Amen."

"Amen!" Shayla chirped.

I kissed her face and returned her hug, then headed out to the living room while Scott said good night again. I was sitting on the couch when he joined me, though he chose to sit on the chair nearer the window.

"I'm sorry, Scott," I said. "I know you were being sincere, and I went and opened my big mouth and ruined it. . . . And I'm sorry. Really, Scott, I'm sorry. I'm an idiot—like that's anything new to you."

He steepled his fingers in front of his face, his eyes on me, and kept silent for a moment. There was neither frustration nor disappointment in his gaze—though they'd been there before, when my Scarlett O'Hara had put a damper on our day. Now it was just pensive. Subdued.

He took a breath and held it, then exhaled loudly, the sound filling the room that had become too quiet. He spread his hands out in front of him and said, "I'm not sure where to start—or how to say it. I'm not even really sure of what *it* is, actually."

"What were you going to say at the restaurant? Can we rewind and play that over? I promise Scarlett's gone for good."

He withdrew into thought again, his eyes on me but his mind clearly elsewhere. When he finally spoke again, it was in a tentative way, weighing each word and scanning my face for a reaction.

"What I was going to ask you at the restaurant was if it would be okay for me to hold your hand—like at the tree lot—and if it would be okay for me to spend more time with you. With you and Shayla." He paused. "But given your reaction . . ."

"I didn't mean it! It was just a knee-jerk thing!"

"Given your reaction, I think I need to change my question. And given your reaction, I'm really scared of doing so."

I didn't want him to change questions. I knew the answer to the hand-holding one. "Okay."

"I know there's stuff you haven't told me."

"Like my David Hasselhoff fantasies?" He gave me a look and I threw up my hands in defeat. "See?" I groaned. "I can't help it!" I gave myself a mental kick in the butt and continued. "Other people twist their hands or get twitchy when they're nervous, and I just go straight for the sarcasm—straight for the zinger—but it's not because I'm trying to be hurtful! It's just—it's a reflex thing. Like screaming when I'm scared or eating when . . . well, just about anytime. That one doesn't work."

He raised an eyebrow.

"See?" I was all out of steam and Scott hadn't moved, except for the smirk on just one side of his mouth. "Ask me your question, Scott. I promise I'll be good." There was a six-year-old sound to the statement, but I didn't care.

Scott levered himself out of the chair and came to sit near me on the couch. He raked his fingers through his hair and dropped his head for a moment. When he looked up, he had his game face on. And I couldn't blame him, as I hadn't exactly made things easy for him so far.

"I'm—and I don't know how to say this without sounding like a teenager—but I'm attracted to you, Shelby. Have been for a while, in case you hadn't noticed. And I'd like to . . . I'd like to pursue you, if you'll let me. Not just hold your hand or spend time with you and Shay."

And that was when the warm, Scott-shaped glow in my chest froze, then paled, then coiled in on itself into a solid, icy core. There were voices in my head, but they didn't belong to me. They belonged to spent circumstances, to pain, to crushed expectations and juvenile bravado. They were so loud, so overpowering, that they contracted my muscles and chilled my skin, numbing me to all but the piercing agony of impotence.

I could have said yes to holding his hand. I could have said yes to curling up beside him and letting myself bend into his care. I could have said yes to spending more time together and saying bedtime prayers with Shayla and sharing Christmas trees. But accepting his affection? Allowing his pursuit? Opening myself to the pain of dashed hopes and faded love?

No.

I couldn't.

Scott was instantly concerned, the suddenness of my transformation bridging the abyss of his guardedness. I saw him clasp my arm, but I didn't feel his hand. I felt his breath against my face, but I didn't hear his words. I had reached an impasse a lifetime in the making, and there was nothing, not even Scott's kindness, that could draw me back from my self-inflicted sanction.

I rose from the couch, and the motion subdued the clamor in my mind. "I'm sorry, Scott," I said. And truly I was. I was sorry for him and sorry for me and sorry for my daughter, who so deeply loved this man.

"Shelby, I was only saying—"

I shook my head and felt a jagged emptiness crushing my heart. "I know what you were saying, and, Scott . . ." The tears were too close. I wouldn't allow them. I took a calming breath. "You're so kind, Scott. So loving to Shayla. So . . . so a lot of things. All of them good. But I'm Shelby. I'm Shelby, Jim Davis's daughter, and I can't let you in. Not this way. Not with . . . You said *attracted* and *pursue*—and I know what those mean. And I like you too much to—to inflict myself on you."

He was standing too, his hand on my arm, his eyes boring into mine with confusion and worry and something like affection. It was the affection I found most terrifying.

"I can't care for you, Scott. Not the way you want. So . . ." I heard a sob and felt a spasm in my chest. There was grief on my face, dripping in hot regret down my neck. "I'm sorry."

I went to the door and held it open—my eyes averted, my resolve firm—and tried to wrap some poise around my tears.

Scott stopped in front of me. "I can't leave you like this."

"I'll be fine."

"Shell . . ."

"I'll be fine, Scott." The anger in my voice took him aback.

"Can I call you tomorrow?" A muscle was working in his jaw and his eyes seemed edgy.

"I'd rather you didn't."

He took his coat from the rack near the door, clearly tortured at the thought of leaving me this way.

"Thank you for . . . Thank you for saying it, Scott. It means . . ." How could I tell him what it meant to me? "It means a lot to me." I hoped he could distinguish my sincerity behind the layers of fear and distress and pain.

He nodded, slipped into his jacket, and with a final, laden glance, he left.

I wasn't sure how long I lay on the couch, flooding the silence with inconsolable despair. I had found a friend in Scott, a kindred spirit, a source of comfort and contentment and challenge and joy. And in my ignorance, I'd hurt him. I'd let him imagine the impossible and dismantle my reserve. I'd crushed us both. And the desolate places in my heart groaned in solitude and grief.

I'd spent my life until then clinging to God while I'd raged against the people at the root of my brokenness. But on this night, my world had shifted and I found myself railing at God as

I clung to the people I loved—like Scott, who deserved so much more than I could give him, and Shayla, whose innocence I feared crippling. Why had I been born into a destructive vortex that had made the thought of loving so intolerable? Why hadn't God intervened? Why hadn't he stilled the forces that had rendered me powerless and damaged? Why couldn't I trust myself enough to love sufficiently? How was I supposed to live the rest of my life in this paralyzing fear of personal failure? My anger was opaque and rough, craggy and raw and frantic.

It was nearly 4 a.m. when I woke. My eyes felt bloated and my limbs impossibly heavy. The numbness in my mind was a relief. There was nothing else to do but pick up the phone and dial.

"Hello!"

"Trey?"

"Shelbers! What time is it over there?" He'd become a pro at time-zone calculation, but this middle-of-the-night call had made him doubt his expertise.

"Nearly four."

There was a beat while he made note of my tone of voice and came to conclusions. "What's happening, Shell?"

I sighed. I couldn't find the words.

"Is it Shayla?" His voice was sharp, his worry audible.

"No. She's fine, Trey. Really. It's not her."

"So . . . ?"

"I need a Rolo."

"That bad."

"Yup."

"Have the Germans been nasty to you? 'Cause I can fly over there and give 'em a piece of my mind, if you want. Really. Just say the word."

"We got a Christmas tree today."

"Okay."

"And then we went to the toy museum for supper."

"Strange, but I'll allow it."

"And we came back and had prayers with Shayla."

"Always a good plan. Just a question, though—who's 'we'?"

I moaned a little. "Scott and Shayla and me."

He didn't say anything. He just waited, my ever-patient brother who would read between the lines and understand the source of my dysfunction without need for explanations.

"He's great, Trey. You'd like him."

"And you like him."

I sighed. "And he told me tonight that he'd like to pursue me."

"What—is he Victorian?"

"Trey."

"Sorry."

"He's so careful. So . . . noble."

"And you said . . . ?"

"I pulled a Shelby on him."

"Shell . . . why?"

"I don't know. I panicked. Told him he shouldn't care about me. That I can't care for him—not that way."

"How many times are you going to do this?" There was a hint of anger in his voice. "How many times are you going to sabotage something good because you're too scared to risk it?"

"I don't know, Trey; how long are *you* going to keep at it?"

"We're talking about you!"

"Well, I don't know! It's not like I set out to be this way!"

"I know."

I knew he did.

"There should be a switch somewhere," I said. "Some kind of existential breaker that allows us to disarm the past. Seriously."

"It's looking for that breaker that landed me in the hospital," my survivor-brother said.

There was no arguing that point.

I allowed myself to think about my parents for a while—something I rarely did—but it seemed appropriate, as they were so entangled in the moment. "When do you think Dad turned into . . . well, Dad?"

"I don't know."

"I mean, Mom wouldn't have married him if he was as bad then as he was later, right?"

Trey thought about it for a moment. "Probably not," he said. "I hope not."

"So there's a good chance that he was a nice guy at one point in his life—nice enough for Mom to fall in love with him."

"I guess it's possible."

I sighed. "It's more than possible. She told me herself—with pictures and letters to prove it."

"When was this?"

"Right after her stroke."

"And I'm just hearing about this now because . . . ?"

I shook my head in frustration. "Because I didn't like it. The part about Dad being romantic and lovable. I tried to forget it, actually."

"But she said he was."

"Yup."

"So . . ." I could hear his reluctance in the hesitation that preceded "We have to believe her."

I sighed again, more wearily this time. "Yeah, I guess we do. But maybe he was just faking being nice to get the girl. Whatever it was, she believed him."

"And you think Scott's a nice guy too," my brother said with intimate understanding.

"And more."

"And your point is that you think he could turn into Dad, since Dad was probably all sweetness and light before we knew him."

"Yup."

"And the other half of the point," he continued with unerring accuracy, "is that *you* could become Dad."

"There are no guarantees, Trey. We were raised with him. We absorbed some of him in all those years. We had to."

"Or maybe we had such good seats at the Jim Davis horror show that it scared us straight. Ever think of that? Maybe we're not going to become him because we've seen him up close and personal—and because he was so revolting to us."

Something cold trickled through the marrow of my spine. "I hate him."

There was a pause on the other end of the line. "You've never said that before," Trey said quietly, with no reproach.

I sighed and squeezed my eyes shut. "I've never felt quite this derailed before."

"It's . . ." He paused. "I don't think it's a good thing for you to suddenly decide you hate him, Shell."

"Maybe I've spent too much time making excuses for him. That's what you used to tell me, remember?"

"But refusing to hate him is what kept you sane."

"No, Trey, it's what kept me *barely functional.* And there aren't very many upsides to that. Not for me, anyway."

He understood. I could hear it in his sigh. "Don't hate him."

I remembered Scott's face when he'd left my apartment and couldn't quell the heat of fury in my blood. "Dad did this to me," I said.

"Yeah, but he's not around to fix it. So hating him isn't going to do anything except wear you down."

I wasn't sure I could withstand more wearing down. There were enough other factors in my life competing for the honor. Still, I hated him just then with a very childish passion.

"Hating people bleeds a person dry, Shell. It does. You're better off using that energy to figure yourself out."

"I don't think I can."

"I think you should try."

The international connection hummed as we fell silent, me with my pain and Trey with his compassion. "Have I told you I love you, Trey?"

"Uh—that's a bit of an abrupt topic change, there, Shelby."

"There's a line in the play where Joy finally gets to tell Lewis she loves him—right before she dies—and I'm worried I haven't told you often enough."

"You're not dying, are you?"

"Not if I can help it."

"Good—then I'll allow the comparison with Lewis and Joy, but only because you're emotionally distraught. And I know you love me. There isn't a moment in my life that I haven't known that. So it's okay that you haven't said it as much as you wanted to. It got said other ways."

"Yeah?"

"Yeah." We let a pause lengthen. "Think you can sleep now?" he asked.

"Probably not, but I can give it a shot."

"How undoable is this Scott thing? Can you reverse the engines?"

"Not sure. I need to decide first if it's worth the risk."

"Well, take it from someone who's lived through your worst PMS *and* gone jeans shopping with you. Any guy would be lucky to have you."

"I'm damaged goods."

There was a tense silence. "Okay, now you've made me mad. Don't ever say that about yourself again, Shell!"

"Okay," I said in a very small voice.

"Jim Davis might have been your father, but you're worlds apart from him. Planets. Don't give him the power to make you damaged goods—not even in your head."

"Yes, sir."

"Now go to bed!" There was a smile in his voice again and it warmed my innards.

"To the brotherhood, buddy."

"And the Davishood, Sis. For better or for worse."

We hung up.

In the quiet that followed, God spoke. I didn't hear a voice. I didn't sense a presence. But a revelation blossomed in the space between my heart and mind, so elemental in its simplicity that it blanketed the ragged edges of my anger with gossamer appeasement.

God hadn't been idle while my father's words and actions had threatened my sanity and bruised my dreams. He hadn't been passive when rage had battered me and fear had shackled me. He had given me Trey. He had given me a living, breathing, comforting warrior whose devotion had mirrored his own. It wasn't he who had so wounded me—it was he who had rescued me. And though the consequences of my father's depravity were still mine to bear, I knew at that moment, more clearly than I had ever known, that God had been faithful. And it was because he'd been there that the horror had been survivable.

The thought quelled my anger but not my grief as I walked slowly, heavily toward my bedroom.

16

NOTHING MUCH HAD CHANGED in the house. It still smelled of fried onions and laundry soap, and it still seemed cluttered with the overflow of too many lives lived in too small a space. Mom sat in her La-Z-Boy, her feet propped up and a glass of water within reach. She hadn't moved much from this position since her return. We'd made her as comfortable as we could, and I'd spent a couple of nights in the overwhelming perkiness of my old room just to make sure she was really all right. The doctors had called it a ministroke, which sounded a little too cheerful for something that had left Mom temporarily without a memory, weak, and confined to a hospital bed.

But she was feeling better now. Her eyes weren't as scared and her skin looked a little less like Marcel Marceau's. She'd called me earlier and asked me to come by, so I'd swung over after my day of student-teaching and found her sitting there, Oprah blaring from the TV set and a book open on her lap. I had to agree—Oprah was a lot more bearable diluted with some reading. It crossed my mind that Mom had her own version of Oprah's Book Club going on.

"Sit down, Shell," she instructed, her voice as rice-paper thin as her skin. "And hand me that box, will you?"

I fetched a small, ornately decorated wooden box from the coffee table and laid it in her lap. Mom turned watery eyes on me and seemed to dig into her brain for a prepared speech she'd stored there. "My . . . episode . . ." She halted, reaching for her glass with unsteady fingers.

I wanted to say, "Your episode was a stroke, Mom. 'Episodes' are what make incredibly obtuse shows like *Dynasty* into palatable televisual bites. 'Strokes' are what nearly kill people. Get it right." *But she appeared to be gathering courage, so I didn't interfere. A lifetime in the Davis household had taught me that courage was rare and precious. It got us through the tough stuff. Like Rolos and wit.*

"My episode," she resumed, "made me remember this box."

Strange—it had made her forget everything else, at least for those first couple of hours.

I observed in silence as she lifted the lid off the box and rummaged around inside. It struck me that her hair had gotten grayer—much grayer—and I wondered when that had happened. She seemed older than her years, and for a very brief moment, I couldn't remember what had caused her premature aging. A framed photograph on the mantel slammed me with the answer. Jim Davis. Absent husband. Abusive father. Immortalized in a pewter frame. But Mom was unaware of the bitter nostalgia in my mind. She pulled from the box a stack of envelopes tied with a red ribbon, their edges yellowed by time but still intact.

"I want you to have these," she said.

"Mom . . ."

"Hush, Shelby."

Mom wasn't prone to giving orders, so I obeyed.

"While I was in the hospital . . ."

There was a strength to her voice, a purposefulness I'd seldom heard before. She was trying to be bold, for one of the few times in her life. I found it disconcerting.

"While I was in the hospital, I had a lot of time to think."

What with the being catatonic and all.

"And I remembered this box. And . . ." She blinked hard to disarm her tears. "Shelby, I want you to have these. And the rest of the things in here." She put down the letters and took from the box a dried rose, a blue garter, and a handful of dog-eared pictures. "I need you to promise me that you'll keep them."

"Mom, what are they?"

"Even if I die, you promise me you'll keep them."

There was something in her eyes that frightened me. Where they had been a bit befuddled moments before, they were now laser clear—focused and demanding and damning.

I pulled my chair closer to hers and took the stack of letters from her lap. The ribbon gave easily, like it had been undone before, and I glanced through the envelopes. They were addressed alternately to Jim Davis and Gail Sanders. As I fanned through them, the scent of White Shoulders, like wisps of memory, drifted up to me. It was the aroma of young love and middle-aged heartbreak, of tentative hope and obliterated dreams.

"You and Dad?"

"Five months of correspondence while he was still in the Navy."

"And the pictures?"

"The two of us when we were young. Dancing at the prom, water-skiing, our engagement party . . ."

She held the stack of pictures out to me, but I shook my head and moved back in my chair. "Mom, I'm not sure I'm the right—"

"He was your father, Shelby. And the man I loved. And if you don't keep these, no one will know him after I'm dead."

There was a stubborn set to her chin and, again, that obstinacy in her gaze. This meant enough to her that she was willing to fight for it—and I'd never really seen my mother fight for anything before. It made me angry.

"Why do you want to keep these, Mom? What difference does it make if everyone forgets him?"

"He was my husband."

"He was a jerk."

"He—was—my—husband."

I was stunned. "Yes, Mom, your abusive husband. Your screaming, offensive, and brutal husband. I should know—he was my father too."

"But he was a good man once," she said, pleading. She shoved the sheaf of letters toward me. "Read these, Shelby. Read them and tell me that he wasn't once kind and romantic and—"

"I don't want to read them, Mom."

"Then look at the pictures. They're—"

"Mom, no."

"He was another person once. He was good enough for me to love him, Shelby. He was funny and engaging and . . ."

The lights seemed to dim as the walls around me regurgitated their embedded memories. My dad's voice crashed across the stillness, his words slashing at my fragility with sadistic precision. His savagery overwhelmed my defenses and annihilated the child in me once more, reducing her to an empty shell, swollen with bravado but translucent in her pain and helplessness. I felt the room tilt a little as my mind fell deeper into the remembered vortex of a merciless destruction, a calculated obliteration of all that was strong and soft and yearning in me.

When my mom pushed up to the edge of her chair and covered my hand with her own, it was all I could do not to fling it away along with the letters I still held and the nauseating powerlessness crushing the resolve from my courage.

I rose and moved to the window across the room, the letters falling like dead leaves from my hand to the blue carpet. I stared at the tree where Trey and I had swung as children, and I tried to remember the happy moments but found them all marred by my father's contempt. I breathed—and in breathing found solace. I was still alive, despite his murderous rages. He hadn't destroyed me.

"It wasn't entirely his fault—the way he was," my mom said quietly, her voice a little raspy. "His father was a drunk who abandoned the family when he was nine. How was he supposed to know how to be a good parent to you?"

I shrugged. There were no valid excuses.

"He grew up poor. Had to work hard—too hard for a boy his age. But he made it to college, got a good job, started his own business. . . . He made sure you and Trey would never be as poor as he was."

"Hurray for Dad."

"He tried, Shelby. It . . . it just wasn't in him to be sensitive."

"His problems went well beyond insensitivity, Mom."

"Yes," she conceded. "They did. But— "

"And whether he was raised by a drunk or by a pack of wolves, it was still him shoving me into the wall of that kitchen," I said, pointing at the kitchen door, "his hands around Trey's neck, and his voice reducing you to . . . to this!"

She lowered her gaze as I motioned toward her with my arm, presenting the human incarnation of my father's degradation. She was a fragile woman, broken by age and devastated by her marriage to a tyrant, yet as toxic as the memories were, she wouldn't allow them to alter her devotion to the man who had destroyed her. Her willingness to look past my father's sins was revolting to me. I'd tried that too, even long after he left, but I was beyond it now. He deserved no mercy or extenuation from me.

I turned to the window and tried to wrestle my mind back into the present, away from the images and sensations suffusing the air of this house that still smelled of my father's maleficence.

I stayed there, looking out, until the chaos in my mind receded, saying nothing until I was sure I could speak without harm to the woman whose life had been as scarred as mine, but whose heart didn't appear to have been as hardened.

"Sit down, Shelby. Please."

I turned reluctantly and went back to my mother. She held the letters I had discarded, her knuckles white with strain, her eyes overflowing with tears.

"I know how much he hurt you," she said, grasping my hand with her birdlike fingers and leaning close to look into my face. "And I know he nearly killed your brother. . . ."

"Then why remember him, Mom? For a stack of letters that only prove that he used to be able to fake being human? For a bunch of pictures that only prove that you used to be beautiful and feminine and . . . and strong before he broke you?" I reached into the box and pulled out the dried rose, dusty and brown and impossibly weightless. "For this, Mom? For a dead flower? Why should I want to remember the man whose imprint on my life has been nothing but shame—and pain—and brokenness?"

I wasn't sure when I'd crushed the rose. I hadn't meant to. One minute it was in my hand, held up for my mom to see, and the next . . . the next it was reduced to splinters on my palm. Disintegrated. Dust.

My mom took my hand and brushed the remains into hers, holding them like fragile flakes of all of us. "This flower," she said, "this rose—your father gave it to me the day Trey was born." She took a feeble, uneven breath and said, "Your father gave me you, Shelby. He gave me you and Trey. And to erase him—" she looked at the letters and pictures and garter—"to erase him would be to erase you."

I nodded. She leaned forward to brush a tear from my cheek.

"So I have to remember him, Shelby. I have to remember that the person who created you was not all bad—not all cruel. He was a troubled man. I know that. But he was part of you. I can't deny his legacy without denying you." She replaced the letters and pictures in the box, then sprinkled the rose's ashes over them. "Will you remember him, Shelby, please? Please remember him—for me."

❋ ❋ ❋

Shayla and I spent our first Christmas morning together opening the presents we'd wrapped and set under our hideously decorated tree. The tree had become something of a bone of contention, as Shayla was of a more contemporary-slash-chaotic decorating school and I had graduated summa cum laude from the International School of Anal-Retentive Christmas Tree Design. I liked things symmetrical and matching. Shayla liked things random and clashing. I liked things classy and she liked them homemade with a pair of kitchen scissors and a bunch of out-of-ink markers. We were polar opposites when it came to trimming trees, and the end result proved it.

Every night when Shayla went to bed, I'd sneak around the tree and rearrange things just so, and every morning when she got out of bed, Shayla would boldly march up to the tree and put things back exactly as they'd been. Which led me to conclude that there had to be some kind of rhyme and reason to her artistic deviance.

When we opened the presents—my gift from Shayla was a clothespin hot pad she had made at kindergarten—I gathered up my courage and talked with Shay about her dad. It wasn't the first conversation we'd had about him, but he had died just before

Christmas last year, and it felt important to acknowledge him that day.

"Do you remember what you used to do for Christmas with your dad?"

She squinted a little, trying to remember. "We had a twee," she said.

"Did he give you presents?"

Vigorous nod. "My blue wabbit."

"That's right! That came from him, didn't it."

"It used to be pwettier, but it's still soft."

"It's really soft, Shayla. Because you've loved it so much, probably." Her eyes veiled with melancholy, and I drew her in, planting a kiss on her temple and holding her close. "What else do you remember about your dad?"

"He was funny," she said.

Funny. The man I had known had been anything but funny. But I was thankful all the way down to the bottom of my emotional scars that Shayla had been loved by this father I couldn't imagine, this man who had given her bunnies and made her laugh.

"Do you still miss him a lot?" I asked a little reluctantly.

"I miss his Wondoh Bwead," she said, and I could tell by the unsteady breath she took that she missed more than that.

"It feels sad to not have your daddy anymore, doesn't it?" I tried to picture another man when I said *daddy* so the images of Jim Davis in my mind wouldn't interfere with my compassion.

"Uh-huh." Her chin puckered a little bit and her eyes welled with tears.

"Maybe we should draw a picture and leave it under the tree for him. Would you like that?"

She turned her watery blue gaze on me and nodded eagerly—gratefully.

"It can be your Christmas present for him, okay?"

She was already heading for the dining room table, where she liked to draw.

"What do you want to draw for him?" I asked, going to the box next to the couch where we kept her paper and crayons.

"A volcano," she said without hesitation. And she did just that in the minutes that followed, giving special care to the lava that flowed from the mountain's red peak. When she'd finished the drawing, she recruited my help to write *For Daddy* at the top. My hand shook as I spelled out the words in green block letters. *D-a-d-d-y.*

We hung the drawing from the lowest branch of the tree and propped Shayla's blue rabbit next to it. It was her way of thanking him, I guessed. For the rabbit. For the Wonder Bread. For the love.

❧ ❧ ❧

Christmas afternoon at the Johnsons' was a down-home family affair, complete with a perfectly prepared meal, an exquisitely decorated tree, and the kind of general cheer that radiated a warm glow. Scott, who had been invited to the celebration long before our falling-out, arrived shortly after we did. We'd met a couple of times in the intervening days, always with polite reserve. The first time had been at church on the day following our Christmas tree purchase, and Scott had deliberately approached me, concern on his face.

"Are you okay, Shelby?"

"I'm okay, Scott. Thank you."

He'd turned to leave but changed his mind. "If you need anything—you know, like your tree falls over or something—just give me a call."

I'd thanked him again and watched him go. Shayla, on her way back from her Sunday school class, had launched herself at him, showing him her Noah's ark drawing with pride. He'd smiled and complimented her, then kissed the top of her head and walked into the sunlight, headed home.

And now, we both sat in the Johnsons' living room nursing glasses of Christmas punch as Shayla played with her new German-speaking doll and Bev and Gus scurried around the kitchen putting the final touches on our meal.

Scott was trying his hardest to diffuse the tension by making conversation, but I could tell it was putting a strain on him. I'd hurt him, and I wasn't sure he understood why. But I wanted him to know that I hadn't dismissed him—erased him from our lives. I glanced at Shayla, who was so engrossed with her doll that she was oblivious to anything else, and gathered some courage.

"We've missed you around." As conversation starters went, it was pretty lame. I rolled my eyes and saw his smile deepen. "What I'm trying to say is that I'm sorry we've seen less of you."

"Yeah? I am too."

I felt a sigh shoving its way to the surface and held it down. "I don't know how to do this," I said earnestly, searching for the right words. "What I said the other night—it's true. And I can't change any of it. But . . . but I don't know how to do this anymore."

"How to do what?"

"How to go back to being friends after . . . after what you said—and what I said."

His eyes connected more intently with mine. "You still want to be friends?"

"I . . ." I hesitated. There would be safety in cutting off all contact, and yet . . . "Yes—of course I do."

He looked at me consideringly, weighing his response. "After what happened the other night," he finally said, "it might be hard to go back to the way things were."

"Scott, if I could . . . If I could, I'd—"

I saw traces of frustration in his expression when he interrupted. "Why can't you?"

"It's . . . complicated."

I tried to say with my eyes what I couldn't articulate, but he was looking away, lost in his own thoughts.

A silence stretched thin before he spoke again. "I should have waited—been more sure we were both on the same page before I—"

"Wait. Scott, you can't take the blame for this—"

"I should have given it more thought before just blurting it out."

"It's my fault too. I should have been . . . I should have been clearer—sooner."

He didn't contradict my statement. "Well . . ." He paused. "At least we know what we're dealing with now."

"Yes."

"And I guess that's a good thing," he said, expelling a breath.

"I hope so."

He rubbed his hands over his face and shifted in his chair, leaning forward with his elbows on his knees. "And since we're the same people we were a week ago—and those people were friends . . ."

"Maybe we can still be?" I offered hopefully.

He stretched his neck, side to side, and I heard two pops. "We can try," he said. "I mean, we're both grown-ups, right?"

I hesitated on that one. "Sure. We're both grown-ups."

"So we just . . . try to make it happen, I guess. I put the lid back on what I talked about, and—"

"Can you?"

The look he gave me teemed with emotions I didn't dare identify. He sighed and shook his head. "I'm not sure," he said, "but I'll give it a shot."

I bit my lip and looked at Shayla, grateful for this man who saw beyond his own pain and embarrassment enough to stay our friend. "Okay," I said with a smile, and there was relief in the word—more than I'd expected.

The smile he returned was kind and sincere and slightly strained. It tore a little at my resolve. "So, here we are," he said. "How do we start this thing?"

I shook my head in amazement at his kindness. "First, we thank God that people like you don't hold grudges."

"He'll be happy to hear about it. It's a new skill I'm working on."

I realized at that moment how difficult this was for him. For a man as confident and driven as he was to admit defeat and allow ongoing contact was a testament to the goodness of his heart.

"And then what?" he asked, sitting up straighter as if preparing for a challenge.

"Well . . ." I racked my brain. "I tell you about my David Hasselhoff fantasies and you tell me about . . . I don't know. What kind of skeletons do you have in your closet?"

He thought hard and I could see a lightness coming back into his expression. "Well, there's the high school prom where I stage-dived into a crowd of adoring fans without warning and they all moved out of my way. I broke a tooth."

"What were you doing diving off a stage?"

"I was in the band."

I raised an eyebrow.

"Guitarist. For—" he made a gesture like he was reading a marquee—"the Raging Atoms."

"The Raging Atoms."

"We were science geeks. And my parents threatened to ground me if we went with our first choice for a name."

"The Raging Test Tubes?"

"The Raging Hormones."

"That would probably have been more accurate."

"Probably."

I smiled at him and felt new buoyancy attenuating the bleakness in my mind. "So—now that we've emptied out our closets, wanna go see if Bev and Gus need help?"

"You haven't told me about David Hasselhoff yet," he said as we headed out of the living room.

"That's a conversation best had after a couple mugs of well-spiked eggnog."

"Cheater."

"Raging Atom." I halted him with a hand to his arm. "Thank you, Scott," I said, my voice soft, sincere. "I . . ." Would it muddy the waters to tell him I needed him? Probably. So I shook my head and kept it to myself as I led the way into the dining room, feeling happy-sad in a mustard-yellow kind of way.

Gus had just placed the largest, most beautiful turkey in the middle of the table when we entered the room, and Bev was busy pouring the drinks.

"Don't mind the draft," she said, nodding toward the open window. "We're getting rid of the burned-Tupperware smell."

"Been helping around the kitchen again, haven't you, Gus?" Scott said.

"She loves me for my slicing skills, but she could do without the rest."

"No one feels sorry for you, Gus," I said without a trace of sympathy.

"Better get Shayla in here," Bev said. "The turkey's getting goose bumps."

"Shayla! We're eating!"

"Not yet," came a stubborn voice from the other room.

"Shayla—now."

"Wait a minute, Mom!"

For a moment, I wasn't sure what had happened. I'd been about to use hollow threats to get Shay into the dining room when it dawned on me that no one else was moving anymore. Bev was frozen in midpour. Gus was staring at me with his trademark Santa Claus grin, and Scott had something that looked suspiciously like deep emotion in his eyes.

"Did I miss something?"

Bev put down her pitcher and looked at me with a smile that was warmth and victory and relief and love all rolled into one. "She called you Mom," she whispered.

My heart did a jig. "What?"

"She called you Mom."

I looked at Scott for confirmation, and he just beamed his dimpled joy at me.

"I missed it!" I wailed.

"Call her again!" This from Gus, his twinkling eyes alight.

I cleared my throat and tried to sound convincing. "Shayla, come here now!"

And from the other room, right on cue, my sweet, strong-willed child answered, with frustration in her voice, "But Mom . . . !"

I covered my gaping mouth with my hand and looked wide-eyed at Scott. He crossed the room and whispered, "She called you Mom, Shell," and wrapped me in a hug.

In more ways than one, I felt like I'd finally, perfectly come home.

❋ ❋ ❋

The canopy hung too low, weighed down by time and dust. The pillows were moth-eaten and smelled of abandonment. Fibers were coming out of the rug we lay on in little tufts of red and black and gray. Our Huddle Hut was decomposing before our eyes.

"You think maybe we've outgrown it?" Trey lay on his side picking at a bag of peanuts, his head too close to the sagging sheet above us. Even the quality of our snacks had deteriorated. And when snacks deteriorated in my life, I knew an ending was beginning.

Trey's legs extended well past the edges of the sheet and he looked scrunched up, somehow—a giraffe trying to fit into an African hut.

"Yeah. I think maybe we've outgrown it."

I was lying on my side facing Trey, head propped on hand, trying to absorb all the fragments and nuances of this ritual that had grown out of our fear and need. There was nothing salutary in the dusty sheet above us, nor in the Christmas lights, nor in the filtered sun petering in from the single attic window. And yet . . . this place had nursed our wounds and buffered our resilience and bolstered our resistance. It had mothered our survival in ways I couldn't fathom.

This was our last visit to the Huddle Hut. Mom had now had a series of ministrokes, and she needed to live in a smaller place, with emergency care nearby—just in case. So Trey and I had come over this afternoon to pack up the last of her things before the movers came tomorrow. The past weeks had been a slogging journey through mountains of accumulated life-fragments—shelf-fulls of LPs, and closet-fulls of outdated clothes, both hers and his, and drawer-fulls of everyday junk, and cabinet-fulls of china and silver and crystal and pewter. We'd finally had to send Mom to her new apartment, ostensibly to clean it, in order for us to box up and dispose of the inordinate amount of irrelevance—physical and metaphysical—she so desperately wanted to keep.

We'd even cleared out the attic, tossing a dumpster-load of garbage from which we'd rescued only a few old toys and a pair of fifty-year-old roller skates. Trey thought he might be able to get something for them on eBay.

And here we lay in an attic empty save for the Huddle Hut, contemplating the shrunkenness and fragility of the structure that once had felt so grand and safe. Trey rolled onto his back and dropped a fistful of peanuts, one by one, into his mouth. I hadn't seen him grow up, but in this intimate refuge from our childhood trauma, he suddenly seemed old and strong and calm. My sensitive, fragile brother had deepened into a prevailer who excelled as an "apprenti-chef" in a French restaurant in St. Charles, led his own support group, helped in a homeless shelter, spent time with a handful of good friends who shared his priorities and views about life, and still, somehow, found time to be with me. I was glad to see him developing relationships with so many others, mostly because he'd devoted his entire childhood to just us. And it was good to hear him talk about seeing places and living adventures and investing in people when he'd spent so many years hiding from the outside world because of the stigmas of Davishood. But on this final afternoon on Summer Lane, it was just the two of us lying uncomfortably in our deteriorating hut and contemplating life. That much hadn't changed.

"You think she'll be okay?"

I pictured Mom in her new, bright apartment and had no doubt. "Once she gets over having to part with, oh, a couple tons of her most treasured junk."

"She couldn't take it all."

"She couldn't take a fraction of it, Trey. This place was a Salvation Army warehouse."

"Speaking of the Salvation Army, you need to go to your senior formal."

"Who told you?"

"None of your business."

"And what does the Salvation Army have to do with my formal?"

"Uh—nothing. Just trying to make a smooth segue."

"Yeah?"

"Old dog—new trick. So tell me about the price of fried okra in Louisiana."

I gave him my have-you-lost-your-mind? look, but he didn't see it; he was still dropping peanuts into his mouth.

"Just joking," he said. "Tell me about your shindig."

"Not much to tell. I'm not going."

"And you're not going because . . . ?"

"Because I'm twenty-two years old and there's more to starting a new life than dressing up like Taffeta Barbie and spending the night being cut in half by my support hose."

"You're not fat and your hair is fine."

"I didn't say anything about my hair."

"Just covering all the bases."

"Besides, Keith wants to take me, and I'd rather get stuck under the limo and dragged three miles."

"Keith's a good guy."

"Keith's a great guy. For someone like Kay Schuler."

"Because . . . ?"

"Because she'd jump at the chance to be his date to the formal and his bride and the mother of his one-point-eight children."

"One-point-eight?"

"It's the national average. Read a little, will you?"

"See, here's the deal. Keith asked you to the formal. Period. I'm pretty sure he didn't have church bells and national averages in mind."

"Yeah, but, you know. One thing leads to another and the next thing you know . . ."

"What? You're happily married and trying to figure out how to fit a standard diaper around your point-eight child?"

"Yeah. Something like that."

"Well, pardon my bluntness, but you're an idiot."

"Gee, thanks, Trey."

"Go to the formal, Shell."

"And then what?"

"And then come home from the formal. What's got you so spooked?"

I marked a pause and tried to figure out how not to sound juvenile when I answered the question. "I think he likes me," I said. Yup. Juvenile.

"Tell me where he lives and I'll go beat him up."

"It makes things weird."

"Weird how?"

"Weird none-of-your-business."

"Shell."

"I don't want . . . I don't want to be liked. There. Happy?"

"Because . . . ?"

"Oh, for pete's sake, eat a peanut."

Trey turned to face me. "Because if he starts to like you . . ."

I sighed. "Because if he starts liking me, there's a good chance he'll stop—someday. Or realize he never really did. And then he might—you know—be mean to my one-point-eight children."

"So you'd rather grow old ungracefully in a cat-infested apartment, eating donuts and watching your girdle stretch into oblivion, than maybe—just maybe—be loved by someone who isn't going to break your heart and destroy your children."

"Uh, you lost me a little with the girdle part, but yeah, that's the general gist."

"You're an idiot."

"You're repeating yourself."

"Shell . . ."

"Besides, he's a hunter."

"So you're turning down his invitation to the formal because he kills rabbits?"

"No, stupid. Because he hunts on Sundays."

"Huh?"

"I'm holding out for a guy who goes to church on Sundays, Trey."

"You're weird."

"Yes."

"Really? About the church thing, I mean."

I nodded and looked at him with as much sincerity as I could muster. "If ever—and by ever, I mean probably never—but if ever I get relationship-tempted by a guy, I want him to be accountable to the Big Man. I'm just hedging my bets in case, you know, the church bells and national average thing."

"You want it."

"I do not."

"Go to the formal, Shell."

"Eat another peanut, Trey."

17

Chaos had overtaken the auditorium. And not the *Steel Magnolias* variety of chaos with the wedding and the dog and the squawking Ouiser. This was the Armageddon variation on the theme. All that was missing was a colossal asteroid hurtling toward the earth. What was hurtling, instead, was the school play, and it was aimed right at a three-week deadline that had me losing sleep. Big time.

A wonderful lady by the name of Nancy had signed on to do costumes for us, and I was pretty sure the process was going to put us all over the edge. It wasn't so much the time it took out of our rehearsals as the sheer impossibility of forcing teenage boys hyped up on adrenaline into too-tight slacks with high waistlines, à la Oxford circa 1953. They whined and haggled and generally gave sweet, patient Nancy a hard time. The girls in the cast, amazingly, just did what they were told and got back to work. My divas were half the trouble of my divos.

Not only did we now have to contend with costuming interfering with our play rehearsals, but the sets committee had installed themselves in the cafeteria space just outside the auditorium as well, like there was no other place in the school for them to paint and drill and quibble about perspective. The downside of our space-sharing was the added noise and distraction. The upside, however, was the fact that my just-friend Scott had become the official carpenter in charge of designing and creating the stage's centerpiece—an oversize wardrobe whose doors would open as if by magic on a specific cue in the middle of our performance. He'd set up shop in a corner of the cafeteria and, now that our rehearsals were going later, would often come by after his practices to fine-tune the mechanics and enhance the aesthetics of his creation.

I liked knowing he was there. I had to admit it. And I liked it when he'd wander in and say something positive about the scene we were doing or bring me a cup of coffee or ask me for some guidance with his building project. And I think he liked that we'd invite him to join us for supper during our extended rehearsals. The kids would banter with him and give him a hard time about the progress of his wardrobe, and every so often, when I'd glance in his direction, I'd catch his eyes on me. Speculative, sort of. Double axel without the lutz. It was a comfortable kind of flip.

We'd almost gone back to the way things had been before the toy museum and our relationship-defining talk. We still did things with Shayla like driving up to Hochblauen to watch hang gliders and going to the stork refuge in Holzen. That particular outing had been a bit traumatic, as we'd arrived just at feeding time and no one had warned us that the graceful, orange-legged birds immortalized by nursery rhymes ate live chicks for lunch! The stork-keeper had tossed a bucketful of chicks over the fence, and the storks had descended on them like murderous science-fiction monsters. Shayla had screamed and I had gagged and Scott had pretty much manhandled us both back to the car.

But Shayla wasn't always at the center of our outings. There were times when Scott could tell that I was teetering on the brink of being overwhelmed. On those occasions, he'd arrange for Bev to watch Shay and whisk me away to a rigorously just-friends dinner at a cozy art café like the Mezzo in nearby Müllheim. We'd sit at the table in the dimly lit interior, trying to keep our eyes from lingering on whatever nude paintings were hanging on the walls that week, and we'd talk about the weather, the sin nature of man, Shayla's progress in German, the sovereignty of God, my latest mini meltdowns—they were getting rarer—and relational evangelism. You know—typical missionary fare. Except for the part where I wondered what was wrong with me for keeping him at arm's length and the part where he looked at me like he thought I should be wondering what was wrong with me too.

Much as Shayla and I enjoyed his company, however, I'd tried to make Scott less of an automatic addition to our activities—just so his number one fan wouldn't think he was becoming a fixture of our little family. But as she had pointed out after we'd driven to Switzerland together on her fifth birthday so she could see the real Heidi mountain, "It's not as much fun without Scott!" And she was right, of course. It really wasn't. But we'd made the most of her special day anyway, visiting the small museum in Maienfeld and taking dozens of Heidi pictures of her as she frolicked, beaming, in a cow pasture in front of snowcapped peaks jutting into the sky. We'd decided on our way home that Scott would have loved our day in the Alps.

Meanwhile, opening night kept hurtling.

It was after a particularly taxing rehearsal that I received a call from Trey.

"You ready for this?" he asked without preamble.

"Depends on what 'this' is."

"Um . . . I just got a letter from Shay's mom—her birth mom. She sent it through Dana, addressed to you and me."

My breath caught and I felt the world tilt a little on its axis. I had visions of Shayla being taken away from me, being returned to the woman who had abandoned her so soon after her birth. "She wants her back?"

"No! Shell, no! And even if she did, she has no legal rights. You know that."

I felt a rush of relief. "What does she want?"

"Well, it appears she just heard about Dad's death and, out of the kindness of her heart and all, wanted to write us a sympathy letter."

"Really. What does she say?"

"Want me to read it?"

"Trey! Of course!"

"Okay. Here goes." There was a rustling of paper, then, "Ready?"

"No. But go ahead."

"'Dear Trey and Shelby, I was saddened to hear about your father's heart attack through a friend.'"

"Stop reading with a Southern accent, Trey. She lived in Michigan."

"Oh—right. I just picture trailer trash and the Southern accent comes out."

"You don't know she's trailer trash. Read."

"All right. Here goes. 'I know that you had no contact with Jim in the years after he moved out. I want you to know he often talked about you. Mostly with regret. He knew he'd done you harm.'"

"Warms the cockles of my heart."

"Want me to stop?"

"No." I heard him take a breath and blurted, "Yes!" before he could continue.

"Yes, you want me to stop, or—?"

"Can you just . . . I don't know, summarize it for me?"

"Listen, if it was more entertaining with the accent, I can—"

"It's not the accent." I wasn't sure what it was. "It just feels . . . I don't know. Too connected. I don't want to be connected to him again."

I could picture Trey doing his squinty confused look. He did that a lot when I got kooky.

"Okay," he said, like he'd decided to let this one slide. "So the summary is . . ." I could hear the paper rustling again. "Basically, she's sorry for our loss, she's glad Shay's with you, and she wants us to know that he tried to change."

"Tried? Not exactly a ringing endorsement."

"Nope. She sounds sincere enough, though. I mean, what did she have to gain from writing?"

"Thankfully, not her daughter." I was still getting over that fraction of a second when I'd thought she was suing to regain custody of Shayla.

"Makes me wonder what Shayla remembers of him," Trey said. "You think she ever saw the Godzilla in the guy?"

"All she ever says is that she misses him and he was funny."

"Really?"

"Yup."

"Not distant? Short-tempered? Violent?"

"Not exactly in a four-year-old's vocabulary, but no." I didn't like to admit it. "The first few months she was with me, I kept looking for signs that he'd hurt her."

"And?"

"Haven't found any yet."

"Maybe he was better with babies than with teenagers."

"Yeah, maybe."

We both pondered that for a moment—the fact that our brutal, ruthless father might actually have been kind in another life, in another fatherhood role, and genuinely so. It seemed impossible, yet the woman's letter had certainly hinted at a change.

Trey cleared his throat. "So this is the way I see it, Shell. If the original Jim Davis somehow managed to debastardize himself . . . you know . . . maybe, just maybe, those genes aren't as potent as we thought, and maybe we'll be okay. You know. In an I'm-not-going-to-turn-into-Hannibal-Lecter sorta way."

"You think?"

"Well, I wouldn't put a million bucks on it just yet, but I think it's a pretty good theory. You should give it a whirl and see if it's true."

"No, Trey, *you* should give it a whirl."

"Except that I'm married to my job."

"You're married to your bakery?"

"I'm married to my vocation as a wannabe French baker with a slightly Italian flair."

"And I'm married to my conviction that it's wiser and saner to play it safe rather than risk perpetuating the Davis family curse."

"Time for a divorce, babe. Take the leap. Teach a lesson to the guy who nearly strangled me to death and show him how parenting is done."

"That's asking a lot."

"You owe me a lot."

I had a brief vision of Scott sitting on my couch with his heart in his eyes, asking if it would be okay for him to pursue me. And fear curled into my stomach like a leaden, malevolent stain. "I'll think about it," I conceded.

"You do that, Shell. And don't take too long. You don't want him to go the way of the Keiths and Daves and Vinnies that came before him."

"He's on a different planet than any of those guys."

"A better one?"

"You have no idea."

"All the more reason."

"I'm hanging up now."

"Enjoy the muddlehood."

"Great help you are."

⌘ ⌘ ⌘

Joy was dying. The room was hushed and reverent as Seth and Kate, teenage actors who appeared too young to know the full weight of such a moment, brought the scene to such a powerful conclusion that none of us—not even the set crew—were unmoved. There was a simplicity to the scene that allowed for nuances so profound and intimate that Seth could pour the entirety of his pain into the lines, enrobing them with soul-purpose and heart-meaning.

"Still here?" Kate whispered, her voice somehow carrying to the back of the auditorium where I sat, script in hand, mind in England.

"Still here." Seth sat on the edge of her bed, his hands gentle on her arm, her face, her hair, his eyes so intent on her that it seemed he'd dimmed the world beyond her next breath.

"Go to bed. Get some sleep."

"Soon."

"Jack. Has it been worth it?"

"Three years of happiness?"

"Tell me you'll be all right."

"I'll be all right."

Kate shifted a little, slightly grimacing with pain. Seth helped her adjust on her pillow and brushed a strand of hair off her forehead. "Are you afraid?" he asked quietly.

"Of dying?"

"Yes."

"I'm tired, Jack." There was profound weariness in her voice. "I want to rest. I just don't want to leave you."

"I don't want you to go."

"Too much pain," she said, wincing.

"I know."

"Other worlds. It has to be more than we can imagine. Even more than you can imagine."

Seth nodded, clinging to that hope. "Far more." After a pause laden with reluctance, love, and loss, he added, "I don't know what to do, Joy. You'll have to tell me what to do."

"You have to let me go, Jack."

"I'm not sure that I can."

I rose from my seat, clearing my throat, and took a couple of steps toward the front of the room. I spoke softly, as if the ghosts of Joy and Lewis might be disturbed by anything louder. "That's all we have time for today, everyone. Thank you, Seth, Kate. Now go home, all of you. Do your homework. Get some sleep. In that order." I looked around at the faces of stressed and tired actors and wondered, not for the first time, how I'd been blessed with such a hardworking and devoted cast. "I'm so proud of you all."

There were some blushes and some thanks as the students gathered up their belongings and headed for the door. Meagan stayed behind to help me gather mine.

"You think they're doing okay?" she asked, handing me the to-do list I'd asked her to compile.

I smiled wearily. "I think they're doing great."

Her eyes traveled to the spot where the scene had just ended, and she shook her head in awe. "How do they do that?" Her Southern accent was enchanting. "I mean, did you see Seth? I think there were actual tears in his eyes!"

I shouldered my bag and started flipping off the lights. I didn't like talking about displays of emotion. "He's pretty amazing."

"'Specially when you consider how tough it was at the beginning. I mean, could you believe the stress between those two?"

It dawned on me, suddenly, that there had been a bit of a thaw lately in Seth and Kate's months-long awkward stage. "You're absolutely right, Meagan! What happened to them?"

"Don't you know?" She gave me a where-have-you-been? look that put me in my place.

"I've been a little preoccupied, Meagan."

"Well, the way I heard it is that the two of them finally started to mouth off at each other one day after practice. Kate kept yelling at him that he was a wuss and he kept telling her that she was too bossy and they finally just got madder and took off."

"And that solved the problem?" The warped minds of teenagers. I locked the auditorium door behind me and headed through the foyer to the double doors that led outside.

"It only made things worse!"

I needed to get to Bev's and pick up Shayla, and this story was keeping me from my daughter.

"So . . . ?"

"So they went to the kebab place the next day and were in the middle of duking it out—you know, for the sake of the play and all—and right in the middle of this major argument, Seth says something like, 'It's because I like you, okay?' And then she went all Helen Keller and stuff."

"Helen Keller?"

"Like, quiet."

Right. I was fascinated. "How do you know all this, Meagan?"

"Jenny was sitting at the table next to them. She told me all about it." She took a quick breath and rushed on. "And then Kate went all ballistic and stuff, but then she had to admit that she liked him too."

"Wait a minute," I said. "Are you telling me that Seth and Kate were acting like kooks this whole time because they *like* each other?"

"Yup. This whole time." She was walking with me toward my car, which was the opposite direction from the van waiting to take her home to her dorm. "And then, once they told each other it was like, *poof!* And now they're fine. And they're acting great too, so that's good news for the play 'cause it's only, like, three weeks away."

I laughed. "Well, thanks for catching me up on the news, Meagan."

"No problem!" She stood there nodding at me, happy as a lark that she'd been the one to tell me the story.

I took her by the shoulders and turned her physically toward the van. "See those lights over there?"

She nodded.

"That's your van." I put on an ominous voice. "Go to the light, Meagan."

She giggled and did a zombie walk for a bit.

18

Shayla was licking cookie dough off a set of beaters when I got to the Johnsons'. She seemed in no hurry to go home, so I sat down at the kitchen table and debriefed my day with Bev. When I got through telling her about the Seth and Kate transformation, she seemed to have nothing to say.

"Isn't that amazing?" I prodded. "I mean, that they've been so uptight about something good that they've made it uncomfortable for everyone else—including themselves."

Bev made a production of washing up her mixing bowl and measuring cups. "People can be silly that way," she said.

"Silly is a bit of an understatement. If your feelings for someone get in the way of your other obligations, you're better off just blurting it out and putting everyone else out of *your* misery."

"Uh-huh. Couldn't have said it better myself."

I crossed my arms and tried to figure out what my suddenly enigmatic friend was talking—or not talking—about. At the table, Shayla shoved not one, but two whole cookies into her mouth, distracting me from the pondering at hand.

"Shayla! What are you doing?"

I think she tried to say, "Eating cookies," but it came out sounding like an ancient Germanic dialect, accompanied by a virtual meteor shower of cookie bits. Bev lunged for her dishcloth, Shayla started to giggle, and I made a mental note to tell Scott about the incident when I saw him at school tomorrow.

It was at that precise moment that the sky opened up and God—sounding a lot like George Burns, actually—bellowed something like, *"Get a grip, Shelby! You're wasting daylight here!"* I figured it would have been disrespectful and dangerous to point out that it was actually closer to nighttime, what with the Big Guy's ability to zap people from heaven and all.

To be completely honest, the sky didn't actually open and there's a good chance George Burns was only in my mind—sharing billing with George Clooney, perhaps—but I was struck with a truth so clear and so urgent that there was no avoiding the corresponding action. My rejection of Scott's pursuit hadn't prevented anything. He was *already* a part of my life. He was *already* the person I wanted to tell about Shayla's misbehavior, the person I wanted to make laugh, the person whose opinion mattered more to me than anyone else's. He was *already* anchored in my life, and the thought of losing him to my desperate independence was intolerable.

I left Bev standing at the sink and set off toward Scott's apartment in a haze of revelation and resolve, but I hadn't made it halfway there before my courage began to wear thin. Thirty-five years of disclaimers and denials were squawking in my mind like the Aflac duck.

I'd done my job well, as the daughter of a tyrant. I'd learned all the lessons and internalized them to such a degree that they had become part of my emotional landscape, a landscape littered with the corpses of aborted and abandoned desires, of stifled needs and evaded longings, of emotional calluses so thick and deep and embedded that I feared nothing short of surgical intervention would remove them. An image of God as the Great Physician popped into my mind and I wondered if he'd answer just this one prayer, if he would give me just this one moment to reclaim a bit of the woman he had intended me to be—pre–Jim Davis, pre-maiming, pre-survival.

I walked down the silent, rain-burnished streets with a growing urge both to flee and to prevail, my steps emboldened by a sudden consciousness of need, my strides restricted by a fear of scorned endeavors and disemboweled hopes. My dread deepened as my urgency increased, and I longed in a flash for the return of the woman I'd been just moments before, whose rejection of risk had yielded a stable, predictable, safe, and stunted life. But in that instant when realization had dawned in a spray of crumbled cookie, when my mind had finally understood my heart and seen the stranglehold of my past on my future—in that moment I'd become too certain to hesitate. I was Seth and Kate encased in self-denial. I was Trey, my protector, shackled by his scars. I was my father, my tormentor, enslaved by his own terrors. I was my mother's helplessness. I was my future's emptiness. I was all I had pledged and purposed to abhor.

My turmoil must have showed on my face when Scott opened his door, because the smile that was growing there froze, then dissipated. He ushered me through the entryway into his apartment, and I sank gratefully onto his couch. My limbs felt flaccid. My breathing was short and shallow. My hands were cold—stiff and shaking. But my head was clear. For the first time in a very long time, my head was clear.

Scott sat at the other end of the couch, his gaze intense, cautious. I took in my surroundings, knowing they would reflect their owner's heart. The space was tidy, though not immaculate by any means. There were a few dirty dishes in the sink, a coat slung over the back of a chair, papers strewn over the dining room table, and shoes lying where they'd been kicked off. The furniture was sturdy and modest, the dark leather couch well-worn and needing care. This was a soothing space—warm, masculine, restful.

"Are you—?"

"I need to say something," I interrupted, too scared of faltering to waste any time. "And it might take a while, so . . ."

He smiled a little confusedly but nodded his agreement. There would be no censure here.

"I am Jim Davis's daughter," I began, linking my fingers to stop them from shaking. And the story unfolded from there, carried on the ebbs and flows and lashes of a past mired in the sinking sand of shame. I didn't hold back—there was no use in that—as I carefully unwrapped the soiled and sordid, tattered shreds of who I was. He heard about the violence, the maiming words, the threats, the abuse. He heard about the Huddle Hut, the hospital, the car, and the abuse. He heard about the pancakes, the zucchini, the ties . . . and the abuse. He heard about it all. Right up to Shayla. I faltered at that hurdle.

"The reason I'm telling you all of this," I said, when the lumbering, restorative tidal wave had passed, "is that I want you to understand who I am."

His eyes hadn't left me. I'd felt them on me from beginning to end, though I hadn't looked at him very much. I'd spoken with determination, with the kind of focus and resolve that had dimmed my senses and sapped my strength. I felt wrung out.

"I don't know what to say."

I was grateful for that. Any platitudes would have cheapened my vulnerability.

"Is your dad still alive?" There was a trace of anger in his gentleness.

I shook my head. "Only his legacy." And this is where my words ran out. How could I . . . ? What would I . . . ?

"I guess you're . . . a miracle," he said, and I could tell he was choosing his words carefully. "That someone as—" he paused—"*good* as you could come from him. And be so different from him."

"You're basing that assessment on limited experience."

"On consistent behavior."

"You don't see behind closed doors."

"Is there anything to see?"

I shook my head. "Not yet. But sometimes . . . sometimes I wonder if it's just going to hit me one day. If something unimportant will happen and I'll just . . ."

"I've had a lot of time to observe you, Shell. With Shayla. With the students. I have never seen a trace of the man you describe."

"Maybe it'll turn up tomorrow."

"And maybe it won't."

I scratched at my scalp with my fingertips. There was a headache coming on.

"You're so good with the students. And with Shayla. Shelby, you're more patient with that child sometimes than she deserves."

"But on the inside," I said. "On the inside there are times when I just want to shake her." Tears were coming, and I covered my mouth to mask my trembling lips. "And sometimes I just want to yell—to yell at her to be quiet or stop whining or straighten up or just obey the first time for once!"

"True confession?"

"You're turning me in to social services?"

"No—but I've had the same thoughts as you a few times."

"With Shayla?"

He nodded.

"No way. You're always so calm with her."

"Remember when she threw that tantrum at the McDonald's in Basel? It was all I could do not to sling her over my shoulder and find the nearest fountain to dump her in."

I didn't know whether to laugh or be worried. "You wanted to dunk her?"

"Dunk her. Yell at her. Shake her."

I gave him a disbelieving look.

"Sorry," he said, hands up in concession, "it looks like I'm as warped as you. The good news is, neither of us has done anything to act on it."

"But you don't have my heritage."

He sighed. "Nope. I'm the son of a business owner and a beauty consultant—which means my flaws are probably being dictatorial and wearing too much blush."

I had to laugh. "You're one of the few men I know who knows what blush is."

"Don't assume that your legacy is all bad, Shelby," he said with so much conviction that I wanted to believe him. "There might even be something good that comes from it someday."

I took a deep, calming breath. "There already is."

"Really?"

"Shayla." It was out. "She's my father's daughter, Scott. She's my half sister."

He shook his head as if he were doubting his senses. "I've thought of a lot of scenarios, but . . . not this one." He looked bemused. "How . . . how did it happen?"

"Oh, you know, the usual way. Man abandons wife and children. Man meets much younger other woman—not necessarily in that order. Man has baby with much younger woman. Woman abandons baby. Man raises baby. Man dies. Grown daughter inherits baby. You know—the usual way."

"And her mother was . . . ?"

"Gone. Uninterested in being a mom. She gave up her rights when Shayla was a baby."

"Shelby, I . . ." He couldn't find the words. And I couldn't blame him.

"I know. It took me a while to wrap my mind around it too."

"And now?"

"And now she's mine. I am the guardian of my dad's illegitimate child. Call the soap opera people—this is a winner."

"Shelby."

"The problem is, I love her. And no matter how much I tell myself that she can't be the daughter of the man who raised me, that there's no way I could love her so much if she was . . . I just can't help it." I laughed a little bitterly. "How ironic is it that the greatest gift of my life came from him? And after he'd died, at that."

"He knew what he was doing. You're the best mother she could hope for."

"He didn't know me at all. The last time he saw me, I was lying on the couch with a sprained wrist, a scraped face, and a bump on my head. I was cowed. And probably being funny. That's the standard Davis Junior response to anything unpleasant like, say, having the tar beat out of you."

"And yet . . ."

"And yet he left her to me. The daughter he apparently loved with the daughter he clearly despised." Unwanted tears blurred my vision. "And the real kicker is, if I'm going to love her, I'm going to be forever linked—and indebted—to my dad."

"You already do."

"So I already am."

He shook his head again. "I don't know what to say."

"So you've said."

A brimming silence settled between us. At some time during the course of our conversation, Scott had moved a little closer to me on the couch. His arm was stretched across the backrest, not touching me, but there was comfort in the gesture, a protectiveness and companionship I'd missed until now. After a long moment in which we'd both been lost in thought, he cleared his throat and said, "What made you come over here tonight, Shelby?"

It was a valid question—what with never having been inside his apartment before and having avoided any deeply personal conversations for some time. The face of Colonel Klink appeared in my mind, as German as *Schnitzel und Pommes*, commanding, *"You vill say vat you came to say, Shelby. You vill say it now."* And with such a gentle invitation to disclosure, what was a woman to do?

"I wanted you to know more about me—about my dad and stuff—because I wanted you to understand how I've been acting since . . . since you've known me, really."

He smiled.

"I've been scared. Actually, I was scared at the beginning, and then when we became just good friends, I was less scared. And then when we bought the Christmas tree and the hand-holding and stuff, it felt good and just . . . normal. But when you asked about, you know, pursuing me—I panicked. There's no other word for it. I just panicked. I've never wanted a relationship—I've never wanted to be pursued. And the truth is, I'm pretty sure I'd be really bad at both of those. There are a lot of things that scare me in this world, Scott, and most of them have to do with exactly what you seem to want."

"What scares you so much about being pursued?"

"Oh, you know . . . everything."

A smile deepened on his face, and there was something optimistic in his eyes.

"So just in case I go a little crazy on you again—this way you'll know why. Not that I'm planning on it, but . . ."

"What are you saying, Shell?"

I stopped fidgeting and took a long moment to look him in the eyes. I decided I liked his eyes. They made me feel brave. "What I'm saying," I said in a mock-annoyed tone, "is that you're welcome to pursue me if you still want to."

He imitated my mock annoyance and said, "Oh, well, fine then. I'll pursue you, okay?"

"Really?" It was the six-year-old voice again—the one that showed up when I didn't dare hope for something.

"Shelby."

"But I can't promise anything," I added hastily. "I can't promise that I'll be any good at . . . at anything. Or that this will become something serious. Or—"

"I'm not looking for promises."

"And there's a good chance you'll realize I'm not what you thought I was, and you need to know that that's okay. Just tell me, and . . . and I'll get out of your hair. Because I know I'm not, well, normal. Not where stuff like this is concerned and . . . and that's all." I took a deep breath. "For now."

"Done?"

"One more thing." I paused, taking the time to reduce my swirling thoughts into words that would make sense to Scott. "I don't want you to think that I'm expecting you to fix me," I said, my breathing shallowed by the statement. "I mean, you don't need that kind of pressure, and I don't need that kind of dependence."

"What makes you think I'm capable of 'fixing' you?" he asked in a voice that held neither condemnation nor condescension. "I'm not here to change you or undo anything someone else has done to you. I'm here because I want to be near you and know you and, well, pursue you. So how 'bout I just concentrate on that and leave the fixing to God?"

I had a flash of certainty just then—as though God said, *"Maybe bringing someone like Scott into your life is just one small part of my plan for healing."*

I wanted to believe it. "You've got a deal," I said to Scott. "But," I added hurriedly, before the last shreds of my courage dissolved, "I really want you to know that it's okay if you decide you don't want to pursue me anymore. I mean, once you get to know me better, if you change your mind . . ."

"Shelby . . ."

"I'm serious, Scott. There have been some guys who . . . who *thought* they liked me. And then they didn't anymore. And that's just the way things go sometimes, so if you change your mind, just tell me."

"Did any of them ever keep liking you?"

"I don't know."

"You don't know?"

"I never stuck around long enough to find out."

"I see."

"So this is a bit of a new approach for me." I attempted a smile and found that it felt good.

"Well, here's to new approaches," Scott said with an answering smile as he pushed off the couch. "Wanna start with a cup of coffee?"

I was torn. "Actually, I left Shayla with Bev, and . . ."

He sighed and shook his head. "The downside of pursuing a woman who has a daughter."

"A half sister that I'm raising as my daughter."

"Your daughter, Shell. Take a look at yourself when you're with her."

I recognized his good intentions, but the statement struck me as odd. "How exactly does a person look at herself in your scenario?" I raised an eyebrow as I stood. "I mean, it's a good suggestion and all, but do I have to carry a mirror? Or just look at my bottom half? 'Cause from this vantage point," I said, looking down at my feet, "all I can see are shoes that need polishing and a couple of things in between."

He was laughing when he pulled me in for the kind of hug that had my blood singing "Zip-a-Dee-Doo-Dah." It was a really nice hug. I especially enjoyed the arms-around-me part, which made me feel a little like a roasted marshmallow squeezed between two yummy wafers. It was "lumpscious," to use one of Shayla's words. But my daughter was waiting for me at Bev's and it was way past her bedtime, so I levered myself away from Scott and did an awkward hair-tuck gesture. "I'd better be going."

"Yeah?"

The happiness in his eyes made my heart crinkle.

"Thank you for coming. Really."

Okay, so I've got to admit that the combination of the, well, affection in his gaze and the intimacy of his voice made my toes curl. Right there in my scuffed shoes, they curled up and sighed. All ten of them. It felt really strange, in a toe-sighing kind of way.

Scott walked me to the door and helped me on with the coat he'd retrieved from the couch. Then he took my hand and kissed my fingers. "I'm glad I get to pursue you," he said.

"Yeah? I'll let you know how I like being pursued."

"Is that a challenge?"

"Take it however you want, Coach Taylor."

"See you tomorrow?"

The thought of it made my blood launch into the second verse of "Zip-a-Dee-Doo-Dah."

"Yup. I'll be the girl with the stressed-out hair and the expanding waistline."

"I'll be the guy with the 'I'm pursuing an idiot' T-shirt."

"Good—then we should recognize each other."

I left his apartment and tried not to laugh out loud as I walked down Kandern's darkened streets. I did a Dorothy heel click instead.

⌘ ⌘ ⌘

The funeral director's heels clicked by on the tile floor outside the empty viewing room. Trey and I had sneaked in there moments before to get away from the chaos of sympathy and empty words. We'd been relieved, once inside, to find the Wedgwood-blue room absent of caskets and flowers and guest books and tears. It was a space that smelled of air freshener and wood polish, and it was blissfully uninhabited by the dearly departed. Trey and I slid down the wall just inside the door and found comfort in the lush carpet and even lusher silence.

"You're cremating me when I die," I said, my voice a little rough from too many days of grieving.

"You can Cuisinart me for all I care, just don't do a viewing."

Mom had died just four days ago, and we'd been in full-on funeral mode ever since. She'd been considerate enough to have most of it planned, from the coffin to the plot to the Bible verses and music, but the days of grief-tinted activity had still taken their toll on us.

"You think Saccharine Psycho will pull the alarm when she figures out we're missing?"

"Let her."

The funeral director was one of those women so intent on masking their clout with artificial sweetness that she'd quickly become "the bane of Mom's burial," "the inhumanity of her inhumation"—and that was just a small sampling of the terms we'd coined for her intrusion into Mom's death. She had avalanched us with so much gushing sympathy in the past few days that we were still reeling from the kindness overload.

"She was such a lovely woman," Trey said in a syrupy voice, imitating Saccharine Psycho to perfection.

"And isn't her makeup tastefully done?" I continued in kind. "She looks like she's just resting peacefully."

We let out simultaneous sighs and listened to the muted voices reaching us through the viewing room's thick wooden door.

"This is probably the most socializing Mom's done all her life," I said after a few moments.

"No kidding."

"She's taking it well," I said. "Barely breaking a sweat."

"She looks good," Trey said.

She did. They'd done her hair and makeup well enough to hide some of the wear and tear of Davishood.

Trey and I had spent as much time as possible at her bedside during the five weeks she'd been seriously ill and beyond medical help, though my teaching and his chefing had sometimes made it difficult. She'd been lucid almost to the end, sweet with the nurses and loving toward us. Talkative, too—like she'd needed to retell all the highlights of her life just one more time.

We'd listened to her stories and smiled at her embellishments and patted her hand when she'd teared up. We'd filled in the blanks of dates and details erased from her mind by the rigors of survival. And we'd taken deep breaths and counted to ten when she'd tried to reframe some of our family stories in a saner, brighter light.

She drifted into sleep midstory and drifted into eternity midsleep, weakened by her strokes and by the cancer rotting her resistance and her will. It was the gentlest, quietest death I could have wished for my mother, the woman who had gently and quietly endured the lashes and lacerations of a life spent with my dad. She'd set a high standard of dignity despite the degradation, of poise despite the poisonous contempt, and she'd honored her ex-husband to the end. It was that stubborn loyalty that galled and humbled me.

"She was a good mom," I said.

Trey nodded. "She did her best under some pretty tough circumstances."

A question had been nagging at me since Mom's life had fluttered to an end in her tidy hospital room. "She knew we loved her, right?"

He looked at me with weary certainty. "She knew."

I took a shaky breath and pressed the corners of my eyes with unsteady fingertips. There had been too many tears since Tuesday—too many questions that had seemed to come too late.

"You think Dad will drop in?"

"He might. If someone tells him or he reads the obit."

"Will you talk to him if he does?" My courageous brother would have to speak for both of us. He always had.

"And say what?"

I didn't know. None of the lines that came to mind seemed appropriate with Mom lying in her favorite blue dress in a casket across the way.

"He probably won't come," Trey said.

"Probably not. That would be too much like admitting he knows us."

A swollen moment passed. "I hope he doesn't come," Trey said softly. "He doesn't belong here after what he put her through."

The high heels clicked past the door again, a little faster this time, and I could picture Saccharine Psycho scanning the halls for us, externally smiling, but internally cursing.

"You think she was happy? I mean, for the last few years?"

Trey thought about it for a while. "I don't think she ever really knew what happy was. And since she didn't expect anything better . . ."

"Ignorance is bliss."

"Sometimes."

"She should have been happy."

Trey turned his head toward me, alerted by the angry edge to my voice.

"She should have been more than a brutalized wife," I went on.

"She should have been a lot of things," he said.

"And she could have been," I retorted too firmly, my insurrection strengthening. "She could have done things and had things and been things . . ."

"But she got Dad instead."

"He killed her. And he killed her a long time before last Tuesday."

"We should send him the funeral bills."

I swiped at the tears on my face, tired of the grief so horribly distorted by a sense of waste. "Maybe if she'd gotten out while she still could."

"She wouldn't have. She didn't even leave when he started taking his frustrations out on us, and she was supposed to be our loving mom, so . . ."

"She was," I said. "She really did love us. She just never figured out how to love us and Dad at the same time."

Trey nodded. "I know."

"She should have been happy," I repeated, but the words sounded desolate this time, much less convicted than they'd been before. Maybe there hadn't really been an option—not after meeting and marrying the man she'd claimed to love until the end.

Trey breathed silently beside me, and I found comfort in his nearness.

"I don't want to be like her." I hadn't intended to say the words, but there they were, suspended in the air above us. I'd thought them frequently enough. Most fervently, perhaps, when I stood by her casket for the first time and looked down at her delicate hands clasped lightly on her stomach. Lightly *was the word for it. For her hands and for her life. She'd never given me the impression of feeling anything really intensely or doing anything full-throttle or rushing into anything headlong. Everything had always been predictable and discreet. And I felt like her life had consequently been too delicate and largely unlived.*

"Then don't be like her," Trey said.

He had a way of making monumental processes sound simple.

"Oh, well, okay then. And how do you suggest I go about that?"

"Figure out where she went wrong."

I laughed. "Starting where?"

"I don't know. Just figure it out and do something about it. That alone will make you different from her."

"Well, I'm not going to marry a jerk, for one."

"At the rate you're running off the good guys, there may only be jerks left."

"That's not the point."

"No, but I'm pretty sure it's a symptom of Davishood."

I gave the theory a moment of thought before discarding it. My mom's questionable taste in men had little to do with my singleness. Or so I chose to believe. "I think I need to steer clear of polyester, too, if I'm going to avoid being like her."

"Wise decision." Trey rocked his head slowly from side to side, trying to loosen the tension of the last four days. "You think she would have gone on in nursing if she hadn't met Dad?"

"Probably."

"Think of how different her life would have been. She'd have gotten a job, tried new things, met new people. . . ."

"I know."

"We should have taken her bungee jumping or something," Trey said.

I laughed. "That would have required taking risks, and she wasn't ever really good at those."

"She never met a risk she didn't run from," Trey said wearily, his head rocking against the blue wall. "And look where that—"

"Shhh!" I whispered urgently. The heels were moving faster yet, this time, and they stopped abruptly outside the door of our refuge. Trey and I both had our friendliest smiles in place when Saccharine Psycho walked in.

"Looking for us?" Trey said.

"Where have you been?" she asked, the spark of impatience in her eyes in contradiction with her soothing tone. "Your guests have been waiting to pay their respects, and I've been searching high and low for you."

Trey stood and extended his hand to help me up from the floor.

"We're sorry," I said. "We just needed to get away for a couple minutes."

She placed a hand on my arm in a gesture calculated to be comforting. "These are sad times," she said quietly. "Losing a mother is one of the hardest blows life deals us."

I wanted to laugh. I really did. But unexpected tears somehow shoved their way past my strained sense of humor. Trey saw them and wrapped an arm around my shoulders, walking me from the shadowed quietness into the pastel bustle of grief.

19

THE FADED COLORS of Lewis's living room and the austere grandeur of the professors' dining hall had replaced the blank, bare stage. We'd even constructed a backstage area and wings by hanging temporary curtains from the beams high above and propping up makeshift walls with two-by-fours and bricks. The transformation had sublimated the performances of the students as they were carried by the sets and props to a time and context none of them had known. The only unfinished item was the wardrobe, the centerpiece of the set, critical to the story, which Scott was in the process of assembling onstage. He'd recruited the help of some of his basketball players for the job, but it still was proving to be a frustrating, unwieldy task. The pieces weren't coming together as planned, and after two hours of effort that should have taken only minutes, with ten cast members waiting to take possession of the stage for a critical rehearsal, things didn't seem anywhere near a resolution. I approached him to ask when he thought he might be finished, but his only answer was a scowl followed by "I'll be finished when I'm finished."

So I retreated to my front-row seat and tried not to let his shortness get the best of me. Meagan and I spent the wait going over a laundry list of small details needing attention, while the cast occupied their time in various forms of stress release and Shayla wandered around the stage in tight circles engrossed in a loud and seemingly endless version of "London Bridge Is Falling Down." Seth paced back and forth across the back of the room, practicing his final monologue at breakneck speed. Two other guys made ape sounds and flounced around in the balcony in a semblance of jungle warfare. And several others were involved in an animated discussion about the social and cultural importance of Paris Hilton. Jessica thought it was commendable that she'd made such a name for herself when all she'd been before was a pretty girl with a pedigree, while two of my more outspoken male actors compared the hotel heiress to a hollow-headed manipulator masquerading as a trashy debutante. It was an entertaining conversation, to say the least. As their voices blended with the ape noises coming down from above, the murmured lines at the back of the auditorium, Shayla's singing, and Meagan's incessant commentary on the goings-on around us, I wondered if I might have somehow gotten trapped inside the psychedelic chaos of Ozzy Osbourne's mind.

"Hold that side higher, Kenny," Scott instructed in a tight voice, lightly hammering his side of the structure so it would line up with the set wall next to it. Kenny strained to lift the bulky frame a little higher off the ground, and in doing so, raised it so high that he pushed Scott's side off-kilter.

"No, Kenny!" he said in exasperation, wiping sweat from his

forehead with his sleeve. I heard him mutter something under his breath as he slammed down the hammer and used brute strength to force the heavy wood back into place.

Thomas and Kate chose that moment to step onstage and begin a sort of demented parody of the play, their voices raised in a comical British cacophony of ridiculous dialogue. On the other side of the stage, a Korean stagehand named Simon nearly stepped off the edge as he tried to maneuver a large, framed painting around the professors' grand table. Meagan jumped into action, screaming his name as she rushed over to catch him if he were to fall.

The noise and confusion were increasing exponentially, and as I found out too late, so was the frustration of the amateur carpenter onstage. He managed to control himself right up until the moment when Simon, who was still trying to position the frame, rammed the end of it into the wardrobe door. Kate screamed in mock horror at the gouge in the wood, which attracted the attention of the rest of the students in the room. The apes in the balcony started yelling down at Simon, giving him a hard time, and Simon started yelling back that actors were an ungrateful bunch of egotists. It was all in good fun, of course, and I was chuckling in the front row when Scott stopped what he was doing and rounded on the students with so much impatience that it scared me.

"Hey! Would you all mind keeping it down?" he yelled, hands on hips and anger like shrapnel in his voice. "Kenny can't hear a word I'm saying and he's only two feet away! Just . . . chill out!"

And he turned back to work with a stiffness I'd never seen in him before, ordering Kenny to put more pressure on the base of the wardrobe structure.

Standing in the middle of the stage in her favorite purple corduroys and matching flowered shirt, Shayla was dumbstruck. Her bottom lip came out, her chin started to tremble, and she looked at me as if willing me to leap onto the stage and whisk her away from the man she'd never heard yell before. I felt the same way she did.

Behind her, Scott had stopped working and was kneeling there, hammer in hand, doing nothing. Kenny still held his half of the wardrobe and seemed rather unfazed by what had just happened. Then again, he'd probably witnessed similar displays on the basketball court. So when he saw Shayla's face, he let go of the wardrobe without hesitation and went to her before I'd had time to rise from my chair.

"Hey, Lady Shay," he said, crouching down beside her, "whatsa matter?"

She didn't say anything. She just turned her head toward Scott as her chin started to quiver in earnest.

"What—him?" Kenny said in a nonchalant voice, pointing over his shoulder. "He's just ticked off 'cause he can't get his wardrobe to work."

"He yelled at me," Shayla said in such an unsteady voice that someone at the back of the room giggled. That seemed to release the tension enough that others started to talk. The crisis had passed. But not onstage. Scott straightened and walked over to where Shayla stood. She watched him come with a frown so thunderous that it would have been comical under different circumstances. Kenny squeezed her arm and moved aside.

Scott took a moment to look down at her, considering the expression on her face and probably assessing the risk. Then he sat down cross-legged in front of her, looked directly and sincerely into her eyes, and said, "I messed up, didn't I?"

She took a shaky breath and said, "You yelled at me."

"You're right, Lady Shay. I shouldn't have."

"You sca-yod me." She gave a little hiccup and swallowed hard.

"I didn't mean to scare you—"

"You should say sowwy."

Scott raked his fingers through his hair. "I am sorry, Shay. I wasn't mad at you. I promise I wasn't. But I was mad at that wardrobe because I can't get it to work right." He took her hand and kissed her fingers. "I'm sorry I scared you."

She seemed to consider that for a moment, then propped her fists on her little hips and said, "Don't do it again."

Scott smiled, though I could still see tension in the lines of his face. "I'll try not to." He tweaked her nose. "Forgive me?"

She hesitated, playing a little hard to get as all good girls do, but then she nodded and Scott scooped her up and sat her down in the crook of his crossed legs. She leaned back against him while he whispered something in her ear that made her giggle. They sat like that for a while, and I looked on from the first row of the audience, blinking hard.

I'd learned three things in the simplicity and spontaneity of an impatient moment. One, Scott was human—which was a great relief to me, because I'd started to think I was the only one with monumental flaws like bouts of verbal diarrhea, a tendency to cry at Hallmark commercials, and an occasionally runny nose. Two, anger didn't always harm, at least not long-term. He'd lost it, he'd realized it, he'd fixed it. Period—pass the donuts. And three, I could think of no more beautiful, heart-stirring sight than my daughter wrapped in the arms of a man who loved her and whose tenderness toward her was stronger than his anger.

❋ ❋ ❋

As opening night drew closer, the days grew longer. I woke up with a to-do list screaming in my brain, and I went to bed dejected at how little I'd actually accomplished. And in between? In between,

I tried to wrangle ten actors hyped up on adrenaline into some semblance of performance, I taught English classes that were sadly ill-prepared, I spent hours with Shayla learning the German words for shapes, colors, and animals, as her teacher had encouraged me to do, and I reveled in the luxury and mystery of being pursued.

My educated and researched view on being pursued was this: good stuff—even though my brain still told me to be careful, to expect disappointment, and to enjoy Scott while I could, because all good things invariably came to a bitter, painful end. So each moment with Scott hummed with the delicate tension of absorbing the wonderfulness and bracing for the horribleness. I found that our times together galvanized me and elevated my emotions to a level of optimism they'd seldom reached before. But I knew that the second I was alone at home again, I'd relentlessly relive the moments in my mind and sift through the happiness in search of something wrong. He hadn't decided to dislike me yet. But a ghostly voice told me that if I gave him more time, he eventually would.

To be honest, my expectations for being pursued were slightly skewed, for which I blamed Keith Jacobs, my almost-date to my college formal. He'd made pursuit into a competition sport in which I'd said no in every way I could and he'd ignored me. I'd rather have played croquet. Keith had been the Arnold Schwarzenegger of pursuit, blending the subtlety of Conan the Barbarian with the romance of the Terminator. He'd attempted to woo me with a kind of rabid sense of purpose that had bordered on maniacal, and I'd spent my last semester of college developing running skills I neither wanted nor enjoyed.

But Scott was different—in every important way. He wasn't out to convince me of anything. Nor was he attempting to seduce my hormones into overtaking my brain. He was simply there, coming in and out of my life during the day with casual touches and healing smiles, helping when he could, and always willing. We laughed together, we took walks together, and we even prayed together, which was teaching me more about his nature and about my own faith than any amount of conversation might have done.

On Monday nights Shayla and I headed to the gym, where I watched BFA's male staff members trying to prove they were still fit by engaging in merciless games of geezer-ball. It had all the trappings of basketball, but apparently none of the rules. We usually played in the bleachers until an injury on the court forced me into my unofficial paramedic role. I found the geezer-ball tradition dangerous and pointless, but who was I to interfere with Scott's need to be macho once a week?

Shayla had caught some of his excitement for the sport. He had taught her how to dribble a basketball, and she now walked around the apartment yelling "swoosh" at random moments, which, I decided, was one of the greater downsides of being pursued by a sports enthusiast. The other was that he was determined to coax me toward at least an appreciation of football, which meant spending hours on his couch with his laptop on a tray table in front of us, watching the Chicago Bears getting beaten by other teams.

It would have been excruciating except for the sitting-on-the-couch part. That much I liked. So I pretended to be horrified when the quarterback dropped the ball and used my horrification to snuggle a little closer to the man whose strength and character made me proud and who seemed adept at only this one form of multitasking. He could watch a game and hold me, which was a pretty cool trick indeed.

"I'm getting shoulder pads," I said on one occasion, when Shayla was sleeping in the armchair next to the window and Scott and I were in our usual places on the couch watching the Bears getting trounced again.

"Yeah?" He was only half with me. I'd discovered that the rise in testosterone caused by football had a direct relation to hearing loss. Go figure.

So I tried it again. I nuzzled his neck a little—because I was allowed to do that now that we were pursuing and all—and said in as husky a voice as I could muster, "Scott? I'm getting shoulder pads."

I had his attention. And his confusion. "Planning on taking up football?"

"No, but look at those guys!" I was back to my own voice as I motioned toward the TV. "Their shoulder pads make their butts look tiny."

"My girlfriend the athlete."

"Your girlfriend the bored nonathlete who sits on the couch and watches games with you because she knows it makes you happy. Your girlfriend who has, however, been sitting on this couch too long tonight because her daughter is asleep in your armchair and should really be home in bed. Your girlfriend who still thinks it's a little bit weird for adults in their midthirties to be using the term *girlfriend* when really this is just a game of if-you-pursue-me-I'll-put-up-with-your-blasted-football-game."

"You through?"

I thought about it. "Yup."

"Good. For an English teacher, you sure use a lot of run-on sentences."

"For a phys ed teacher, you sure do a lot of sitting on the couch."

He raised an eyebrow at me. "Should we break up?"

"Sure—I have to go home anyway. Can we make up in the morning?"

"Sounds like a plan." He got up and slipped into his coat. "I'll carry Shay out to the car."

"Thanks—I'll wait here for your second run."

"I'm not carrying you."

"You couldn't lift me anyway. I've got my first-performance bulge going on."

"You're not fat, Shelby."

"My love handles have grown into a love steering wheel."

"You're not fat," he said again, lifting a limp Shayla into his arms and arranging her against his shoulder. "But your lips should be a lot skinnier for all the flapping they do."

Any talk about mouths or lips always got my brain thinking about kissing, and thinking about kissing always made my toes curl, so I put the thought out of my mind, what with having to walk out to the car and all. Curled toes made it ungainly.

I followed Scott outside and waited while he installed Shayla in her car seat. It was a lesson I'd learned only recently. It went something like this: wait for the cute guy to open your car door or he'll get all huffy and make you get back out of the car so he can be a gentleman. Scott was trying to break me of my single-girl habits. When he got around to my door, he reached for the handle but didn't open it right away.

"So are we going to talk about the kissing thing or just have a moment of panic every time it crosses our minds at the same time?"

I put on my Scarlett accent. "Why, Scott, I have no idea what you're talking about."

"Flapping lips."

My toes did the sighing thing. "Fine. Go ahead and talk about it, then." I hated that I still went a little junior-high when I was out of my comfort zone.

"You want subtle or nonsubtle?"

"I want quick. Shayla's freezing in the backseat."

He glanced into the car where Shayla slept peacefully and warmly under the blanket Scott had wrapped around her. "She's not complaining."

"Okay, let's go for subtle."

He cleared his throat, and I thought I saw a bit of a blush working its way up his neck. "All right," he said, "here's the deal. I've known you for, what, six months now, and we've spent a lot of them being just-friends—which, by the way, was your idea."

"Are you blushing?"

"Hush. I'm trying to be subtle."

"Whatever."

"But we're not just just-friends anymore and . . ."

"All right, enough of subtle. I don't have time for this. How 'bout you go for nonsubtle and get whatever this is over with?" There was an elf tap-dancing on my stomach and he was driving me nuts.

"Nonsubtle?"

"Please."

"All right, here it is. I really, really want to kiss you, and if you don't say no in the next three seconds, I'm going to do it."

One. *No, no, no, no, no . . .*

Two. *Okay, well, if you have to, let's get it over with.*

Three. *What are you waiting for?*

One minute I was standing there feeling three seconds tick by, and the next . . . and the next, a warm hand was snaking through my hair to the back of my head and drawing me in. I had a moment of panic right before his lips touched mine, because it felt so conclusive somehow—in a what-are-you-doing-for-the-rest-of-my-life? kind of way. But then his lips were on mine and his breath was on my face and my hands were clinging to the front of his jacket because my legs were doing a limp-noodle imitation.

Zip-a-dee-doo-dah, quadruple axel, knotted-up toes, tap-a-tap-tap, and all that stuff.

It was nice, in other words.

He pulled away just enough to take a look at my eyes—like he expected me to have fallen asleep or something.

"Still here," I said.

"Yeah?"

"Yeah."

"For the record?"

"Uh-huh?"

"I haven't stopped liking you yet . . . or wanting to pursue you."

"Oh." My turn to blush. "Well . . . give yourself some time. It might still happen."

"See you tomorrow, Shelby." He said it against my lips, and my innards did a twist.

❋ ❋ ❋

"Shut—your—mouth," Trey said with so much pent-up impatience that I clamped my jaw shut and ordered myself to be quiet. Apparently he wanted his surprise to be a silent one.

I'd never been into surprises. Maybe because they were by definition something I couldn't prepare for, and preparing was a critical issue for me. I blamed it on the drama of my seventh birthday, when Mom had asked a few girls from my class to my house for a party. I hadn't expected it. Trey and I had gone to the library to return some books and pick new ones for the weekend, and the house had seemed really quiet when we'd returned. Right up until we'd walked into the living room and Vira Snurdly had popped up from behind the couch yelling, "Happy birthday!" loudly enough to scare the crows out of the tree in the yard. I was so surprised that I fell backward over the

La-Z-Boy's footrest, legs in the air, and exposed my Tuesday undies to the assembled guests. It wasn't showing my Tuesday undies that had humiliated me so much as the fact that it was Saturday. My day-of-the-week panties were a big deal at the time.

So when Trey had insisted on covering my eyes with a scarf several minutes ago, then shoved me into the passenger seat of his car and driven around town for a while, I'd had flashbacks to that fateful birthday party.

"I don't like surprises."

"You'll like this one." He sounded sure of himself, and that scared me even more.

"Just give me a hint."

"Nope."

"Is Vira Snurdly involved?"

"Be quiet, Shell."

"Well, at least I'm not wearing day-of-the-week panties."

"Huh?"

"Remember the day we got books at the library and then went home and Vira Snurdly was hiding behind the couch with Jocelyn Hicks and Carrie Smith and they jumped out at me and yelled, 'Happy birthday!' and I fell over the footrest and they saw my panties and—"

"Shell." There was a warning in his tone. A kindhearted warning, but a warning nonetheless.

"Wait, you don't understand—they were my Tuesday *panties!"*

There was a pause before a reluctant "And?"

"And it was Saturday! Saturday, Trey! They saw my Tuesday panties and it was Saturday, and I'm telling you, I just knew that Vira would never let it drop because she never let anything drop, like the time Corrie split her pants and—"

That was when Trey told me to shut my mouth. Which I did. But I opened it again to explain to him that surprises scared me and that blabbing soothed me, at which point he said a "Shell!" that crackled a little too much for my own good. So I shut my mouth and sat there in silence while we drove around long enough to make me sick to my stomach. He eventually parked, turned off the engine, helped me out of the car, and ushered me through a door into some sort of resonant room.

"You ready?"

I was standing there blindfolded, trying not to throw up, but yes, I was ready.

"Keep your eyes closed until I tell you to open them," he said, his fingers fiddling with the scarf's knot. "Okay—open."

I opened my eyes and found myself standing in an empty room with unpainted walls, a semifinished tile floor, plastic-covered windows, and dangling wires where light fixtures should have been. Trey was looking at me with so much expectation that I didn't dare react.

"Where am I?"

He looked around the room with a deep smile spreading across his face. "Picture it," he said. And he proceeded to describe in minute detail every invisible item he could see in the space, from the wall decorations to the window treatments, from the espresso machine to the whipped cream dispenser. He was still talking exultantly about the bakery of his dreams when I interrupted.

"You bought your bakery?"

He nodded and smiled like he'd swallowed the sun. "Signed the papers this morning," he said with so much excitement that his voice and eyes danced. "I start renovations next week."

"You bought your bakery!" I threw myself at his neck with so much force that he teetered, and then we both did a ridiculous hopping routine that had us turning in circles in the middle of the echo-chamber room, waving our arms above our heads, and whooping like drunk cheerleaders.

When I'd whooped myself hoarse and hopped myself breathless, I plopped down in the middle of the floor, mindless of the dust and dirt, and looked around at the vision Trey had described. I could see it all, every hue and nuance of the dream he had bought with dogged pursuit and relentless dedication. He sat down next to me and leaned back on his hands, taking in the half-finished space with the eye of an artist.

"You think it'll fly?" he asked.

"With you as the chef? You bet your booty."

He exhaled loudly. "Tell me I'm not an idiot."

"You're not an idiot."

"It's financial suicide opening this kind of thing, Shell. Even with Mom's money. I mean, the guy who had it before me only got halfway through the renovations before he threw in the towel."

"But you've worked it all out, right?"

"Down to the last penny. With a bit of a cushion in case of emergency."

"Then you're not an idiot."

"I'm calling it L'Envie."

"So it's a Chinese bakery?"

His head dropped back and he stared at the ceiling with his usual my-sister-the-moron expression. "That's French, Shelby."

I smirked. "I know." I looked out the plastic-covered front window at the cars going by and savored the moment. "So what now?"

"We paint the walls, and the tile guys come next week to finish this up." He motioned at the front part of the room, where the beige tile ended and rough cement extended to the door. "Kitchen gets installed after that. Then I have the inspectors come in to make sure it's up to snuff, design flyers, put ads in the paper, maybe hire some help, organize a grand opening . . ."

"So you're going to be busy, in other words."

"For the foreseeable future."

I nodded and inhaled the brightness of his dream. "It's going to be fabulous, Trey."

"I'm thinking of maybe serving meals, too. Maybe one meal a day—single-item menu."

"As long as the single item is calorie-loaded and mushroom-free, I'll be your designated taster."

I giggled at his goofy, happy grin and lay back on the dusty floor, bending my knees and getting comfy while the grime of construction got into my hair. There wasn't much to look at from that position. Then again, there wasn't much to look at from any position yet. He joined me in the dust and let out a happy sigh.

"I like the postmodern light fixtures," I said.

"Yeah? The French are big into the tangled-wire look."

"And the ripped plastic on the windows is a really fancy touch."

"Thanks. I ripped it myself."

"This is your dream, Trey."

"Yup."

"You made it happen."

"I did."

"God's not spitting anymore."

"He never did."

I turned my head to look at him. "You used to think he did."

"We were only kidding."

"Yeah, but remember after you killed the bird? When you went downstairs and started throwing things around in your room? You kept yelling at the ceiling, 'Stop spitting on me, you . . .' And then you used a word I won't repeat because I don't want to damage your fancy new bakery with a lightning bolt from heaven."

Trey chuckled and breathed deeply. "I remember," he said. "But I think I knew even then—way down—that God hadn't spit on us. Dad had."

"Literally and figuratively."

"But not God. God does things like this instead," he said, basking in the accomplishment and miracle of L'Envie.

"Took a while."

"Well, he kinda wanted me to be part of the process, and I spent a few years getting over the Dad factor, so . . ."

Something bittersweet breathed across my mind, but since I didn't recognize it, I let it glide on by. Trey must have sensed it too. He captured it before it passed.

"You'll get your dream someday, Shell."

"Yeah?"

An ambulance went braying by, its siren jarring the hope-laden air. Our celebration settled, mellowed, dimmed.

"How did you figure it out?" I asked, with inner eyes exploring the dull blankness of my hopes.

"My dream?"

I nodded.

"I don't know. It just kind of came."

A shadow crept across the weary gray of jadedness. "So what's mine?" I asked. "What's my dream?"

Trey grabbed my hand as we lay on the pale, hard tile—so plush, moments before, with the joy of dreams come true. "It's out there, Shell. Just wait." He squeezed my hand, exhaled. "Life isn't finished with you yet."

20

All things considered, life could have been a lot worse. My greatest problems, two days before opening night, were that Kate had a cold, Seth hadn't slept in three days, Thomas still thought all the English accents stank, two of the auditorium's spotlights were out, the wardrobe's pulley system only worked once in every five attempts, Shayla had tried to walk out of the house wearing one of my bras that morning, and there was a cannonball where my stomach used to be. I was nervous. I was nervous enough that I'd forgotten to eat several times in the past few days. And forgetting to eat was a scary thing indeed for this ingestion addict.

This was very much the students' play—and they'd earned every bit of praise they would receive for it—but it was also my directorial debut, and though I hoped I'd done things right, I wouldn't be sure until the final blackout after our first performance.

Scott had come by my classroom earlier in the day to ask if Shayla and I would like to go out for an early dinner with him before the forty-eight-hour circus we knew was ahead. As I was in a particularly astute and intelligent mood at the time, I accepted, though I did disinvite Shayla, whose lack of sleep in recent days had transformed her into a human version of the Tasmanian Devil. Since she'd be sleeping at the Johnsons' for the next three nights anyway because of the play, I figured it wouldn't hurt to add one more evening of being spoiled by Bev to her vacation from me. I just hoped my daytime hours with her would compensate for our separation at night. The thought of not having her under my roof made me weepy.

Scott took me to the Café Inka that evening, a tiny family restaurant in the village of Ötlingen, where renovations in the late eighties had revealed paintings dating back to 1819. The owners had exposed and cleaned the valuable artwork and, as a preservation measure, had imposed a smoking ban on the café. This was probably the only restaurant in the area where smoking was not allowed. As accustomed as I'd become to the thick air of German restaurants and to the strong smell on my clothes when I got home, it felt wonderful to be in a smoke-free environment for the evening.

I ordered a slice of broccoli quiche and Scott got a pork steak. It was one of those evenings when I was acutely aware of the calm before the storm, and I felt an expectancy and eagerness that made it hard for me to sit still. I just wanted to get to opening night and find out if this play could fly.

Scott did his best to distract me from the tension, but my state of mind was undistractable.

"How's your quiche?"

"Do you think the pulley system will work if we lay hands on it and pray really hard?"

"That's a lot of vegetable for someone like you. Try not to have a health overdose."

"I could just leap onto the stage and yank the doors open if they stick. A little directorial cameo. Bet they haven't done that in a BFA play before!"

"Did I tell you I have a surprise for you?"

"A surprise?" Scott didn't know how much I disliked them.

"Yup," he said, and I could tell by the dancing lights in his eyes that it was a doozie.

"You're scaring me. . . ."

He pointed with his chin toward the doorway behind me. "It's right over there."

I was concentrating so hard on looking for a wrapped present or a bouquet of flowers when I turned that I didn't immediately see the blond guy with the silly, jet-lagged grin leaning against the doorframe.

I was about to turn back to Scott in frustration when the U of I shirt worn by the gentleman holding up the doorway registered in my mind. My breath caught.

"Trey?" He was too out of context, too unexpected to be real.

"Hey, Shell," he said, sauntering over to my table with a goofy smile and pulling me out of my chair.

It wasn't until I smelled his Drakkar Noir aftershave that I believed he was really there. If he'd been taller, I think I would have climbed him like a tree. He was Trey. Trey was here. My brother, Trey, was in Germany, in the same room as me and . . .

I turned on Scott. "You knew he was coming?" My voice was a little too loud for the environment, and every German head in the room turned to frown at the insensitive American making a scene.

"I did." He was smiling with so much affection that I didn't know whether to leap across the table and strangle him or leap across the table and hug the living daylights out of him.

"This is Trey," I told him with all the love of thirty-five years of tandem survival.

Scott stepped forward and shook Trey's hand. "Good to meet you, man."

Trey shook back. "You too."

"Well, sit, sit!" I forced Trey into a chair, mainly so I could sit too. My legs had been through a lot recently, what with performance jitters and first kisses and long-lost brothers showing up, and they weren't doing a very consistent job of keeping me upright.

I just stared. I stared and grinned stupidly and occasionally opened my mouth to say something, but lost my train of thought before the first word was even out. I looked from Trey to Scott, from Scott to Trey, and just kind of beamed—like the Cheshire cat on crack. I was kind of happy.

"How was your flight?" Scott asked when it became clear that I wasn't conversationally competent yet.

"No problems. Just a three-hour layover in Frankfurt before the flight to Basel. Gus drove up to the curb just as I walked out, and . . . here I am!"

I found my tongue. "When did you get here? Where are you staying? When did you decide to come? Who else knows about this? How did you get to Ötlingen?"

Scott and Trey exchanged glances, then did a kind of tandem shrug. It was the gesture of men who knew me well and found my weirdness endearing, so I allowed it.

"Well, 2 p.m., on your couch, three weeks ago, just Scott and the Johnsons, and . . . what was the last one?"

I smiled. I was going for the gold medal in smiling.

"Want something to eat?" It's a good thing Scott was playing host, because my hosting skills were comatose.

Trey, my brother Trey, who was supposed to be in Illinois—that Trey—shook his head. "Maybe just coffee. I had something to eat at the Johnsons'."

"Are you exhausted? Have you slept?" Me again—still slightly demented.

"Easy on the decibels, Shell. I took at nap at the Johnsons' before coming out here, so I'm good to go. Bev told me I had to sleep because you were going to keep me awake all night, and she's a pretty convincing woman."

"She's the best."

There was something a little odd going on at the table. We were all being friendly, but there was an underlying vibe that was making me a little uncomfortable. Trey leaned over to give me a sideways hug, then turned his attention on Scott.

"So . . . you're Scott."

"Been practicing that opener all the way over here, Trey?" I smiled.

"I've heard a lot about you," Scott said.

"Yeah? I've heard a little about you too."

On a scale of one to ten, this conversation was scoring a twenty-three for lameness. It felt like a face-off—subtle, mind you, with no guns drawn, but something was definitely going on here.

Trey stared at Scott for a little too long and Scott returned the stare, unflinching.

"So what's with the two of you?" Trey asked.

"Oh, great, Trey. Way to be smooth." I was finding this comical—in an unfunny kind of way.

"I'm serious. I'm the brother. I'm supposed to know."

"Shelby and I are . . . What are we, Shell? Dating?"

"You don't have to answer him, Scott. He's just playing King of the Sandbox with you."

Scott turned his eyes on Trey, smiling. "We're dating."

"Cool. And . . . what are your intentions?"

"His intentions? His intentions! Maybe you should have taken a longer nap, Trey."

Scott sat back in his chair and crossed his arms. "What do you want to know?"

"Are you treating her right?"

"I am."

"Are you leading her on?"

I was outraged. "Trey!"

"No, I'm not."

"Do you see this going somewhere?"

"Okay—earth to moron! Trey, stop it. You're embarrassing yourself and you're humiliating me."

"I hope it's going somewhere. I pray to God it's going somewhere." Scott was undeterred.

"And where would that be?"

"Hello?" I looked from one staring man to the other staring man. "Is anyone hearing me? 'Cause I'm pretty sure I'm talking, but I'm not getting a whole lot of response from either of you."

Scott, still ignoring me, leaned his forearms on the table and assumed his most serious, responsible expression. "I love your sister," he said, "and my 'intentions' are to be the kind of man she can love enough to want to marry." There was a bit of a challenge in the smile he aimed at Trey. "And since you're the brother who's kept her sane all this time, I'm happy to answer any other questions you have."

I thought of saying something witty about the "sane" thing, but the *L* word was messing with my zingers—not to mention the

M word turning my cognitive skills to mush. Scott hadn't ever told me that he loved me—not directly, anyway. He hadn't been shy about expressing it in other ways, but hearing it so unexpectedly in a crowded café with my newly reunited brother sitting next to me awoke a cacophony of voices in my mind, each of them speaking from a different fragment of my heart.

"He's lying," said my daughterness.

"He'll hurt you," said my woundedness.

"He doesn't know how warped you really are," said my brokenness.

"You can't afford to trust him," said my betrayedness.

"Maybe . . . just maybe . . . ," said my uncertain hopefulness, the part of me that wanted to cheer—and dance—and cry—and laugh—and beg all the other voices to be wrong.

I was too fragile to address Scott's declaration at that moment. Too stunned. Too confused. Too terrified. So I stayed mute and hoped the two men whose lives were so entangled with mine wouldn't notice my withdrawal. Scott reached across the table and squeezed my hand just as Trey reached to do the same. We all froze for a fraction of a second; then Trey withdrew his hand as Scott twined his fingers with mine. An invisible page turned with such finality that it grieved, frightened, and sobered me.

My brother just sat there looking at our hands, biting the inside of his lip like I'd seen him do a thousand times when he was thinking. His eyes met mine, and he smiled in a way that said he knew. He understood.

"Just so you know," he said to Scott, "she's stubborn."

"Trey . . ."

"So is my sister," Scott said. "I've had practice."

"And she drags her feet like no one I've ever known."

"Trey!" Consternation was quickly overtaking my confusion.

"I've noticed." Scott smiled, bringing my hand to his lips.

"And she has a hang-up about the whole 'love' concept—never believes it's for real."

"And expects people to change their minds about it once they get to know her?"

"That's Shelby."

I slid down in my chair and covered my burning face with my hands. "I am so humiliated."

"And," Trey continued, raising a finger to punctuate his statement, "she can build some pretty thick walls around herself to keep people at arm's length."

"Any advice?"

"Oh—that's right. You've been up against a couple of those, haven't you."

I groaned.

"Well," Trey continued, ignoring me, "if you run into them again, my advice is to storm the barricades."

"Storm them?"

"Blast 'em to smithereens."

"Really." Scott seemed to be warming to the concept.

"Don't give her any wiggle room."

"Thanks, man. That's good advice."

"I'm sitting right here, boys," I said in a weary voice. "Sitting right here."

The inquisition had apparently ended and Scott seemed relieved, though he had a purposeful look about him—like a warrior readying for an assault. My brain was suddenly exhausted from the surprise, the face-off, the *L* word, the *M* word, and the look on Scott's face. We all let the loaded silence stretch for a while. A few moments later, Trey slapped Scott on the shoulder and settled back in his chair, relaxing for the first time since he'd arrived. Scott smiled and continued to hold my hand, idly toying with my fingers and leaning in to kiss my temple.

"So," Trey said with enthusiasm, "how 'bout them Bulls?"

And they were off—a little awkwardly at first, what with the rather brutal introduction to the evening—but once they got going, it was like listening to childhood friends. I realized, about ten minutes into their conversation, that I was going to have to do some serious brushing up on my sports if the three of us were going to be spending any amount of time together.

Trey went inside ahead of me when we got home, and I was thankful for a few moments alone with Scott in his beat-up old Volkswagen.

"So that was painful," I said.

"It was fun."

"The beginning part, I mean."

"It didn't really surprise me."

"He's not usually that . . . forward."

"He was just checking out the guy who's been hanging out with his sister."

"Hanging out, huh?"

"Sure. Hanging out."

"Um . . . About that 'love' thing."

He cocked an eyebrow.

"You know, the whole 'I love your sister' thing. . . ."

"Yes?" His grin told me he'd been expecting the topic to arise.

"Well . . . it's just that I've never really heard you say the word before. I mean . . . not directly to me. So it kinda took me by surprise when you just blurted it to my brother."

"What are you getting at?"

I sighed and weighed my words. "You've only known me a few months," I said.

"Yes."

"So . . . really, you don't know me very well at all."

He looked at me for a moment before responding. "I know you well enough."

"It's just that . . ."

"I'm sorry I blurted it out to your brother before having said it to you," he said softly, running the back of a finger down my cheek. "I just wanted him to know that you were safe—that I wasn't out to harm you."

I nodded, unsure of what to say, of where to begin, of how to explain.

"I love you," he said, and something in me softened a little with the words. Something resolute and hard. An armored vestige of my childhood's pain.

"Do you remember the second part of what I told him?" Scott asked, breaking into my thoughts.

"The part about marriage?" I asked, my voice husky from the tears I was striving to restrain.

"Yeah."

"I've been trying to forget that part."

"Why's that?"

"It gives me the heebie-jeebies," I said with an unsteady giggle, emotions wreaking havoc on my poise.

"In a good way?" He was a little perplexed.

"In a heebie-jeebies kind of way."

"I meant it, you know."

I was trying to reach the point where I could consider "love" without breaking out in hives. Adding "marriage" to the mix was making me itch.

"Are you going to pull a Scarlett O'Hara on me again?"

I shook my head. I'd learned my lesson at the toy museum.

Zingers at crucial moments were not worth the collateral damage. "Scott . . ." I squeezed my eyes shut and tried to put my thoughts in some order. He seemed so casual about the subject, and it made me a little leery. "Do you talk about marriage a lot?" I finally asked, opening my eyes to scan his face for sincerity. "Because it strikes me that if you've always been as casual about it as you were tonight, you should have been married a few times over by now."

"I've seldom ever talked about it—or thought about it—except in theoretical terms."

That gave me pause. "Why not?"

"My youth pastor when I was in ninth grade."

My curiosity was fast overcoming my distress. "He made you take a vow of celibacy?"

He shook his head. "Sam Collier. A General Patton–esque man with all the people skills of Attila the Hun."

"Sounds pleasant."

"He was actually perfect for the job—imagine ten guys like me in the same youth group." I crinkled my nose in sympathy. "He was former military, actually. And he had this really infuriating ability to predict just how stupid my next idea was going to be."

"And he's the reason you're still single at age thirty-six?"

"Thirty-seven in a few weeks." Scott leaned his head back on the headrest and seemed to be picturing the scene. "One of the guys in our group asked the colonel—that's what we called him—what he thought about divorce, and he told us what he thought about marriage instead. He said, 'Gentlemen, my best advice to you is never get married. Respect marriage. Fear marriage. And absolutely do *not* get married!'"

"What?"

"He had a point. There were so many marriages, even in my church, that were falling apart, that he told us we should only consider getting married if we were absolutely, fiercely determined to fight for it with all our worth for the rest of our lives. And if we didn't have a kind of warrior's zeal and compulsive commitment to give to it, we should run from it as fast as our scrawny legs could take us."

"So he wasn't an optimist, is what you're saying."

"He was a math guy—he knew the stats and they weren't in our favor. And most of what I've seen since then has proved him right."

"So you've followed his advice—been a good little boy?"

"I was a stupid teenager who did some really stupid things," he said. "But after I grew up a little, I had a couple more serious girlfriends and gave his theory some thought."

"Get very far?"

He shook his head. "Every time I stopped to wonder if I was willing to invest in a lifelong battle to keep the relationship alive, I decided I didn't love her enough or I didn't want marriage enough."

I let the silence stretch, mostly because I had no idea how to fill it.

"And now?" I resisted the urge to clap my hands over my ears and sing loudly enough to drown out his response. I was a little nervous.

"And now," he said, "I've reached the ripe old age of thirty-six . . ."

"Nearly thirty-seven."

". . . and I'm in a bit of a predicament."

Here it was. "Predicament?"

"Having found someone I'm willing to go to war for."

My stomach somersaulted. Not the confession I'd expected. "And that's a predicament because . . . ?"

"Because I want it with all my might," he said, his eyes lighting with intensity and determination, "but I don't know yet if you're up for the battle too."

"I see." The voices were rising in my mind again.

He sighed and leaned his head sideways on the headrest, staring at me. "Still no Scarlett?"

"I think she might be giving you the time to change your mind."

"She can stop whenever she wants, you know."

I nodded. "I've never been very good at battles, Scott. I'm the type who runs for the cellar, not the armory."

"I'm in no hurry," he said.

Years of cynicism streaked toxic stains across the genuineness of Scott's gaze. I wanted to believe him—with every insurmountable scar of my past.

"I don't know how to trust you," I said. I saw his gaze cloud over and a muscle work in his jaw. "That's not what I mean," I rectified. "I know I can trust *you*. But it's your . . . your . . ."

"Love?"

"Your love," I said, and the word sounded foreign and unwieldy on my tongue. "It's your love I have trouble with. And if I can't believe that . . ."

He turned toward me in his seat and looked at me like the answer was written in hieroglyphics on my face. "What will it take?" he asked in a voice whose huskiness matched mine. "How can I convince you?"

I bit my lip and shook my head, begging him with my eyes not to hate me for my uncertainty. "I don't know."

There was a flicker of frustration in his gaze, quickly quelled and softened with a patience that humbled me. "I'll keep trying until I get it right," he said, and I knew from the edge in his voice that my hesitance was hurting him.

"I'm sorry, Scott."

"There's no need."

His hand was gentle as he cupped my face. His smile held

something deep-flowing and sure. "You should get some sleep," he said. "You've got a couple big days coming up." His voice was still a little tight, but his eyes were soft and ember-warm.

"You're right," I said, reluctant to leave him but relieved to defer the conversation. "And I've got an early morning tomorrow, so . . ." I looked into the serenity and depth of his smile, and I wondered what I'd done to earn his love. But Trey was waiting for me in my apartment, probably half-asleep on the couch by now. "I'd better go. Trey and I still have some catching up to do."

"Glad he's here?"

"I can't even tell you."

"I like him, Shell."

"And all you've seen is his caveman side!" It felt good to smile.

"He loves you. That's all I really need to know."

"I'm so . . ." I paused. How could I explain to him the fullness of my heart? "I'm so very grateful to know you, Scott. To . . . to have you in my life. And Shayla's. I just want you to know that. Whatever happens." I reached up to touch his face and let my fingers drift over his features. What had I done to deserve this man who made me laugh and think and wish for an impossible future?

He took my fingers from his face and kissed my palm. "Good night, Shelby."

"Good night, Scott."

21

THE ACTORS WERE strangely calm as they went through their final preparations—makeup touch-ups, costuming, line reviews, and all the other minor details that grow to enormous proportions in those minutes preceding the opening scene. Some actors lightened the mood with quiet banter, talking about the teachers and friends who would be in the audience that night and trying to predict what their reactions would be. Seth and Kate had found two chairs in a corner of the room and were talking through Joy's dying scene despite the chaos all around. Their eyes were closed as they very slowly, very emotionally, went through their lines. After a couple of minutes, Kate reached out and, eyes still closed, found Seth's hand. It was one of the most moving sights I'd witnessed—two high school students sitting in a crowded changing room, tears in their voices, feeling the pain of another man's loss.

I tended to the actors between walkie-talkie calls from the soundmen, the props crew, and the ticket-sales ladies. Aside from a few small glitches, things were going smoothly. My stomach was knotted and my mind was in overdrive, but I felt an energy and excitement I'd seldom known before. This moment had been months in the making, and despite my deepest qualms, I had a feeling it was all about to pay off.

Meagan came rushing back to let us know the auditorium was full and the ushers were closing the doors. I gathered the actors in a huddle for a final moment together. Their eyes were bright and eager. We prayed for the performers, asking that they would enjoy each moment on the stage regardless of anything that might occur, and I added a special prayer that the wardrobe doors would open on cue. Just in case. Not that I didn't trust the builder. Then we walked backstage in a flurry of silent anticipation and waited for the lights to rise.

❀ ❀ ❀

Seth was finishing the play with a monologue that was at once his story and his faith. "God loves us, so he makes us the gift of suffering. Through suffering, we release our hold on the toys of this world, and know our true good lies in another world." He scanned the audience with weary, hopeful eyes, unfathomably confident despite his age and fragility. "We're like blocks of stone, out of which the sculptor carves the forms of men. The blows of his chisel, which hurt us so much, are what make us perfect. The suffering in the world is not the failure of God's love for us; it is that love in action. For believe me, this world that seems to us so substantial is no more than the shadowlands. Real life has not begun yet."

Seth didn't wipe away his tears. He didn't flinch away from the audience's eyes. He stood his ground. Tall. Proud. Certain of the truth he spoke and emboldened by his own healed wounds. He finished his last line and let the words settle; then he turned and exited the stage in slow, unhurried steps. I met him in the wings and ordered him to bend down so I could hug him properly. I felt his tears against my cheek and wondered at the depth of this young man whose quest for truth had somehow redeemed the fury of his pain. He seemed a healed person, and C. S. Lewis, whose faith had reached beyond the grave, had contributed to making him whole.

Once the lights came down, the actors erupted. They jumped on each other and punched the air and slapped high fives until I yelled to them to line up for the curtain call. Of course, we didn't have a curtain—only lights that came up with the brilliance of victory. I watched as the actors marched to the front of the stage one by one, beaming smiles on their faces, and took a bow. They were the newest conquerors of the theatrical world, and their happiness was contagious. The audience urged them on to three more bows, then I used my walkie-talkie to order the room lights up and the doors open.

I'd never been on the receiving end of performance praise before, so it was all a bit overwhelming. Scott gave me an enormous bouquet of roses and gerbera daisies arranged tightly in a wide green paper cone as the Germans often did. Trey told me he'd spent the afternoon making his first German cheesecake, with ingredient help from Bev, and it was waiting for me at home. I gave him a hug that made something in his neck pop. There were flowers and chocolates and notes of congratulations and so many pats on the back that I lost track of who was giving them. It took half an hour for me to coax the actors back into the changing room, where Nancy would collect their costumes and wash them for our next performance. They carried on a nonstop commentary about the evening while they undressed behind the sheets we'd hung for privacy. It was all high-spirited and adrenaline-fueled and thoroughly entertaining.

Nearly two hours later, I sat at my dining room table with Scott and Trey across from me, but my entire, undivided attention was on the first piece of cheesecake I'd eaten in six months. Actually, I was on my third piece, but no one seemed to be counting.

"Trey, my friend, you're my hero," I said as I shoveled another bite into my mouth.

"You know, Shell, I just realized there's one thing I haven't missed about you."

"Her zingers?" Scott asked.

"Her eating habits," Trey said.

I swallowed and gulped down half a glass of milk. "It's the nerves," I explained. "Imagine what this scene would have looked like if the performance hadn't gone well!"

They both smirked, and I was struck again by their similarities. Though there were major differences, too. One of the greatest of those was their energy level—Trey was Tigger, and Scott was . . . Scott was everything I wanted. I choked a little and had to gulp more milk.

"I've got to hit the sack," Trey said, pushing back from the table. "This jet lag's a killer."

"What he means," I translated for Scott, "is that we're sitting in his bedroom, since the couch is longer than Shayla's bed, and he'd really like for you to leave and for me to go to bed so he can get some sleep."

"Nice that one of you got the diplomatic gene." Scott was feeling comfortable enough around Trey to be sarcastic. I thought that was a good sign.

"Hey, don't hurry on my account," Trey said. He grabbed his toothbrush and went off toward the bathroom.

Scott came around the table and pulled me into his arms for a long hug. "You were wonderful," he said right next to my ear.

"Yeah?"

"Yeah."

"Coming again tomorrow?"

He pulled away and took his time tucking a strand of hair behind my ear. "You bet."

"You make me happy—have I mentioned that?" I squashed an impulse to look around for the person who'd said the words. I had a sneaking feeling it had been me. My mouth was developing a mind of its own these days, and it made me a bit skittish.

Scott smiled a little dangerously and kissed a spot beneath my ear.

"Not that kind of happy," I said, trying to sound bored.

He stopped kissing me, and I immediately gave myself a mental kick in the butt. "Really?" he asked.

"Actually, that kind of happy too." I was blushing like a twelve-year-old, so I did a quick check to make sure I hadn't developed braces along with teenage hormones.

"So how's the battle coming?" Scott asked.

I gave it some thought. "I'm contemplating it."

"Yeah?"

"Yup."

"From the cellar or the armory?"

I had a vision of a narrow shaft of light piercing the darkness of a dim and musty space.

"The cellar. But I think the door might be cracked open."

He raised an eyebrow.

"Just a teensy bit," I added, not wanting to raise his hopes.

He smiled in a warm, dimpled assault on my few remaining shreds of sanity and wished me a good night.

❋ ❋ ❋

I hurried through the door and threw my book bag into the nearest chair.

"Trey?" There was a worried edge to my voice as I looked around the living room, then headed down the hall. "Where are you?"

Trey had called the school during the morning and left a message for me to come home as soon as possible. The receptionist had found me holed up in the staff room, feverishly checking items off my endless to-do list. Mop the stage floor? Check. Write cards to the actors? Check. Sedate Meagan? Check. The moment she said "emergency," I was out the door and headed for my car. There was nothing dramatic about Trey, and if he used that word . . .

I was halfway down the hall to the bedroom when a smell from the kitchen halted me midstride. It was a familiar odor, the type that made an otherwise-bright day feel bruised.

"Trey?" I said again, unwilling to take a single step toward the kitchen.

He came out into the hallway, all casual and calm, wiping his hands on a dish towel. "Shell! You're home!"

I squinted my suspicion. "Where's the emergency, Trey?"

He shrugged.

Two steps brought me close enough to smack him in the shoulder with my purse, suddenly sure that I'd been duped. "Do you have any idea how crazy my day is?"

"I'm sorry." He was almost contrite. "But would you have left school if I hadn't made it sound important?"

"You are such a . . . What's this about?" I demanded, hands on hips. My teacher voice didn't seem to faze him at all.

"You."

The aroma coming from the kitchen was getting stronger. And making me more leery. I pasted on a casual smile. "Tell me that smell isn't what I think it is."

"Come here." He grabbed my hand and led me into the dining room.

I stopped short when I saw what he'd done. The table had been moved aside, and in its place were two chairs, a coatrack, and a floor lamp, all of which were draped with one of Shayla's fairy sheets.

"Couldn't find four matching chairs?" I asked, as if the fact that the construction was there at all were the most normal thing in the world.

"I figured we needed a couple of higher corners now that we've grown up and all."

"You realize I have a play performance tonight, right?"

"Yup."

"And you realize I have, oh, about forty-three thousand things to do before that happens, right?"

"Yup."

"And yet you called me away from school under false pretenses to stage a Huddle Hut revival?"

My voice had risen to an incredulous pitch, and Trey held up his hands in self-defense. "You wouldn't have come if I'd told you the truth!"

"Correct!"

"Except that this is more important than the list you spent half the night writing," my brother said. The certainty in his eyes scared me a little.

"Trey . . ."

"Be quiet and crawl under," he said, turning on his heels to head toward the kitchen.

"There's an expiration date on childhood traditions, you know!" I called after him, eyeing the lopsided Huddle Hut with a mixture of nostalgia and frustration.

"How 'bout your attitude?" came Trey's voice from the kitchen. "Is there an expiration date on that?"

"I'm going back to school."

"Stay put! I'll be right there."

"I'm not staying put and I'm not eating whatever that is I'm smelling."

"Get in the hut and we'll discuss it."

It felt stupid to be having a conversation in two rooms, but the kitchen smelled like pain and the Huddle Hut looked counterfeit and Trey's scheme—whatever it was—felt morbidly intriguing, so I really couldn't figure out what I should do next. I stood there and yelled, "This is making me nervous!" toward the kitchen.

"Get in the hut!" He was in drill-sergeant mode.

"Not until you tell me what's going on!"

I looked at him like he'd lost his mind when he came sauntering out of the kitchen with two steaming dishes in his hands. "We're reliving a brotherhood milestone."

"If it's what I'm thinking of, you're going to be reliving it alone."

"Don't be such a crybaby."

I stared at him long and hard. "You're acting crazy, Trey."

"Just following orders." He saw my confused glare. "Geronimo."

I rolled my eyes. "Not him again."

"And I like Scott," Trey said. My brother, Master of the Segue.

"Come again?"

"We need to do this." He smiled pleasantly and installed himself under the sloping Huddle Hut roof, his bush of blond hair turned pink by the sun slanting through the rosy sheet.

"What does this have to do with Scott?"

He patted a pillow and waved me in.

"No," I said.

He sighed and raised an eyebrow. It was his are-you-going-to-be-a-sissy? look, and I didn't like it one bit.

"No," I said again.

"Shell."

"You can't make me."

"What—are you three? I'm not 'making' you anything. I'm inviting you."

I wrinkled my nose at his attempt at manipulation and struck a rebellious pose. "He's dead. We've grown up. It doesn't matter anymore."

It had been a long time since Trey had looked at me that way—with equal parts compassion, strength, and resolve. He came out of the Huddle Hut and wrapped me in a hug that brought tears to my eyes. "He's dead. We've grown up. And it matters more today than it ever has," he whispered against my ear, so urgently that I shivered. "We need to do this," he said, pulling back. "We need to remember who we are."

I closed my eyes, expelled a breath, and let the past wash over me.

⌘ ⌘ ⌘

"You think maybe we're mutants?"

Trey stopped drumming his fingers against the Huddle Hut floor and turned his head to look at me. The motion dislodged the earphone I had so carefully arranged to fit against my ear. I reached between our heads to find my half of the earphones and press it back into place, resticking the masking tape that held it there.

"Stop turning your head when I talk to you," I said. "It unsticks the tape."

"This wasn't your most brilliant idea, you know."

"I didn't hear you coming up with anything better."

"Maybe we should get two Walkmans with two sets of earphones. Ever think of that?"

"But then we couldn't listen to the same tape at the same time." It seemed obvious to me.

"You're right," he sighed in halfhearted frustration. "It's much better to lie here with a Walkman between our heads, listening to Toto with two disconnected halves of earphones masking-taped to our ears." His sarcasm made my mind feel brighter. Toto did too. It was our courage music, and we'd be needing it soon.

"So . . . about the mutant thing."

"We're not mutants."

"This is what I've been thinking . . ." I had to pause because I didn't really have my arguments all organized in my head yet.

"You making outlines in your mind again?" We'd been doing persuasive speeches in Miss Reeser's seventh-grade English class for a couple of weeks, and Trey didn't like it. He got frustrated when I stopped midsentence to plot out the best way to say things, and he especially got antsy when I tried to convince him of the nutritional value of, say, butter, instead of just asking him to pass it. So I didn't take too long organizing my thoughts before plowing ahead this time.

"Mom's a decent person," I said. "I mean, she's nice, right?"

"Too nice."

"So let's say she comes from Planet Nice." Trey started humming the theme from Star Trek, *and that kind of impressed me as he still had*

Toto playing in his left ear, but I wasn't deterred. "And Dad is . . . well . . . not such a nice guy."

"So he comes from Planet Bast—"

"You can't swear if you're trying to be persuasive, Trey." I felt him smile. "Dad comes from Planet If-I-Knew-You-Were-Using-My-Masking-Tape-I'd-Blast-You-to-Jupiter."

"Betcha they have trouble fitting that on their license plates."

"And we're kinda half and half, right?"

"Nice to see you've been paying attention in biology class."

"So we're mutants."

"More like hybrids."

I had no idea what the word meant, but it sounded right.

"So as hybrids, how do we decide which planet we belong on?"

Trey turned his head again, which unstuck the tape—again. "Huh?"

"If I had to choose, I'd want to live on Planet Nice. Not that Planet Nice would be a party. Actually, I think I might die of terminal boredom. But it still would beat the smell on Planet Masking Tape."

"Dad's planet smells?"

I nodded. "Like burned coffee and garlic breath."

Trey seemed to mull that one over for a minute. I let him do that because Miss Reeser had told us that it was important to give the audience enough time to figure out what we were talking about.

"It's no fun being a hybrid," I said when the silence got a little too long. I was really hoping we'd be able to keep the topic going and avoid the horrendous exercise Trey had planned for our Huddle Hut session.

"You ready?" he said.

My diversion hadn't worked. I gave his question some thought and decided I might as well bite the fungal bullet. I needed the milestone like Madonna needed a stylist. Trey must have read my mind, because he grunted up to a sitting position at the same time I did. We pulled the remaining masking tape off the sides of our faces, cringing as little hairs came off with it, and took simultaneous deep breaths.

"You still sure about this?" I asked, kinda hoping he'd changed his mind.

He nodded with absolute conviction. "Too many signs," he said. It made me uncomfortable when Trey talked about signs. I was the one who was supposed to see invisible things, and he was the one who was supposed to fix real-life things. "Mom hasn't made mushrooms or zucchini in months," Trey continued, certainty lending weight to his words, "and today, right after I had that dream about going to boot camp for zucchini delinquents, both vegetables turn up in the fridge. On the same day as my dream, Shell. The same day. I'm telling you, this is Geronimo's way of getting us to prepare for next time. We can't ignore the signs."

Trey had started calling God Geronimo. I wasn't sure why. Maybe because the Big Guy felt more like a warrior that way, the type of God who would unleash a swarm of arrows on anyone who tried to hurt us.

"You dream weird things," I said.

He wasn't finished making his point. "And then Dad went to that seminar and Mom went to get her hair done, and we're both alone in the house with the fridge. That's a sign too."

I stifled the urge to tell him that me being alone with a fridge was nothing unusual. "What are we going to say when she asks us where the mushrooms and zucchini went? She's not going to believe the 'Geronimo's boot camp' thing."

"I don't know," he said, but I could tell he wasn't really giving it much thought. He had the same look on his face he'd had earlier, when he'd stood by the stove stirring one pan of zucchini and one pan of mushrooms. He was hard-eyed and square-jawed, obviously taking this boot camp thing seriously.

"Geronimo has no idea how much I hate mushrooms," I said.

"Yes, he does."

"I don't think I can do it."

He reached for the bowl of fried mushrooms and handed it to me; then he took the bowl of fried zucchini wedges and held it up to his face.

"What does it smell like?" I asked.

"Zucchini. You?"

I sniffed at the mushrooms without bringing them too close to my face, just in case my gag reflexes were smell-sensitive. "Mushrooms. Cold mushrooms. And a little bit like the boxes of bait we used to buy at the cabin. You think they'd taste any better if we warmed them up?"

He shook his head and used his fingers to take two pieces of zucchini from his bowl. That Toto music had really made him brave. "You take some out too," he instructed, his eyes riveted to the green triangles he held.

I gagged when my fingers touched the slimy mushroom slices. "I can't."

"You can."

"Trey . . ."

"Come on, Shelby." There was something desperate in his voice. Like my failure would make him look weak too.

I picked up a couple pieces of mushroom and watched them flop against my fingers like slices of slug. "I can't eat them, Trey. There's no way." It was all I could do to quell the impulse to fling them off my fingers into a far corner of the attic.

"Just do one of your persuasive speeches on yourself," Trey said with growing tenseness. I could hear him swallowing loudly from time to time. "Tell yourself it's not going to kill you. . . ."

"I might throw up."

"But you won't die. And then next time Mom fixes them and Dad's

all Godzilla, you'll be able to eat them." He was trying so hard to be persuasive, but I could tell he hadn't made an outline in his mind.

"I can't."

"You have to."

"I can't, Trey!"

I felt him gathering himself next to me. When he spoke again, it was in a quiet, certain voice I'd seldom heard from him before. He sounded deeper somehow. And farther away too. "If you can eat those mushrooms, he won't be able to scare you with them anymore. He won't be able to make you cry . . . or feel like dirt . . . or less than dirt . . . or . . . or anything. Not with the mushrooms. Not anymore."

"There'll still be all the rest."

"Yeah, but there won't be this. It's one less thing, and we're deciding he can't have it."

I watched him drop the zucchini into his mouth and chew methodically, a red flush growing out of the collar of his Bulls T-shirt and moving up toward his jaw. He swallowed hard, froze for a moment, then swallowed again. "See?" he said, looking at me. There was sweat on his upper lip.

I closed my eyes and brought the mushrooms to my mouth. I gagged when they touched my tongue, then again when I tried to chew. I felt tears eking out between my eyelids as I gagged over and over, finally forcing the mushrooms to the back of my mouth to swallow them.

Trey was handing me a glass of water when I opened my eyes. He had more zucchini in his other hand. "You need to chew them this time," he said.

"You're eating more?" I asked incredulously, awed and humbled by my brother's outrageous courage.

"Geronimo wants us to practice," he said.

And emboldened by my brother's fierce conviction that Geronimo had orchestrated the challenge to defeat my father's next assault, I took another deep breath and reached for more mushrooms.

"The second time's easier," I heard Trey say. And all I could do was gag and believe him.

22

Our second performance wasn't quite as clean as our first. With the excitement from the first night still pumping scattered energy through their minds, the actors made a few small mistakes, none of which the audience probably noticed. I walked around in the dark, mobile cocoon of backstage shadows and spoke in soothing whispers to the actors as they entered and exited the stage. There was something magical about the convergence of effort, inspiration, and accomplishment, a magic amplified by the presence of spectators who laughed, gasped, and cried on cue. I felt the performance like a constant hum in my marrow, a low-key intensity of purpose and emotion that was at once galvanizing and calming. I stood in the wings and absorbed it all until I felt swollen with the warmth of achievement and the overflow of gratitude. But my thankfulness was for more than the play. It was for the plenitude of

God's love for me, displayed in human form under the spotlights and in the audience beyond the stage.

When Seth ended his final monologue as transparently and movingly as he had the night before, I felt a sunset-warm fullness I'd seldom experienced before. But the serenity of the moment was short-lived. After their second curtain call, Seth and Kate stepped into the wings, each taking one of my arms, and dragged me into the spotlight with them. I didn't want to be there. Backstage was my comfort zone. But there was little I could do to quell the surge of their post-performance elation. Seth stepped to the front of the stage and, in the warm-chocolate voice I'd come to love, simply said, "This is Shelby. She believed in us and inspired us, and we want to thank her."

Kate gave me a bouquet and a long, hard hug, and I did a little half bow, extending my arm toward a cast that had, in many ways, altered my life. They smiled at me with emotions I knew I didn't deserve, and I hoped my love for them was evident on my face.

Nearly an hour later, when the audience had filtered out of the room and the actors had started to realize that their journey together was truly over, I heard a commotion by the auditorium door and saw Trey, my wonderful, pseudo-French brother, rolling a *pièce montée* into the room on a metal cart, sparklers pointing out of it like glowing porcupine quills. As much as I loved cheesecake, I loved this French tradition more. Nothing said celebration like a *pièce montée.*

"Trey . . ." There was such happiness in my throat that I didn't know how to continue. The actors scattered around the room approached the tall tower made of stacked cream puffs and drizzled with hardened caramel, their appetites suddenly outweighing their melancholy.

Trey wheeled the cart up to me and gave me a quick peck on the cheek. "I figured your finale warranted something special."

"You're absolutely right," I said, my thoughts flashing back to the mushrooms he'd prepared for me earlier that day. I reached around a sparkler to pull off the top cream puff, the brittle caramel around it snapping loudly, and sank my teeth into the decadent treat. I heard someone clear his throat behind me but paid no attention to it. There was a tower of culinary fascination in front of me that had the full focus of my calorie-addicted brain. It was possibly because of my absorption in the *pièce montée* that I didn't immediately sense what was going on around me or register the animated silence that fell the second time that same someone cleared his throat.

Someone, as it turned out, was Scott, but it wasn't until I heard Shayla's earnest "Are you going to eat it *all*, Mom?" that I turned and found him standing there, my daughter in his arms.

I didn't know whether to be delighted or outraged. "Scott, what are . . . ?" Shayla was wearing her Cinderella pajamas and a mile-wide grin. I felt my heart do a cartwheel. Then my mom reflexes kicked in. "What is Shayla doing here?" I said to Scott. "She's five and it's going on midnight. Do you see anything wrong with this scenario?"

Trey stepped in to take Shayla from Scott, saying, "She kinda had to be here for this." He winked at me and moved to stand by Gus and Bev, both of whom had somehow materialized out of nowhere. Kenny was there too. And Simon, my clumsy props guy. Thomas, the epitome of British decorum even at the age of fifteen. And Meagan with her dancing eyes. Seth—solemn, peaceful Seth—standing just a tad too close to his feisty, untamable Kate. All my actors were present, lined up and waiting, exchanging the kinds of knowing glances that convinced me that I was the only one in the dark about what was going on here.

"Scott," I whispered, though in the hushed room, my words reached to the balcony. "What are you doing?"

"Giving you certainty, I hope." He paused, arresting my thoughts with the temerity of his gaze. "And storming the barricades. I'm multitasking." He cast my actors a conspiratorial half smile.

I glanced at my daughter, up way past her bedtime, and all I could think of was that she'd be a monster tomorrow. But when I looked from Shayla to my brother, I saw a family there that took my breath away. Trey, the defender to whom I owed my life in so many ways, and Shayla, the daughter of the bitter, violent man who had devastated my childhood but gifted me with the miracle of motherhood.

Scott's hand on my arm brought my attention back to him. He stood in front of me with so much earnestness and determination on his face that I felt a giggle bubbling to the surface. "What—are you going to make a speech or something?" I asked, distracted from my gratitude by a sense of impending significance. He nodded, and I felt the air constrict a little around us. "Really?"

When he spoke, his voice was soft and uncharacteristically unsteady. "I'm not sure if this is the right way to do this, Shelby," he said. "I mean, I know you're a pretty private person, but the private approach hasn't been working, so I thought . . . I thought maybe I'd . . . storm the barricades with a little public humiliation."

"For you or for me?"

"Probably for me." He smiled a little crookedly and added, "I'm the guy with a killer case of stage fright who's trying to come up with the right words and pretty sure he'll fail. And all you have to do is stand there and watch me suffer."

"Sounds equitable to me," I said. Something weird was going on with my lungs.

He cleared his throat—again—and looked down, gathering his thoughts. "Here's the deal," he finally said, his eyes rising to connect with mine, capturing my mind with their bold and gentle intensity. "I am convinced that nothing in our lives happens by chance and that the best things in life require taking a risk. So this . . . this is me taking that risk."

I glanced at Trey, my Huddle Hut chef, and began to suspect a conspiracy.

But Scott wasn't done yet. He took my hands in his and pulled me closer, linking his gaze with mine. There was a muscle working in his jaw and a sheen of sweat on his forehead. My skin felt electrified with apprehension. I tried to think happy thoughts of cows coming in from pastures and dolphins frolicking in the waves to calm my nerves and still my fear. But the cows ended up herding themselves over a cliff and the dolphins, in their enthusiasm, beached themselves on a rugged shore, so neither was exactly helping.

"On the first day I met you," Scott said, nodding toward Gus and Bev, who waved when I caught their eyes, "Gus introduced you as my future wife. I didn't take it too seriously, as he's a bit of a . . . how should I put it? A creative thinker."

"Ain't that the truth!" came Bev's happy voice. She did a high five with Shayla and there was a little laughter from our audience, quickly hushed by anticipation.

"Scott . . ." There was fear in my voice as a burning panic moved from my stomach to my throat.

Concern flashed across his face. "This isn't what you're thinking," he said, holding my hands a little more tightly.

"It isn't?"

"It's not a proposal. You know that's what I want—sometime—but not yet. Not until we've gotten this other thing straight."

"And thank your lucky stars for that," Kate said with the certainty of experience. "This guy proposes like a hippo does ballet."

Scott shrugged and smiled. "So I'm not an actor."

"No, but you're turning into quite the public speaker," I said a little hoarsely, unaccountably disappointed that this wasn't the proposal I so desperately feared.

"As I was saying," Scott continued, leveling a well-aimed look at Kate to quell any further interruptions, "this isn't a proposal. But it's equally important to me. Something I promised you I'd keep trying to get right." He took a deep breath and smirked at his own nervousness. "And I'm hoping that doing this in front of all these friends comes close to that."

Meagan giggled and clapped a hand over her mouth, and Seth met my gaze with a warmth and affection that made me want to weep. Kenny lifted a gaping Shayla out of Trey's arms to whisper something in her ear as Scott took a moment to look around at our friends and students. His eyes stopped on my daughter. "Is it okay if I do this now, Lady Shay?"

Shayla nodded and beamed him a glowing smile, throwing an arm around Kenny's neck and yelling, "Yes, yes, *yes*!"

Scott took another deep breath and smiled at his mesmerized audience. I could tell his nerves were getting to him. "You all know Shelby," he said, addressing them but staring at me, "so you may be surprised to hear that she's not very good at believing people love her." He glanced at Trey. "And I have it on good authority that this isn't a recent thing either." I tried to roll my eyes at my interfering brother, but they stayed anchored to Scott's.

"We love you, Miss Davis," Meagan singsonged. Seth hushed her with a hand on the top of her head.

"Exactly," Scott continued. "And you're not alone, Meagan. That's why I find it so hard to understand how a person as well-loved as Shelby can be so unconvinced of . . . well, of her lovableness."

The students voiced their agreement with murmurs, nods, and

smiles, while Gus let out a hearty chuckle and gave Scott a thumbs-up. Our audience was clearly warming to the Scott Taylor Show.

"Is *lovableness* a real word?" I whispered to Scott, emotion constricting my throat.

"I don't know," he whispered back, smiling. "Give a coach a break, will you?"

There were tears in his eyes, and he blinked at them as he continued. "Shelby," he said, his fingers holding mine with so much gentleness that I feared I might forget, in months and years, just how they felt, "I need you to know, in front of the people who mean the most to you, how I feel about you."

"Scott . . ."

"This isn't a passing or casual thing. It's not something I need to wait and think about some more. And it's not something I've ever said with this degree of conviction or hope before. It's something I *know*—and I'm so sure of it that I want everyone here to know it too." He took a deep breath while Shayla scrambled out of Kenny's arms and came to stand right next to me, looking up with wide, ecstatic eyes, her arms hugging my legs.

"Am I doing this right?" Scott asked, his insecurity endearing.

I laughed a little raggedly. "You're doing great."

"I love you, Shelby Davis," he said softly.

The bottom dropped out of my stomach, leaving a dizzying void behind, a buoyant space that brimmed with unimaginable promise.

"And I don't need you to feel the same way I do," Scott continued, a tremor in his voice, "and I certainly don't expect this to make Gus's prediction come true. This isn't about bribing you or pressuring you. I know you're still dealing with a lot of stuff, and that's for you and God to wrestle with. So for now—" he brought my hand to his lips and kissed it, eliciting a high-pitched "awwww" from Meagan—"for now, all I want is to present you with my love in a way I hope you'll believe, in front of all these people who know you and love you too, so you'll have this memory to come back to the next time you have trouble accepting what I've said."

He sighed heavily, a smile softening his eyes and seeping through my reserve into my most protected weakness. "I wouldn't be saying this with so many witnesses if I weren't sure of myself. I'm for real, Shelby. I'll probably mess up and disappoint you and fail in multiple ways, but my love is real. And I'm not going anywhere. So—" he wiped a tear from my cheek with his thumb—"please, please believe me."

I blinked. Twice. Then I reminded myself to breathe. There was a convergence in my mind of so many images that dizziness made me reach for Scott's arms and hold tightly to his strength.

He saw me, I knew, in all my healing imperfection. He saw me as I was and somehow—by some miracle—still wanted me. He was the living, breathing, nurturing expression of God's love for me. So was Shayla. So was Trey. So were the students and friends bolstering my weakness with their comfort and support. They were God's rescue from my pain.

I could feel a surge of joy growing out of the ashes of my past as a peaceful certainty clicked into place like a missing puzzle piece. No need for cows and dolphins. No need for zingers and barbs. No need for fear of the unknown. My only need was for boldness to enter the battlefield and for courage to face the risks head-on. Every particle in the room turned golden and converged in a burst of sudden, luminous clarity. The Davis genes, above all else, were cowardly. And I refused to give them the power to determine my future. I looked at Trey—he smiled at me. He knew. My courage was God's answer to the mushroomness of fear.

In that moment, I saw the fullness of my life like a crystalline mosaic in which shards of rejection and survival and despair and love and horror and redemption swirled into the luminescent revelation of God's abiding love. I saw it all—I embraced it all. And with my eyes riveted to the sureness of Scott's gaze, I nodded through my tears and whispered, "I believe you."

A Note from the Author

SOMETIMES AN AUTHOR sits around for weeks charting plotlines and developing characters before beginning to write. And sometimes an author is engaging in the glamorous task of vacuuming her apartment when the freckle-dusted face of a four-year-old pops into her mind. I was still living in Germany when Shayla's soulful eyes first distracted me from my chores. I can remember the exact section of ratty carpeting I was working on when her gaze flashed across my consciousness with a hint of complex history. I turned off the vacuum and gave the apparition a moment's thought, then shook my head at my flight of fancy and resumed the job at hand. But not for long.

Minutes later, the vacuum stood abandoned in the living room while I curled up in my bed with my laptop and began to type. I had no idea, at that moment, of the zigzagging path the story would take between present and past, nor did I foresee the characters who would come to flesh it out. But as Shelby appeared and stole the spotlight from Shayla, as Gus and Bev ushered Scott into her life, and as present-day muddlehood led back to darker huddlehoods, I realized that Shayla's face might have been more than merely an excuse to stop Saturday chores.

For the better part of the following nine days, I let myself be guided by the characters—watching them evolve as they suffered, dreamed, and overcame. The Huddle Hut emerged out of Shelby's and Trey's minds, not mine, as did Geronimo, swinging chins, and that crazy Vira Snurdly. Trey himself was unplanned, yet he wove his way into the fabric of the narrative. He started out as "Kerr," but my fingers kept typing "Trey," so I gave in to the story's wishes and dutifully made the change. Even now, with the novel approaching publication, I feel it as a creation that breathes in spite of me, and the process that birthed it remains in great part a mystery.

But I hope *In Broken Places* is much more than a tale of huts, hurdles, and the power to overcome. Child abuse is a destructive force. It slithers and marches; it whispers and roars. It either weakens or hardens its victims, but it never leaves them unscathed. If you or someone you know is being victimized, please call the National Domestic Violence Hotline: 1-800-799-SAFE.

My sincerest prayer is that the pages of this book will shed a compassionate light on the ravages of child abuse, its soul-crippling tyranny and deep-rooted legacy. Pain need not win. There is life beyond bleeding. There is love beyond fearing. There is hope beyond despairing. I should know . . .

I am a survivor.

Discussion Questions

1. Why does Shelby feel the need to move to Germany with Shayla?
2. Is the relationship between Shelby and Trey healthy or unhealthy? What evidence do you see in the story?
3. In what ways did Shelby's abuse influence her in adulthood? Can you think of at least three examples?
4. Faced with the chance to take in your abusive father's daughter, would you do what Shelby did? Why or why not?
5. Should Scott have walked away from Shelby after so many early rejections? Was his persistence a sign of weakness or strength?
6. What could/should Shelby's mother have done differently? Can her choices be forgiven? What responsibility does she share with her abusive husband?
7. What role does the Huddle Hut play in both Shelby's and Trey's survival? Can you think of a place or ritual in your life that fulfills a similar role?

8. Can you recall three or four places where the book refers to a bird? What is its symbolism?

9. What do you foresee happening in Trey's future? What is the trajectory for his life emotionally? Professionally? Spiritually?

10. Can Shelby and Scott have a healthy relationship that leads to a strong marriage? Why or why not? What steps might they take to increase the chances of a "happy ending"?

About the Author

Born in France to an American mother and a Canadian father, Michèle Phoenix is an international writer with multicultural sensitivities. A graduate of Wheaton College, she spent twenty years teaching at Black Forest Academy, a school in Germany for missionaries' children.

Michèle fought two different forms of cancer in 2008, a challenge that caused her to reevaluate the direction of her life. In 2010, armed with a desire to broaden the imprint of her remaining years, she returned to the States to launch a new ministry for and about missionaries' kids (MKs).

Now living in Illinois, Michèle serves with Global Outreach Mission as an MK advocate, speaking, writing, and educating the North American church about the unique strengths and struggles of missionaries' children.

Her first book, *Tangled Ashes*, was released in 2012. Visit michelephoenix.com for more information.

ENJOY MORE GREAT FICTION FROM

MICHÈLE PHOENIX

TANGLED ASHES

A NOVEL

Michèle Phoenix

"Phoenix weaves these two darkly enticing stories together in a fast-paced novel leaving the reader guessing until the very end." —*Booklist*

Available now in bookstores and online.

www.tyndalefiction.com

CP0632